{Between} Boyfriends

{Between} Boyfriends

michael salvatore

KENSINGTON BOOKS
www.kensingtonbooks.com

This book is a work of fiction. Names, characters, places, and incidents either are products of the author's imagination or are used fictitiously. Any resemblance to actual persons, living or dead, events, or locales is entirely coincidental.

KENSINGTON BOOKS are published by

Kensington Publishing Corp.
119 West 40th Street
New York, NY 10018

Copyright © 2010 by Michael Griffo

All Kensington titles, imprints, and distributed lines are available at special quantity discounts for bulk purchases for sales promotion, premiums, fund-raising, educational, or institutional use.

Special book excerpts or customized printings can also be created to fit specific needs. For details, write or phone the office of the Kensington Special Sales Manager: Attn. Special Sales Department. Kensington Publishing Corp., 119 West 40th Street, New York, NY 10018. Phone: 1-800-221-2647.

Kensington and the K logo Reg. U.S. Pat. & TM Off.

ISBN-13: 978-0-7582-4683-7
ISBN-10: 0-7582-4683-8

First Kensington Trade Paperback Printing: June 2010
10 9 8 7 6 5 4 3 2 1

Printed in the United States of America

For all my friends who are like family,
and for all my family who are like friends

{Between}
Boyfriends

Four Years Ago

The greatest thing about being gay is that moment when you walk down the street holding your boyfriend's hand and you *forget* that you're holding his hand. Gay becomes natural. You don't think about it anymore, you don't question it or celebrate it; it simply is who and what you are. That's the way it was for me and Jack as we strolled down Sixth Avenue to do some Saturday afternoon shopping after a morning of kissing, fondling, and HGTV-watching while munching on bowls of Cinnamon Toast Crunch cereal. At that time Jack DiRenza had been my boyfriend for three years, my live-in boyfriend for one year, ten months, two weeks, and six days of that time. I'm not counting, I just have a really good memory.

"Hey, Stevie B.," Jack asked in between sips of a Starbucks grande mocha Frappuccino. "Do we need a new butter warmer?"

"Does anyone need an *old* butter warmer?" I asked in between sips of my iced grande skim mocha, which is my summer Starbucks drink as opposed to my most favorite Starbucks drink, which is a Venti skim, extra-hot, light-whipped peppermint mocha that I drink from Labor Day to Memorial Day. All my friends know that I like my coffee to be like my boyfriend—consistent.

"Your birthday is coming up and I'm planning a surprise lobster dinner," Jack said. "And what's a lobster dinner without warm butter?"

"Sounds yummy," I said. "But honey, the surprise lobster dinner is only a surprise if you don't tell me about it."

Jack smirked like a Catholic schoolboy on the verge of committing a venial sin and said, "I didn't tell you what I'm going to do to you for dessert."

Smiling like the happiest gay in the world I held on to my boyfriend's perfectly calloused hand, sipped my Starbucks, and entered Bed, Bath & Behind to buy an unnecessary kitchen appliance. Because that's what you do on a Saturday afternoon in Manhattan when you're gay and in love. Who knew that exactly two weeks later my perfect boyfriend would kick me out of his apartment and his life with barely an explanation and force me to take up residence in the mad, mad, mad, mad world of the single gay man.

On that terrible night, while the rest of the gay world went out clubbing or stayed in snuggling, I slept on my best friend Flynn's pull-out Jennifer Convertible trying to figure out how I could shoot my ex-boyfriend without winding up on Rikers Island. When thoughts of homo-cide had left my brain, I wondered how I had gone from being deliriously happy to devastatingly miserable in less than twenty-four hours. Four years later I still don't have an answer. All I know is my name is Steven Bartholomew Ferrante and I am still a single gay man living in Manhattan. Welcome to my world.

Chapter One

The bed was enormous, a California king squeezed into a Chelsea queen's apartment. Unfortunately the adjective attributed to the bed could not be used to describe Ely, the guy who lay asleep in the bed. Not only was Ely not enormous, he wasn't large, biggish, or even the thicker side of medium. Ely was small. And I'm not referring to his height or personality, I'm strictly commenting on his penis. And by penis I mean cock. Though I don't think a penis no larger than an adult male thumb should be called a cock. There is a hierarchical system in the gay world and nowhere is it stricter than below the waist.

As I watched Ely sleep, I was filled with a mixture of sadness and awe. When I first met him in the wee hours of the morning of this very day, I sensed he possessed an ebullience and intelligence that I had not encountered for the longest time. I truly thought, as I sipped on my fourth cosmopolitan, this one with a bashful hint of mango, that this man who stood before me was brimming with PRM—Potential Relationship Material. It was for that reason alone that I decided to ignore my no-sex-until-the-third-date rule, a rule that naturally would have been ignored if Ely was a Puerto Rican Male, a PRM of a totally different color and, of course, size, and accepted Ely's invitation to go home with him. I got excited when he whispered in my ear during the cab ride to his apartment that he was a dominant top, and was borderline breathless when his key finally opened his door on the third try. Within moments and without any further conversation, I yanked Ely's pants to his ankles, then I yanked his underwear to his pants, and then I realized that there would be no more yanking. The reason Ely calls himself a *dominant* top is that the only way his thumb/penis can enter an asshole is to threaten it with execution.

I don't mean to convey that Ely's penis was a deformity on a par with the Elephant Man; it just wasn't an invitation. And let's be honest, we all like to be invited places. So while little Ely lay in his big bed, I quickly got dressed, rearranged his refrigerator magnet letters to spell out THANK YOU, and fled quietly into the midafternoon October sunshine. The morning's attempt at a fling would need to be flung from my memory and I only knew of one way to do it successfully. It was Starbucks time. If a Venti skim, extra-hot, light-whipped peppermint mocha couldn't erase from my mind the vision of Ely's tiny penis, sheathed in a condom imported from Japan, trying desperately to enter the, by comparison, overwhelmingly enormous cavity that was my asshole, then I was a doomed gay. Yet as I clasped the gunmetal handle of the Starbucks door, I knew being a doomed gay was better than having to call your cock a penis.

From the first lip-smacking sip of my Venti skim, extra-hot, light-whipped peppermint mocha I knew I would be triumphant and Ely would permanently be part of my past. The caffeine-cum-heroin flirted with my throat in areas that Ely never could. The escapade with Tiny Man was officially over and I had reclaimed my life, yet again. It was time to begin another chapter in the saga of Steven Bartholomew Ferrante, thirty-three-year-old, Italian-American, former Jersey-ite, single-yet-looking-really-really-hard, soap opera producer. Thus began Chapter 822—give or take.

I was in mid-performance of a Star-turn, which is a complete, yet nonchalant, 360-degree turn at a Starbucks condiment station to check out the customers—or as defined in the Starbucks employee manual, the guest list—when I heard my name being shrieked by either my friend Lindsay Wilde or my great-aunt Matilda Barziano. I could never tell the two sounds apart.

"Steven! You look like you spent the a.m. with a dick up your a-hole!"

I still couldn't tell who it was, so I was forced to turn all the way around.

"Lindsay," I said, only partially relieved. "You couldn't be more wrong."

"Really? Tell me. Tell me everything."

An uncontrollable smile grew on Lindsay's face, for he loved nothing more than to hear other people's tragitales. And if the tragedy was sprinkled with a smattering of smut, his smile would grow even wider. Lindsay had been this way ever since I first met him on the set of *If Tomorrow Never Comes,* the long-running soap opera that I produce. It was 1994 and Lindsay had just lost his chance of winning a figure skating medal by coming in fourth at the Lillehammer Olympics. He had entered Norway as the three-time U.S. men's national figure skating champion and left a bona fide loser. His devastation was only a few notches deeper than that of the American figure skating audience. And since roughly the entire American figure skating audience also watches American soap operas, my executive producer asked Lindsay to visit Wonderland, the fictional town of *If Tomorrow Never Comes* or *ITNC,* as *Soap Opera Digest* has acronymed us. It was on that day, after take sixty-seven, that Lindsay realized he had absolutely no talent as an actor. Well, he realized it after I told him. At first he was upset that a mere mortal like me would point out that a god like Lindsay could have a flaw, but then I told him that the star-crossed lovers on the show used to be lovers in real life until one gave the other genital herpes. We've been friends ever since.

Brimming with the joy another person's tragedy would soon bring him, Lindsay flopped his bubble butt onto a chair and flipped the *New York Times* that was on top of the table (presumably left there by some Starbucks Sunday Regular as a table-saving device) onto the floor. He took a sip of his iced grande soy vanilla latte—Lindsay drank an iced grande soy vanilla latte all year long, iced because he said he was hot enough without help from fluid and vanilla because that's how he liked to fuck—tossed an unruly lock of unnaturally blond hair from his unnaturally sun-tanned forehead and gazed at me with the steely determination that defined him as the former figure skating champion he was.

"What happened?" Lindsay demanded.

"I broke my rule," I confessed.

"Which one? You have more rules than Dick Button."

"My no-sex-until-the-third-date rule," I mumbled, knowing full well the Wilde-wrath that was about to come.

"That rule is as outdated as Dick himself!" Lindsay growled at precisely the same time the Starbucks Sunday Regular came back to what he thought would be his saved table.

"I enjoy Mr. Button's commentary," said the Regular.

"And you probably rooted for Nancy Kerrigan!" Lindsay shouted back. "Now get the hell away from my table!"

I couldn't really concentrate on the next few things Lindsay said as I was trying to steal glances at the handsome sort-of-Italian, could-be-black-Irish Starbucks Sunday Regular collecting his *New York Times* from the floor. However, I did hear Lindsay mention something about the genius of Tonya Harding never being fully understood by the elitist figure skating community or something of that ilk. And even though I thoroughly enjoy Lindsay's outbursts, at this moment I was more interested in the crooked smile the *very* handsome Starbucks Sunday Regular beamed in my direction. But was he smiling because he was self-conscious after Lindsay's public scolding, self-confident that Lindsay was a deranged former figure skater, or self-content that his feelings for me were real and had to be expressed in the form of a Jake Gyllenhaalesque shy, yet seductive, smile?

"Are you listening to me?" Lindsay said with an exasperated air.

"Of course," I answered, startled out of my reverie.

"And you agree?"

"Yes," I said slowly, stretching the word into four syllables since I was not at all sure what I had agreed to.

"Good," Lindsay said. "Because I hate to think I'm the only one who feels Peggy Fleming should fly solo. It's just not fair that Dick gets to commentate on the men's *and* the ladies' competitions, while Miss I-Reinvented-Modern-Day-Figure-Skating-*and-*

Conquered-Breast-Cancer has to share the microphone with Mr. Button. Did Dick ever have his own TV special? I think not. And don't even start me on Dick's protégé, Peter Carruthers."

"I like Peter. He's hot."

"You're just like all the others. All you want to do is watch the pretty boys do figure eights in sparkly sequined costumes! Figure skating is hard work. My ass might look beautiful, but it's covered with scars from years of practice."

"As are the asses of every gay man in Chelsea," I observed. "And before you go into a tirade over why you should have won the bronze in Lillehammer, lille man, don't you want to hear about my night?"

"Do you know how frustrating it is to come in fourth?" Lindsay spat.

"Do you know how frustrating it is to hear that you came in fourth for the forty millionth time!" I spat back.

"They compound the misery by awarding you a pewter medal. Did you know that?"

"Yes, Lindsay, I know that," I said. "You told me."

"The fourth place loser gets a pewter piece of shit," Lindsay continued, obviously ignoring me and transported back to the Olympics next to, but not on, the third podium. "Worst award I ever received for the most humiliating experience I ever lived through. I gave it to my mother."

"Are you done reminiscing?"

"Yes. Thank you for listening. I can't keep the bile inside all the time; it's destructive."

"That's why I'm here," I replied. "To collect the bile."

"Now tell me, Steven," Lindsay said, much more calmly now that the bile was released. "Why *didn't* you spend the a.m. with a dick up your a-hole?"

"Got socially acceptably drunk, went home with a PRM, took off his pants, and silently screamed for my mother to whisk me away from the horror that I saw inches in front of me."

"What was he? Pre-op?" Lindsay asked.

"Worse."

"One testicle, lots of scar tissue?"

"No," I said. "Toddler-penis."

"Damn those 'roids!" Lindsay shouted as he slammed his fist onto the table. "I can deal with hair loss and acne-back, but toddler-penis is unforgivable. Steroidables should live at the gym and never leave!"

"He wasn't on steroids. His affliction, as far as I could tell, was perfectly natural."

Lindsay's mocha-chocolate eyes grew two inches wider, which made him look as if I had just told him Starbucks had gone bankrupt and was selling its chain to Folgers.

"Then for crissakes why doesn't he just do the steroids and at least have a conversation piece, a point of blame?"

"Who can understand these people?" I said. "The kicker is he said he was a top."

"Of what? Charlie Brown's Christmas tree? Why can't gay men assess themselves the same way they do every other gay man who crosses their path? Small penis equals bottom. Big cock equals top. It's simple, it's math, the universal language," Lindsay explained. "A deaf-mute from Ukraine understands, and I'm not being geographically random: the son of one of Oksana Baiul's coaches was a deaf-mute *and* very well endowed. There was never a problem in the bedroom. If Nikolai could understand, why can't a Chelsea boy?"

"Everybody wants to be what they're not supposed to be."

"What's that supposed to mean, Steven? That I'm *not* supposed to be an Olympian? That my bare, chiseled chest was never meant to bear anything more than Olympic pewter?" Lindsay fumed.

"Loser boy! This isn't about you."

"Sorry. You know how I get when anyone mentions figure skating or the Olympics."

"You're the only one who *ever* mentions figure skating or the Olympics!"

Lindsay stared at me for a moment as the truth settled into his heart, then his mind, then his voice: "It's all I know!"

I allowed Lindsay several seconds of uninterrupted fake tears during which time I checked out the Starbucks Sunday Regular again and to my surprise he was checking me out too. Color me bashful as I felt my cheeks flush and my eyes dart away. I could see him smile at my involuntary response and so before I became a complete second grader in the midst of a schoolgirl crush, I focused on Lindsay and attempted to change the subject away from his Olympiphobia and toward a more manageable, non-blushable subject.

"Before you lapse into endless chanting of 'Why me?' let's use this time productively and figure out what we're going to do for Gus's birthday. He's going to be forty on the twelfth."

Lindsay was instantaneously pulled out of his own misery by this news that he considered to be even more catastrophic.

"God, that's sad. Officially forty-something and single and gay and living alone in the big, wormy apple that is the city. Why would anyone want to celebrate that?"

"Gus will be forty, not forty-something. He can't be forty-something until next year, when something comes after the forty," I explained. "And it's not sad. He's got the best apartment of us all in the Village, he made a mint on Wall Street before it went bust, and he's got an accent."

Lindsay pursed his lips, then formed a smile with only the right side of his mouth.

"But every night Gus goes to bed alone."

"We all go to bed alone," I retorted.

"But we're years from being forty-something," Lindsay cried. "We still have hope!"

He had me. I hate when Lindsay barks a truism, but sometimes amid all his rantings, non sequiturs, and sentences that start with the word *I*, there exists a kernel of truth. And turning forty in a city, or at least a gay section of a city that worships youth, is an unfortunate happening. But as with all happenings in the gay section of any city, it was a happening that would be celebrated. So even though all Gus's friends were glad that he was the one turning forty and not them, all Gus's friends would gather together and throw him a celebration worthy of a happier happening. It made no difference that during the celebration all of us would be praying that when we turned forty we looked as good as, were as successful as, and had the financial portfolio of Gus Aldwych. To his face we would simply call him old.

"Whatever you do, I'm in," Lindsay said, "but remember I have that Fox retrospective on the third and I need you all there for support. This could be very lucrative for me."

"I thought it was just for Olympic medalists."

"They've expanded their coverage, okay? They've opened themselves up wider than a certain male figure skater did for the entire French bobsledding team!"

While Lindsay saw red, I noticed that the Starbucks Sunday Regular was still eyeing me from behind the *New York Times* Arts section. Only in New York is it possible to upgrade from toddler-penis to literate lover in less time than it takes for Lindsay to expose the sexual secrets of every male figure skater who ever lived. God bless gay New York. And God bless the chutzpah on the Regular, for before I could look away this time, he got up and walked directly toward me.

"I'm done with the paper if you want to check it out," the Regular said.

"I'd love to check you . . . I mean *it* . . . out," I stumbled, causing the Regular to smile crookedly.

"Page three has a great article," the Regular said, maintaining eye contact with me. "It was nice meeting you."

As he started to walk away he looked directly at Lindsay and finished his sentence, "Both." He gave me one more knowing glance and, I think, yes I believe, he actually winked at me. I was too startled to wink back, which is a good thing, because I can't wink, so I probably would have looked like I was squinting or suffered from an uncontrollable Tourette's-like twitch. Neither would have been construed as flirtatious. So I just sat there with my mouth open, which he could have perceived as a response to his Sunday afternoon brazenness or an invitation from me to be brazen on a Sunday afternoon. Effective either way.

"Can you believe that guy?" Lindsay said, guzzling the last drop of soy 'n' vanilla. "Caffeine makes people rude."

I wasn't listening to a word Lindsay said because I was staring at something much more interesting on page three of the *New York Times* Arts section. In between an article begging people to write a new musical for Patti LuPone and another article begging people to stop writing musicals for *American Idol* finalists was the Regular's phone number. A real number followed by a real question—*Call me?* The Regular had actually managed to be forward and shy at the same time. And to top it off, all of this information was signed. The Regular had a name and it was Frank. A perfectly regular name for a perfectly regular guy.

I ripped Frank's number and query from the paper, making sure to also rip out the entire Patti LuPone article, for I too believed it was time for the once-and-future diva to return to the boards in a brand-new musical and not a lame revisical, and told Lindsay I had to run. We kiss-kissed and he said he would hang around and boy-watch for a bit before heading to the gym. Luckily I have a degree in Lindsay-speak and understood that meant he hadn't gotten laid the night before and was still horny.

As I was leaving Starbucks, who walked in but Ely. We looked at each other and without breaking our strides another understanding took place. He knew that I was not up for a sunlit encounter and I knew that he knew that he had a small penis. At times of necessity, gay men can understand each other. As I walked down the street toward my future I glanced back and looked through the window to see Ely and Lindsay exchange glances. How I would have loved to hear Lindsay's reaction when he came face-to-face with Ely's steroid-free mini-pee, but luckily I had better things to do.

Chapter Two

An hour later I was still aglow with the possibilities of romance. It was therefore appropriate that I found myself at my second favorite location in all of New York City—the first, of course, being any Starbucks coffee bar. I stood on the southwest corner of 20th Street and Fifth Avenue, right in front of Club Monaco or more precisely the entrance to what I call Gay Men's Shopping Mecca—or GMSM, which should not be confused with Gay Men's Sado-Masochists, unless you stand at the entrance with a maxed-out credit card.

GMSM is so named because if you walk south on either side of the street you will stumble across Gap, Banana Republic, J. Crew, Zara, Kenneth Cole, Pier 1 and, at the lip of the retail river, Paul Smith. To be honest I have never bought anything at Paul Smith, but I did briefly date an androgynous Pan-Asian Paul Smith salesclerk, whom I christened Ho-Sale, just to get a few free Paul Smith multicolored vertically striped shopping bags that I absolutely adore.

So there I stood in front of Ralph Lauren's Canadian bastard child with the number of my future life partner tucked into my pocket next to a credit card that demanded to be exploited. I always spend money whenever I feel my life is about to change in a positive way. I did it when I first got promoted to real producer at *ITNC* and not a yogurt smoothie–fetching, phone message–taking associate producer; I did it when my first, and *only*, case of gonorrhea cleared up; and now on the threshold of the most significant romance since Miss Barbra Joan Streisand married some former TV doctor, I would do it again. And although this was a spiritual celebration it was also a practical one—I needed a new wardrobe for my new life with Frank.

As is typical on a retail shopping excursion in the GMSM, you're bound to run into people you know or see at the bars or have had sex with once or twice before. While I was deciding if I should try on a pair of distressed jeans, size 32, thank you very much, Frank's face was momentarily pushed out of my mind as I noticed a familiar guy wearing the Chelsea Uniform: baseball cap pulled down low, light blue Abercrombie & Fitch zip-front sweatshirt, navy blue Nike track pants with a white stripe down the side. This particular guy was someone I affectionately called Fuck Counter. He earned his nickname not because his ass could double as a folding tray, but because he literally counts the number of times his dick enters you while fucking.

The first time Fuck Counter and I met was during Gay Pride in front of the Duplex Cabaret. Shaved down and horned up, we drank Bud Light out of plastic rainbow cups and sang Carol Channing's more memorable tunes with a bunch of other drunken partygoers, mocked the physically impossible alien-spawn Splash employees who do nothing but tend bar and work out, then went to his apartment and tried our hand at conversation, but realized we both just wanted to have sex.

Like so many sexual encounters south of 14th Street it began with a promise and ended with a lie. "Great cock!" somehow always ends up becoming "I'll call you." Here's what happened. Fuck Counter started fucking me and I was mentally airlifted to that place you think is only attainable for dewy Bel Ami models and their siblings and then I started to hear mumbling. I assumed Fuck Counter was being airlifted to the same place I was about to enter and he'd chosen to speak in tongues to the Bel Ami children. Then I realized he wasn't mumbling words, but consecutive numbers, and by the time he got to twenty-five I realized he was counting the number of times he had entered my ass. I felt like a Tootsie Roll Pop and he was the Owl trying to figure out how many thrusts it would take to get to my center. I tried to turn off my ears, but the Owl's counting only grew louder and my erection softer.

"Are you actually counting cock thrusts?" I finally asked.

"Forty-seven, remember that number," Fuck Counter ordered before pausing, but not exiting. "I tend to ejaculate prematurely. So my therapist suggested I count thrusts to control my sperm and teach myself not to come until I reach a certain number."

I digested this information like a sexual trouper who has seen much and done some.

"And are we approaching that magic number?" I queried.

"Well, my personal best is one-fifty-three, but your ass is pretty tight, so I don't know if I can make it that long," said Fuck Counter with a dopey grin.

In spite of my disappointment that he'd broken one of my cardinal rules and used the word *sperm* during sex, I'm a sucker for a challenge as well as a dopey grin. I felt my inner Mary Lou Retton grow along with my dick, and I tried to loosen up my inner ass. However, as my proctologist once told me, "Steven, you have the sphincter of a straight man." I had to face facts: my asshole is tight. If I couldn't help Fuck Counter by loosening up my ass, I'd have to help him another way.

"You want to count thrusts, boy?" I bellowed.

Fuck Counter was startled at first, but quickly realized I was totally on his side and willing to act as his sex coach.

"Sir! Yes sir!"

"Well, counting costs. And right here's where you start paying. In sweat!"

I kept shouting like Debbie Allen instructing dancers whose only chance at fame would be as chorus members of the bus and truck tour of *Fiddler on the Roof* starring Eddie Mekka and it seemed to do the trick. Fuck Counter was energized. His hands gripped my ankles like two vises, his face became a mask of focused concentration, and his dick swelled.

"Fifty-five!" he shouted.

With each thrust his shouting got louder, so by the time he reached 178 I could swear I heard the parade watchers outside counting along with him. Soon he gasped, "Two hundred and ten," orgasmed, and collapsed on top of me in a pile of muscle and sweat. His body felt wonderful and I rode an emotional roller coaster lying underneath him as I realized Fuck Counter could be a fun boyfriend if he wasn't so fucked up. Once I resigned myself to the fact that I couldn't explore this relationship emotionally, but only numerically, I was able to shoot my load and rush back to catch the end of the parade leaving Fuck Counter to clean up.

Heading to the Club M dressing room with my size-32 distressed jeans I walked by Fuck Counter and gave him a smile that said, "Hey, how are you doing?" "You look great," and "Glad to see you're alive and well, but I have no desire to get naked with you again." Comprehending my silent comments, Fuck Counter just leaned into me and whispered, "I'm up to three-twenty-five."

As I entered the dressing room, I carried not only my merchandise, but also an unexpected erection. Shopping satisfies on so many levels.

By the time I got to J. Crew, I had five bags and felt like Joan Collins sauntering down Rodeo Drive, if Joan Collins carried her own bags, which everyone knows is an activity relegated to a paid employee, i.e., her husband. I clutched one side of the J. Crew door as another good-looking Sunday-strolling gay retail whore clutched the other. Much to my joy I realized it was my best friend, Flynn McCormack.

"Ahhh!" Flynn shrieked.

"Ahhh!" I shrieked back.

"Bad night?" Flynn asked, eyeing my bags.

"Yes," I confessed. "But now I'm in love."

"Ooh, baby got bounce. I want to hear all about it, but first Mama needs some argyle."

Steven Ferrante and Flynn McCormack would make the perfect homo-couple if only we were in love. But, alas, some things are just not meant to be. I met Flynn when we were both at Boston University and he was an out-of-the-closet junior and I was a please-don't-unlock-the-closet-door freshman. Mutual friends set us up on a blind date not so much because they thought we'd be compatible, but because they knew Flynn would rip open my closet door and fling me out into the real world like a skilled obstetrician ripping a baby from the comfort and security of its mother's womb. And that's just what Flynn did. He reached into my symbolic vagina and yanked out my true self. He was the first person who taught me what it really meant to be out and proud. And even though we physically looked like a couple you'd be jealous of—Flynn's auburn hair, freckled cheeks, pale complexion, and six-foot-two swimmer's body perfectly complemented my dark brown locks, olive skin, high cheekbones, and five-foot-ten nicely muscled frame—there were no real romantic sparks between us. We did engage in a hot make-out session that resulted in my first facial burn, which still makes me wistful whenever I think about it, but something better than romantic sparks grew out of our first meeting, a flame of friendship that still burns to this very day. No one knows me better than Flynn and no one knows Flynn better than me, so for better or worse we're stuck with each other, which is just the way we both like it.

"Did you measure it?" Flynn asked in reference to Ely's penis, as we walked further south on Fifth Avenue toward Washington Square, carrying multiple bags of queergotten merchandise.

"No, but when I went to stroke it, it got lost in my fist."

"Ah jeez, poor guy. Perhaps I should send him this book I'm reading—*You're the Top: How to Be a Better Bottom in Twelve Easy Steps*. It's changed my life, it could change his."

"Thank you, but I think it's best if Ely and I go our separate ways."

"Sometimes that's best," Flynn agreed, "like me and Andy."

"I thought he was the new love of your life?"

"He was until I realized he's a freak," Flynn said. "Like every other man I've ever had, except you of course."

"You never had me," I corrected.

"I know," Flynn said. "Just testing you in case this latest setback made you embellish your memories."

"How thoughtful," I said, then asked tentatively, "Did he get upset when you told him?"

"No, he was fine with that," Flynn said.

"Good."

Flynn has been HIV-positive for the past ten years and on occasion it has gotten in the way of a budding relationship. Fortunately, healthwise, Flynn has never had a serious problem. At first we were both frightened and devastated by his diagnosis, but those feelings quickly gave way to the survival instinct—we both wanted Flynn to live. So I helped him find a wonderful doctor who found the right combination of medicine; he got to the gym more often, started eating healthier and, most important, clung to his optimistic spirit. It's what I love most about Flynn; he truly believes life is worth living. The only caveat being that there has to be good musical theater—so now that *Cats* has finally closed Flynn should live for a good long time.

"So what elevated Andy to freakdom?" I queried.

"Last night we were about to have sex for the first time," Flynn began. "We're on his bed and his dick is almost all the way in and he stops. I figure he wants to take it slow, which I love, so I close my eyes and get ready for him to crank up the volume, but there's no sound. I open my eyes and I see him smoothing out the sheets and fixing the pillows. So I said, 'Are you gonna fuck me or make your bed?' The freak pulls out and starts making his bed!"

"Losing out to bed linen, not very good," I said, trying to console him.

"No, it's not. He said, 'I just got these sheets from ABC, let's do it on the couch.' To which I respond, 'The moment's passed, hon, like Elton John's Broadway career.' "

"Really? What about *Billy Elliot*, I hear that's supposed to be great."

"That's a West End transfer, it doesn't count!"

"You theater queens are so harsh at times."

"Listen, Elton's said good-bye to the Yellow Brick Road, it's time he said good-bye to the Great White Way too. Especially after that *Lestat* debacle. That show sucked so bad it made *Dance of the Vampires* look Tony-worthy."

"I was talking about Andy."

"Oh yeah, him," Flynn continued. "I just got dressed and

left. Last thing I heard him say before the elevator doors slammed shut was 'Those sheets are seven hundred count.' Fuck him! I am worth nine hundred count at least!"

"It's like I always say, if you're gonna fuck a man, be a man and buy your sheets at Target like all the other cheap Marys," I declared. "Never mind, I didn't really like him anyway."

"Thank you," Flynn said.

"He had that birthmark on his earlobe. I always thought he was wearing an onyx clip-on. And each tooth was a different shade. Didja ever notice that? One was off-white, one was ecru, a few were mother-of-pearl."

"I said thank you," Flynn interrupted tersely.

"Sorry, I wasn't sure how bad I had to mock him to ease your pain."

"I'm eased," Flynn said, then smiled that warm smile I have grown to cherish. "Now tell me about you: my baby's in love?"

"Well . . ."

So as we entered Washington Square Park I told Flynn about my fateful meeting with Frank and how I totally understood love is not born from a few glances in Starbucks, but that I had a good feeling about him. And even if that feeling turned out to be completely wrong and Frank joined Andy as the newest resident of Freakville, it couldn't hurt to be a little happier for a few hours.

"My optimism seems to have rubbed off on you," Flynn said with a smile.

"I'm trying."

"I'm happy for you," Flynn said with complete honesty. "I'd give you a hug, but Frank may be stalking you right now and I don't want your love life to turn into a *Three's Company* episode where Mr. Roper mistakes our friendly bonhomie for full-out man-to-man love."

"You really think he could be stalking me?" I asked, trying desperately not to look around the park.

"Steven honey, I've lived in this city for twelve years, nothing shocks me."

* * *

That night when I got home I had four messages. The first two were from Lindsay. Message number one was placed from the bathroom of some guy whose appendage, Lindsay claimed, might rival Ely's thumb/penis. Message number two was placed by a hysterical Lindsay from the street three minutes later after he discovered the man whose thumb/penis rivaled Ely's was none other than Ely. The last two were from my mother and compared to her messages, Lindsay's seemed tame.

"Steven, it's your mother. I need you to do me a favor. Call me!" my mother's voice, a nasal mix of northern New Jersey and southern Italian, bellowed.

"Steven! It's your mother! Are you ignoring me?" my mother's voice bellowed even louder than before. Her tirade continued, each word hitting the air like the heels of an angry, post-menopausal flamenco dancer. "I called you almost an hour ago, why haven't you called me back? Where can you possibly be on a Sunday? You said you liked to rest on Sundays. That's why you can't come over to have dinner with me. Are you lying to me, Steven? Have you become a son who lies to his mother? Are your restful Sundays an elaborate lie? I would really like to know so I can adjust my positioning on the chart of what's important in your life. I thought I was in the first box, Steven, but obviously I am mistaken!"

Contrary to popular opinion, my mother is not Jewish, she's Sicilian, which means she's like a Jew, but has access to a gun. At sixty-seven, Anjanette Ferrante is a forceful woman who has only taken no for an answer once, when she asked my father's doctor if the operation he suggested would save his life. I knew that if I didn't call her back immediately she would be at my office tomorrow morning wearing a black mourning veil.

"Ma, it's me," I said after she picked up the phone before the first ring ended.

"Me who?" she countered.

"Your favorite son!"

"Paulie, how nice to hear from you," my mother said over-dramatically. "I wish your brother Steven would return my phone calls as quickly as you do."

"Oh shut up, Ma! I was out shopping. It's how I relax."

"Where's your cell phone? What if I died, how would anyone contact you?"

"If you die, it doesn't matter when I get the call. You'll already be dead!"

"Don't yell at your mother!" my mother yelled.

"Don't leave crazy messages on my machine!" I yelled back. "I save them, you know. When I accumulate enough I'm going to use them against you in a court of law and have you committed."

"Like your father didn't try that a hundred times," she replied.

"Anjanette, I'm ignoring you," I said, then braced myself and continued, "Now what do you mean by 'favor'?"

My mother's tone of voice immediately changed from marked to telemarketer.

"As president of the Salvatore DeNuccio Tenants Group it is my responsibility to entertain the tired, the hungry and the poor of our small, impoverished village."

"You live in a retirement community in Secaucus, Ma, not Ellis Island!" I said. "You have tennis courts, a pool, a bingo hall, and a piano bar. I can't wait until I'm sixty-five so I can move in. I've already put my name on the waiting list."

"We want more, Steven! We're in the twilight of our years and we want more than a few laps in a heated pool and Sing-a-Long with Jerry Herman night," she shouted back. "I ask you as a gay man who knows a thing or two about the musical theater, how many times can you sing about corn husks and bougainvillea?"

Finally my mother was speaking my mother tongue.

"All right, what do you want from me now?"

"I want one of your soap people to come here and sing for our Christmas party," she said nonchalantly.

"Christmas isn't for another two months," I shot back without a trace of nonchalance.

"A good president plans early," she responded with a trace of disdain. "So which star can I say is going to sing? The pregnant nun or the blind obstetrician?"

"You know I can't help you," I said, trying to reclaim my calm.

"Remember the songs need to be happy ones, nothing about Jesus freezing in a manger or wise men bribing innkeepers," she said calmly, ignoring me. "Ideally we'd only like songs that Bing Crosby might have sung. Everybody loves Bing."

"Ma, we've been down this road before. I need to separate my personal life from my professional."

"Oh really?"

My heart missed a beat. I knew that this tone of my mother's voice meant that she had found something out about me that she was about to use against me. It was the same tone of voice she used when she found the *Playgirl* magazine under my bed when I was seventeen and then asked if I wanted to hone my organizational skills by cleaning up the garage.

"Then perhaps you can explain why you are quoted in this week's *Homo Extra* magazine as saying, 'I'm thrilled that I was able to work out our production schedule so Lorna Douglas—one of the top stars of *If Tomorrow Never Comes*—will be the showcase of this year's Gay Men's Health Crisis holiday show. It gives me such real satisfaction when my professional life can merge with my personal.' "

My mother had so blindsided me with this stunning revelation that for a second I almost missed the obvious.

"Why the hell are you reading *Homo Extra?*"

"Lenny Abramawitz recently became homosexual and his granddaughter who lives in the city brings him gay materials to help him cross over," she explained. "Loni is very sweet. Bucktoothed, but sweet."

"Ma, the GMHC gala is a very high-profile gig for Lorna," I said. "She wants to transition to Broadway and this is a great opportunity for her."

"And what is the Salvatore DeNuccio Tenants Group Christmas celebration?" she asked. "I'll tell you what it is. It's what the Secaucus *Herald* called '*The* annual holiday treat for mature adults.' And they put the *The* in italics!"

"Ma, I really don't think I can help you out," I said, knowing full well that by the end of our conversation I would have committed to help her out and agreed to run the lights for the show myself.

"Stevie, you have to do this for your mother," she began. "I already told my ladies that one of your soap people will be appearing live to sing and perhaps dance."

"Well, you shouldn't have committed yourself," I said, exasperated. "You watch *I Love Lucy* every day. Have you learned nothing?"

"I was put on the spot! Paula D'Agostino started talking about her kid who works on that friggin' *Today* show. She said Katie Couric—who Paula said *still* talks to her daughter—is going to come here and demonstrate what a colonoscopy really is and I just couldn't take it anymore. I told Paula, 'Katie can shove her colonoscopy up her ass, my Stevie is going to bring us the gift of music this holiday season.' My ladies cheered me on," my mother added proudly. "You cannot make me disappoint my ladies, Steven."

Before I could even utter a reason why Lorna could not perform at Mr. DeNuccio's retirement villa, she continued.

"What did I tell you the day you told me you were homosexual when I found you trying to squeeze into my Easy Spirit beige pumps? What did I say?"

"You said you weren't disappointed in me," I responded sheepishly.

"That's right. I was disappointed in your choice of shoe, but I was not disappointed in you because you were gay."

"I know," I said even more sheepishly.

"So don't disappoint me now, Steven. I need you more than ever."

"I will do my best to get someone to sing at your show."

"That's my boy," my mother said proudly. "Now I have to go, bingo starts at seven and Mama need a jackpot!"

So many things raced through my mind after my mother hung up on me. Why it should never surprise me that I get sucked into her hijinks, how I secretly love to get sucked into her hijinks, and how Flynn and my mother both refer to themselves as Mama. I made a mental note to ask Lorna Douglas if she'd like to tour as I pulled the torn piece of the *New York Times* Arts section out of my pocket. I took a deep breath, happily realized that I hadn't felt this nervous since I asked out Johnny Sanducci, the premed student who became my first boyfriend, and dialed Frank's number. After four rings the machine clicked on. As I listened to Frank's deep masculine voice assure me that I had called the right number, that I should leave a message with my date and time, and that he would get back to me as quickly as humanly possible, I thought that perhaps I should hang up and call him back later. But then I realized my number would be electronically saved on his machine so when I called him back later he'd know I had called him previously and hung up. Damn technology!

"Hi Frank, this is Steven," I started. Then I coughed. "Sorry. This is Steven from Starbucks. You, um, gave me your number on page three of the Arts section so I'm calling. I'll keep this short and sweet so I don't scare you off before I ever learn your last name, which I swear is something I've only done to two other guys before. That was a joke. It was actually three guys. That was another joke. Sorry, I guess it's not good to joke when you don't have an audience. Makes you feel like Carrot Top. That was another joke."

It was then that I remembered what Johnny Sanducci said when he broke up with me. "You're a really sweet guy, but you should never try to tell a joke." Taking a deeper breath I continued rambling on Frank's voice mail.

"Please note that if I could erase this message I would, but I can't so this, sadly, will have to count as our first conversation," I said, stifling a nervous laugh. "Please don't use this message against me and give me a call when you can or as quickly as humanly possible—you see I do listen, even though I have a tendency to ramble when I'm nervous. Okay, that's all, I'll talk to you later."

I left my home number and my work number on his machine and was about to give him my cell phone number when I realized I had already blown it with Mister Devastatingly Handsome Regular Guy so it really didn't matter if I gave him my Social Security number, he was never going to call and my love life, which had been so promising less than an hour ago, was now as infertile as Lorna's character, Ramona, on *ITNC*.

Two hours later, Frank still hadn't called me. I stood in front of my bathroom mirror for about twenty minutes trying to figure out why I felt so handsome when Frank's green eyes stared down at me and why I felt so ugly when I stared at myself. When I finally tore myself away from the mirror, I immediately picked up the phone and started to dial Frank's number, then stopped. I started several more times, stopped several more times and once got all the way to the sixth digit before slamming the phone down in frustration because I realized if this relationship stood any chance of survival Frank had to return my first phone call. It was the least he could do.

For the rest of the evening, I putzed around my apartment, cleaned then re-cleaned my mini-kitchen, and finally watched an *I Dream of Jeannie* episode on TV Land, which simply made me long for a simpler, more magical time. But no matter what I did, I kept wondering why Frank didn't call me back. A few minutes before midnight, I finally turned off the television and accepted that my day would end like it had started, with me being duped by a man. As I dragged my taut-yet-single ass into bed and pulled the charcoal gray Calvin Klein comforter and complementary pale pink sheets up to my chin, I clung to one saving grace: my full-size bed is much smaller than Ely's, so chances were good that at least one other gay man in New York City was feeling lonelier than I was tonight.

Chapter Three

Monday mornings on the set of *If Tomorrow Never Comes* are like Willy Wonka's chocolate factory before the tiny Oompa-Loompas stick their tiny chocolate time cards into the tiny chocolate time card machine and man their tiny chocolate stations. It's all boring book scenes without the jaunty yet repetitive music. And like Mr. Wonka's factory it can also be a dangerous place to be. Unless you learn to follow the instructions from the network brass, ignore the phone calls from every actor's agent, and stay far, far away from the show's resident diva.

Miss Loretta Larson hates every morning, afternoon, and evening spent in fictional Wonderland, but she hates Monday mornings the most. Mainly because she spent Saturday and Sunday in a drunken stupor trying to forget that on Monday morning she once again has to take up residence as Regina O'Reilly, the grande dame of Wonderland. Loretta is a bitter, angry, lonely actress, but the fans adore her so even though she is also a bad actress, she's one lucky lush. For the past twenty-eight years Loretta Larson has repeated the same facial expressions, vocal inflections, and cosmetic injections, yet somehow manages to keep the fans of *ITNC* entertained with her performance and obsessed with her persona. They worship at her 100-percent-proof, liver-unfriendly altar and, thus, everyone else who works with Loretta worships her as well.

"Loretta!" I exclaimed, clutching my Venti skim, extra-hot,

light-whipped peppermint mocha (which I will refer to henceforth as my Starbucks Usual). "Love the poncho."

"Some fuckin' Mexican immigrant wanted to charge me fifty bucks for it on the Upper East Side," she exclaimed in her trademark raspy voice. "I said, 'You're not even *allowed* on the Upper East Side!' I tossed him a twenty and told him to give me the poncho or I was going to call INS."

"Damn those leaky borders," I replied.

Before I could tell her how the yellow angora of the poncho almost perfectly matched the yellow jaundice of her skin, the Loretta everyone knew, hated, and fawned over announced her arrival in typical Monday morning fashion.

"People!" she shouted very much like the male passengers on the *Titanic* when they were told there really were no extra life jackets. "Where's my fucking coffee?!"

Experience had taught me that when Loretta screeched, you had to get out of the way or risk being trampled by the throng of interns, entry-level producers, personal assistants, and nervous executives who inevitably responded to her banshee cry the way the Oompa-Loompas responded to Mr. Wonka's piccolo whistles. (Which I always believed was a nod to Captain Von Trapp's ingenuous way of calling his children to order before Maria swooped in from the mountains and offered the captain two new favorite things to wrap his lips around.) My adrenaline kicked in and I, along with my trusty Starbucks Usual, sought cover in the first office I could find, which luckily was the site of the production meeting I was almost late for.

"Steven!" cried Laraby Simmonson, my boss *and* a closeted homosexual.

To be honest, no one knows if Laraby really is gay, but he is definitely gay-ish. And all that's needed to start a rumor about the sexual status of a single man working in the soap opera industry is the *ish* part. Personally, I never understood the fascination about Laraby's sexual preference because he looked like a cross between Dick Cheney and Jeff Stryker. Even if he did possess an incredibly long, thick and mouthwatering dick, he was also fifty-something, short, balding, pasty, and when he wasn't being arrogant he was being charming in order to persuade you to believe in or do something you knew in your gut was false and evil. But in defense of all the "Is he or isn't he?" rumors, Laraby is the only person I know who can transfeminate from frat boy to sissy queen in three seconds flat. And transfemination usually occurred on Monday mornings as a tonic to thwart Loretta's hungover harangues.

"Dude!" Laraby shouted like my college dorm buddy. "We went up one-tenth of a point in the ratings!"

"That's great news," I said with a fake smile since I had already heard the news over the weekend.

Then Laraby shifted gears and sounded like my other college dorm buddy, who went to bizarre lengths to try and catch glimpses of me partially or fully naked.

"That's *fabulous* news, Stevie! We should celebrate. Is it too early in the morning for canapés? What about a mixed fruit parfait? Chez Vouvez downstairs has the freshest berries all year long, *all year long*, can you believe it? And the chef, Roget, who I think is from Prague, puts them in the most darling parfait glasses that have slender necks and plump bottoms. They remind me of my mother. What do you say, Stevie? Should we do it? Should we celebrate?"

At that moment I realized even if Laraby was gay, I didn't care. I was not the canapés, parfait, or Vouvez type. I like things simple. And he was a very complicated man.

"Why don't we just raise our coffee cups in honor of everyone's hard work?" I said.

A light mist appeared over Laraby's eyes as suddenly as a San Francisco fog. My words had touched him.

"Your simplicity and honesty never cease to amaze me, Steven," Laraby said as his eyes welled with water. "Perhaps one night we can go to dinner. Some place simple, and talk about the simple things."

I took an extra-long sip of my Starbucks Usual (which I will refer to henceforth as my SU) and was contemplating how to articulate a response that wouldn't get me fired or groped, when the rest of the production staff barged into the room. Perfect timing *is* a soap's mainstay.

"Bitchola is in rare form this morning," cried Lourdes, the continuity girl. "She got all up in my face crazy cuz I told her that hot coffee is only gonna make her hot flashes seem hotter."

"Did she throw her coffee in your face?" asked Leon, the lead director.

"No, she spit it on me," Lourdes replied, showing us her coffee-stained shirt. "I'm letting the stains settle, then I'll sell it on eBay to one of her psychotic fans. Give me a bitch, I'll make bitchinade."

"Excuse me," Laraby said as a cue that the Loretta-bashing should cease. "I'd like to propose a toast."

With the same conviction that Brigitte Nielsen once adopted to convince Sly Stallone that she would remain faithful to him even if the *Rocky* franchise went bankrupt, Laraby explained that despite the harsh truth that the world of soap opera had seen much better days, *ITNC* was still able to perform a miracle every now and again. At least one-tenth of a miracle. And before we entered the madness that is Monday morning, he wanted us to raise our coffee cups and pay homage to all of those who helped make this mini-miracle come true.

While no one was looking, Laraby raised his coffee cup one-tenth higher in my direction and winked at me, just like Frank had at Starbucks less than twenty-four hours before. I smiled weakly; was this a sign from above that I should sprint to my office to call Human Resources, or to call Frank? Regardless of what signals I was being sent, the phone calls would have to wait; Monday morning had begun and all else, including my Frank, would have to be put on hold for the next nine hours. When I'm at work, I am all business.

A half-hour later I ran to my office to check my messages while there was a break in taping. Lorna and Loretta were in the middle of a crucial scene that was an extension of last Friday's cliffhanger in which Lorna as Ramona reveals to Loretta as Regina, Ramona's older sister, that she has always known that

Renata, their baby sister, never died in the boating accident five years ago, but has been in a coma in a secret location somewhere near Butte, Montana. It was this final part that was holding up production. Loretta was having yet another emotional breakdown because unbeknownst to the head writer, Loretta was, in fact, born somewhere near Butte, Montana, but had been run out of town when she was sixteen years old after her father discovered she was pregnant by one of the ranch hands. She got a botched abortion, was told she could never have children again, and that she could also never return to Butte or the surrounding area as she had shamed and defiled her family's name. Some people have every reason to drink. And when I checked my machine and realized Frank still hadn't called me back I felt like I was quickly becoming one of those people.

Fortunately I'm obsessed with planning so my day wasn't as horrible as it could have been. I had prepared for what I knew would be a HINE—which is pronounced *Hi-Nee* and stands for Highly Intense Neurotic Experience—and forwarded my home phone to my work phone so during the day I would only have to check the messages left on one phone and not two. Seven years of therapy had not taught me how to corral my uncontrollable neurotic thoughts, but it had taught me how to make them seem more controllable.

Three hours later, while the writers were trying to decide if Renata should be moved from her secret location in Butte to one near Boise, Idaho or Cheyenne, Wyoming, I raced to my office again. Still no message from Frank, just one from my mother asking if Lorna Douglas had agreed to sing for the Salvatore DeNuccio Tenants Group. Frank may have disappointed me with his inconsistency, but my mother never would. At four hours and counting, I made my assistant check my messages, but Frank still remained silent. Five hours later I couldn't help myself and walked out of a budget meeting claiming a weak bladder. When I realized I was still in the no-Frank zone I almost threw the phone out the window. My mother, bless her heart, remained consistent and left two more messages of increased urgency about Lorna and her New Jersey debut. I wrote *Lorna & Salva-*

tore on a Post-it and put it on my desk to remind me to deal with this matter when my head wasn't drowning in thoughts and images of Frank.

Seven hours later Frank still hadn't called me. I didn't care that Loretta was taking valium with a bourbon chaser or that Laraby kept winking at me, all I could think about was that rat bastard Frank and how if he didn't call me I would trump every psychologically challenged actor who ever appeared in our show by having a petit mal seizure right on set. I knew I needed to change direction or else I'd spiral out of control quicker than Jackée Harry's career, so I counted to ten and reacted the only way a normal, red-blooded American gay man would: at five o'clock I sent an emergency e-mail to the boys and told them to meet me at Starbucks at six. I had to vent over a Venti.

"Why hasn't he called me?" I questioned my friends as well as the universe.

"Why are you shaking?" Lindsay asked. "Are you hooked on Dexatrim again?"

"It's my fourth Starbucks today," I replied shakily.

"Honey, did you eat?" Flynn inquired.

"I had some baby carrots around noon."

"Mama need starch," Flynn said, tossing me a Yogurt Honey Balance bar. "It'll absorb all that caffeine."

"Not to mention the shock that your Mister Regular is probably just another regular two-timing, phone-number-tossing, no-good Chelsea boy with a killer smile and a cold heart," Lindsay added.

"Sounds like someone's channeling Patsy Cline *after* the plane crash," said Gus in his perfect British diction that always sounded vaguely pompous and condescending, but because it also sounded more intelligent and superior than any American voice ever spoken, it was a sound that we all loved. "It's only been one day, Steven."

"Could you stop thinking rationally for a moment?" I asked. "I need your support."

Gus ran his manicured fingers through his close-cropped, gray-speckled ebony hair as he pondered this request. He took off his titanium and matte black-framed Modo eyeglasses and stared at me with eyes so blue they would have humbled Paul Newman.

"Can't I do both?"

"No, Gus, you can't!" Lindsay replied. "The only time *both* works is when the Russian pairs figure skating team wins the Olympics because some Russian judge bribed a cash-poor French judge and the Canadians get robbed of their gold medal and the only way to make things right is for the Olympic Figure Skating Commission to give gold medals to *both* teams. If you haven't noticed, that is not happening now. Steven does not need rationality *and* support so stop thinking old-man thoughts and pony up some positive vibes."

"You know, Lindsay, Steven isn't the only one who could benefit from rational thought," Gus said, sounding completely pompous and condescending.

As always, Flynn decided to moderate this impromptu gay men's group therapy session.

"Boys, there is no *I* in gay. But there is a *Y*. So let's remember *why* we're here," Flynn said with a remarkably straight face. "We're here to help Steven."

As expected, Lindsay spent the next several minutes apologizing for his outburst and explaining why some words like *both* make him relive the injustice that is the modern day Olympiad. We all told him that we understood. We didn't specify that what we understood was that he was psychologically damaged from the events in Norway and every four years when the Winter Olympics rolled around his skates had to be confiscated or else he would use them as razor blades to end his pain finally and symbolically. That was something that was simply understood.

"Maybe there's something wrong with his phone," Flynn offered.

"Maybe he got called away on a business trip?" Gus blurted out.

"Or maybe he had a family emergency," Lindsay added. "You love family oriented guys."

This show of support was catching on faster than a daisy chain among out-of-work actors in West Hollywood.

"Ooh! I know!" Flynn shrieked in a higher octave than normal. "Maybe, just maybe someone in his family tragically died. That would be wonderful."

"That would be horrible," I said.

"Yes, but no," Lindsay interrupted. "Horrible for Frank, but a wonderful way for you to show how comforting and consoling you could be to the grief stricken. It's the perfect Boyfriend Test."

"That's right! Show him your Mother Teresa side," Gus offered. "But remember to dress like Princess Diana. Didn't they make the cutest couple? I personally think Mother Teresa died of a broken heart."

"What if Frank's just not interested?" I asked meekly.

Like a bad hostess I had brought the party to a grinding halt and dismantled the chain of supportive daisies. The group was forced to regroup and contemplate a different approach.

"Well, honey," Flynn began weakly. "That is a possibility."

There was another awkward pause as we all reflected on how well gay men can flip-flop even when they're not in bed. Maybe what happened was that Frank got caught up in the magic that Starbucks creates and before he thought it out completely he jotted his phone number on a newspaper and thrust it into my eager hands. Then maybe when Frank got outside and breathed in real air and not Starbucks magic-air he realized offering himself to me was a mistake. Maybe he knew I wasn't worthy.

"What's wrong with me?" I asked.

"Nothing is wrong with you!" Flynn and Gus cried out in unison.

"You don't spend enough time on the treadmill!" Lindsay added.

"Shut up, Lindsay," Flynn reprimanded. "Steven, there isn't anything wrong with you. It's the gay species, our interactions are very intricate. Like the relationship between Carrie and her mother in *Carrie: The Musical*."

Everyone at the table, including me, let out a collective moan, for Flynn had once again compared something important and real to the Broadway stage's biggest flop, the musicalization of Stephen King's horror classic *Carrie*. About five people saw the show in '88 and Flynn was one of them. Since then he had become an evangelist for the singing telekinetic and at any moment could and often would wax rhapsodic over the melody that was Carrie's pain regardless of the fact that it had nothing to do with the present conversation. Like right now.

"Gay men are their own worst enemies," Flynn began. "They, like Carrie and Mrs. White, superbly played by Outer Critics Circle nominee Betty Buckley, are victims of their own psycho-sexual-socioreligious dogma."

"Flynn, we're talking about some bloke who forgot to ring Steven back," Gus corrected.

"It's a symptom," Flynn continued. "A symptom of the society that we have collectively created. Its structure is weak and if we don't mend it, it will crumble."

"Just like the way the gym crumbled at the end of the movie?" Lindsay asked, trying to sound like an innocent commentator when he was really a guilty instigator.

Flynn responded the way we all knew he would. He took the bait.

"I'm not talking about the movie!" Flynn barked. "The movie is a manifestation of Brian De Palma's fear of Hollywood. A fear that made him turn from the source material—Stephen King's straightforward, yet poetic prose—and run into the dictatorial arms of the movie studio machine. Brian didn't trust his source, like gay men don't trust theirs. They want to constantly be like the blockbuster and appeal to a wider audience instead of being happy to appeal to a niche market. *Carrie: The Musical* isn't afraid."

"But *Carrie: The Movie* was scary," Lindsay said, unable to remain silent.

"Yes, it was scary!" Flynn freaked. "Because it was a prime example of how yet another talented filmmaker bent to the whims of the Hollywood dictatorship."

"What about the hand coming up through the grave at the end?" Lindsay asked. "Tell me that wasn't scary?"

"That isn't even in the book!" Flynn screamed. "And now yet another gay man has bent to the whims of the gay male society. 'Here's my number, call me. No, wait, I can't trust my instincts so when you call I won't return your phone call.' If gay men want to be trusted by each other and the hetero world, they have to begin by trusting themselves and stop playing this endless game of push me–pull me."

"Ah yes, the old llama dilemma," Gus commented.

Flynn didn't even hear Gus's *Doctor Dolittle* reference; he was still under Carrie's musical spell.

"We as a community—and I am not including lesbians, bisexuals or transgendered peoples because they need to stop piggybacking and create their own community 'cause they're sucking the life force out of ours—must take a cue from Mr. King and Michael Gore, the wildly misunderstood composer of *Carrie,* and explore the psycho-sexual-socioreligious dogma that we have allowed to dictate our framework before that framework ruptures and traps us within our own fear."

Flynn was finally finished. He took a gulp of his coffee to refuel and waited to see if his didactic words had any effect on his pupils.

"So what you're saying," I started, "is that Piper Laurie really wanted to fuck the shit out of Sissy Spacek and then knife her to death so she didn't have to deal with her emotionally anymore."

"My insight is wasted on you people!" Flynn shouted.

"Give it one more day," Gus said rationally. "Then if Frank still hasn't called you back you can call him again."

"I have a better idea," I said. "Why don't one of you call Frank right now to see if he's around? That way I'll know if he's busy or just uninterested."

"Even if Frank answers, it won't tell you anything," Gus rationalized. "It'll just tell you that he's home."

"And not interested in calling me back!" I said, sounding as pathetic as I knew I would.

"Is this about Jack?" Lindsay asked.

The silence this question stirred was deafening. If this were a scene from *ITNC* the end credits would roll or we'd at least cut to a commercial. Everyone at the table knew that my ex-partner Jack DiRenza had told me to leave his apartment and his life four years ago on July fourth (forever ruining for me a day that to the rest of the country is a cause for celebration) and everyone at the table had shared their advice as to how best to move on, as well as their shoulders for me to cry on when I didn't think moving on was an option. But everyone at the table also knew that Jack was more than just an ex-partner. He was the love of my life and the man I thought I would grow old and happy with. No one at the table, including myself, ever thought he was the person who would push me from his life because he felt tied down, or as he so eloquently put it, "too bored with the whole commitment thing." So like most fragile elements of a person's past, Jack had been carefully packaged and stored somewhere just out of reach. Now Lindsay had ripped him thoughtlessly from the distant emotional shelf I had placed him on and the result was shocking.

"Lindsay!" Flynn scolded. "Don't say the J-word."

"Steven, I'm sorry," Lindsay said. "But it has to be said. This is not the first time you've freaked out since Jack broke up with you. It's becoming a pattern. So before it gets out of hand and you waste any more time hurting yourself you have to admit if your reaction to Frank's tardy response is a result of your split with Jack."

An odd thing happened when Lindsay spoke sense; it caused those listening to pause. But within that pause was quite a bit of action. First the listener had to remind himself that it was indeed Lindsay speaking. Then he had to repeat his comment silently, ignore the surprise that his comment included not one figure skating term, process his comment, ignore the surprise that his comment actually contained sense, and articulate a response. After a few moments the pause was over.

"This isn't about Jack," I said.

"Are you sure, hon?" Flynn asked.

I looked at my three closest friends—Flynn, Lindsay, and Gus—and realized I had to be honest. And I knew there was no reason why I shouldn't be. They chose to be in my life and I chose to let them stay. They had to take the good with the bad, since they knew that I had done and would continue to do the same for them.

"It's not about Jack, it's about me," I said. "I'm really tired of looking for someone, but I'm not ready to give up. I'm scared that I don't know the difference between some jerk who throws his number at me just so he can get laid and a nice guy who would like to get to know me on a deeper level."

I could tell from the looks on their faces that such honesty was not what they'd thought they'd hear when they were summoned to Starbucks. But I could also tell from their expressions that I had hit upon a shared truth. They understood me, which is exactly what friends are supposed to do.

"You have to let go and let gay," Lindsay said.

"What?" I responded.

"Let go of everything that is holding you down and be your gay self," Lindsay explained. "Let go of your impatience to find your soul mate, your preconceived notion that every new guy you meet will *be* your soul mate. . . ."

"And Jack," Flynn finished. "You have to let him go too, Steve. Not only Jack himself, but what the two of you shared. For a while you had perfect. And now you don't. That doesn't mean you're never going to have perfect again. It just means that perfect now means something a little bit different than it did when you were with Jack and now you have to figure out what perfect means to you."

I looked at my friends again, closer this time and without the Pity Party eyes. It was then that the light dawned on me.

"Did you all swallow Dr. Phil pills with your Viagra this morning?" I queried.

"A bit too sappy?" Flynn asked.

"It was fine up until the perfect part," I said.

"I thought that was a bit over the top myself," Gus remarked.

"But I'm British. 'Thank you' is considered over the top in some parts of the U.K."

"I stand by everything I said," Lindsay declared. "You're handsome, you're hot, Flynn tells me you're hung. If I were you I'd be freaking out why loser boy didn't return my phone call. But remember, I saw him too and I don't think he's worth pining over."

"That's 'cause you were on a Dick Button rampage," I said, reminding Lindsay.

"Again?" asked Flynn and Gus, once again in unison.

Lindsay's face scrunched up the way it did when he was about to do some incredibly difficult jump on the ice. He looked like he was going to do a triple-triple combination, but instead he just banged his fist on the table.

"That man just annoys the shit out of me! I'd love to take his two Olympic medals and shove 'em—"

"Thanks, guys," I said politely, shutting Lindsay up.

"For what?" Flynn asked as a representative for the group.

"For reminding me that when a crisis arises I should simply"— I paused for effect—"let go and let gay."

"To letting go," Flynn said, raising his cup.

"And letting gay," we all responded.

So for the second time that day I found myself raising my coffee in honor of some intangible notion. And for the second time that day while I sat with my arm outstretched, my coffee raised, and a fake smile plastered on my face, I was consumed with the same persistent thought: *why hasn't Frank called me back?* And then another thought popped into my head: *why can't I just let him go?*

I answered my questions almost immediately thanks to Lindsay's earlier advice. Like some people just can't be anything other than gay, other people just don't want to be let go.

Chapter Four

The next day was as chaotic and poorly choreographed as a Bollywood musical. It was so haphazard that by noon I was actually considering changing my name to Kumar "Steven" Patel, but I reeled myself in knowing my mother would have a coronary if I turned my back on my Sicilian heritage, even if she was developing a taste for cumin thanks to the latest occupant of the Salvatore DeNuccio Towers, the widow Padma Maharaji. As one madcap hour evolved into another I could almost hear the high-pitched nasal twangings of a chorus of Hindi dancers wearing Western garb and gyrating in front of a huge waterfall. Then in the middle of a sun-drenched desert. Then stopping traffic in the center of Bombay's busy market district. My day, like a screwball comedy in Sanskrit, clung desperately to its through line.

Here's how the day went. Bright and early on Tuesday morning I marched into the *ITNC* studios with the determination of Norma Rae and the optimism of Gidget, resolved to ask Lorna Douglas if she would star in my mother's Christmas celebration. But by our first early morning break my resolve recoiled. I succumbed to the belief that if you think the answer to your question will be bad it's safer to avoid asking the question altogether. By ten-thirty, however, I realized that if I didn't report back to my mother with a yea or a nay as to Lorna's participation pronto, she would use her maternal powers to psychically haunt me from the other side of the Lincoln Tunnel. She had done it before; she would do it again.

Luckily, luck was my lady and I spotted Lorna sitting by herself during a break in taping. Her lips were moving like those of a silent film star on crack, so I could tell she was using her downtime to memorize lines while a few feet away the makeup team surrounded her costar, Lucas Fitzgerald, to reapply a fake scar to his face. I knew it would take them more than a few minutes since Lucas's character, Roger Renault, was a race car driver who had sustained terrible burns from a recent boating accident and the resulting scar started at the left side of his forehead, ran over the bridge of his nose, somehow never made contact with his incandescent blue eyes, and ended on the sharpest point of his right cheek. The implausibility of the scar was matched only by the implausibility of my question getting a positive response from Lorna. But the time had come for me to somehow try and make the implausible plausible.

"Hey, Lorna! Sorry to interrupt, but this December my mother is organizing a Christmas musicale for her senior citizens' group in New Jersey and she'd like you to be the headliner and perform for free," I explained. "So how's about it?"

"Cool," was Lorna's monosyllabic reply.

For a second I thought she was referring to her scene partner's scar, which I had to admit did look grotesquely arousing, and in the next second I understood why Lindsay found the guy in *Mask* a masturbatory fantasy, but in the second after that I realized Lorna had seriously answered my indecent proposal.

"You'll do it?" I asked.

"Sure," she monosyllabically replied.

Just as I was beginning to think Lorna was saving all her dialogue for the camera, she added her disclaimer.

"As long as there's no press, I can use my own band and it's before the GMHC show," she demanded. "It'll be like a rehearsal."

If all women were so accommodating and logical, I might consider heterosexuality as an alternative lifestyle.

"Lorna!" I squealed. "Forgive my zeal, but you are the first woman since Lynda Bertadotto to make me truly happy."

"Who's Lynda Bertadotto?" she asked.

"Sixth-grade teacher," I explained. "She made me sit next to Richie Troisi so I could help him with his sentence deconstruction. He looked just like Scott Baio and I still have the puka beads he gave me as a thank-you for helping him master the intricacy of the adverbial clause."

"God, that's romantic," Lorna said. "Pathetic, but romantic. You should have the writers include that memory in my backstory."

"I'm sorry, but I prefer to keep the puka beads private," I replied. "Richie's married now with three kids and, well, I'd hate to stir up trouble."

"Gay *and* moral," Lorna said with a sad smile. "Another illusion shattered."

I ignored her stereotyping and circled back to the reason for our conversation—I needed to lock her in before the makeup team was finished cosmetically mutilating Lucas's otherwise flawless face and she would be called to the set.

"So I'll get the details from my mother, and her girl—which is me—will be in touch with your girl, who actually *is* a girl," I stammered, "and a mighty pretty one I might add."

Lorna tilted her chin to the left and clenched the skin around her eyes the same way she did when her character, Ramona, put a hit on her sister Renata's psycho doctor, Rodney, when she found out he caused Roger's accident as an act of revenge against Renata's family. I knew that look could not be good.

"You think she's *mighty* pretty?" Lorna queried.

How stupid could I have been? Lorna may be even tempered and cooperative most of the time, but she is still an actress midway through her second contract cycle on a daytime drama and perilously close to her thirtieth birthday. Every producer knows you don't tell an insecure, aging actress that her younger assistant is *mighty* pretty.

"Well, yes," I stumbled, "in that I-was-nice-looking-in-college-why-the-hell-am-I-so-ugly-in-the-real-world sort of way. And by real world I mean your world and not MTV's."

"She does wear a lot of makeup," Lorna rationalized.

"Applied with the restraint of a kabuki," I offered.

This comment seemed to pacify Lorna, and her artificial warmth started to thaw the ice in her veins. Soon the actress was all businesswoman.

"My GMHC gig is December fifteenth, and we have a one-hour rehearsal on the fourteenth. As long as your mother's thing is before then we have a deal," Lorna said. "If not, there's no way I'm hauling my ass to Jersey to entertain a demographic that's not going to be around long enough to do me any good."

Before I could mumble "That's the Christmas spirit," a high-pitched shriek pierced through the studio, sounding like an Indian princess after she's been ripped from her would-be lover's arms by a Hindi villain. In this instance, the Indian princess was being played by Lucas.

"My eye!" he screamed. "Oh dear God! My eye is on fire!"

Lucas's eye wasn't actually on fire, it only felt that way. Some of the glue holding the fake scar in place had dripped into his eye, causing it to turn a bright shade of red and burn like a Vietnam-era soldier's pee the day after he grabbed himself a fine piece of poontang. Not that I have any idea what that feels like, but I've heard stories. Lucas cried and flailed about so animatedly it took a while for the makeup team to flush out his eye with water. He didn't stop moving entirely until Lorna slapped him across the face.

"You're an actor!" she declared. "Use your pain."

I felt as if I was watching Uta Hagen bitch-slap Marlon Brando. Lucas's one good eye focused intently on Lorna, while the other one tried desperately to open fully. It was like watching a mildly retarded baby chick being born. But there was beauty within that ghastly looking inflamed eye. And ratings.

"Action!" the director shouted.

There was a kind of hush all over the set and then the magic of soap opera began. Lucas and Lorna as Roger and Ramona played out their scene with more sincerity and passion than either of them had ever previously produced under the harsh, unforgiving studio lights. At the end of the scene Lucas dropped to his knees, not out of thankfulness that he just delivered the performance of his life, but out of anguish as his reddened eye began to swell. This time when the director shouted, it was for an ambulance.

As they wheeled Lucas away on a gurney I waved good-bye, but since I was on the side with the injured eye I'm not sure that he saw my show of support. The director called for an emergency meeting with the writers to write Lucas's character out of the rest of the script, so I took the opportunity to press speed dial number one on my cell phone and once again call Frank. Just as I was hearing his message I got an incoming call. Could Frank finally be answering one of my many voice messages? Nope, just my mother. Well, if I couldn't be satisfied, at least I could satisfy.

"She'll do it," I said.

My mother and I speak the same language so there was no need for me to explain any further.

"That's wonderful!" she shrieked. "Paula D'Agostino is going to shit a brick when I tell her I booked Lorna Douglas."

"I'm so glad I could help."

"Tell your Lorna dress rehearsal will be the night before the show in the Community Room," she said. "I'll make some refreshments and there'll be a small invited audience so she can get the feel of the room."

"Ma, when exactly is the show?" I asked, then held my breath.

"The eighteenth," she replied.

"No!" I shouted, releasing my angry breath into the spiteful, spiteful air. "You have to push it up a week."

"I can't do that, December is completely booked. I have the Christmas tree lighting, the nativity play, the children's pageant starring Lenny Abramawitz as Santa."

"The gay Jew is playing Santa?"

"The children do not need to know!"

"Ma! Lorna won't do the show unless it's before the fourteenth, you have to rearrange your schedule."

"It's too late! I've already printed up the calendar of events. On heavy bond paper," she replied. "We're locked in until the end of the year."

"Old people need to be flexible! Death is right around the corner."

"I have no room for death in my date book," my mother countered, then paused for effect. "Look, Stevie, just tell Lorna to have her girl call my girl and we'll work this out."

"I am your girl!" I shouted. "And I'm telling you we can't work it out unless you change the date of your show."

"Then get me somebody else. Not for nothing, but Lorna's looking a little tired lately. She's always clenching the sides of her eyes. She's going to wrinkle if she keeps doing that," my mother informed me. "Honey, Mama has to go. Coco, the seamstress, is here and she's going to measure me for my Halloween costume. I'm going as Barbra Streisand."

I involuntarily pulled the phone from my ear when my mother's voice rose three octaves and twenty decibels.

"Come with me! We can be Barbra: Before and After! You can wear a midi-blouse and be Barbra from *Funny Girl* and I'll be Babs from *The Prince of Tides*. I'm due for a manicure anyway."

"How many times do I have to tell you, Ma, I don't dress up like a woman."

"Oh come on! Our only competition for Best Couple will be Sheila and Vinny Caruso; they're going as Myron and Myra Breckinridge. Vinny's going to be Myra, he's got less hair on his legs."

Faced with the realization that my mother was living in a home for aged drag queens, I hung up the phone.

"Lorna," I started. "The Christmas thing at my mother's isn't going to work out."

"No biggie," she replied. "Why don't you ask my assistant? She might be available."

Lorna turned from me in what seemed like slow motion, her bouncing and behaving hair whipping through the air and making her look like a brunette Heather Locklear in a vintage watercooler moment from *Melrose Place*. Until then, I had thought I handled the mighty pretty assistant near-fiasco rather well.

"Kidding!" Lorna squealed.

Obviously I had.

"That bitch who picks up my dry cleaning might be a few years younger than me," Lorna said, "but damn, I can act!"

Learning from my earlier faux pas, I remained quiet and gave Lorna one of my I'm-such-a-proud-producer stares.

"Tell your mother I'm sorry and ask Lucas to do the show."

Lorna once again started a slo-mo turn away from me à la Heather, but paused to glance back, allow her collagen-improved lips to slink into a smirk, and add, "I hear he's itching to sing."

The *Melrose* theme music pounded in my head as I contemplated what Lorna's smirk suggested. Could it be that hunky Lucas Fitzgerald—two-time *Soap Opera Digest* award winner for Best Male Lips, one-time contender for the coveted role of young Bob Barker in the E! original drama *Is the Price Right? The Untold Story of Bob Barker*—was gay? He did shave his chest, contour his eyebrows, and highlight his hair, but what guy didn't these days? Unfortunately, I didn't have time to play the gay guessing game because at that very moment there was a scene change and I saw Lindsay striding across the studio.

"Stevie!" Lindsay yelped. "Do you know how hard it is to get onto this set? Doesn't anyone remember that I was once the star of this sinking soap?"

"You were a day player. No better than nine out of ten waiters in the city," I reminded him. "What are you doing here?"

"I've come to take you to lunch," Lindsay replied. "Rudy Galindo opened up a new restaurant in SoHo called Blade. Isn't that a great name?"

"I give it a perfect six."

"Ahh! Skating lingo," Lindsay yelped again. "I *am* rubbing off on you."

"Linds, I'd love to go, but we're in a bit of a crisis mode here. One of the actors was rushed to the hospital."

"Drug overdose?"

"No."

"Alcohol poisoning?"

"No."

"What else is there?"

"Inflammation of the eye," I said, trying to make it sound deadlier than it was.

Lindsay leaned in confidentially and whispered in my ear.

"Is 'eye' a euphemism for 'dick'?"

"No!" Now it was my turn to yelp. "Why is your mind always in the gutter?"

"Sorry. I'm pre-horny."

"What are you talking about?"

"I didn't just come here to invite you to lunch, I also got an invitation to a sex party tonight. Say you'll come with me. I never go to these types of functions, but I feel like shaking things up a bit."

I thought for a moment and realized a sex party might be just what I needed. Forget my troubles, come on get . . . laid. And Lindsay was actually the perfect person to attend a sex party with. He really just liked basic missionary sex, with him on the bottom of course, and wouldn't force me to do anything outrageous. Plus he upheld the gay motto that what takes place at a sex party stays at a sex party and would never mention anything that took place ever again even if he and I were having a private conversation. Lindsay's offer seemed almost too good to pass up, until I remembered the other man in my life.

"What if Frank's there?" I asked.

"You can finally have sex with him."

"I want more than sex with Frank."

"Then what a perfect setting to discover if Frank is the right guy for you," Lindsay rationalized. "Surrounded by a hundred hot, sweaty, horny men, you and Frank choose each other. If that's not everlasting love, Stevie boy, I don't know what is."

"I can't," I said finally.

"Why not?" Lindsay said fitfully.

"Because I'd feel awkward and stupid if the next time I see Frank I'm standing butt naked with lube on my dick."

"Wear a jock."

"Lindsay, you don't understand," I replied. "And besides, if you're going to a sex party tonight why are you eating lunch? You know your digestive tract is unreliable."

"I was only going to lend my support to Rudy and sample the bar," Lindsay explained. "I hear they have a drink called a Michelle Kwantreau. Served on ice, of course."

"Of course. Well, you enjoy sipping Michelle, I have to put out some fires here."

"Steven, don't look so sad," Lindsay said. "I will ask every man at the party if his name is Frank. And if I find him I will fuck his brains out for not returning your calls. Because even though I'm a bottom, I'm tops with my friends."

"You're also an asshole."

"At least I'm a clean one."

Lindsay gave me a surprisingly supportive hug and waltzed out of the studio waving to the cameramen and the lesbian manning the Kraft food table as if he'd just shot his last episode after an incredible thirty-year run. With charm like that it was certain that tonight Lindsay's asshole would be as popular as it would be clean.

The rest of my work day became a logistical nightmare. I was forced to meet with the director and the writing team and together we decided to extend Lucas and Lorna's scene to include Lucas's emotional fall to the ground. Lorna, as Ramona, would later explain that Lucas's character, Roger, had suffered a mild stroke brought about by the emotional confrontation. This way they could exploit Lucas's true pain, plus explain his damaged eye if it never returned to its original state. Unfortunately, this also meant that we had to bandage the face of one of the extras to play Stroke Roger, turn all of Lorna's dialogue into monologues, and still shoot the rest of the script, which included a dream sequence in a Las Vegas casino, the pregnant nun going into labor in a secluded cave, and the blind obstetrician trying to find his way out of a cornfield maze after being lured there by none other than Rodney, the homicidal physician. It was just a typical day in Wonderland.

After work, I decided to pay Lucas a visit in the hospital. It was, after all, my duty as producer, but more importantly, I had a variety show to cast. My actions could be judged as selfish, but anyone who has ever fallen victim to the wrath of Anjanette Ferrante would understand and temper their judgment with mercy.

Like most things on the Upper East Side, Mount Sinai Hospital was devoid of any personality. It was a commanding structure and a powerful presence, but left little impression once you hopped on the 6 train and fled downtown. There was a reason that most gay men never strayed anywhere north of East 90th Street except for a quick visit to a sick friend or the occasional desperate hookup with a bi-curious married man.

As I entered Lucas's hospital room, I thought that either the network is doing something right or I'm doing something wrong, because his room was almost as large as my apartment—and furnished with more flair. He was propped up in bed surrounded by a smorgasbord of flora with a bandage covering his eye, watching a rerun of *Will & Grace*. I wondered if he was watching it out of professional curiosity or personal connection.

"Hi, Lucas," I said. "It's me, Steven."

Lucas turned and when he saw me his one good eye widened with surprise.

"Hey, Steven, I can't believe you came to see me."

"It's what they teach in Producing 101," I replied. "Always visit sick employees."

"Well, that's very thoughtful of you," he said, forming those award-winning lips into a genuine smile. "Thanks."

I put my cactus plant, which had seemed quirky when I bought it, next to a gorgeous spray of yellow roses and daffodils. Bending over a bit more than necessary, I was able to read the gift card attached to the yellow floral arrangement: *With one eye or two, you're still the sexiest man alive. Feel better. Love, M.* If that card had been sent to me, *M* would probably have stood for *Mother*, but that's an issue for me and my therapist. If I could find out who *M* stood for in Lucas's life, I would know if Lorna was telling the truth or setting me up for a fall. Being Italian, subtlety is not my forte, so I asked him point-blank.

"Who's M?"

"An ex."

"M's an ex?"

"Yup."

"Sounds like M wants to be an ex-ex."

"For some time now."

"So will M get . . . *its* wish?"

My choice of third-person pronoun did not escape Lucas. He might have been visually impaired, but he wasn't stupid. As he stared at me with one gorgeous blue eye, I thought there was subtext underneath that gaze, but it could have been the side effects of the Percodan.

"I think the real question is will I get mine."

Another smile, another intent one-eyed stare, another insipid plot twist involving Jack, Karen and a leaking fire hydrant.

"What wish would that be?" I asked, forcing my voice not to crack.

"Lorna phoned earlier and said you might have a proposition for me," he replied. "One that *sings* with opportunity."

It was my turn to catch the clever turn of phrase. So, Lorna had called Lucas to alert him that I might offer him the chance to star in the biggest show Secaucus has ever seen. That's why he was acting so coy and demure. It wasn't the Percodan, it was ambition.

"Can you sing?" I asked.

Like every wannabe starlet, from the little girl who wears her mother's false eyelashes and dances on her dining room table to the businessman who squeezes in tap lessons between meetings, Lucas answered my question the only way he knew how, by channeling Ethel Merman and singing the chorus of "There's No Business Like Show Business." It was a stirring rendition and Lucas displayed a powerful belting ability and the hint of a lovely vibrato. Moreover, I really didn't have the stamina to search for another star so I told Lucas the job was his.

"Thank you, Steven, this is the break I've been looking for," he effused.

"Let's see if you thank me after you've met my mother," I said.

"She can't be nearly as bad as the narcissistic drunk who reared me," he confided.

I flushed. Even if Lucas wasn't gay, maybe we did have something else in common: we were the products of questionable parenting.

"I owe you one, Steven."

"I was counting on it."

On my three-block walk to the subway I noticed not one, not two, but four Starbucks, which was quite a high concentration of retail outlets even for the Queen of Caffeine. I took it as a sign and decided to pop into a certain Starbucks in Chelsea that held fond memories for me. But when I got close to the door my optimism waned. Was I so lonely that I clung to the possibility that a chance encounter with a stranger in Starbucks was meant to be important and life changing—when it was more likely just a random footnote in a lifetime of romantic disappointments? Before I could answer, the bad Hindi movie that was my day provided yet another scene change as another friend popped up unexpectedly. Looking through the window, I saw Flynn surveying the room like a Connecticut housewife at a rival's dinner party. When he caught my eye, he beckoned. The next thing I knew I was sitting across from Flynn drinking my SU in the exact same seat I had occupied a few days earlier when I thought my love life was about to take off.

"What are you doing here?" we asked each other simultaneously.

"You first," I said, not completely willing to reveal my true intentions.

"I thought I might find Frank," Flynn admitted.

"Me too!" I squealed, ignoring my intent.

In a tone remarkably free of pity, Flynn explained that he was concerned about me and thought it might help if he stalked the Starbucks customers in case a certain dark-haired regular-looking guy walked in alone looking for someone. I was touched by Flynn's concern, but also felt foolish. Perhaps my behavior was

a by-product of my job: it's easy to blow things out of propor-
tion when you're accustomed to people regularly coming back
from the dead or marrying three weeks after a first hello. Evidently,
I had begun to live my life in the exaggerated terms of soap
opera. The truth was, I could remain seated for the next three
days and Frank wouldn't waltz through the Starbucks doors accompanied by his own personal theme music and soft lighting.

"I can't make any excuses," I said. "Clearly, Frank's not interested."

"How does that make you feel?" Flynn asked.

I thought about it for a moment and realized I was feeling
lots of conflicting emotions, but one rose to the surface with
more strength and speed than the others.

"Sad."

Flynn grabbed my hand and looked me right in the eye.

"Well, get the fuck over it already."

A little bit of Starbucks came out through my nose as I snorted
in response and even though the sadness didn't dissipate completely, a familiar happiness was growing. If I didn't have a new
boyfriend, at least I had an old friend to keep me company. Two
seconds later and that number doubled, as our mutual second-
tier friend, Sebastian Santiago-St. Clare, appeared and plopped
down beside us.

"*Hola, señoritas,*" Sebastian purred. "Are you two fucking
again?"

Flynn and I let go of each other's hands and pishawed all over
Sebastian's ludicrous accusation. We should have expected such
a comment since everything about Sebastian was ludicrous. If he
were to file his taxes tomorrow, he would have to list college
Spanish professor, fitness model, masseur, and dance instructor
as his jobs. He was gorgeous, trilingual, and extremely intelligent, but also self-involved, twenty-something, and borderline
sociopathic, so it was only possible to take him in small doses.
Sebastian was a living, breathing recreational drug.

"I thought for a moment that the late Carl Sagan was actually right and I had stepped through a time tunnel," Sebastian
sneered. This, while sipping a double docchio.

"We were just having an after-school special moment," Flynn explained.

"You and your TV references," Sebastian snapped. "You boys need to get out in the natural light more often. Cathode ray tubes create lines on the face, and trust me, neither one of you needs any more lines."

Flynn and I forced separate, though similar, smiles to appear on our lined faces; Sebastian was perilously close to receiving a social pink slip. But Sebastian could, as the Italians might say, turn from prick to paisan in the flick of a wrist, so it was no surprise that his next comment made us jump for joy instead of the exit.

"I have the greatest idea for Gus's fortieth birthday," Sebastian exclaimed. "Incidentally, can I just say that I pray to my spirit guides every night that when I turn forty I look as hot as Gussie Gus. Anyway, I propose we *celebrate* Gus's age and not run from it like so many scary Marys do. Let's cuddle up to his youth and throw a roller boogie party at Splash."

For the second time that night Flynn clasped my hand. "That's discotabulous!" he shrieked.

"We'll be like Steve Guttenberg in the opening credits of *Can't Stop the Music*," Sebastian 'splained in a Spanish accent that he only employed when he was truly excited. "Buff, carefree, and so very, very gay. I think Gus'll go for it."

"He'll love it," I said. "And who would scoff at the chance to wear a tight midriff T-shirt and daisy dukes in public without being puked on by the fashion police?"

"Then it's settled," Sebastian declared.

It was decided that since Sebastian's Thursday night fuck buddy did PR for Splash, he would handle booking the party, Flynn would deal with food and alcohol, and Lindsay would steer the decorations committee because history had taught us that he would redecorate whatever decorations were put up anyway. I, being the most organized, would put together the guest list and send out the invites.

"Now if you'll excuse me, boys, I gotta run," Sebastian announced, downing the last of his double-D. "I'm late for my Tuesday night blow job."

"Oh, is it Tuesday already?" I queried.

"Time to be the highlight of some lonely queen's week," Sebastian declared. "I'll be free in an hour if you guys want to be rounds two and three."

We watched Sebastian's denim-swathed ass wiggle out of Starbucks and we were confronted with the gay man's age-old dilemma—sometimes the ass you wanted to boot out of your life was the same ass you wanted to rim. Sebastian, much more so than any of us, embraced his sexuality and didn't care if he teetered on the edge of slutdom. Collectively, we tsk-tsked him; individually, we envied him.

Pushing X-rated thoughts from our minds, Flynn and I started to sketch out ideas for Gus's party and soon we had come up with this: each guest had to come as a character from *Can't Stop the Music* or a major icon from the disco era. Anticipating an influx of Donna Summers and Grace Joneses we decided to adapt a technique mastered by heterosexual women: the bridal registry, or what I refer to as the scam of the century. Along with the animated e-vite that we would create, we would include a list of appropriate disco era personalities that people could impersonate. Each time a guest chose a name it would disappear from the roster, thus ensuring that each guest would attend as a different disco star. To satisfy the popularity of such megastars as Donna and Grace we would allow them, and a few certain others, to have multiple listings that would reflect the range of their careers, such as Grace from her "Demolition Man" video and her grunt 'n' glama role in *A View to a Kill,* and Donna as the whore of "Love to Love You Baby" and the paid whore of "Bad Girls." I was filled with an emotion that took me higher when I decided I would break another one of my rules and don drag to attend the party as Samantha Sang. And then another emotion grounded me as I realized that no matter how hard I tried, I somehow always gave in to my mother's wishes.

"Do you know what just happened?" Flynn asked.

"Anjanette picked out the perfect pair of pumps for me?" I guessed.

"No! You went thirty minutes without thinking about Frank," Flynn said.

"Excuse me, Maureen McGovern, can you read my mind?" I asked.

"Stop joking, Superman, I'm serious."

I didn't want to get serious, but I also didn't want to contradict Flynn. As a producer I had learned the art of multitasking and that's what I had been doing. While laying out the groundwork for Gus's landmark party, I was planning what I would say if Frank walked through the door.

"Wow, maybe I'm moving on," I lied.

"Well, it's a start," Flynn said. "I guarantee you, Stevie, that by the time Gus's party rolls around you'll have a boyfriend who loves you almost as much as I do."

Sometimes truth flows effortlessly into the air. When it does it's important to catch it so you can remember it at a later date like when you're just about to fall asleep and you're feeling a little bit lonely. I mentally stored Flynn's comment, certain that I would need to use it later that night.

I watched Flynn walk down the street for a moment, then continued on my way. It was a balmy night, which meant the streets were packed, but I felt like a ghost floating through the horde of happy-go-luckies. Every once in a while when one of the happy boys brushed against my shoulder, I thought I got a fleeting idea of what they felt like on the inside. Many of them were as depressed as I was. If it weren't for the ringing of my cell phone, I would have walked the entire way home in my dismal reverie.

"Lindsay?"

"Stevie! Sebastian just called me about Gus's party!" he exclaimed. "Disco rocks!"

"I thought you had plans tonight," I said. "Where are you?"

"The sex party," Lindsay confirmed. "When Sebastian called he was getting a blow job. How surprised was he when I said 'So am I'?"

"How surprised am I that none of us can sustain a romantic relationship," I said, obviously still connected to my dismal reverie.

"Oh, please! One underwear optional party doesn't define who I am."

"I know, I'm just in a bad mood."

"Well, stop it!" Lindsay yelled. "No, not you! My friend. You keep doing what you're doing."

At this point I became aware of the thump, thump, thumping of house music and the clang, clang, clanging of chains and realized Lindsay was most likely spread-eagle in a sling. I could hear an occasional grunt and labored breathing so I could tell that he was also getting slung in the sling. Outside, the clouds rebelled and suddenly I was being slung by a fierce downpour. Darting in between pedestrians and partygoers, I tried to run alongside buildings to escape the raindrops but when another call came, I was already so drenched I couldn't see clearly and inadvertently hit CONFERENCE instead of HOLD and wound up in a three-way conversation with Lindsay and my mother.

"Stevie!" my mother shouted.

"Stevie!" my friend shouted.

"Can you hear me now?" my mother shouted louder.

"Can you hear me now?" my friend shouted even louder.

"Ma!" I shouted. "Hold on, I have Lindsay on the line and I need to disconnect."

"Lindsay!" my mother shouted again.

"Hello, Mrs. Ferrante!" Lindsay shouted back.

"Um, Lindsay, now's not the time," I whispered.

"How've you been, honey?" my mother rattled on. "Have you heard from Nancy Kerrigan lately? Is she still complaining?"

"Yes, and it's still 'Why me? Why me?' I'll give you 'Why'—ahhh!"

"Lindsay!" I shouted, desperately trying to disconnect the call but unable to see the touchpad.

"I'm sorry, Lindsay, I forget how badly the skating world treated you. You're always asking, 'Why pewter? How could I lose?'"

"Who's your daddy?" said the man fucking Lindsay.

I felt my ulcer exploding deep within my abdomen as I frantically started hitting buttons on my phone.

"Ma! Hang up and I'll call you back."

"I said, 'Who's your daddy?'" the man fucking Lindsay repeated.

"Steven," my mother started, "I did not know Lindsay was adopted."

"Ma! Would you please, for once, do as I say and hang up?"

"Tell him I'm very good with genealogy. I found out your father was the fourth cousin of Sophia Loren's brother-in-law."

"Oh God! Yes!" Lindsay cried.

"That's right, honey!" my mother cried in reply. "Mama can help you too!"

Finally, the Lord helped me and I was able to shut off my phone so my mother could let Lindsay get fucked in peace. If only she would extend me the same courtesy, my life would be a little less complicated. Or would it?

Before I went to bed I made one final phone call. Once again I got Frank's answering machine. I listened to his deep voice one more time, then turned off my cell phone, not bothering to worry whether or not Frank was on the other end screening his calls or getting a late-night cup at Starbucks or lurking in the shadows at Lindsay's sex party. Wherever he was, he wasn't in my life because he chose not to be there. Flynn was right; I was already surrounded by love. Once I realized that, it was easy to look at my life like an audience member watching a nonsensical Bollywood movie. I didn't analyze it, I didn't judge it, I simply accepted it for what it was.

Chapter Five

Thank God It's Friday. Catchphrase, Academy Award–winning motion picture, truth. Even though I'm not like most nine-to-fivers and I truly love my job, I still get that lightheaded feeling whenever I wake up on a Friday morning. It's the feeling of possibility.

This Friday turned out to be one of those exceptional Fridays that come along once every six months or so. One of the actresses who recently graduated from her anorexia outpatient program brought in a dozen boxes of Krispy Kremes for breakfast, our ratings shot up another three-tenths of a point, and each scene was shot in one quick take, including the cliffhanger when Stroke Roger uttered his first word to Ramona. *Purloin.* Because Roger had always joked that Ramona stole his heart.

I got out early enough to fit in a quick workout before heading home to find my answering machine blinking madly and I knew one of those blinks had to be an invitation to party like it was a Friday in 1999. Sure enough the first message was from Gus imploring his mates to gather tonight at Marys and meet his latest fling. This would actually be the latest in a string of flings that had started almost a year ago when Gus determined to sow each and every one of his wild oats before turning forty. By the lustful sound of Gus's voice on my machine this latest boy toy might prove to be the wildest oat of all.

The three other messages were from Flynn, Lindsay, and Sebastian, all telling me that we should meet at Marys at ten o'clock,

with Sebastian adding that he had secured Splash for Gus's birthday bash and that his Thursday night fuck buddy needed to
switch to Wednesdays so if I knew of anyone looking for a regular Thursday hookup I should feel free to give them Sebastian's
number. I didn't think our human resources department intended
for our community bulletin board to be used as a networking
opportunity for sex addicts so I shelved the idea of posting a notice at work. Sebastian might have to watch TV on Thursday
nights like the rest of us.

I made a quick dinner out of leftover Chinese takeout while
watching white-hot Anderson Cooper on cable and soon I was
eating bok choy with a boner. It was time for porn.

From my favorite cable bottom-liner to my all-time favorite
porn top, I watched Aiden Shaw plow the ass of Tag Adams, in
some triple X-travaganza entitled *Perfect Fit*. Tag was the perfect poster boy for the conflicted gay bottom. His grunts of absolute delight were in total opposition to his facial expressions,
which made it seem like he didn't know if he could take another
inch of Aiden's huge uncut dick. All I knew was that my cock fit
perfectly in my right hand and I was able to stroke myself to cli-
max while my man Aiden pulled out and shot an incredibly
powerful load (and I choose to believe it was an angry one, in
response to Tag's mixed messages) all over Tag's stomach.

The beauty of imaginary porn playmates is that they are often
the most satisfying. My pretend partner, who in most cases is
Aiden, is always a consistent performer so I never have to feign
interest. The extra beauty of these early evening imaginary play-
dates is that I get sex out of the way so I can concentrate on ini-
tiating conversation and not inevitable copulation while cruising
the bars. Masturbation, for me, is a survival technique.

Dressed in a vintage purple and gold Duran Duran T-shirt, low-
rise jeans, and color-coordinated Pumas, I waltzed into Marys a
few minutes after ten grinning like Simon Le Bon on a VH1-
sponsored comeback tour and immediately saw Gus towering
above some blond, barely-out-of-his-teens waif wearing a vintage Human League T-shirt. How dare he?

Gus introduced the waif as Brady, a bloke he'd met yesterday online in a chatroom for gay anglophiles. Before I could ask for proof that *straight* anglophiles exist, Brady launched into an animated monologue about the first time he laid eyes on Gus. He rhapsodized and gesticulated in a manner that would shame any anglophile, gay or straight, and told me how he and Gus were just supposed to have hot sex but wound up having hot sex plus stimulating conversation, breakfast, a quick lunch at Gus's office (and by lunch Brady informed me that he meant blow job), dinner, more sex, and now a night at Marys.

"Are anglophiles allowed to be so spontaneous?" I queried.

"I'm really not an anglophile," Brady confessed. "The accent just gives me a boner!"

Gus smiled hard and slapped Brady's ass harder, which prompted me to get the beginnings of my own boner. Then Brady went on to confess that his parents had named him after their favorite sitcom family, which prompted me to lose my boner completely since *The Brady Bunch* was also *my* all-time favorite sitcom and I suddenly felt very, very old. I spied Gus's index finger introducing itself to Brady's ass-cleft and realized I was the only one bothered by the fact that nearly two decades of reruns separated us from this Brady boy. I firmly believe that chicken-love has its time and place, but I just couldn't imagine how Gus could enjoy a blow job from a man named Brady without it conjuring up images of three very lovely girls with hair of gold. Perhaps *The Brady Bunch* never aired in Britain. Perhaps I got too emotionally invested in television as a child. Perhaps life is sometimes just as annoying as Cousin Oliver. Whatever the reason, I knew I would be thankful when Gus inevitably told Brady he had been canceled.

Luckily Lindsay has the comic timing of Ann B. Davis and was soon standing by my side, drink in hand, jabbering away about the details of his recent foray into the world of the sex party.

"I loved it!" Lindsay squealed. "I felt free, like a kid again."

"You were in a sling, not a swing," I corrected.

"You had your childhood playground," he said, "I had mine."

While ordering another round of drinks for us all, Lindsay

announced that he had seen several familiar faces at the party, including an Academy Award Best Actor nominee who made his partners wear gold condoms so he could imagine he was being fucked with an Oscar.

"I assume he wanted to know what it's like to be the former Mr. Hilary Swank," Lindsay declared. "That lucky broad's got his and hers Oscars. When they were married I bet they lay side by side to see who could take more of the phallic gold statuette."

"Jodie Foster can do the same thing," I reminded him.

"Do you really think Jodie does anything with her Oscars except stare at them and envy their slim, boyish hips?"

"Well, I'm sure many Academy Award winners have had sex with their Oscars. What about Barbra Streisand? She's got two Oscars too," I responded.

"Do not take the name of La Streisand in vain!"

"Bette Davis had two," I said, feeling very knowledgeable in gay cinema all of a sudden. "And she was a wild one."

"The Oscar reminded her of her uncle," Lindsay reminded me. "Even she wasn't kinky enough for that."

"Oh, my God! Katharine Hepburn had four!" I shouted.

Lindsay's face went white as the blood drained from his face and raced to his dick. "Just imagine the sex party possibilities," he sighed.

Before I could imagine the endless possibilities of a group of horny, naked gay men and four Oscars, Flynn and Sebastian joined us at the bar.

"*Hola, chicas!*" Sebastian cried, then noticing Brady he added, "And chiquitas."

It looked like Sebastian was going to make a Chiquita hawk comment, but a remix of a remix of a Madonna classic blasted through the airwaves and he declared it was time to get into the groove.

One Madonna remix led to an Amber remix, which led to another musical attempt by Dolly Parton to have a hit song post– "9 to 5," and soon an hour had passed. My lungs begged my body to stop moving, so I grabbed the boys and we huddled at the end of the U-shaped bar, which was manned by a strapping, hairless man-boy in a boy-sized jockstrap, and ordered ourselves a round of cosmos. Before the first sip, Brady took control of the conversation and announced that he was attending graphic design school and was looking for opportunities to perfect his craft.

"Isn't that what you're doing with Gus?" I asked, allowing myself a moment of bitchiness.

"No!" Brady squealed. "I'm letting Gus perfect his craft at being the perfect top with me!"

It sucks when your own bitchiness comes back to bitch-slap you in your face. The boys all saluted Gus's quest for perfection and I felt like Dolly reading the latest, unkind *Billboard* charts.

"Maybe Brady can design the invitations for my upcoming birthday bash," Gus suggested.

"We're not throwing you a birthday bash!" Lindsay protested.

"You, Lindsay Wilde, are a gay liar," Gus said. "And you know what happens to gay liars?"

"They grow up to become Scientologists?" Flynn suggested.

"Yes," Gus answered. "But they also get spanked with an Olympic pewter medal."

Before spittle could form at the edges of Lindsay's mouth, Sebastian intervened and admitted that we were planning something special for Gus's fortieth birthday, but would never divulge what that surprise was unless, of course, Gus fucked it out of each and every one of us, starting with Sebastian. Being the proper Brit that he is, Gus declined to go to such extremes, but he did allow his eyes to glance lasciviously at Sebastian's extremely round ass, causing Brady to snuggle closer to Gus and hyperextend his own bulbous backside even farther away from his spine. Then, once he realized his friends had not forgotten his milestone, Gus showed that most improper of British emotions: joy.

"I can't wait for the surprise!" Gus gushed. "But I have bad news for you boys."

"Bad news has no place at your birthday surprise," I replied.

"Bad news will not attend, and, unfortunately, neither will Wendolyn," Gus said.

Flynn, Lindsay, Sebastian, and I didn't dare look at each other, but gave each other imaginary high-fives.

"Oh, that's too bad," I lied. "You're sure that there's absolutely, positively, no chance in the entire whole wide world that Wendolyn will be able to attend?"

"Sorry, mate, she'll be in Nepal with Richard Gere on my birthday weekend."

"Your sister knows Richard Gere?" Brady asked.

"Yes, she hobnobs with the stars."

"All of a sudden you're even hotter than you were like five seconds ago."

Gus and Brady started to make out with each other as if oblivious to our presence, so we decided it was time to give Daddy and Son some alone time. Almost instantly, Sebastian got sucked into the crowd by one of his many paramours, leaving the three of us alone to revel in our luck.

"I was so afraid we were going to have to invite psycho-sister!" I exclaimed.

"I know! Let's tell Brady all about Ms. Wendolyn," Lindsay suggested. "Guaranteed he'll disappear quicker than my last crab infestation."

"You still get crabs?" Flynn asked.

"Only when I have sex on the beach," Lindsay replied. "We should find out if Brady's last name starts with a *G*!"

We laughed hysterically, downing our cosmos like good homos, and wondered if Gus's boy toy would still be so young, carefree, and gay once he found out the truth about Gus's sister—that she is certifiably insane. And not just eccentric in that irrepressible Maggie Smithish sort of way, but undeniably nuts. It's always difficult dealing with the mentally challenged, but the situation with Wendolyn is worse because Gus doesn't think there's anything wrong with how her brain works. To him, she's his wacky baby sister. We think she's missing a chromosome.

Among Wendolyn's many symptoms is that she is mortally afraid of the letter *G*. Her real name is of course *Gwendolyn,* but she changed it before she hit her teens. It seems that when she was a little girl she got into her father's collection of G-Man comics from the 1940s that was stored in the attic of their lovely country cottage. Gwendolyn was a shy child and preferred the solidarity of a stuffy attic to the overpopulation of a family outing, so while the rest of her family was enjoying a picnic on the rocky shore near the beach, Gwendolyn rummaged through the comics and spread them out in a circle around her until she was surrounded by the red, white, and blue uniformed G-Man, upholder of all things true and just. The floorboards of the attic, however, were not as strong and just couldn't hold up Gwendolyn's ample weight and she fell through. Actually, she only fell halfway through, as she got stuck right at the point where her size 35 waist bulged out over the wooden slats.

Clutching at the floor around her, Gwendolyn frantically tried to pull herself back up, but only succeeded in getting fists full of splinters and pulling the G-Man comics closer to her. Hysterical, she began to scream for help, but alas the family couldn't hear her cries over their own laughter and the crashing of the waves. They went on frolicking about, assuming sensitive Gwendolyn needed some private time.

As night began to fall, the mice in the attic came out to play and exhibited the same interest in G-Man comics as Gwendolyn. Not as a way to spur the imagination, but a perfect place to poop—and Gwendolyn's frizzy red hair the perfect place to nuzzle. When her family finally found her, they recall that she was maniacally pushing away the comics and the curious rodents screaming, "No *G!* No *G!*" And from that day forward Gwendolyn became Wendolyn and has been afraid to say any word with the letter *G* in it. Therefore, she refers to Gus as "Us" and he rationalizes her unique nickname for him as being symbolic of their close relationship. Long ago, I decided not to try to get Gus to accept his sister's madness like I have accepted my mother's, because I realize the British deem mental instability as weakness, while the Italians see it as standard.

I was about to raise my hand to order another round of cosmos and completely enter the world of drunken madness, when Lindsay yanked it and pointed it toward the dance floor.

"See that guy in the black Henley tank top?" Lindsay gasped.

"You mean Fuck Counter?" I announced.

"*He's* Fuck Counter?" Flynn asked.

"He was also at the sex party," Lindsay explained. "And he's up to five twenty-seven."

There was a moment of silence as we all realized what an accomplishment that was and what a pleasure 527 continuous penetrations could be. I watched Fuck Counter dancing with some hot boy and allowed myself a moment of pride in knowing that I had helped him on his way to becoming the super top that he obviously was. I noticed a stirring in my jeans and wondered if perhaps I had been too hasty in rejecting Fuck Counter or was I just getting horny again, even though it was only three hours since I had made imaginary love to Aiden? All thoughts of sex, however, were thrust from my head as I spied Sebastian dancing on top of the bar, thrusting his hips wildly, wearing only a stained white jockstrap. He would now have to add *go-go boy* to the career blank on his tax returns.

"Do you think he does it for the ego trip?" I asked.

"I think he does it for the tips," Lindsay corrected.

We watched Sebastian gyrate and grind in front of an eager throng of barflies, allowing eager fingers to stick dollar bills in his jockstrap, his socks, and even in the crack of his eager ass. Then we noticed he kept stopping to gyrate in front of one pair of eager fingers that belonged to a man who had to be at least seventy years old. A real-world seventy, not a gay seventy, which would be around fifty-two. These eager fingers belonged to an honest-to-goodness gay senior citizen.

"What the hell is he doing now?" Flynn asked.

"He's encouraging that poor old thing!" Lindsay cried.

It definitely looked as if Sebastian was encouraging the senior sinner, for he was poised directly in front of him, kneeling on one knee, pushing his crotch oh-so-close to the man's wrinkled face, and whispering into his most likely hair-filled ear. Lindsay squinted and then opened his eyes in stunned disbelief.

"That's no poor old thing!" Lindsay declared. "He's shoving fifty-dollar bills up Sebastian's ass!"

Suddenly Sebastian jumped off the bar and started sashaying toward us. When he got close enough he waved a fifty-dollar bill under our noses and I caught the faintest whiff of vinegar.

"I'm off to get ramgeezered," Sebastian announced.

"You're going to let that old man fuck you?" Lindsay asked.

"*Mi amiga,* papi need a new Jack Spade bag," he said. "It'll be worth it."

We watched Sebastian walk toward the go-go boy changing room, his perfect ass flexing and unflexing with each stride as if it were waving good-bye to the boys who would have to wait yet another night, or at least another few hours, to have the chance to make an entrance.

"Do you think he has a Granddaddy complex?" I asked.

"No," Flynn answered. "He's just a whore."

"Now every time he slings his bag over his shoulder he'll be reminded that he slung his legs over the shoulders of some old bag," Lindsay added. "Even Jack Spade's not worth a memory like that."

After a few more drinks we decided it was time to go. Actually I decided it was time I should go. Gus was off with Brady somewhere, Lindsay was dancing near Fuck Counter hoping it might add up to another chance encounter, and Flynn had bumped into an old flame and decided to see if the embers could still burn for one more night. On my way out I had a bump of my own.

"Sorry," I stuttered.

"That's okay," the bumpee responded.

Fighting every urge to speak, I forced myself to remain quiet and just take in this moment. The music was blaring all around me, the lights were flashing above and below, sweaty arms were brushing against me, but I kept silent and stared ahead into one of the most beautiful faces I had ever seen. Full red lips, smooth ivory skin with creases at the ice blue eyes and around the mouth to prove it was real, and a thick mane of blond hair that fell loose and carefree on the forehead. This face looked back at me with what I interpreted as equal wonder and all the insecurities

Frank had ignited in me were extinguished. I wasn't a loser like the last time and the time before and this beautiful man in front of me would prove that. Unfortunately, the beautiful man behind him would unravel my newfound confidence and take from me another chance for happiness with one sentence:

"Come on, Brian, I love this song!"

With those words Brian's beautiful face was whisked away from me and dragged onto the dance floor as a Cher tune pulsated through the air. I saw him glance back at me and I tried to follow him, but just then the DJ sampled an old Go-Go's hit and I was nearly trampled to death by a swarm of gay men who just had to get the beat.

My luck had gone from bad to worse. At least Frank had given me his number before rejecting me; Brian didn't hang around long enough to do the proper thing and create the façade that he wanted a relationship before giving me my rejection notice. Thank God Friday was officially over.

Alas, that meant Saturday had arrived and this Saturday meant having lunch with my mother and her best friend, Audrey, at the Secaucus Diner. Normally it was a fun event during which I would let the ladies tell me all about the wild adventures of the tenants of the Salvatore DeNuccio Towers and allow myself to get caught up in the pandemonium, but this Saturday would be different. It would be the Saturday after losing not one, but two, potential boyfriends. I would have to wear a smile tighter than Priscilla Presley's.

"Steven, what's wrong with you?" my mother asked instead of saying hello.

"Hello to you too, Ma," I replied, ignoring her question. "Hi, Audrey, how are you?"

Audrey Pizzarelli is my mother's best friend. She is a Sicilian widow like my mother and similar to her in almost every single way except that she dyes her hair jet black, is thirty pounds heavier, wears polyester twill jumpsuits from the '70s with color-coordinated neckerchiefs, and has been dying for the past twenty years. It's a self-diagnosis disputed by every doctor in the tri-state area, but one that Audrey clings to as tightly as I cling to the dream that I will someday meet the man of my dreams. Everyone has to cling to something.

"I found a lump," Audrey declared with undeniable pride.

"It's a mosquito bite," my mother corrected.

"Since when do mosquitoes bite in October?" Audrey asked.

"You were down at the swamps again."

"I was not."

"Yes, you were! Rosemary saw you."

"That friggin' Rosemary! She's always spying on me!"

"You were on her daughter's property. Lori Ann lives right next to the swamp."

"That is no reason to spy on someone."

"Excuse me, Audrey?"

"Yes, Steven dear?"

"What were you doing down at the swamps?"

"Stealing flowers," my mother answered. "Again!"

"Orchids! I wanted an orchid."

"So buy one. Rocco left you a very wealthy widow."

"Why should I spend Rocco's money when they have perfectly fine orchids in the swamps? My granddaughter, Caitlin, told me that her science class grows the most gorgeous orchids in the swamps."

"So you've made Caitlin an accessory to theft!" my mother declared. "You should feel very proud of yourself, Audrey. Very proud."

"Anjanette, enough!" Audrey shouted, causing heads to turn at the Secaucus Diner. "Is it a crime to steal beauty? Is it? No, I do not think so. Now Steven, what's wrong with you? You look unhappy."

If Audrey was a criminal, she was a perceptive one.

"I'm fine. Just a little tired. We went out last night."

"We as in you and your friends?" my mother asked. "Or we as in 'Mother, I'd like to introduce you to my new boyfriend'?"

"Ma! Could you save the humiliation for when we're alone?"

"Oh please, your mother tells me everything about your personal life. Nothing is sacred between us. I'm so glad your rash turned out to be nothing."

"Waitress!"

Luckily the only thing my mother loves more than prying into my life is prying into her meal. She loves her food immensely, so while she ate I had a few moments to talk about the more superficial aspects of my life and make it appear as if everything was fine in the Land of Steven. I wasn't sure if my mother was buying it, but the second I mentioned Lucas Fitzgerald and how excited he was to be part of their upcoming Christmas variety show, all thoughts of her son's potential depression were overshadowed by her own thoughts of superstardom among the senior set.

"I cannot wait to see Paula D'Agostino's face when Roger from *If Tomorrow Never Comes* starts to sing 'White Christmas' at my show. He will sing 'White Christmas,' won't he, Steven? He knows how much we love that song, does he not?"

"Everybody loves Bing," Audrey confirmed.

"Yes, Mother, Lucas knows 'White Christmas' is a deal-breaker."

"Good. Paula is going to have a heart attack and drop dead before we serve the main course once she hears that. And she deserves it, after all the grief she has put us through."

"You are so right, Anj," Audrey said. "Between her size-four dresses, which I think are really eights if you want to know my opinion, and her friggin' daughter. . . ."

"Do not even get me started on her kid! I hate her!"

"Ma, what did Paula's daughter ever do to you?" I asked.

"She has given her mother years of bragging rights! All that comes out of Paula's mouth is how successful her daughter is because she works on the *Today* show. I thought for sure the show would tank after Katie left and then Paula would have to admit that working in the soaps isn't such a dumb career move."

"Paula D'Agostino thinks working in the soaps is a dumb career move?"

"Yes! She ain't so nice anymore, is she, Stevie?"

"I never liked her," I finally declared.

"That's my boy."

I had to admit that my mother was right. Maybe if I stripped myself of all social decorum and allowed myself to really listen to someone's comments, I too could be insightful. But I would soon realize that even my mother didn't know everything about everybody.

"Lenny, come join us," Anjanette demanded. "Steven, this is Lenny Abramawitz. He, like you, is gay."

As Secaucus's only Jewish "out" senior citizen, Lenny Abramawitz had a certain reputation with the ladies. As he sat down and I got a good look at him, I realized he also had an old-fashioned reputation. Lenny was Sebastian's ramgeezer.

Thank God I had already taken the last bite of my chicken parmigiana sandwich, so there was no danger of it getting lodged in my throat. But Lenny's skin grew so pale the liver spots on his hands stood out like neon signs. If you connected the liver dots they would probably spell out I AM A DIRTY OLD MAN.

"Hello, Lenny," I said. "It's nice to . . . *finally* meet you."

Sometimes acting as if you actually lived in a soap opera did have its benefits. I waited for Lenny's response and something curious happened: Lenny acted like the perfect soap opera villain. He regained his composure, straightened his posture, and spoke in an affected whisper.

"Hello, Steven," Lenny said. "I've heard so much about you. It's a pleasure to . . . finally meet you too."

To paraphrase the soldier from *Les Miserables*, I was agog and I was aghast that Lenny mimicked my timing and paused before uttering the word *finally* while arching *his* eyebrow. The old geezer knew that I knew that he was a dirty old geezer, but he also knew that I was put into the age-old gay dilemma. Should I expose Lenny for the go-go boy–buying old fart that he was, thereby confirming what many already believed—that gay men were hedonists and only looking to flit from pleasurable experience to pleasurable experience instead of settling for a life of heterosexual misery? Or keep Lenny's secret, thereby con-

doning Lenny's morally questionable behavior? But who was I
to judge someone else's actions when only a few days ago I had
run out on a man cursed with a minipenis and then fallen head
over heels in love with a guy whose last name was still a mystery
to me?

"Will you be performing any special acts in the Christmas
show?" I asked.

"Why yes, I hope so," Lenny replied. "Though I haven't found
the perfect costar yet. Would you like to audition for the role?"

I could not believe my ears. Lenny Abramawitz was coming
on to me in front of my mother! If only I had Priscilla Presley's
smooth, expressionless veneer of a face, so it wouldn't be so hard
to hide my outrage.

"I don't think that would be fair to all the others who could
really benefit from your generosity. Mother tells me you're a
very giving man."

"He is," Anjanette confirmed. "Lenny was just telling us that
he likes to help out young men of mixed-race descent who are
having trouble financially."

"We think it's a beautiful thing," Audrey added. "Something
we would never do because we're widows and cannot afford to
be so generous, but a beautiful thing all the same."

"And do you engage in such activity for purely altruistic pur-
poses, Leonard?" I asked, "Or do you benefit from your generosity as well?"

"My only benefit is the joy of knowing I've helped point
some young man's head in the right direction."

My chicken parmigiana gurgled violently in the pit of my
stomach; the only direction Lenny wanted a young man's head
to go was south toward his withered dick. I choked out my next
sentence: "That is a beautiful thing."

Like two teenaged girls at their first boy-girl dance, my
mother and Audrey left the table to use the restroom, leaving me
face-to-face with Lenny. Horrified, I felt as if I was staring into
the face of my future. If I didn't find a man to share my life with
I could end up living the life of Lenny Abramawitz: having sex

with strangers and then lying about my escapades to Anjanette and her friends. The horror I felt worsened as I realized this was in some ways the life I was already living.

"What will it take to keep you quiet?" Lenny asked, cutting right to the chase.

"What makes you think anything can prevent me from telling my mother the truth?"

"I have a reputation, young man, that I do not want spoiled," Lenny began. "I also have needs that I need to fulfill and I think you may have noticed that there aren't a lot of romantic possibilities for me at the Salvatore DeNuccio Towers unless I want to go back into the suffocating closet that I called home for the first seventy-four years of my life. Is that what you're suggesting I do?"

For a moment I was torn between applauding his speech, which I vaguely remembered from an Ida Lupino movie, and slapping his wrinkled face indignantly, which would have made me the star of an Ida Lupino movie, but I decided to simply answer the question.

"I'm not suggesting anything. If you can live with yourself, I guess I can too."

"So you won't tell your mother about last night?"

"No, I won't," I replied.

"Wonderful!" Lenny squealed. "I knew I could count on a brother. Maybe I can show you my generous side sometime."

Lenny accented his statement by placing his clammy palm on top of my hand. I flinched at this outrageous act of chutzpah right in the middle of the Secaucus Diner and blanched when I realized my mother and her cohorts thought this man was respectable. So I did what any respectable Italian mama's boy would do: I defended my mother the only way I knew how.

"You listen to me, you old Jew fag. I will keep your secret because I do not want my mother to know what a creep you are. Just because you chose to live in a closet your whole life does not make it all right for you to go to bars and pay for sex when you should be in your own bed watching Jay Leno. You should be reminding young gay men that they don't have to wind up like you, and that they can choose to be proud of who they are—not teaching them it's okay to take money from strangers for sex. And if I see you at the auditions for the Christmas Show I will take that moment to tell the entire Salvatore DeNuccio Tenants Group just what you do on your Friday nights. And it goes without saying that you will not be playing Santa! I may not be able to stop you from degrading yourself and the men you buy, but I can stop you from degrading my mother and her friends. You aren't worthy of their friendship."

My anger surprised me more than it did Lenny. The night before, when he'd been a nameless, faceless old man shelling out money to help Sebastian buy a new accessory, he'd been a punch line. Now, as I watched him scurry out of the diner, he was a joke. And I was truly frightened that in a few more decades I would become that same joke. When my mother and Audrey returned from the bathroom, I explained that Lenny had forgotten he had to run some errands. Audrey thought it probably had to do with all the volunteer work that he did and I nodded in agreement. If my mother suspected anything had taken place between her son and her friend she didn't mention it. But the way she hugged me good-bye told me that she knew there was something wrong.

When I exited the Port Authority bus terminal later that day, I wasn't ready to go home so I started walking downtown. It was good to feel the familiar New York concrete under my feet and the cool air brushing my face. I was tired and I needed to wake up. It was time to face up to certain truths.

I was at a crossroads: I wasn't young and I wasn't old. Thus far, I had lived an interesting but mostly emotionally unfulfilling life. I could continue to live that type of life very easily as many others have, but my heart kept reminding me that I wanted something more than just spending my nights at Marys bar and my mornings getting out of some Mary's bed. I said the words out loud: "I want a boyfriend." I wanted what my mother had for most of her adult life—a partner, someone to share life and bad jokes with, someone to fuss over and argue with. Seeing how Lenny Abramawitz spent his evenings had made the feeling stronger. The thought of being a lonely, single senior citizen frightened me. As I turned the corner onto 23rd Street, I bumped into a stranger who wasn't really a stranger at all.

"Oh my God, it's you!" I cried.

For the second time in less than twenty-four hours I found myself staring into the most beautiful face I had ever seen. And once again that face was smiling back at me.

"Hi, I'm Brian, from last night."

I took a deep breath and finally found the courage to speak. "Hi, I'm Steven. From right now."

Chapter Six

Suddenly I understood what it felt like to be one of the nuns in *The Sound of Music*. I wasn't frustrated because I still had to wear a habit in the hot Austrian sun while Maria got to frolic in a lake wearing a window dressing, or furious because I knew I was fated to become a mere notch in Rolf's shiny black leather belt while Maria became a Swiss Mrs. with an instant sugar-coated family, but I was downright confused, out of focus, and bemused. One moment I was confident that I would spend the rest of my life living alone in an overpriced one-bedroom apartment with an alley view, very little closet space, and a stove that doubles as a mouse hotel and the next moment I had confidence in confidence alone. Was Brian a darling, a demon, a lamb? I didn't yet know, but my stomach knew something good was happening and whirled like a dervish.

"I can't believe this! I've been thinking about you nonstop since last night," Brian admitted.

"Me too," I said. "What happened?"

"It was Cher's fault," Brian said.

"Isn't everything?" I replied. "I mean first she single-handedly made the world question the infomercial, then she made Epstein-Barr tiresome, and now her endless concerts. She has given the farewell tour a bad name."

"Totally agree," Brian began and then continued to speak slowly in one of the most melodic voices I had ever heard. "But I meant that it was my buddy Rodrigo's birthday and he loves

Cher, so when "Take Me Home" came on he got all maniacal and when you get to know Rodrigo you'll realize that you cannot interrupt him when he's riding the maniacal merry-go-round, you just have to hop on and go along for the ride. So that's what I did. And then the DJ sampled "We Got the Beat" and it was like the whole bar turned into an "I Love the '80s" convention and when I turned around to pull you onto the merry-go-round with me you were gone. I spent the rest of the night looking for you and I figured you got taken home by some hottie and forgot all about me. But now here you are. And I'm the only one talking, I'm sorry. I do that when I'm nervous or when I see a guy I've been thinking about nonstop."

"Well, why don't you shut up, take a deep breath, and come have a cup of coffee with me?"

Startled, Brian smiled wickedly.

"A take-charge kinda man," Brian said. "I kinda like that."

And so I took my charge to Starbucks so we could discover a bit more about each other while drinking liquid ambrosia. As we entered the shop that had redefined how the world drank coffee, my stomach whirled again, and this time it was definitely in anticipation of something not-so-good happening. No matter how hard I tried to masquerade as a confident, take-charge kind of guy, I couldn't mask the fact that this was an important meet 'n' greet. It couldn't simply be coincidence that Brian should round the corner at the exact moment I was contemplating my future; I tossed my request for a boyfriend into the universe and the universe responded by tossing me Brian. Universally speaking, this meeting could end in one of three ways and only one of those ways would ensure my future as a fulfilled, nonbitter, and chronically happy adult gay man. Either Brian would gulp down his Starbucks and flee once he realized I was unworthy of nonstop thought; we would go back to his place and have incredible, porn-worthy nonstop one-night-stand sex; or he would ask me out on a date so we could begin our passionate, nonstop miniseries-worthy love affair. Feeling much more like a chaste Richard Chamberlain from *The Thornbirds* than the take-charge Richard Chamberlain of *Shōgun*, I decided that my whirling stomach was an indication that this encounter would turn into something heartfelt and not heartless.

"So why don't we start at the very beginning," I said.

"That's a very good place to start," Brian replied.

"What's your full name?"

"Brian Patrick Oldsboro. And you?"

"Steven Bartholomew Ferrante. Age?"

"Thirty-two."

"I'm thirty-three."

"Perfect, I like older men."

"I'm Italian Catholic from Jersey."

"Lapsed Baptist from Alabama."

"Really?" I said, not hiding my disappointment very well.

"Is that a problem?" Brian asked.

"You know something, it's actually a good thing," I replied. "My mother is going to have to find a flaw in you anyway. It might as well be religion."

"You have one of those mothers too?"

"Anjanette is the president of the club."

"Oh, I don't know about that. My mother's held that position for years."

"No, seriously, my mother's the president of the tenants' group in her senior citizens' building. Or as I like to call it, the insane asylum."

Brian stared at me intently and then said, "I can't wait to meet her. And the rest of the inmates."

With that one sentence I knew that Brian wouldn't be chugging his coffee and that we wouldn't be having passionate yet meaningless sex within the hour; we would have a relationship. Sometimes you get the vibe and the vibe, like Brian's vibrantly blue eyes, cannot be ignored. And so I didn't ignore them, but held his gaze as Brian filled me in on some of the major moments of his life that I had missed. His family's move to Alabama from New York when Brian was two courtesy of his father's employer, his move to New York from Alabama when he was twenty-two courtesy of his first employer, his move up the corporate ladder to his current position as Senior Editor at *Upgrade*, the men's magazine unofficially targeted to men of confused sexual orientation whose official tagline is "For men who want to be on top," and his move downtown from a long-term sublet on the Upper East Side.

"Now that I live in Chelsea I finally feel like a gay man," Brian declared.

"Seriously?"

"Well, yeah. I can walk around and be who I am. If I feel like wearing a too-tight T-shirt I can and I don't have to worry that some breeder couple with two kids is going to roll their eyes at me as I strut by. I know the area can be a gay cliché, but it really is freeing. Where do you live?"

"Hell's Kitchen. Forty-seventh between Ninth and Tenth," I said. "Not very glamorous, but I can walk to work. And I'm close to Port Authority so when my mother has a crisis, and you have been warned, Anjanette—that's her name—is Italian for *panic*, I can be at her place in roughly twenty-five minutes. Twenty if I catch the express bus."

"You're close with your mother?"

"Well, she's a widow. My younger brother, Paulie, lives over an hour away in Sparta—wife, two cars, his own dental practice, he's got his own issues. . . ."

"You're all she has."

"Not all, just most. But I don't mind. She drives me absolutely bonkers, but she loves me, she's always accepted me, and has never judged me. Except for when I make a really bad fashion choice, and she's always right. Like the time I wore plaid on plaid. I don't know what I was thinking except that it was the eighties and like you said, there's something about that decade that made people act freaky."

"I know! Summer 1986, I was totally asymmetrical. Every hair on the left side of my body was shaved and I let the right side grow out. I still have to fill out my left eyebrow with a pencil. See?"

Brian leaned forward so I could get a better look at his eyebrow. His hand brushed against my forearm and I got a whiff of his smell—a little sweet, almost citrusy. I liked it. I noticed his eyebrow and it was obvious that he was very skilled with an eyebrow pencil, but then I looked down just a bit and into his eyes and surprised myself. Instead of dwelling on how long it had been since I had such a spontaneously intimate encounter with a man, I allowed the simplicity of the moment to waft over me and didn't look away. This was the way a meet 'n' greet should be, easy and filled with promise.

"I have to go now," Brian announced.

And abrupt segues.

"I'm sorry, but I have to get home and do some work."

Brian explained that he had two articles to edit for freelance assignments and was already past his deadlines. One article was "How to Organize the Perfect Closet,"which he knew nothing about since he was a self-described slob with a Venezuelan maid named Viva who came in once a week. I refrained from telling him that I was the most organized person I knew other than Martha Stewart's personal assistant, but made a mental note that it might be worthwhile to invest in a French maid's outfit. The second article was on "Man Boobs," which he admitted he did know a little something about, but he was adamant that it was only for one summer when he was thirteen, overweight, and hormonal.

"Petey Verderammo had man boobs in eighth grade," I recalled. "His mother was a lunch lady and very strict. Whenever he cheated on his diet she made him wear a bra."

"That's fabulous! Do you have Petey's number so I can interview him?"

"Sadly, no one knows where Petey is today. Rumor has it he had a sex change, but, really, how could you tell?"

"Well, the only way I can afford to be a Chelsea Boy is to do lots of freelance work."

"I understand," I said. "I've been engaged to my job for some time now as well."

"Would your job be jealous if I took you out to dinner on Monday night?" he asked.

"She'll just have to get over it," I replied. "Because I can't think of a better way to start my week than with a Monday night date."

"Beats *Monday Night Football*."

Unless you're beating off watching the hot, sweaty, football players pound the shit out of each other on the hard, uncompromising Astroturf.

That last sentence I kept to myself, but being in Brian's presence was very arousing. Instead of swapping saliva, we swapped cell phone numbers and engaged in a clumsy hug. For a moment it looked like our first kiss was going to take place right next to the Starbucks condiment station (which for me would have been further proof that the universe understood me), but Brian sort of blushed and whispered that he didn't want our first kiss to be under fluorescent lighting or in front of an audience. Personally I find the lighting in Starbucks to be quite diffuse, but I was glad to hear that Brian wasn't an exhibitionist. Public sex is fun in your twenties, but after thirty it makes you look needy.

We parted ways, he going downtown, me going up, both happy in the moment and hopeful about the moments to come. On my way home I said a prayer to Baby Jesus asking him to allow me to survive until Monday night. I bartered that if he kept me safe until my date with Brian I would see the inside of a church one more time and not just for a wedding or a funeral, plus make a moderate donation. Then I realized my bartering was a form of blackmail accented with an amen, and no matter what religious angle you looked at it from, blackmailing Baby Jesus wasn't a good thing. So I said another prayer asking for forgiveness for my first prayer and tagged on the simple request that Baby Jesus allow me to enjoy myself Monday night and open up my heart to all of Brian's goodness. I was rather impressed with myself as this prayer not only acknowledged that Brian was virtuous, but put the onus on me to have a successful date. The quest for morality and the potential for guilt all in one prayer: it was quintessentially Catholic.

As was my mother. Before I could even undress and plug in my vibrator to engage in a masturbatory session starring Brian and me as quarterbacks for rival high school football teams, she called.

"Steven, are you all right? I'm worried."

"I'm fine, Ma."

"You weren't yourself today. You were preoccupied and distant. You reminded me of your father."

"Funny how things can change in just a few hours."

"Really? So what's his name?"

That Anjanette had the instincts of a bloodhound.

"If we ever get to the second date, I'll tell you."

"You've had a first date already?"

"Not an official one, but soon."

"Have you set a date yet?"

I hesitated briefly, then decided as much as I loved my mother full disclosure wasn't wise. "Not yet, but we will."

The next day I met Flynn for coffee and filled him in on the events of the past twenty-four hours. As expected, he was thrilled for me. Like the rest of us, Flynn bobs and weaves amid the emotional waves that define a gay man's personal life, but ever since he tested positive he has decided to let optimism reign in his world, so his cup is always half full. What's more, he's always willing to share his cup with his friends.

"Since Frank didn't pan out, let me buy you an outfit for your official first date with Brian," Flynn exclaimed.

And we were off. I don't usually let Flynn buy me clothes, but this was a special occasion and since his promotion to Senior Vice President of Business and Legal Affairs at one of the top talent agencies in the city he has a few more zeros at the end of his yearly salary than I do. We decided I should wear something classic to prove that I was a grounded gay, but something with a hint of trendiness to remind him that I was still, after all, gay. After some debate we settled on Banana Republic because that's where all the straight men go to look just a little bit gay and vice versa. Flynn convinced me that the olive green French cuff dress shirt would make my green eyes pop and the simple black straight-leg pants with a tinge of Lycra would show off any popping that might take place down yonder. The black side-buckle cuff-boots were the finishing touch in an ensemble that shouted husband material to any sexual orientation.

"You can wear the black onyx cufflinks that were your father's," Flynn suggested.

"Great, I always wanted my dad to chaperone my dates."

"Better your dead father than Anjanette."

Reveling in our girlie-girl shopping escapade, we almost didn't see the spectacle of Gus and Brady making out in the sale section. When I saw Brady sucking face with Gus underneath last season's marked-down paisley pants and white collar 'n' cuff dress shirts, I felt vindicated. Brady was cheap.

"Gussie, look! It's your friends!" Brady shouted.

Gus looked nonplussed. Brady, in contrast, was nondiscreet.

"We just had sex in the dressing room!" Brady declared.

"I *thought* the salesboys were looking rentable these days," Flynn said.

"Not with the retail staff, silly, with each other!"

Our heads snapped toward Gus, searching for either confirmation or denial. Much to our surprise Gus impishly smiled, indicating that while Brady was being inappropriate he was also being honest. Before I had a chance to give in to my immediate desire to burst into the dressing room that doubled as their *plage d'amour* and breathe in the intoxicating smells of Gus-sex, Brady got even more inappropriately honest.

"And it was full out-and-out anal sex, not just a quickie blow job like usual."

"However did you make the transition?" Flynn asked.

"I was trying on a pair of purple corduroys, you know, something fun and a little pansified for fall, and Gus tells me that purple is his favorite color so he just has to see them on me. So before I can come out to show him, he comes in. And then his dick comes out, well, because I took it out and then it goes back in, if you know what I mean. You know what I mean, right? He fucked me. Right in the dressing room, he fucked me!"

"We know what you mean, Brady," I said. "Older folk like us do understand subtlety."

"Good thing I always carry condoms with me. Magnum Extra-Large because Gus is fucking huge! And the lube is a must, I always carry those little one-night-stand lubey packets because I can take a lot, but did I mention that Gus is huge?"

"Yes, you did," I said. "And for that piece of information about Gus's piece, I would like to personally thank you."

By now I noticed that Gus's impish grin had turned limpish and he did not look at all like a forty-year-old man who had just gotten a little something-something from a twenty-something that cost absolutely nothing. Before I could wrack my brain to decipher what lay behind Gus's silence, the train wreck that was Brady kept chugging along.

"I can't believe no one stopped us. I bet someone was watching on the surveillance cameras. At least that's what I was thinking while Gus was fucking me. I know they had to have heard something. Gus was really rough, which I love, but he kept making me make my sounds. Gus loves when I make my sounds; they're like Pee-wee Herman's laugh, only higher. Now I have to buy these cords and I really don't even like them, but they have Gus's jizz all over them and Gus wasn't born in this country so it's not like he's going to become president some day, so they'll just be like a souvenir."

"From Slutworld."

"Don't be jealous, Flynn, 'cause you're not getting any from Gus and I am! Gussie baby, I'll go pay for these and then we'll go be slutty at J. Crew. They have tweed pants with a purple motif running through them."

As Brady was heading off to the register to purchase his cum-stained purple corduroys, he nonchalantly tossed yet another revelation to us in a not-so-subtle stage whisper.

"I'm gonna get fucked twice. On a *Sunday*!"

Left alone with Gus, Flynn and I jockeyed for position much like Charles Nelson Reilly and the manlier Brett Somers Klugman must have on the set of *Match Game* and determined through a complex combination of facial expressions and hand motions that I should take the first shot.

"Brady is such an articulate boy, Gus," I said. "I didn't know they taught elocution in the gutter."

"I was actually going to go with 'I didn't know Slutworld had a new mayor,'" Flynn said. "But yours was more character driven and less a one-liner. I bow before you."

"Thank you, Flynn. And Brady bows before Gus. Twice."

"Gentlemen, I hate to break up this witty repartee," Gus said. "But I must escape whilst I can. Please inform Brady that I am no longer in need of his services."

We scurried after Gus as he attempted to peel out of the Banana. Over at the register, Brady was entertaining a middle-aged out-of-town couple who were buying matching cable-knit sweaters in cherry red and lime green. Flynn pulled me back to reality.

"Gus! Do they not sell the Gay Manual over in Britain?" Flynn asked. "It clearly states in chapter fourteen that you cannot fuck a boyfriend in a dressing room stall and then dump him."

"I have to! He's like this balmy gay sex-pig in heat."

"And isn't that what you wanted? To be a balmy gay sex-pig before you turn forty and your youth is history?"

"Yes, but not every bloody day! I'm popping Viagra like aspirin and it's beginning to get dangerous. I shot a load so hard last night my nipple got a black eye."

"Which one?" I asked.

"I fucked Brady so brutally in that dressing room I thought I broke his coccyx bone and all he did was beg me for more."

"I bet it was the left one," I said. "Right?"

"No, I can't see him anymore. I'm tired! Just tell him we're through. I can't break a bloke's heart."

"But ya got no problem with breaking a bloke's ass," Flynn reminded him.

"Please, boys, save me! Tell him anything. I know! Tell him Wendolyn rang and I have to fly back to England. It's an emergency."

"Don't worry, Gus, we'll take care of it."

When Brady returned he glanced about and asked, "Where's Gussie?"

"Gone," Flynn said. "He left you, Brady. He wanted us to make up a lie and tell you he had to leave the country to take care of his mentally unstable sister, but we're not going to do that."

"No, we're not," I added, following Flynn's lead.

"And do you want to know why?"

"Why?" Brady and I asked in unison.

"Because you deserve the truth," Flynn said. "And the truth is . . . you're like our friend Sebastian. You're a whore."

Brady looked stunned. "Oh, I know that." But not shocked. "It's what attracted Gus to me in the first place."

"Well, then, you know a whore is like a butterfly. It's pretty, it's hard to pin down, and after three days it dies."

"Oh my gosh, Flynn, that is so beautiful," Brady said.

"So move on, pretty little gay butterfly whore."

"Yeah, move on," I added.

"I will. I will move on," Brady declared.

But standing there in the doorway, Brady made it clear that he didn't want to move on alone.

"Do you two want to come to J. Crew with me?"

"No, Brady-whore. We don't like purple."

Like the slutty underage mistress in *Evita*, Brady nodded that he understood his time had passed and left on his mission to defile yet another dressing room. Having dressed me for my date with my latest potential boyfriend and having spared Gus from any further potential emotional injury, Flynn decided it was time he go on a mission to search for his own potential. I spent the rest of the day cautiously optimistic that my love life, for the first time in quite a while, had some real potential as well.

The next morning on the set of *If Tomorrow Never Comes*, I was still as happy as a flibbertigibbet, a will-o'-the-wisp, a clown. I was dying to tell everyone around me about my impending date, but I didn't want to jinx it in case Brian turned out to be the new Frank, so I decided to keep it a secret. Some other people, however, were trying to have their own secrets exposed.

"Stevie!"

"Laraby," I said. "I haven't even had my morning coffee. Can't this wait until later?"

"Oh, but Stevie, I just have to tell you I rented *Cruising* this weekend. I never knew such wild shenanigans went on in the seventies."

"Why? Have you developed amnesia?" I asked.

"I mean I only rented it because I adore that Mister Al Pacino . . . what? Amnesia?"

"You *were* living in the city in the seventies, weren't you?"

"Of course. The lure of the world's media mecca called to me and so I left home to move here."

"So you know all about the Manhole and the Spike."

"The . . . Manhole," Laraby said dreamily. "Well, um, theoretically yes. One did hear stories about the carousing and the sweat-soaked orgies that spontaneously erupted in the musk-scented back rooms thanks to the intricate, yet necessary, language of the handkerchief. But, Stevie, I never partook; I was married in the seventies."

"To your career?"

"No, to a Canadian woman. Midge did so love her golf."

Before I got to the point where I screamed to Laraby that his secret was out and everyone, except perhaps a golf-loving woman from Canada, knew he was a homo in hetero clothing, Loretta Larson did something she so rarely did these days. She stole the scene.

Right after Loretta as Regina helped Sister Roberta give birth to a baby girl in a cave somewhere in the mountains she passed out drunk, her face landing right in the fake placenta. The scene looked more authentic than any Loretta had been in since her debut almost thirty years ago, yet everyone knew it was not in the script. Silence reigned until a trembling voice came over the loudspeaker.

"Did Loretta pass out on the *stunt* baby?"

An intern wearing rubber gloves and an absolutely terrified expression was pushed forward to investigate and after much tentative prodding and poking, he found that yes, the baby lodged underneath an unconscious Loretta was indeed the anatomically correct stunt baby doll. The director called for a break and the crew, including a network paramedic, surrounded Loretta not

to conduct CPR, but to stare at a fallen star. Lourdes was clicking her digital camera like a young Annie Leibovitz and was
overheard saying that if these pictures turned out to be the soap
queen's final photo op she would be able to sell them to the
tabloids, retire, and finally have enough money to take back control of her family's sugarcane plantation in the Dominican Republic. Her camera stopped flashing when at last someone rolled
Loretta over and announced that she was still breathing.

"Damn! I'll never get that plantation back!" Lourdes cried.

At that point I noticed Lucas on the set, wearing a black leather
eye patch and looking gayer than a pirated Johnny Depp. He informed Laraby and me that he was feeling much better and his
doctor had told him his eye should heal completely in a few
days. The eye patch, he confessed, was a gift from M. Of course
I wanted to push the conversation further, but Laraby pushed all
social boundaries first and attempted to hug Lucas, pressing his
flesh into Lucas's and letting his head rest in the cradle between
Lucas's firm chest and solid shoulder blade, a truly fine place to be
for a repressed homosexual.

"And the haggardsnatch blows!" Lucas cried.

"Oh, I'm sorry," said Laraby, backing away from Lucas. He
ran out of the room, his hands covering his privates.

"Not you, Loretta," Lucas said as if Laraby was still there.
"The tired cunt just threw up all over herself."

And indeed she had. Vomit poured from Loretta's mouth, or-
angey brown in color and chunky, like she had mixed her tequila
with Orangina and washed it down with brownies. Lourdes's
camera caught it all in its gory Technicolor glory.

"That plantation *will* be mine!"

I don't know if it was because Loretta was shitfaced drunk or
because she had come to that point in her life that Laraby still
hadn't reached and simply didn't care what the world thought
of her, but she rose like a boozy phoenix, pushed away the paramedic and the terrified intern, and demanded that shooting resume. Covered in vomit, which surprisingly looked a lot like
afterbirth, Loretta handed Sister Roberta her stunt baby. When
the scene was over there was no applause, only slack-jawed

shock as Loretta wiped a little vomit drizzle from her chin and stumbled toward her dressing room. A few feet behind her the intern followed, armed with a towel in case the volcano spewed forth again.

After work I rushed home, took a shower, and started to masturbate to an old fantasy that featured me, Aiden Shaw, and a schoolroom, but then decided that it would better aid my flirtations with Brian that night if I were somewhat horny. With my left hand holding my dick, I raised my right hand and swore to Baby Jesus that I would not have sex with Brian and would only pleasure myself in a frenzied solo jerkfest after our date. It was the absolute closest I was getting to abstinence and the Baby would have to accept it.

One last look in the mirror—not so bad. My hair was just messy enough, not one pimple had decided to join me for the evening, and my green eyes did indeed pop. In the safety of my apartment I felt ready. But when I stepped outside all that self-assurance disappeared and I went through as many personalities as Sybil. For a few blocks I felt completely inferior to this guy who I didn't even know, then I was excited to get to know this guy who I was very attracted to, then for a block or two I was apathetic because I knew this guy would turn out to be a jerk, and for several blocks I was so nervous that I had to walk with my arms sticking out from my sides so I didn't get sweat stains in my armpits. Why was I sabotaging myself? It was a date, not a commitment ceremony. I literally had to stop on 29th Street and go into the frozen foods section of a Korean deli to dry out my armpits and get control of the situation. If this date didn't go beyond this first dinner I wasn't any less of a man. I was just a man having a first date with another man. Nothing more, nothing less. I really didn't know why I was putting so much pressure on myself. Or did I?

"Stevie!" Flynn cried from my cell phone when I answered. "Is my boy nervous?"

"I just got over my first panic attack, but keep talking, I'm sure you can induce another one."

"Don't worry, this date is going to be perfect. You are wearing the outfit I bought for you, right? You didn't switch at the last minute to something from your own closet?"

"There is nothing wrong with my own clothes," I pouted.

"Stevie, the last thing you need to do is try to go all suburban and wear your Dockers and flannel."

"The Dockers were on sale."

"They have pleats, Steven!"

"Hold on, it's my mother," I said, switching lines. "What?"

"Are you wearing your father's cufflinks?"

"Are you psychic?"

"Flynn told me you have a very important date tonight and that you were taking a piece of your father with you. I wish you would have invited me, but at least one of your parents can share your joy."

"Hold on. Flynn!"

"Yes, Steven."

"Why did you tell my mother that I have a date? *And* that I'm wearing my dead father's jewelry? You know how jealous she can get."

"She called me because she was worried about you. You, my love, are as transparent as Lisa Rinna's attempts to get back on network TV. I told her about your date so I could put her fears to rest."

"What about *my* fears!?" I cried. "Now she's going to expect a recap before midnight."

"Is she still on the other line?"

"Yes."

"Conference her in."

Wiping away the sweat on my upper lip, I conferenced in my mother so she and Flynn could talk about me as I listened.

"Mrs. Ferrante, it's Flynn."

"Hello, lovey!"

"Steven's a little nervous about tonight."

"I am not!"

"Yes, you are," they both replied.

"Stevie, make sure you walk with your arms outstretched,"

Anjanette advised. "There is nothing more unattractive than a sweat stain. You should've borrowed my dress shields. You could use a maxipad as a substitute; they can absorb a river, let me tell you."

"I am not sweating!" I said as I walked down the street looking like a jet plane.

"Mrs. Ferrante, let's let Steven have his night all to himself and he'll call us tomorrow with a recap."

"Oh, of course he can call me tomorrow. I wouldn't dream of calling him tonight, I understand all about remaining in the periphery of my son's life."

"Ma, don't lie! You've camped out in the epicenter."

"Steven, I don't even know what that means, but I attribute the tone of your voice to your fragile emotional state. Remember this date is not your last chance."

And there it was. The ugly voice from way down deep in my gut finally channeled itself through my mother and shot its contaminated comments into the air. I did feel that my date with Brian was my last chance at a happy future. This feeling was unwarranted, unsubstantiated, but undeniably real. It was also a feeling that had to be shaken off before I met Brian so my part of the night's dialogue would be dazzling and not desperate. Just then another call came through and instead of fighting fate I conferenced Lindsay in to join the cell party.

"Hi, Lindsay, my mother and Flynn are also on the line. Go ahead, tell me not to be nervous."

"Hello! I'm with Gus and we want to wish you good luck tonight."

"Have a brilliant time, Steve, you deserve it. And hello, Mrs. Ferrante. When are you coming across the pond to have a night out with the boys? It's been too long."

"Oh, hi ya, Gus. You know I don't like to wedge myself into Stevie's life. He likes to keep his affairs in New York private and so I respect that."

"You can't even spell respect, Ma!"

"And Steven hasn't had any affairs in years, that's why this date is so important."

"Oh, Lindsay, did Steven tell you that I could help find your father?"

"He did and thank you very much, Mrs. Ferrante, but I did find my daddy, he is everything I could have hoped for, and I will be seeing him regularly on Tuesday evenings."

"That's wonderful, Lindsay, I'm so happy for you."

"Will you be able to handle a weekly meeting with Dad?" I had to ask.

"As a son, Steven, you should know that children need to make sacrifices for a parent's love," Lindsay said. "I may hurt in some specific places, but the pain is worth it to see a sneer—I mean a smile—on my daddy's face."

"To hear you talk like that, Lindsay, brings a tear to my eye," Anjanette said.

"Oh, I do hope Daddy brings several tears to mine."

About a block from 23rd Street I saw Brian walking toward me talking on his cell phone too. It was time to see if the problem of my love life could be solved quicker than a novice named Maria.

"People! My date is here, I gotta go."

A chorus of *good lucks* and *have funs* erupted and I clicked off my phone. I couldn't be mad at them, they were just as excited as I was. Hopefully, Brian would be too.

"Your friends wishing you luck too?" Brian asked.

"Yeah," I admitted. "It's been a while since I've been on a real date."

"Me too. Let's promise that no matter what happens we'll just enjoy ourselves tonight."

"That sounds like a perfect plan."

East of Eighth is the type of gay restaurant that can work for every type of gay. The flamboyant, butch, just-out-of-the-closet, or married-with-two-kids-in-Westchester will all feel at ease. It's my favorite first-date restaurant and I was thrilled to be going back after such a long dry spell.

Part of the reason the restaurant is such a safe haven is the wait staff. They're all gay without being in-your-face obnoxious like Mario Cantone wannabes auditioning to be the host of

Steampipe Alley: The Next Generation. They can also recognize a relationship that's fresher than the other side of a pillow. Instantly they become more friendly than flirty, ask a few more personal questions so you can use them as a springboard for conversation if there's a lull in the air, and they always give that one-sided smile and wink that translates into "He is sooo incredibly cute, make him your boyfriend now or I'll have him for dessert in the break room as four Mexican busboys cheer us on." They may not mean a word or gesture they convey, but it doesn't matter, their attention and support keep those childhood friends—emotional pain and self-doubt—at bay.

Wearing a pale blue dress shirt with tiny-tiny light yellow vertical stripes that perfectly matched his blond hair and navy blue pants that had a touch more Lycra in them than mine, Brian looked more like a Southern California man-boy than a Southern Alabama transplant. But it was more than his physical beauty that I found attractive; he had a calm, serene air about him despite the fact that he was a workaholic. He was one of those people who seemed laconic, but was really just comfortable in his own skin. He spoke evenly and in full sentences, he didn't stutter or interrupt himself, so even when he rambled from one tangent to the other, he sounded fluid and vocally hypnotic. It also helped that his voice was deep and smooth like bourbon with a splash of fruit juice. Whatever the reason, he made me quiet.

". . . So between my job, freelance assignments, the bowling league, and the Sci-Fi Channel," Brian said, "my life is pretty busy."

"You're a sci-fi fan?"

"Love it. I'm a closet geek."

"And a sportsman. Though you look more like a surfer than a bowler."

"I feel it's important to get in touch with my inner lesbian."

"Me too. That's why I have a pair of Dockers and some flannel shirts in the back of my closet."

"Dockers are very underestimated. They're stain-resistant,

cheap, and the pleats add emphasis to your entertainment center. Not that your center needs more entertaining."

"Thank you."

"You're welcome. You have beautiful eyes."

Apparently, Brian was also a segue master. Or just one of those people who said what was on his mind, like Lindsay. But unlike Lindsay, Brian didn't seem to offend when he observed.

"Thank you. I wish I had a more clever retort."

"No need. Just keep focusing your beautiful eyes right over here."

I actually blushed. I would have laughed out loud if Flynn, Lindsay, Gus, and especially Sebastian had told me that his date said that to him. But Brian was sincere and that was wildly refreshing. Was his sincerity his strategy? Maybe, but I wasn't allowing my thoughts to focus on anything other than the here and now just as I wasn't allowing my eyes to focus on anything other than Brian's effortless beauty.

"I must say your Southern charm is irresistible," I declared. "But is there an accent buried beneath your laid-back charisma?"

"The only time my drawl starts to come out is when I get tipsy," Brian said.

"So I guess when you start saying *y'all* it means that it's time to go home?" I asked.

"Or that the night's just started."

We smiled, we flirted, we giggled like girls then tried to cover it up with guylike guffaws, only to giggle louder, and the dreaded lull never swooped in to destroy our conversation.

"You majored in English lit too?" I asked.

"Yup. I almost became a teacher, but I feared I would end up reliving my high school angst."

"I am such an anomaly. I loved high school."

"Really? I hated it! So much so that I graduated early. Luckily I had my books to lose myself in. *Wuthering Heights* made me forget about my troubles more times than I'd like to recall."

"*Jane Eyre* did it for me. I still grab for the tissues when she marries Mr. Rochester."

"Steven."

"Yes, Brian."

"I think we *are* lesbians."

Over coffee and a shared dessert of hot apple crumble pie with vanilla ice cream I sighed with relief. Unless Brian revealed that he had to check in with his parole officer before midnight or that he was Republican, this date would go down in history as my most successful and least awkward. And then the waiter placed the check in the middle of the table.

Awkwardness prevailed and I was instantly filled with hetero-envy. If we were a heterosexual couple the waiter would have put the check in front of the man because the man always pays. Or at least that's what my blue-collar Italian Catholic upbring-ing taught me. But we're both men, so even the most gay-savvy waiter gets confused. I subscribe to the theory that whoever does the asking should do the paying. Maybe I'm hopelessly subur-ban, but if I'm on a date I want to be treated as such whether I'm the guy or the girl. Luckily, Brian and I had something else in common.

"I asked you to dinner so I'll get this," Brian declared, pick-ing up the check.

"Thank you," I said.

Once the check was paid we had another decision to make. This was the one that most hetero couples didn't have to ponder on the first date and could involve two men unclothed and hor-izontal. I was just about to explain my no-sex-until-the-third-date rule when Brian interrupted.

"I know I'm going to sound like an old-fashioned fag, but do you mind if I walk you home? It's not a ploy to be invited up to your place, but it's such a beautiful night I'd like to share it."

On the way home we giggled some more, took some time to just look at each other, fought the urge to grab hold of each other's hands because we both knew that it was a little too early for such a statement, but did let our hands brush against each other and enjoyed the hint of warmth. We kept learning about each other: we both had an Aunt Matilda who was a not-so-loveable curmudgeon, we were both morning people, and we both had crushes on Olivia Newton-John. We acknowledged that if we were true lesbians this would be cause for Brian to move in right then and for us to open up a joint bank account online. But we also acknowledged that we were gay men and at the foot of the steps to my apartment we paused.

"There's a part of me that wants to run upstairs with you, throw you on your bed, and ravish you," Brian said breathlessly. "But I've done that before. . . ."

"And the relationship petered out as quickly as your peter."

"Exactly."

"I'd like to see you again."

"Good. Me too."

"So I guess this is good night," I said.

"No. This is."

Like the end of a good Julia Roberts movie, one where she doesn't die or play the maid to a drug-addict doctor, Brian leaned in, pressed his warm hand against my chest, and kissed me gently. His lips felt moist and I responded by pressing in just a little to make sure he knew he wasn't on his own. We kept the kiss going long enough to let our tongues meet and our breath quicken. And then we pulled back and stared at each other. Was it a defining moment in my life? Was it the beginning of a problem-free romance-filled future? Did it unlock the mystery of how to catch a cloud and pin it down? I couldn't say. All I knew was this was the best first date of my life and Brian Patrick Oldsboro was officially my new favorite thing.

Chapter Seven

The waves caressed our toes with a lazy bonhomie. Brian held me ever-so-tightly as a breeze drifted over and through us making his white linen shirt billow to expose a glimpse of supple, tanned flesh. I was right, Rakiraki on Fiji's Sunshine Coast was indeed the perfect place for a commitment ceremony. Blue sky, bluer water, bluest eyes. Raising my chin proudly, I mouthed my new name to the Fiji air—Steven Bartholomew Ferrante-Oldsboro—and squinted as the sunlight bounced off my new platinum and 24-karat-gold wedding band creating a prism of light that turned the tropical skyline into a radiantly happy rainbow. I closed my eyes and arched my back in such a way as to permit the sun *and* Brian to kiss my skin. Our embrace grew so intense that we fell to the beach and rolled around on the sand like lovers from the alternative ending of *From Here to Eternity*. How wonderful to be gay and in love and in Fiji. And how wonderful to allow myself a moment during my busy Wednesday morning to succumb to a moment of GRIFF—Gay Relationship In Fast-Forward. Major emotional don't, but common practice by gays who haven't been in a real relationship for four years, three months, two weeks, and three days and suddenly find themselves on the brink of coupledom.

"Oh Steeeeeeeeeevie!"

Judging by the tone of Laraby's voice I was on the brink of yet another uncomfortable moment with my might-be-homo-boss.

"Yes, Laraby," I said.

"I need you!" he barked. "I need you *now!*"

"And what *exactly* do you need from me?" I said, praying the answer wouldn't be undying love or an article of used clothing.

"A bulletproof vest."

A near miss.

"Sorry, but I just donated all my Kevlar to a marine I met on-line."

"Really? What's the Web site?" Laraby asked. "No! Stop confusing me, Steven, I'm serious. I have to do something terribly dangerous, *terribly* dangerous, and I'm afraid for my life."

Hmmm. What could possibly make a possibly homosexual businessman fear for his life? Could the X-rated photos have resurfaced? Could he be living a *second* alternative lifestyle involving the selling of drugs and/or black market army surplus? Could his ex-wife Midge be blackmailing him for the entrance money to the LPGA tour?

"Laraby, leave the drama to our cast. What could possibly be that dangerous?"

"I have to fire Loretta Larson."

Talk about a cliffhanger. If the writers of *ITNC* could come up with storylines like that, we'd never be cancelled. Loretta might be a raging alcoholic bitch diva, but she had also been a daytime staple for the last three decades and the life force of Wonderland. If she could get the axe, then nobody was safe. And if Laraby didn't want to wind up in the morgue he would have to make sure there were no axes around when he broke the news to her.

"Fire Loretta Larson!?" I asked in disbelief. "Tha . . . that . . . that's like firing Arnold from *Green Acres*."

"I know! Every fictional town needs its pig," Laraby squealed. "What am I going to do?"

"Sudden agoraphobia? Witness protection program?"

"I don't need a plot device, Steven, I need real-life advice!"

"I'm a soap opera producer, my real-life advice *is* a plot device," I said. "Now back up a second. The network really wants you to fire the star of our show? Why?"

"When she turned the set into a vomitorium it was the last

straw," Laraby said. "Oh, God, she's going to kill me! And then vomit on me!"

"You'll be lucky if it's in that order."

"I can't do it, Steven, I can't! I'll show them. I quit!"

My dream was in reach; Laraby Simmonson was about to quit his job and consequently quit being my boss. But like so many dreams of adulthood, this one came with a tarnished silver lining. If Laraby quit, I would get his job and by default the responsibility of firing Loretta. I could not let that happen.

"Laraby, harshness is sometimes appropriate during lovemaking, but never during decision making," I said sternly. "You are a producer and every once in a while a producer has to produce something that is vile and painful and this is one of those times."

"Did you say something about lovemaking?"

"Focus! When Loretta comes out of her dressing room I want you to march right up to her, bring her into your office, and explain to her that while we have enjoyed her presence in Wonderland these past thirty years, the time has come for her to move on to a land even more wonderful. Tell her that cable television awaits."

"You think I can do that?" Laraby trembled.

"I know you can," I fibbed.

"Your support means more to me than you will ever know, Steven," he said, clutching my arm to steady his trembling. "How will I ever repay you?"

"Get rid of the pig."

Oddly, Loretta was nowhere to be found. Laraby checked her dressing room, the ladies' room, the men's room, even the outdoor smoking room on the third floor and still he couldn't find her. I wondered if someone had tipped Loretta off and she had decided to go AWOL, but I quickly realized that Loretta was not the type to react peacefully when betrayed.

Half of the day's episode was already shot and still no sign of Loretta. Every time I tried to have another moment of GRIFF and fantasize about what Brian and I would name our adopted Malaysian children, I thought I saw her entering the soundstage and instinctively ducked for cover. According to the shooting schedule the wait could soon be over—Loretta was supposed to be in the next scene, the day's cliffhanger.

All around me it was business as usual and it was clear that no one else but me, Laraby, and the network executives knew that Loretta was soon to be a tele-footnote. The scene began with Lorna and Lucas's characters, Ramona and Roger, waking up from a night of passionate sex, joyful that they had rekindled their love affair. Lucas looked ultra-sexy wearing just his ultra-tight jeans and his eye patch, and Lorna was so sultry and seductive you could just sense the network censor's finger stroking his hot-button, ready to press down hard and put a stop to the afternoon delight if things got too steamy. But everything went sub-zero when Loretta, as Regina, entered the scene.

Lorna, still clutching Lucas's bicep, lifted her eyes to meet Loretta's and I knew that she knew. Peripherally, I saw Laraby open his mouth in a silent gasp and knew that he knew that Lorna knew as well. But the most important fact was still not known: did Loretta know?

How I longed to be back on the shores of Fiji with Brian and our children, Leilani-Anjanette and Montgomery, but I was forced to bear witness to what could be the single most pivotal moment in daytime television history. "I know all about Ramona's past disgrace," Roger said. "And I don't care. I don't care, I tell you!"

"You see, Regina," Ramona purred. "You really are nothing but an *old* woman without ammunition."

Fury flared across Loretta's face, for Lorna was supposed to call Regina *stupid* and not *old*. But if throwing up on camera couldn't derail Loretta, a scene partner throwing her lines hardly had any chance of throwing her off course.

"I guess if I'm an old woman, Ramona, that makes you . . . middleaged."

Lorna gripped Lucas's bicep so hard his good eye winced. Loretta's eyes darted to where Leon, the director, was standing when she didn't hear his familiar "Cut!" that always rang out whenever the ad-libbing went too far. Her eyes darted back to Lorna, then to Leon and back to Lorna again. She was acting like the only laboratory mouse left in its cage, happy for its freedom, but perplexed as to why a latex-gloved hand wasn't swooping in for the kill. Her confusion was about to end.

"Better to be middle-aged than . . . *unemployed*!" Lorna screamed.

Laraby screamed even louder and in one apoplectic move spilled his coffee all over himself. He wanted to run from the room, but he was as transfixed as the rest of the crew.

"What did you say?" Loretta said in a dangerously hushed tone.

"Not only are you old, Loretta, but you're fired! You got the axe, lady! You have officially become Loretta Larson, *ex*–Regina O'Reilly of *ITNC*."

Lourdes scoured the day's script to see if there was any chance that the writers had rewritten history to make Ramona Regina's boss and thus the firing would merely be fictional. But then Lourdes realized Regina didn't even have a job in Wonderland, she owned the town. Lourdes threw down the script and picked up her digital camera, flicking on the video button. That Latina was determined to buy back her plantation.

"You don't know what the hell you're talking about," Loretta said nervously.

"If you don't believe me," Lorna said, "ask them."

Lorna pointed to the crew, causing Laraby to shake so uncontrollably that his flailing arms sent the entire snack table flying. A croissant landed at my feet as I distinctly heard Lucas say, "You're breaking the fourth wall, Lorna." God bless his innocent heart.

"Laraby!" cried the Medusa of mid-afternoon drama. "What the fuck is this ugly, no-talent bitch talking about?!"

Lourdes pushed Laraby forward so he was on the set and lined up her camera so both he and Loretta were perfectly in frame. She could taste the sugarcane already.

"I . . . I . . . I . . ." was all Laraby could utter.

"Stop stuttering, you sycophantic sissy, and start 'splaining!"

"Sh . . . sh . . . she's right," Laraby started. "You're fuh . . . fuh. . . ."

"Fucked?" Lorna suggested.

"Fired!" Laraby got out.

Jaws dropped lower than Dominick Dunne's when the O.J. verdict was announced.

"Why, you overweight, bald, incompetent, coffee-stained faggot!"

"It's ca-ca-ca-cappuccino."

Then every lesson Loretta ever absorbed from every bad acting teacher rose to the surface and she focused her tirade to the powers that be. Channeling Joan Crawford at her most nonmaternal, Loretta delivered *the* performance of her life.

"What's the matter, boys? Dontcha have the balls to fire me yourself?!" Loretta shouted up to the glassed-in executive producer's booth, gesticulating with gusto. "Are you pussy boys afraid of me? Well, motherfuckers, you *should* be afraid!" She circled the set, her boobs heaving and her heels *click-clicking* on the hardwood floor. This was an actress fighting for her very survival and she would not be ignored. "Ask your stupid little selves this: do you really think my fan club will allow you to fire me? All it takes is one e-mail from me to NumberOneLorettaLarsonFan@aol.com and tomorrow morning you won't be able to get your fat asses into this studio because Loretta's Army will form a human blockade!" The *click-clicking* stopped and Loretta positioned herself center stage to deliver the rest of her monologue. "Because let me tell you this, you little pieces of dried-up chicken shit, do not underestimate the power of a mob of bored, bitter housewives and repressed middle-aged queens. My name is Loretta Larson, I am the queen of this fucking shithole we call daytime TV! And those people out there, they are my slaves and they shall do my bidding!"

There was a smattering of applause and slowly Loretta's lips turned into a satisfied smirk. Gently, Lucas grabbed Loretta's elbow and asked, "Loretta, honey, why don't you come with me?"

And God bless his innocent heart for a second time. Whether or not Lucas was gay, the truth was he was a nice guy. While the rest of us were watching Loretta unravel and quite honestly enjoying the performance, Lucas realized she was making a backside of herself and was trying to do something gentlemanly. Unfortunately, Loretta hated gentlemen.

"Get your fucking hands off me, Cyclops!"

She pushed Lucas backward with such force that he spun around and with his open palm slapped Lorna across her face. He stumbled until Lorna pushed him in the opposite direction so she could charge into Loretta. Handicapped with only one-sided vision, Lucas didn't know that he was falling onto Laraby until he heard him whisper, "The haggardsnatch won't blow so quickly this time," quickly followed by the sound of Lucas's left arm breaking in two separate places.

Loretta yanked out Lorna's hair extensions and Lorna tried to dig her nails into Loretta's fleshy bum but only succeeded in ripping her Bumderwear, the posterior-enhancing undergarment Loretta had sewn into every outfit she wore on and off set. As pieces of fake hair and bum scattered all around them like confetti, the women put Alexis and Krystle to shame, catfighting over the couch, the coffee table, Lucas, and Laraby. Lourdes was actually crying tears of joy as she captured all the action on her camera. I would have loved to join in the tearfest, but I was too busy trying to figure out how the events could turn out so incredibly wrong.

Later that night at Starbucks, I brought the boys up to date.

"So we had to re-tape the entire last scene to make it look like Roger broke his arm while having sex with Ramona, a grief counselor had to be brought in when Lourdes's digital camera was confiscated, and in order to get her contract renewed, Loretta had to agree to take a vacation at a rehab clinic in Aruba."

"I love Club Meds," Lindsay said.

"Steven, I must say you have a much more exciting job than I do," Gus said. "The only thing I did today was make a certain gay baseball player three million dollars richer by moving around some of his investments. He's only seven million away from announcing to the world that he's a poof."

"Then poof goes his career," Lindsay interjected.

"Don't be such a cynic."

"I'm a realist. And I know a thing or two about sports-related homophobia. I am an athlete."

"You're not an athlete, you're an ice-skater," Flynn said.

"And you wore sequins, not pinstripes," Gus added.

"Not only are you two nancy boys jealous, you're misinformed," Lindsay said. "I have so worn pinstripes. Did you not see my long program at the '92 nationals when I skated to *Field of Dreams?*"

"Boys! While I love your good-natured ribbing, why hasn't anyone asked me about my new boyfriend?"

"I'm giving you your space," Flynn said.

"I'm trying not to pry," Gus said.

"I'm not interested," Lindsay said.

"Lies, lies, and more lies. Brian is terrific! He's hot, he's got a great job, and he's the best kisser ever!"

"You've already told us that, honey," Flynn reminded me.

"So I'll tell you again and you will act as if it's news."

Flynn, Lindsay, and Gus all took sips of their coffee drinks at the same time, eyeing each other conspicuously.

"Steven, please tell me you're taking things slowly and that you haven't already given names to the children you and Brian will adopt?" Flynn queried.

"I am taking things slowly. I only called him once since our date. Do you think I'd jeopardize our relationship by revealing my OCD symptoms before our one-month anniversary?"

"And the children?" Flynn asked.

"Leilani-Anjanette and Montgomery," I confessed.

"After Montgomery Clift, how sweet," Gus remarked.

"Actually it's in honor of the capital of Alabama, where Brian's from."

"Do yourself a favor! Book Loretta a double room and join her," Lindsay declared. "You're as crazy as she is!"

"I am not crazy. I'm happy."

Without sounding as if I was itching to become the latest member of the Hallmark Hall of Fame, I explained how I knew that Brian and I didn't have a solid relationship yet and that at any moment he could cancel our second date and I'd never see him again, but the possibility that we could have a relationship had made me happy and I was embracing it. Past experience had taught me that a love life is fleeting, so even though I knew men are chameleonic and can change their emotions at will I was choosing to have fun while it lasted.

"Mama like a cockeyed optimist," Flynn said, smiling.

"Always with the dirty remarks, Flynn," Lindsay remarked. "No wonder breeders are convinced gay men don't know the difference between love and sex."

"It's a lyric to a show tune," Gus said.

"Worse! Nelly gay men who don't know the difference between love and sex."

"That's the fag calling the kettle gay," I said. "Among the four of us which one's love for his daddy grows every time Daddy's dick goes up his ass?"

"I am not in love with my daddy! I just want him to fuck my ass in a sling every Tuesday at nine. What the hell is wrong with that?"

The table of tourists next to us didn't answer, but simply took this as their cue to scurry away, the dominant female of the group covering her young daughter's ears and casting a look at Lindsay similar to the one Satan must have seen when God cast him out of heaven.

Gus took this as the perfect moment to change the subject and invite us all to his swanky apartment for a Halloween party the following Saturday night. Of course we all agreed to come and I was thrilled that I would have a date to bring. Lindsay, ever the party planner, declared a TV theme and announced that each of us must dress up as his favorite TV character. Gus sighed and reiterated his belief that the fall of American culture was due exclusively to the overly important status our uncultured society has given television.

"I have two words for you, Gus," I said. "Benny Hill."

The rest of the evening was spent tossing out ideas about what characters we should come as. I felt extremely proud when

I said I couldn't make my decision until I spoke with Brian. Even if I was putting my Gay Relationship In Fast Forward, it was refreshing not to have to decide something on my own.

Another thing I didn't have to do on my own was entertain myself on a Friday night. Two dates in one week wasn't a record for me, but it was a welcome reminder that I was boyfriend material and could attract a gentleman's eye for more than a quick one-nighter. Brian and I decided to extend the lesbian metaphor we started over dinner and go bowling. I gave a lesbian mainstay a homo twist and wore a short-sleeved flannel shirt in green, yellow, and mauve plaid with faux-pearl button snaps. I rolled up the sleeves an extra notch and left the top two buttons unbuttoned in order to show maximum flesh. Twenty quick dumbbell curls to give my arms a little more oomph and I was ready to go.

Brian was waiting for me outside Bowlmor Lanes wearing a quiet smile and a very loud red and black bowling shirt with the name SHIRLEY embroidered on the front pocket. He outlesbianed me.

"You look great," Brian said.

"So do you, Shirley," I replied.

He was still laughing when he kissed me, which made me giggle. With one kindhearted kiss the stress and commotion of my week evaporated. It was as if Loretta, Laraby, and the rest of the energy-sucking *ITNC* crowd didn't exist. It was just me and Brian and, of course, a bowling alley full of rowdy strangers.

I chugged my second Bud Light as Brian bowled his third strike in a row. Hustled, I was. Brian had told me he was a member of A Ball with Three Holes, the premiere gay bowling league in town, but I hadn't actually thought he'd be a good bowler. I figured he had merely joined for the social aspect, which was really the only reason to join any sport. Learning new things about your date is what the whole darn dating thing is about anyway.

"Excuse me, Shirley," I said.

"Yes, Laverne?" he replied.

"You suggested we go bowling so you could show off, didn't you?"

"That depends. Have I impressed you?"

"Yes! But you've also depressed me," I confessed. "I suck!"

"Please don't change the subject, we're talking about bowling."

"Dirty bird! Someone spends a lot of time in the gutter when they're out of the bowling alley."

Sitting next to Brian on the hard plastic bowling bench I got a rush of memory. I remembered sitting on a similar bench at the Columbia Bowling Lanes in Union City, New Jersey next to Tommy Guma in seventh grade. We were on the same PAL bowling league and every Saturday morning we would talk about *Star Wars* or *Planet of the Apes* in between making fools out of ourselves by trying to hit ten pins with one ball. At that time I hadn't yet admitted to myself that I was 100 percent gay, but I knew that I loved spending those Saturday mornings with Tommy. The conversation was effortless and we both wanted to hear what the other had to say, just like now. I hadn't thought about Tommy in years and so I thanked Brian and explained.

"Should I be jealous?" he asked.

"Not at all. Tommy moved out of state the next year and I never saw him again."

"Then I take the comparison as a compliment."

It was my turn to bowl, although with a score of fifty-eight in the ninth frame there really was no point of continuing the charade. But as on those Saturday mornings a lifetime ago, bowling for me was less about bowling and more about bonding.

"Nice ass," Brian shouted.

The ball flew out of my hand and landed with a thud an inch away from the left-hand gutter, which it proceeded to enter and roll noisily down until it disappeared from view. I turned and almost bumped right into Brian, who was standing on the lane. He was smiling his easy smile and I found myself staring at a man who was in total flirt mode. But what I liked about Brian was that his flirting was natural, while mine was often forced and sounded scripted. I desperately tried to think of something clever to say, but decided to follow Brian's lead and take things slow.

"I hope you didn't feel the need to return the compliment?" I asked.

"Nope. I just call 'em as I see 'em. And you have a nice ass. And a nice mouth."

By this time Brian's breath mingled with mine and when he pressed against me to kiss me right there on the bowling lane his boner pushed up against my own hard-on. I closed my eyes and tried not to think that every single person in Bowlmor Lanes was watching me. I wanted to enjoy this moment. When Brian pulled away, his naughty smile told me everything I needed to know. He liked my ass, but he liked me more.

As Brian prepared to bowl another strike, I saw a twenty-something girl a few lanes over staring at me. She smiled and raised her beer bottle in my direction. I saluted her with my Bud Light and beamed because the world recognized that my date was a hot catch.

During our third game I learned that Brian's mother was stopping in New York next month on her way to Budapest. Ever since her divorce, Brian said, his mother was using most of the money she'd won in the settlement to see the world she hadn't while she was bound by the shackles of matrimony. But before he could tell me any more about the prison that was his parents' marriage, I saw that my beer buddy had left and in her lane were Sebastian and some older fat man. Not wanting Sebastian to be the first friend Brian met, I quickly turned around, but alas, not fast enough.

"Steven!" Sebastian cried. "Over here! It's me, Sebastian!"

Waving his arms frantically overhead, Sebastian's tight little tee rose up a few inches exposing his taut stomach muscles and a bit of pube.

"Friend or ex-lover?" Brian said.

"Second-tier friend. I don't even have him on speed dial."

Leaving the fat man to do the prebowling setup on his own, Sebastian sashayed over to our lane and introduced himself.

"You must be Brian," Sebastian said, extending his hand. "I'm Sebastian." He yanked Brian closer and leaned in to kiss one cheek and then the other. "Thank you for asking Steven out. It's been so long we thought he turned straight on us."

"He was just waiting to bump into the right man."

"Speaking of, do you have any Tina?" Sebastian asked. "I won't even bother to ask Nancy Reagan here."

"Sorry, call me Ronald," Brian said.

"You just say no to drugs too?" Sebastian asked. "What the hell is the gay community coming to?"

Perfect. Now the first impression Brian would have of my circle of friends is that they're a bunch of swishy, recreational drug users. I had to shift the conversation.

"Sebastian, who's your fella?"

"Oh, that's Henry," Sebastian said. "We're going to bowl a few games then I'm gonna blow him."

"What?" Brian said, only because I was rendered speechless.

"I met him last week when I was dancing at Marys. He's a software salesman and he just got a huge bonus so he was extra generous with the tips."

"So for an extra twenty you're going to blow him?" I asked.

"Do you think I would really have sex with a man who gives me money?"

"Yes," I said.

"Well, that's true, but Henry bought me a suit and for that he's going to get a nice tongue-whaling."

I was back to being speechless so Brian continued the interrogation.

"Did he at least pay retail?" Brian chuckled.

"Of course! It's a gorgeous John Varvatos three-button pinstriped suit in navy blue," Sebastian explained. "I will look like a fucking designer diva! Ooh, Shamu is ready to roll, see you later, boys."

"Enjoy," I said.

Sebastian took something out from his back pocket and handed it to me. For the third time that evening I was rendered speechless as I saw that I was holding three condoms, one light blue, one red, and the third clearly smelling like apple pie.

"I'm not going to need these tonight," Sebastian declared. "Fat stuff is getting a blow job and *nada más*. It's not like papi bought me Armani." He flounced away.

Mortified, I stared down at the condoms. Suddenly, Brian grabbed them and threw them in the garbage.

"We won't be needing those either," Brian said.

"Oh, really?"

"Look, I'm not into retrocopulation and I do use condoms," Brian explained. "But you might as well know right now that I have a no-sex-until-the-third-date rule. So no matter how hard you try and no matter how much I want to we're not having sex until our third date. But when we do have sex, and trust me we will, I promise it's gonna be really, really good."

I just smiled and told him that we had something else in common. Then I gave him a sexy kiss and told him to bowl me another strike. Goshdarnit if he didn't comply.

This time I walked him home and on the way asked him to be my date for Gus's Halloween party. Without hesitation he agreed and reminded me that it would be our third date. I told him I had already figured that out. We had a spirited discussion about what characters to dress up as, but I told him that since I work in the entertainment industry I should have the final say. Reluctantly he agreed and we decided to go as Felix and Oscar from *The Odd Couple* with me being Felix and he Oscar. It was a much better choice than *Mork & Mindy,* even if Brian thought Mork's rainbow suspenders hid a pro-gay message. If I wasn't so excited to have a date to a holiday party that was going to end with hot sex, I would have been upset that Brian's taste in television was suspect.

The good-night kiss this time was much longer and more intense. I was relieved that Brian didn't cross the line and try to turn our two dates into a meaningful relationship by saying something he really didn't mean. It's okay to daydream about such things, but to act upon them is self-destructive. His blue eyes conveyed just enough honesty without making my green eyes roll.

But the perfect capper to the evening came just before I went to bed—Brian sent me a text message: *Two for two, can't wait for number three.* I'd have to remember to buy a new box of condoms.

The days raced by like calendar pages between scenes in an old MGM musical. Nothing really important happened, but there was always this happy melody playing in the back of my head, something sweet and bouncy to accompany me until Saturday night when I would see Brian again.

It's amazing how the beginning of a relationship affects your day-to-day. Very little bothered me, not the endless meetings at work to deal with Loretta's indefinite absence, not the onslaught of Indian summer, which I despise; not even my mother's incessant phone calls. I didn't get upset when my mother wanted to guest on her favorite quiz show, *Tell Me All about Steven's New Boyfriend,* nor did I zone out when she chattered on about the tenants group's upcoming Halloween costume party. In fact I was thrilled that she had convinced Audrey to go with her as before and after Barbras and even offered advice on how to gussy up their costumes so they could beat Sheila and Vinny Caruso. I told her that if she wanted to win first prize Audrey should not dress up like Fanny Brice, but should wear a copy of the black chiffon Scaasi peek-a-boo pantsuit Barbra wore when she accepted her first Oscar in 1969. My mother, as always, was grateful that she raised a brilliant homosexual son.

During the week Brian and I chatted on the phone and IM'd each other during work just to say hi, share some slightly ribald Internet humor, and plan our wardrobe for Saturday night. We decided that Brian should simply wear a backward baseball cap, a stained dress shirt, and crumpled pants, and stuff his shirt pocket with unlit cigars. On a side note Brian and I discovered that we had both grown up with fathers who smoked and as a result the smell of a cigarette was not only unpleasant but conjured up images of riding in the backseat of a car with the windows open as ash flew into our faces. We couldn't tolerate cigarettes or their smellier cousins, cigars.

As Felix, I would wear a dress shirt, tie, and slacks and a full-length lace apron with a strategically placed can of Lysol. To top off the outfit, Brian suggested I borrow his maid Viva's feather duster. I was going to live out the maid fantasy sooner than expected.

When Lucas entered Starbucks on Thursday night I almost choked on my SU. The poor thing still had the eye patch on and now his left arm was in a cast. If he kept going at this rate, in six months his whole body would be covered in plaster and/or black leather. The thought got me mildly aroused.

"Thanks for meeting me, Steven," Lucas said, sitting down across from me with what looked and smelled like a grande Caramel Macchiato with extra caramel. Lucas must have a sweet tooth.

"No problem. How are you feeling?"

"I'm okay. The eye patch comes off tomorrow so I won't look so pathetic."

"You don't look pathetic," I lied. "Just . . . unlucky."

"Well, hopefully my luck will change starting with the Christmas extravaganza."

Lucas showed me his sheet music for the songs he planned to sing and thankfully "White Christmas" was among them so my mother and the rest of the over-the-hill gang would get their Bing Crosby fix. I also noticed quite a few show tunes.

"You're fond of Broadway, I see."

"Well, duh! Who isn't?"

On perfect cue, Flynn, the king of theater queens, waltzed in and I called him over. He sat in between us and before he even noticed the one-eyed, one-armed soap star, he saw the sheet music for the song "Fine and Dandy" from *The Best Little Whorehouse in Texas.*

"And who, may I ask, feels like a hard candy Christmas?" Flynn questioned.

"That would be me."

Some people believe in Santa Claus, others the Tooth Fairy; I believe in the magic of the Starbucks Mermaid because when Flynn looked at Lucas a spark ignited between them. Was it love?

I couldn't say because Lucas still wasn't officially out of the closet, but it definitely was deep *like*. The kind of deep like that only two show queens can share.

"That musical was so far ahead of its time," Flynn said.

"So was the sequel."

"Say it ain't so, Ethel! You saw *The Best Little Whorehouse Goes Public?*"

"Twice! Opening *and* closing night."

"I was there on closing night too. Row G."

"I was in Row F!"

I listened to the two of them chatter on and on about this flop show and that diva's debut and who should've won the Tony and who should never set foot on the Broadway boards again. I smiled approvingly when Flynn suggested a certain song for Lucas's Christmas show and nodded when he claimed another should be cut. Lucas looked like a lonely gay nomad who is befriended by a kind widower near the end of a long journey; he had found a companion. A few minutes into their conversation and I had no more doubts: Lucas was definitely a full-fledged homosexual and I was bursting with pride that someone so sweet and so handsome was on our team.

"What's your favorite musical?" Flynn asked, nearly breathless.

"Oh, I'm sure you've never heard of it."

"Honey, I saw *Rags, Raggedy Ann*, and *Annie II*."

"*Annie II* only played off-Broadway."

"Just keeping you on your toes, baby. Now answer me. What's your favorite musical?"

"*Carrie.*"

I think Flynn may have started to cry because at that moment he realized his soul mate was staring at him with one beautiful green eye. My eyes got teary too because at that moment I realized my best friend had fallen in love.

Flynn spoke slowly. "*Carrie* is, without question, my absolute favorite musical in the history of modern American theater."

"Really? I cannot believe I found someone who shares my love for the ostracized, yet vocally gifted, high schooler."

"Do you have the bootleg recordings?"

"Yes! The Broadway company with Betty Buckley *and* the original Royal Shakespeare Company version with Barbara Cook."

Flynn moved in closer to Lucas and clutched his hand. I noticed Lucas didn't pull away. "Have you ever heard a recording of the workshop with Maureen McGovern?"

Lucas gasped. "I have been searching for that missing tape for years."

"Well, your search is over. How would you like to come back to my place and listen to it now?"

"I would abso-fucking-lutely love to," Lucas said. "Steven. I'm sorry, but do you mind if we talk about my show some other time?"

"Even if I wanted to I don't think I could interfere with the magnetic pull that is drawing the two of you together. Go on, go listen to the freaky girl sing."

"Thanks for understanding," Lucas said.

I pulled Flynn closer so his ear was next to my mouth, "Remember to sing out, Louise! And call me in the morning."

Flynn guided Lucas to the door and the two of them floated outside on two great big pink musical notes. (Or at least they did in the musical in my mind.)

Typically, I am not what you would call a Halloweeny kind of guy. Perhaps it's because I work in the soap industry and get to watch people dress up and act crazy every day of the year, or perhaps it's because while growing up my father would make us put every piece of candy, gum, fruit, and currency under a microscope to make sure it wasn't tainted with poison or harboring a razor blade. The man may have been looking out for his children's safety, but he took all the fun out of the holiday for me. This year, however, was different. I had a Halloween party to attend and, most important, I had a date.

Dressed as Oscar, Brian looked several years older. Dressed as Felix in a frillier-than-expected apron, I felt a bit submissive. It was an interesting combination and one that we both noticed. By the duration and intensity of Brian's hello kiss, it was a combination he wholeheartedly supported.

"Hello, boys," Gus cheered as we entered. He was wearing what I thought was supposed to be a butler's outfit and a gray wig. "I took your lead, Stevie, and I'm that effing Benny Hill. Who are you two supposed to be?"

"The Odd Couple," I said.

"Well, you do look a bit odd. You're all neat and fussy and your date is quite sloppy and stained. Do you need a washcloth?"

"Gus! We're Felix and Oscar from the series."

"Oh, I don't know why I ever agreed to this cocked-up theme, I never watch TV."

When he was done chastising, Gus gave Brian the once-over and me an approving wink. He then introduced us to the emaciated waif who was dressed as Benny's cheap tart and who also had one hand in Gus's back pocket.

"This is my date, Reuben," Gus said. "Reuben Kincaid."

Reuben smiled at us tartly and Brian and I looked at Gus in disbelief. "You're kidding, right?" Brian asked.

"No, that's my name," Reuben said.

I looked around for a school bus with a Mondrian theme and said, "Gus honey, you really need to get yourself a TV."

He may not have had TV savvy, but Gus had style. His apartment could have been photographed for *Metropolitan Home* or showcased as the "after" segment of an HGTV special on home makeovers. It was impeccably decorated in masculine hues like chocolate brown, pumpkin, and pomegranate and filled with dark wood furniture and backlighting. And unlike most picture-perfect abodes it was also very comfortable. There were no floor cushions or seats without backs; Gus's apartment was filled with furniture that looked good and felt better. It reminded me of Brian.

I brought my BF over to the bar, which was manned by a very hot-looking African-American bartender wearing what looked like the Chippendales' version of a Navy uniform. He introduced himself as Isaac, our gay bartender, and welcomed us to *The Love Boat* bar. When Lindsay threw a party, he sure did pay attention to details.

Brian ordered a Long Island Mr. T, which was a regular Long Island iced tea topped with Goldschlager, and I settled for a Captain Rhoda Morgenstern, which was a rum and Coke with a splash of Manischewitz. After we ordered our second round of TV-flavored drinks, Flynn finally arrived and I was a bit surprised to see that Lucas wasn't on his arm. He explained that Lucas had booked a personal appearance at a shopping mall in Des Moines for the following morning and had had to fly out tonight. I could tell he was lonely, but I couldn't tell what character he was dressed up as.

"I'm supposed to be David Janssen from *The Fugitive*, but it really doesn't work without the one-armed man. But forget about my costume, I have bigger problems. Is Lucas gay?"

"You're asking me? I'm almost certain, but I thought you'd be able to end the mystery."

"Well, he definitely passes the gay test when it comes to musical theater."

"What about the French kissing test? That's a bit more conclusive."

"There was no kissing. Flirting, sitting way too close together, but at the end of the night, he just gave me a hug."

"Hugs are nice," Brian said.

"I am so incredibly rude; you must be Brian," Flynn said.

"And you must be Flynn."

"Wow, Mama like! You really are as cute as Steven described," Flynn began. "I thought he was just making you sound hotter than you are, like *People* magazine does with Ed Norton."

"Thanks, Stevie," Brian said, looking at me.

"The truth is, I'm on edge. I haven't gotten laid in three months and the first man I met who I would like to lay with is on his way to friggin' Iowa and may be straight."

"Well, when he gets back just ask him straight out, 'Are you gay?'" I said.

Flynn was dumbstruck. "Why are you always logical when it comes to someone else's love life? When it's about you, you're completely crazy and irrational."

"Because I'm a homosexual!"

I made Flynn change the subject so Brian could discover why he was my best friend and once the two of them started talking about less volatile subjects like music, television, and, of course, me, they were laughing like Laura Ingalls and Nellie Oleson before Nellie became a bitch.

Soon enough the three of us were standing on the sidelines commenting on the party revelers. At some point, though I don't know exactly when, Brian's hand found mine and our fingers intertwined. Brian's hand felt warm and secure. We didn't have to adjust several times to find that perfect fit and he didn't keep breaking the hold to scratch or brush off some lint from his stained shirt; our hands just stayed together and it felt good.

Flynn noticed our hand holding and smiled at me. I smiled back and although tomorrow I would listen to him blurt out how Lucas's absence made him feel a bit lonely, I knew that as he watched me he was happy for me and wished me and Brian all the happiness we could create for ourselves. But the time had come to stop thinking about ourselves as Lindsay made his grand entrance.

"Well, it's about time the bloody party planner arrived," Gus shouted.

I couldn't believe my eyes. Lindsay was wearing what appeared to be a fat lady suit underneath a blouse, jeans, and fire-engine red cowboy boots. His costume was topped off with a long blond wig that was teased so it resembled my cousin Angela's hair after she gave herself a home perm and tried to straighten the resulting curly horror with an iron. It was dry, frizzy, and in severe need of an Alberto VO5 hot oil treatment. Next to Lindsay stood an African-American midget wearing a track suit and sneakers. For the life of me I couldn't figure out who Lindsay and his date were supposed to be.

"I'm Sally Struthers," Lindsay announced. "And this is one of the third-world children I'm exploiting."

"Actually I'm supposed to be Emmanuel Lewis," the midget corrected. "But Lindsay offered me fifty bucks and I'm a little short on rent."

Emmanuel Lewis announced that he was going to get sauced on the free booze, which I thought would have been more appropriate coming from Gary Coleman, and he scampered over to Isaac the bartender.

Then in walked Sebastian. As expected, his outfit was scant. It was also inspired. He was wearing a simple blue Speedo and on his feet he wore flesh-colored aqua socks that were redesigned to look like there was webbing between his toes. He was the Man from Atlantis, and the reason I knew was that when Patrick Duffy emerged from the ocean every week, my preteen dick bobbed like a buoy in a rough sea. I watched every lame episode of that show and each time Patrick went anywhere near water, I got hard. It was one of the first times I suspected I was gay.

"Sebastian, I love your costume," I said.

"I thought you would. I know how much you lust over Mr. Duffy."

"Fuck your costume, Sebastian, your ass looks bloody hot!" Gus exclaimed, causing Reuben to shoot him a look, as if he had just screwed up the singing family's Las Vegas booking.

"Speaking of, I just got my asshole bleached," Sebastian declared. "Pink is the new brown, you know."

"Liar!" Lindsay shouted. "You cannot have your asshole bleached. I've looked into it."

"Well, you didn't look deep enough because you can and I did. You want to see?"

"Yes!" we all shouted.

So there we were in Gus's posh apartment, me holding Brian's now-clammy hand, as Sebastian bent over, pulled down his Speedo, and spread apart his asscheeks to reveal the most gorgeous pink asshole any of us had ever seen.

"Oooh, Mama like pink!" Flynn exclaimed.

There wasn't a fleck of brown, mocha, or even dark cinnamon anywhere near his hole or the rind surrounding the hole. It truly was pink. And smooth. And inviting.

"Did it hurt?" I asked.

"Burned mostly," Sebastian said, upside down. "But that went away the next day."

"I don't want a dirty tunnel of love," Lindsay declared. "You must give me the name of your doctor."

"He's a magician and he's Brazilian. Plus he's got the fattest uncut prick I've ever taken up my ass."

"Your doctor fucked you?" I asked.

"My doctor fucked me before he was my doctor," Sebastian said. "But once I heal he'll fuck me after too!"

"How long does it take to heal?" Lindsay wanted to know.

"I can't get fucked for a week. I can get sucked off, if anybody's interested, but you can't rim me 'cause you could get poisoned by the bleach and die."

Finally Sebastian stood right side up and wriggled himself back into his Speedos. Most of us had to do some wriggling of our own.

"But like I always say, sex is risky." he continued. "Oh, I almost forgot." And down came the Speedos once again. "Sniff."

Like gay Pavlovian dogs we all bent over so Sebastian's anus was mere inches away and took one collective sniff. We were transported out of Gus's apartment to an English rose garden.

"Doctor Pinga Gigante used a rose-scented bleach. Not only will I have a pink man pussy, but for the next two weeks my shit won't stink."

"Will I really die if my tongue tastes your pink rosebush?" Lindsay asked.

"Yes. But don't worry, I'm inviting all of Chelsea to a tasting party in a week. I'll be sure to send you an invite."

"That does it," Brian declared. "We need to leave."

"So early? The party's just starting."

"Baby, I am so fucking horny if we don't go now I'm gonna mount you on Isaac's minibar."

It was "Man from Atlantis" all over again. We bid good-bye to Gus, the fugitive, Patrick Duffy, Sally, Reuben, Isaac, and Emmanuel and hightailed it out of there. In the elevator ride downstairs, Brian kissed me ferociously, even doing the old two-hands-on-either-side-of-the-face kiss which only works when both parties are completely out of control. When the elevator stopped at the lobby so did Brian.

"I'm sorry, am I being too aggressive?"

The only words I could find to answer his question were on the tip of my tongue so I shoved it into his mouth and he seemed to understand that his aggressive behavior was perfectly acceptable.

We practically kissed the entire way home and when we were naked on his bed and I was watching him put a condom on his beautiful, nicely thickened dick, I laughed. Brian was a bit startled, but he got it and he laughed too. After all, sex was supposed to be fun. And as I grabbed the flesh on his back and felt him penetrate me we stared right into each other's eyes and laughed a little bit harder.

Chapter Eight

Waking up for the first time in a new boyfriend's bed is a lot like being plunged into one of Sid and Marty Krofft's 1970s Saturday morning TV shows. One minute you're roaming through the familiar reality of your own dreamworld and the next minute you're waking up in an unfamiliar land of the lost next to a guy with skin as soft as the smoothest Styrofoam. It leaves you feelin' groovy and just a tiny bit funked out.

As I watched Brian smile in his sleep I felt like I had fallen a thousand feet below into a place where boys could be ladybugs and sea monsters could find refuge at a beach house. It was a magical place, but also a place where I didn't have secure footing. So I closed my eyes and when I reopened them I was happy to see that nothing had changed—Brian was still asleep and smiling. I suddenly felt as sexily innocent as I did as a young boy hoping that yet another button on Will Marshall's tight-fitting khaki shirt would come undone.

Lying there in Brian's queen-sized sleigh bed, swathed in olive green Ralph Lauren cotton twill bedsheets, I breathed in the faint smell of musk that rose from underneath the covers and marveled at how gay I was as a kid. I wasn't a lisping sissy-boy (though one Christmas I did steal my cousin Robyn's Sun Valley Barbie mainly because she wore a cool orange 'n' yellow ski outfit that I totally coveted) but my most profound memories of childhood and early adolescence are those that include feeling special pangs of excitement toward other boys whether they were on TV, in my classroom, or living in my neighborhood. Wavy-haired Wesley Eure as Will Marshall was just one in a long line of crushes that I couldn't really explain, but understood made me a little bit different than the other boys. Luckily, I no longer felt ashamed about feeling different, only pleased that I could still recall the happy pangs. And happy pangs were what I was feeling lying next to Brian.

"Are you staring at me, sexy man?" Brian asked with one eye open.

"Guilty as charged."

"Then you have a punishment coming to you."

"Well, I've done the crime, so I must do the time."

"Your sentence is one really long pre-mouthwash morning kiss."

"That sounds yummy."

Brian grinned as his naked body slinked on top of me. His skin was warm and inviting. Our woodies ground into each other slowly and I reached under the sheets to get a good grip on his asscheeks. I could feel his hot breath hover over my mouth for just a moment before his lips pressed themselves onto mine. Then I got the wake-up call every gay man craves—a deep, penetrating tongue kiss from a handsome guy.

My right hand traveled north and tousled Brian's hair as my left went due south and found the center of Brian's firm and meaty buttocks. Instinctively, my legs spread apart and I wrapped them around his. Our kiss got deeper and harder until our woodies were full-fledged hard-ons and soon Brian was thrusting his pelvis into me with slow, deliberate strokes. In between kissing my eyes and darting a tongue in my ear he said, "You are so fucking hot." To which I responded, "So why doncha fuck me again?" Wasting no time, Brian reached under his bed for his secret stash of lube and condoms and took another ride inside my love tube as I gasped, sighed, spread my legs even wider apart, and smiled because I was having hot Sunday morning sex— which is simply the grown-up and more interactive version of watching dreamy teenaged boys in Saturday morning TV shows as a kid. I was glad to know that some things hardly ever changed.

While Brian was in the bathroom having some private time, the moment I had been expecting finally arrived. My mother called.

"Steven, I am outraged! Outraged, I tell you!"

"Did another bingo caller resign?"

"Worse! Audrey and I lost the Halloween costume competition!"

"Well, you can't win 'em all," I said as I examined my naked body in the mirror. I clutched the mini-paunch underneath my belly button and surmised that if I was going to have sex on a regular basis with the same fella it might prove beneficial to increase my daily number of sit-ups and decrease my daily intake of soft drinks and junk food. How impressed was I that I could carry on a conversation with my mother and contemplate my sex life at the same time? However, my mother's shriek made me rethink multitasking in her presence.

"That is not the response I was hoping for!"

"Sorry, Ma," I said, backtracking. "That is incredibly and enormously unfair."

"My heart is broken, Steven! Broken into many small pieces!"

"I don't get it. I mean seriously, what costume could beat Before and After Barbra?"

"Before and After . . . Judy *Goddamned* Garland!"

Ah yes, a dead diva always wins by a nose. My mother explained that Lenny Abramawitz and his granddaughter Loni came as the beginning and the end of Judy Garland. Loni was the pig-tailed, gingham-clad Dorothy from *The Wizard of Oz,* while Lenny, the oldest friend of Dorothy this side of Chelsea, was Judy from her famed concert days. He wore a Bob Mackie-inspired black sequined dress with boatneck collar and three-quarter length sleeves, black sheer stockings that showed off his bony, manorexic legs, and black pointy-toed pumps that a drag queen would have had to practice walking in for twelve hours before going out in public with any confidence. But it wasn't impeccable attention to costuming detail that won the Abramawitzes the coveted award, it was the fact that Lenny pranced around with a microphone all night and channeled Ms. Garland's repertoire. He was such a flaming success that by the end of the evening every Secaucus senior citizen (except a bitter Anjanette and Audrey) had forgotten their troubles and had gotten so happy that they were slurring their words.

"It isn't fair! Jews don't even like Halloween!"

"True. Their holidays are more somber by nature."

"I tried to have them disqualified since Loni isn't a resident, but the friggin' rules clearly state you could enter with a guest!"

"Didn't you write the rules?"

"Throw my mistakes in my face, why don't you?!"

"Hey Steve, I'm gonna take a shower," Brian called out to me. "Wanna join me? And just so there's no confusion, I'm not asking." Covering the mouthpiece of my cell phone I answered, "Be right there."

"Stevie, who was that?"

I took a deep breath. "That was Brian."

"Ohhhhhh," my mother replied. I didn't even get to silently count to ten before she turned into an Italian inquisitor. "And why are you two boys going to a baby shower?"

"Ma! I have to go."

"You like this one, don't you, Stevie?"

"Yes, Ma, I do. Now I'm going to hang up so I can like him a little bit more."

"Stevie's got a boyfriend," she sang. "So when will Mama be meeting your Mister Man?"

"When he gets his anti-Anjanette shots."

"Don't talk to your mother like that!"

"Gotta go . . . love you, Mom."

"Steven Bartholomew Ferr—"

The rest of my mother's outburst was the rest of the universe's problem, for I had to soap up a well-hung suitor and have sex for the second time on a Sunday morning. If I ever bumped into Gus's ex, Brady, while shopping again, I would have to remember to share that information. And just so there's no confusion, by share, I mean brag.

Well-scrubbed, we went to brunch and then browsed our way through the stores in Chelsea. As we squeezed into one partition of the revolving door and swung into Bed, Bath & Behind, I was stricken with Jackflash. Not an overwhelming desire to jump out of my whiteboy skin and whoop it up like Whoopi Goldberg trying to protect the homeland from Russian spies, but a flashback of my ex-boyfriend Jack. I hadn't had one for quite some time and was thrilled to find that this one wasn't accompanied by the usual feelings of self-pity and sorrow. This was that rare judgment-free memory. Obviously my life was moving forward to a bright future instead of sliding backward toward past blight. I silently thanked Brian and held his hand a bit tighter. His silent response was to give my hand a squeeze.

"So this has been a great weekend," Brian declared.

"Yes, it has," I agreed.

We were standing on the steps of my apartment building, the fall chill making our cheeks and noses rosy, and for the first time all weekend we were a tad awkward with each other. But it was a good awkward and not like we were each searching for a kind way to say, "Your Manhunt pictures were Photoshopped."

"I'll call you tomorrow."

"Sounds good," I said, sounding less romantic than I had wanted. So then I took a chance: "This is good, isn't it?"

I startled him, which is not what I really wanted to do, and I could feel the chilly air around me get hot and thick as I tried to read his face. Had I said too much? I couldn't think of anything else that I could say to him. So I was forced to wait for his response. It was worth the wait.

"Yeah, Steve, it's really good."

And then he leaned in and kissed me softly on the lips. It was a new kiss for us, tender and sweet and knowing. His kiss said that while he didn't know everything about me he knew that he wanted to gain that knowledge. My return kiss said *I'll help you learn anything you want to know.*

For the first time since Jack broke up with me four years ago I felt really hopeful. I gave Brian a little wave and walked up to my apartment wishing I could bottle the moment. That little insecure boy who watched Saturday morning TV and wondered if

he would ever be like the normal boys was wearing a very satisfied smile.

There were no smiles on Monday morning, when I returned
to work to find Lorna Douglas was taking full advantage of
Loretta's absence and trying to claim the position of deranged
diva. She was strutting around the soundstage acting like Benita
Bizarre after she'd taken several puffs on the magic dragon. It
was a performance that would have caused even those koo-koo-
kooky Krofft brothers to flip their lids.

"My sister Regina is a drunken *whore*!" Lorna as Ramona
declared during taping, causing Laraby to turn a bright shade of
Witchipoogreen. He tried to scream "Reshoot" but his throat
was burned by acid reflux and all he could do was swallow the
acrid fluid.

Midweek Lorna was busted while swallowing a much tastier
fluid. Lourdes caught her in the denouement of a blow job she
was giving Lionel Smythe, the hunky Brit actor who recently
started playing her long-lost nephew, Rick (who bore a striking
resemblance to a young Jack Wild), in the cave where Loretta
had recently thrown up while helping Sister Roberta give birth.
Between the vomit and the semen that cave was going to have to
be disinfected by the local hazmat crew. Afterward, Lourdes was
heard demanding that her confiscated digital camera be given back
to her so she could commemorate special moments like these.
And, of course, so she could sell the prints and add to the down
payment she was going to put on the plantation in the mother-
land.

I thought I was going to have a special moment of my own
later that evening, but Brian had to cancel our dinner plans because his friend Rodrigo was having a crisis. He didn't elaborate
as to what kind of crisis Rodrigo was going through even when
I deliberately paused to give him the opportunity. Try as I might
I couldn't stop my mind from going all psychotic and imagining
that Brian and Rodrigo were actually renting a movie or hosting
an orgy or doing something that was fun and Steven-free. It was

the first time I'd gotten an anxious twinge in the pit of my stomach with Brian, but I shrugged it off and attributed it to the fact that I was a bit nauseous from the smells emanating from the cave. Determined to be proactive and not spend the night wondering what friend's crisis could be more important than a boyfriend's romantic dinner, I invited Flynn over. It turned out he was having a crisis of his own.

"Steven, I'm fine," Flynn protested as he took a sip of his second glass of red wine.

"Well, you're not yourself," I said. "Have some more chicken?"

"Don't pull out the meal card, please. Your chicken parm was delicious, but I'm full. And I have not lost any weight so as the soccer moms in Ohio like to say to their Ritalin-resistant offspring, 'don't go there.' "

"Then what's wrong?" I asked.

During dinner Flynn had listened to me prattle on about Brian and the joys of new boyfriendhood and he'd smiled and nodded and mmmhmmmed in the appropriate places, but he hadn't asked sexually inappropriate questions or squealed with delight or uttered the word *mama*—in short, he was very unFlynn-like. He was silent for a bit too long and I could tell that he was wrestling with himself to choose the correct words that would address his present state of mind. When he finally spoke, he was quiet and definite.

"Steven, I love you like a brother, you know that," he started.

"Right back at ya," I replied.

"And I am very happy that you've found someone to make you happy, I really am. But it's made me think about my own circumstances and how I don't have that. And how I need to accept the fact that while I will always have you as a friend, I might never have that type of intimacy in my life."

"Mama no like talk like that," I said, sounding as stupid as Flynn sounded sincere.

He smiled at me like an older and wiser brother. "You wouldn't understand."

I watched Flynn finish his wine and, regrettably, I did understand. It was time to peel off my happy suit and acknowledge that the world could be like Saturday morning TV shows starring has-been actors. It could get ugly.

"What's his name?" I asked.

"That's just it, there are no names. There are no current flames, no could-be flames, no exes to call up in the middle of the night."

"What about Lucas? I thought you were going to pursue that."

"What's to pursue? At best he's a closeted soap opera actor who loves musical theater. I kind of doubt that he's going to want to enter into a relationship with an openly gay, HIV-positive attorney. Let's face it, I'm not the type of guy you want to bring home to your publicist."

"There are plenty of guys who don't choose their dates based on what kind of media coverage they can expect."

"But there are plenty of guys who choose their dates based on what diseases they can contract."

I wanted to be stunned, but I couldn't be. Because Flynn is my closest friend, I had seen firsthand that someone who is positive is not necessarily one swan dive away from his cemetery plot. And yet I know many men who, if faced with the choice of dating someone who's negative and someone who's positive, would opt for negativity. Survival of the fittest? Fear of the unknown? I don't know. What I do know is that despite all the breakthroughs and medical advancements, being HIV-positive can still mean living a very lonely life.

"You're right," I said.

"Well, thank you for not trying to disagree with me. I appreciate that."

"Please promise me one thing though. You won't give up."

Flynn contemplated this request. "No, I won't give up, but quite frankly I don't know how much time I have left on this planet."

"Flynn, that's nonsense!"

"Steven, it's the truth. I know none of us has a lock on immortality, but for me complications could arise tomorrow. I'm not going to waste whatever time I have left hoping for someone who may never turn up."

"I wish I could change things," I said feebly.

"It is what it is, Stevie. I'm just glad that you're my friend. You're all I really have, you know."

"Flynn," I said, "your mother has tried to reach out to you." I examined my plate and flicked a few pieces of ziti with my fork, aware that Flynn's family was not considered subject matter for pleasant conversation.

"Yes, she has, but it's always on her terms and it's always done because she feels sorry for me. Do you know what that's like? To have your mother feel sorry for you because she thinks you've fucked up your life?"

Fortunately I had no idea. Although any physician would willingly write Anjanette a prescription for anti-psychotic medication, my mother was nurturing and supportive and furthermore she would tell anyone willing to listen that I was the most brilliant and successful young man working in the television industry. And she meant every word of it.

"The worst thing about it is that part of me agrees with her."

"Flynn, don't—"

"I got drunk and made a mistake. I knew the rules and tossed them out the window and now I'm paying the price."

Flynn turned away and I could see the tears well up in his eyes. Watching your friend at his most vulnerable is a powerful moment. It's also a moment of privilege. The fact that Flynn would expose himself like that to me and share his private thoughts and actions without censoring made me feel honored. We both knew that it would be much easier to force a smile and say, "Oh, I'm a little depressed right now, but I'll feel better tomorrow." But easy isn't always best.

I moved next to Flynn and put my arm around him. The tears had stopped, but the sadness remained. We sat there for a while in silence, neither one of us feeling it necessary to speak.

"Isn't this more fun than having dinner with your boyfriend?" Flynn joked.

"Well . . . fun is such a subjective word."

Flynn looked directly at me and laughed. It was wonderful to see his crow's-feet crinkle again. If I didn't know that it would make him even more depressed, I would have told him how handsome he looked with the crinkles next to the tiny flecks of gray in his sideburns. And how happy any man would be to look into that face night after night. But there are some things that are best unsaid, even to your best friend.

Before I went to bed I gave my mother a quick call, knowing that she was the resident night owl of her high-rise. I was surprised to find that she had company at such a late hour.

"Audrey and I are practicing," my mother announced.

"For what?"

"Tomorrow night's bingo tournament."

"It's Winner Take All," Audrey shouted from the background.

I wondered how much the winner could take considering they all lived on fixed incomes. "That's terrific. But can you really practice playing bingo? It's all luck."

"That's where you're wrong, Stevie. There is skill involved and Mama need to win."

"So does Audrey!" shouted Audrey.

"Ma, you're becoming very competitive, you know. Why's it so important all of a sudden that you win?"

"We're playing for bragging rights against the Martha Salvatore Tenants in Hoboken. My cousin Antoinette, the bitch who tried to seduce your father when we were first going out, she's the reigning bingo champion. I'm finally going to knock her down a peg."

"Or two!" shouted Audrey supportively.

"Easy on the vendettas, ladies."

"No one offers to make my husband lasagna," Anjanette said. "With imported mozzarella!"

"I hate to disrespect your family, Anj, but that one was always a tramp."

"How can you disrespect, when it's the truth? Steven, did you need anything, we really have to practice."

"I just wanted to say hi."

"Do you hear that, Audrey? Steven just wanted to say hi."

"He's such a good boy, Anj! I wish my Albert was a gay."

"Albert's too fat to be gay."

"I know. But he could diet."

"Gastric bypass, Audrey! All he needs is a staple gun and a dream."

"Ladies, I hope you beat the support hose off of Martha Salvatore and her peoples."

"We will, honey, don't you worry."

Why should I worry? My mother wasn't the most educated woman in the world and she would never be a millionaire no matter how many bingo tournaments she entered, but she enjoyed her life and that's the greatest lesson a mother could ever share with her son.

The only thing more enjoyable—and gayer—than a Krofft super-show is an ice-skating revue. While they both have over-the-top characters, elaborate costumes, and a once-famous cast, the world of ice-skating has the edge as it has some of the best male butts this side of the porn industry. It also has Lindsay Wilde.

Since Lindsay was one of the former skating celebrities taking part in Fox's skating retrospective, *Back on the Ice III*, at Madison Square Garden, we all got seats in one of those glassed-in booths that comes complete with your own bathroom, bar, and catering staff. I would have preferred to be a little closer to the ice action, but this way we could make like Dick and Peggy and have our own running commentary on the skating icons. Or as Lindsay calls them, the *Ice Whores*.

"I have to admit, I think I cried when Lindsay just missed getting the bronze medal in Lillehammer," Brian admitted.

"Steven! Didn't you warn him?" Flynn asked.

"No, sorry," I said. "Brian, when it comes to the Olympics Lindsay is highly sensitive, some might say insane."

"Who can blame him? I mean really . . . pewter?"

"Blimey! Don't ever say the *P*-word in Lindsay's presence!" Gus shouted.

"Or the *O*-word," Flynn added.

"Or the *D*-word," Sebastian offered.

"What's the *D* stand for?" Brian asked.

"Dick."

"How do you not say *dick* in front of a homo?"

"Not *dick* as in *cock,* the most beautiful, mouthwatering organ that God ever created," Sebastian explained, "but Dick Button."

"Lindsay thinks the Button should button up and retire," Flynn explained.

"Brian, don't ever tell Lindsay," I said. "But I have a little crush on Mr. Button."

"You do not!"

"I think it's the bow ties."

"You're a freak," Brian declared, then gave me a kiss.

I caught Flynn watching us out of the corner of my eye and despite myself I felt as if he had caught me doing something improper, like Rock Hudson must have felt when Mrs. Hudson came home just a little earlier than expected. I didn't want to flaunt my relationship, but I didn't want to temper it either. Flynn eased my confusion when he came over to me and gave me a hug and a peck on the cheek.

"Thanks for the other night."

"Sshh! That's how rumors start."

"You should be so lucky as to be involved in a scandal."

"Did someone mention scandal?" Sebastian asked from across the room.

"How'd you hear that?" Flynn asked. "Did your doctor give you superhearing along with your new and improved asshole?"

"I didn't hear what you said, I felt it. I'm like that Melody girl on *Josie and Her Pussies.*"

"You mean *Josie and the Pussycats.*"

"Whatever. When she senses danger her ears wiggle. When I sense danger, my dick twitches."

"I thought you didn't watch TV," I said.

"Sometimes I keep it on in the background if I'm getting serviced. I thought it was a lesbo pussyfest and the occasional meadow munch turns me on. Of course I was disappointed to find it was a cartoon, but I think that Alexandra girl is a dyke. If you ask me, her obsession with stealing Josie's boyfriend is merely a ploy to mask her true feelings. She wants to snuggle up to Josie herself and make her purr like a satisfied Miss Kitty."

"Another Saturday morning cartoon ruined," I declared.

"Listen up, gay folk, scandal is brewing," Sebastian announced. "My dick is still twitching. Feel it. C'mon, feel my dick!"

Of course that was the moment the only straight cater waiter in all of New York City chose to walk into the room carrying a tray of buffalo wings.

"I'm telling you all right now," the cater waiter said, "anybody touches my ass and I'll make you wear the Bunsen burner as a cock ring."

We were all rendered speechless. Except Sebastian.

"Like I haven't done that before."

Nearly twenty minutes into the show the hostess, a luminescent Rosalynn Sumners—who just happened to be my favorite ice-skater ever—introduced Lindsay. I felt so proud at that moment I wanted to grab Rosalynn's microphone and announce, "That's my friend!" but my friend was nowhere to be found. The spotlight shined on empty ice, the audience screamed, but there was no Lindsay. Uncertain, Rosalynn made the announcement once more.

"Ladies and gentlemen, the three-time U.S. men's champion . . . Lindsay Wilde."

Rosalynn looked as nervous as she had when she was competing against that Teutonic temptress of the ice, Katarina Witt. Once again the spotlight shined and this time the audience chanted "Wilde Boy!" as they did when Lindsay was in his prime, but still he didn't appear.

"Oh my God! Do you think he's having a backstage breakdown?" Flynn asked.

"When I spoke with him he sounded great," I said. "He was really looking forward to putting his skates on again."

"Brian, are you sure you didn't mention the *P, O,* or *D* words in front of Lindsay earlier today?" Gus asked.

"No, I didn't even see him."

"Look at my dick! It's twitching like Kate Moss after a couple of rides on the white line."

And it was. Sebastian's dick could barely be contained by his Levi Offender jeans—it looked like he'd shoved a ten-inch Mexican jumping bean into his underwear. Could Sebastian's penis actually be prophetic? Could it really know when danger was about to develop? Or were Latin dicks like Latin men, always craving attention?

"There he is!" cried Flynn.

At last, Lindsay made his entrance and the crowd erupted. The sound technician didn't turn Rosalynn's microphone off fast enough and she was heard thanking God that pewter boy had shown up. Luckily, Lindsay was too busy tucking his shirt into his pants to hear her comment, which would have undoubtedly spun him into an emotional death spiral and landed him as lead story on *Inside Edition*.

"Look at his dick!" Sebastian shouted. "Wilde Boy just had wild sex."

Much like Sebastian's jeans, Lindsay's black stretch pants couldn't conceal his erection. Evidently, the guy who ran the spotlight noticed too because Lindsay's spot got so small that you could only see him from his waist up. Sadly, this made it easier to see Lindsay's disheveled hair, melting makeup, and the large kidney-shaped hickey on his neck. This event was supposed to be a comeback of sorts for Lindsay, to see if he could get back on the touring scene after taking a break from the ice-skating world. Unfortunately, it looked like he was coming back as Tonya Harding's sex-crazed brother.

"He's really good," Brian said. "Even though he probably took it up the ass five minutes ago."

"I told Lindsay not to wear the stretchy pants," Sebastian said. "They feel too good, too sensual . . . my dick is twitching again."

"Another scandal?" I asked.

"No, now I'm just horny. I have to go jerk off."

When he got to the bathroom door he turned and stared directly at the straight cater waiter. "I'll leave the door open in case you'd like to join the home team."

The straight cater waiter didn't take the bait, but the milk-fed Abercrombie clone manning the sundae station made a beeline for the bathroom, armed with a can of whipped cream. I would have to remember to eat my sundae sans topping. I turned back to the arena action just in time to see Lindsay land a triple axel perfectly on the downbeat of the music. Obviously he had lost his erection, because he was now being filmed without restrictions, and he was skating spectacularly despite his shaky start. When the show aired the following week his delayed entrance would certainly be edited out, so hopefully this would mark his return to professional skating. I was more curious as to what, or more accurately who, delayed him from returning to the ice on time.

Lindsay skated another solo that was even better than the first and then joined the rest of the company in a Broadway medley culminating in all the skaters forming a line and skate-dancing to "One" from *A Chorus Line*. Flynn was in his glory and if Sebastian hadn't made it passé, he would have jerked off with a cater waiter in the bathroom. Flashing a beaming smile, Lindsay seemed to be in his glory too, and I hoped he was smiling because he could feel that the audience had missed watching him perform and not because he was flanked by Vladimir, a hot Russian pairs skater, and some hairy-chested French ice dancer.

After the show we waited at the stage door with a horde of suburban housewives wearing red hats and embroidered sweatshirts and pimply faced gay teen boys wearing fedoras and mascara to watch the ice stars exit. Brian tried, but couldn't prevent me from accosting Rosalynn Sumners. "Oh my God, you're my favorite!" I exclaimed.

"Thank you, that's so sweet."

"All my friends in school cut our hair just like yours after the Olympics. *I* even got blond highlights."

"The next time I see Dorothy Hamill I'll have to tell her she's not the only one whose hairstyle inspired a generation."

After that I attacked Paul Wylie and got his autograph, then I was attacked by Oksana Baiul, who said I reminded her of her childhood friend, Boris, who had died mysteriously in a sheep-herding accident back in the Ukraine. Her bodyguard apolo-gized (which I had a feeling he did often), then led Oksana, who was staring at me and chanting something under her breath, into her waiting limo. It would be a very long time before I ate lamb again.

"Where in the sodding hell is he?" Gus asked.

"I don't know," I said. "He told me he'd meet us outside the stage door."

"Well, I have an early meeting tomorrow so I have to beg off. Tell the bugger he made the Brit proud."

"Will do. And we'll see you next week for your birthday bash."

"I'm going to leave too," Flynn said. "I have a conference call with Tokyo tomorrow and I have to prepare. Those people are always a day ahead, you know. I'll call Linds tomorrow and tell him how wonderlicious he was."

"Brian, it's late, why don't you go home," I said.

"I don't want to leave you here alone."

"That's all right. I have to figure out what happened to Lind-say and I don't want to keep you up all night."

"You're sure?"

"Absolutely. I'll call you in the morning and let you know if Sebastian's dick was right."

"Okay. I had a great time."

"Me too. But that's nothing unusual with you."

We kissed under the lights of Madison Square Garden, caus-ing some drunken Long Island businessmen to titter, but we didn't care. I wasn't going to let some boozed-up, poorly dressed ac-countant from Ronkonkoma force me back into the closet. As I watched Brian walk down the street Lindsay finally made con-tact via a text message: *MEET ME IN THE BASEMENT. THE SECURITY GUARD HAS YOUR NAME. HURRY!*

All caps! How exciting! It was in wacky moments like this that I longed for a cape, knee-high boots, and a sidekick so I could transform into my favorite superhero, Electra Woman. She was athletic, smart, and had gorgeous hair—she was everything a homosexual hoped to be. Channeling my inner EW, I stealthily opened the stage door and bumped into the stomach of the jimongous security guard whose evil villain name would be Dr. Securitron. Wishing my trusty cohort-in-crimefighting, Dyna Girl, were there to watch my back, I told Dr. Securitron my name and although it was clear that he wanted to stun-ray me into submission and keep me prisoner in his secret evil villainy lair, he let me pass through. I followed the signs down to the basement and with each step my rush of excitement was turning into feelings of trepidation. Had Lindsay pissed Dick Button off one time too many and was *he* now being held prisoner in the bowels of Madison Square Garden with his hands and feet bound by jaunty bow ties? Had he publicly condemned Rudy Galindo's new eatery and become the victim of his wrath? Or was he trying to lure me into a four-way with Vladimir and the hairy Frenchman? With the steely determination of EW I pressed on in search of the answers and shortly found myself standing in front of the basement door.

Tossing back imaginary, yet well-coiffed, blond supertresses, I turned the doorknob and braced myself for what evil was lurking on the other side of the door. When I entered the room I was crestfallen to see that it was actually a dressing room and that it was empty. Where was Lindsay? Without a crime to prevent would my superhero status be revoked? When I closed the door I saw that Lindsay had been hiding behind it. I also saw a different kind of evil.

"Why are you naked?"

"You have to help me get hard," Lindsay said.

He was standing with his black stretch pants pushed down to his calves, his shirt was rolled up to his pecs, and his hand was wrapped around his flaccid penis. It was the first time I had seen Lindsay in the buff and although I approved of his well-toned ice-sculpted physique, it yanked me back to reality and all kitschy thoughts of Electra Woman, Dyna Girl, and their evil nemeses were destroyed in one heartbreaking instant.

"I have told you repeatedly I will not have group sex with

you!" I searched the room for his partners in this ice sexcapade. "Do you hear that, Vladimir, you ain't getting any from me!"

"I'm serious! You have to help me get an erection."

"Why didn't you text Sebastian? He lives for stuff like this. And he knew something indecent was going to happen, his dick was twitching all night."

"I don't want Sebastian touching my dick, he's got cooties. I need you."

"Lindsay! I am not going to touch your dick. I mean, no offense, but what the hell's gotten into you?" Then I saw it and I rephrased. "What the hell's gotten on you?"

From what I could tell Lindsay had gotten his dick tattooed. The artwork looked to be a series of Chinese characters in black ink that ran up and down the length of his penis. I could only assume that it spelled out SUCK ME OFF in Mandarin.

"It's not a tattoo," Lindsay said. "It's a Sharpie!"

Lindsay was often exasperating, but this was extreme even for him. My confusion apparent, he composed himself and explained that during the pre-taping he discovered that one of the Fox cameramen was our friendly neighborhood Fuck Counter. His real name was Donald and he'd been doing behind-the-scenes camera work for years. They were pleasantly surprised to meet each other once again and reminisced about the sex party where they had initially met, which got them aroused and so they gave each other quick blow jobs in Dick Button's dressing room. Just before Lindsay was to make his entrance Donald had to run backstage to switch cameras, one thing led to another, and suddenly Donald was sucking Lindsay's dick again. But then the sucking stopped and Lindsay smelled something strong like video-head cleaner. He assumed Donald was taking a whiff of poppers, which Lindsay would have loved to do, but he knew it wouldn't be wise if he had to perform a three-minute routine in front of a packed house in about thirty seconds. But he was wrong, Donald wasn't sniffing poppers, he was writing on Lindsay's dick with a Sharpie.

"He wrote his phone number on my cock," Lindsay said. "Isn't that sweet?"

"He couldn't find a Post-it?"

"I don't think a Post-it would stick to my dick."

"So you almost screwed up your chance to rejoin the skating elite because Donald couldn't punch his number into your cell phone?"

"Oh wow, we never thought of that," Lindsay said.

"Well, maybe if you were thinking more and sucking less you would have."

"Stop badgering me and get me hard!"

"I told you already, I am not getting you hard."

"You have to! Right now Donald is on a flight to Hawaii to cover some stupid golf tournament and I have to call him when he lands so he knows that I'm interested. If I don't call he'll start counting thrusts up some sarong-wearing tiki boy's ass and stay in paradise forever while I become angry and bitter like Karen Black in that TV movie where she turns into the tiki warrior with really bad teeth."

"Have you ever thought about hooking up with Oksana Baiul? I think the two of you would have a lot in common."

"Oh my God, it's working. My tirade got my dick hard."

It was true. Lindsay's dick was starting to grow and thicken and I couldn't believe I was actually standing there watching his dick grow and thicken.

"Am I hard enough so you can read the numbers?"

Dutifully, I squatted and started reading Donald's cell phone number. I tried to concentrate on the task and not on the fact that I felt as dirty as a Korean whore relieving herself in a trough. "Nine-one-seven." With his free hand, Lindsay punched the numbers into his cell phone.

"Go on."

"Three-one-eight. No wait . . . three-one-three. I think it's a three, but I'm not sure. All your jerking off smudged the numbers."

"Sorry, I was trying to jerk dry, but I can't help it, I have a juicy cock."

"I do not need to know that!"

"And when I skate I sweat. Does it smell funky down there?"

"I wouldn't know, I've been breathing through my mouth!"

"Don't freak out on me now, Steven! Are you sure it's a three? From here it looks like an eight."

"It's a three!"

"Four more numbers, that's all I need to start my life with Donald."

I ignored the absurd Lindsay-speak and continued. "Okay, four-seven . . . no, I think that's a one."

"Get closer!"

About an inch from Lindsay's graffitied dick I was certain. "It's definitely a one."

"Keep going."

"And then . . . um . . . it's a two."

"What's the last number, Steven!? The last number?"

"I can't tell. Your dick is all shriveled again."

"No, no! Steven, you have to help me."

"I'm trying, but it's all scrunched up."

"Tweak my nipples. That'll get me hard."

"Lindsay, it's nothing personal, but I feel very uncomfortable tweaking your nipples. I feel uncomfortable just saying it."

"It's just a nipple! Don't be such a prude."

I scrunched my face up into my best Lorna Douglas expression conveying the threat of vengeance. "You owe me, Wilde!"

Closing my eyes, I twisted Lindsay's left nipple.

"That's it, Steven, play with my nipple. Yes! Oh yeah, twist it, baby."

"No sex talk!"

"Sorry, but you are really good. Brian is one lucky boy."

"And you will be very unlucky if Brian ever finds out about this."

"Don't worry, it'll be our little secret. Okay, I'm hard. Get down on your knees and do your job."

Back down in squatting position, I was able to read the last number. "It's a five! His number is nine-one-seven, three-one-three, four-one-two-five. Now please pull up your stretch pants."

"Yes, Lindsay, please do pull up your stretch pants."

We both turned around at the same time to see Dick Button

himself staring at us, wearing the cutest red and yellow striped bow tie and holding a video camera. As Lindsay attempted to cover himself, Mr. Button informed us that he had overheard Lindsay and Donald in his dressing room earlier so he borrowed a camera and paid one of the interns to tape Lindsay while he was commentating, thus capturing the Wilde Boy's dalliance on video.

"Excuse me, Mr. Button," I said. "Is my face by any chance on that video? FYI, I am a huge fan of yours."

"Don't worry, I'm only interested in having leverage against Pewter Boy."

I steadied Lindsay so he didn't topple over and listened as Dick told him his terms. He didn't want to hear a disparaging word about him or the figure skating community from Lindsay or else he would release this video to the media. And if they weren't interested he would invite the cast of *Stars on Ice* to his home and have a private screening in his media room.

"You wouldn't dare," Lindsay said.

"Just try me. I *am* men's figure skating, bucko. Your renegade days are over. Do I make myself clear?"

Fighting the urge to strangle him with his own neckwear, Lindsay merely replied, "Yes."

"Yes, what?"

Lindsay's pale complexion was replaced with something crimson. "Yes . . . Mr. Button."

"That's better. And Steven?"

"Yes, sir? Mr. Button, sir?"

"It was a pleasure to meet you."

I blushed. "No, sir, the honor was all mine." My cheeks were still a bit flushed after he'd left. "He's *so* not a dick."

"I will not take orders from him!"

"Okay, but if you piss him off and he has you kidnapped and his hired goons write a ransom note on your ass in Magic Marker, do not call Electra Woman to transcribe!"

When I got home it wasn't too late and I was too excited so I gave Brian a call. Color me a deep shade of surprise when an older woman answered his cell phone.

"Oh, I'm sorry, I must have the wrong number," I said.

"That's all right, honey, who're y'all lookin' for?" said the Southern-accented stranger.

"Brian Oldsboro?"

"You don't have the wrong numbuh, sugar," she drawled. "Brian's my baby boy."

That nervous feeling in the pit of my stomach that I'd felt when Brian canceled on me to help out Rodrigo returned. If Brian's mother was answering his cell phone that meant she was in town. And if she was in town why didn't I know about it?

"Hey, Steve, is everything okay with Lindsay?" Brian asked after he'd come to the phone.

"Yeah, he was, um, just tied up backstage with reporters and stuff," I stuttered. "When did your mother get to town?"

"A few days ago. Remember I told you she was swinging by on her way to Europe? She pushed up her schedule so she came a few days early. She leaves for Hungary tomorrow."

"G'night baby. Your Mama's bushed."

" 'Night, Ma."

"Oh. I didn't realize her itinerary had changed," I said, desperately trying to sound nonchalant and not too much like my mother.

"Personally I can't wait until she gets on the plane," Brian whispered. "Rodrigo and I have had enough of entertaining her."

In my mind I saw a cardboard box being ripped open and several hundred red flags fall to the ground. I shut my mind off and ignored the image. "Rodrigo's been showing her around?"

"Yeah, didn't I mention his crisis?"

"Briefly."

"He was going to take her to that new sushi place in the East Village, Raw something or other, but they couldn't get reservations and she was dying for really good sushi and when my mother is dying for something she has all the Southern charm of a lynch mob. I had to pull some strings with our PR people, but they finally got us into Nobu at the Seaport."

"Oh. I didn't realize that Rodrigo's crisis was really your mother's crisis."

"But tomorrow she'll be halfway across the globe. Life will be crisis-free again."

I started to pace back and forth in my bedroom, head down, eyes focused on the hardwood. "So I guess I won't get a chance to meet her."

"No, she's got to leave early. Trust me, you're not missing a thing."

"It's just, you know, it would've been nice to put a face with the name."

"Don't worry, she's threatened to pop in again on her way home," Brian said, stifling a yawn. "I'm sorry, I have to get to bed, the car service is going to be here around five a.m. Have a good night, sweetie."

"Yeah, you too."

Long after I hung up, the nagging sensation in my stomach lingered. Why did he lie to me? Why didn't he want me to meet his mother? And, most important, why didn't he think meeting her was important? Our perfect weekend and our perfect dates seemed as long ago as my childhood Saturday mornings spent laughing at the silly antics of talking hats and prehistoric cavemen. And I knew that for better or worse, things had just changed between me and Brian.

Chapter Nine

On July 12, 1979, disco officially died. It was a particularly brutal death in Chicago's Comiskey Park, when jealous and most likely overweight baseball fans brought disco records with them to the game so that a rhythmically challenged DJ could blow them up on the field. About twenty thousand pieces of innocent vinyl were destroyed on that sad, sad day, but despite the vicious act the beat thumped on—albeit a bit differently.

For proof, look no further than the transformation of Donna Summer from disco diva to rock 'n' roll wanderer. It wasn't the most successful reinvention, but it was a practical rebirth. She had two choices: try to exist beyond the last dance in a MacArthur Park that had melted beyond recognition or wander for a while in rockier territory in search of her own state of independence. She chose the latter and as a result is now able to work not so hard for her money. I, like Ms. Summer, now had a similar choice.

In the days following Briangate, I had to decide whether to confront Brian about his lie or forget about it and move on. Flynn, the only person I confided in, brought to my attention two important factors that helped me make my decision.

"Let Mama break down," Flynn began. "First of all, you said Brian sounded calm and indifferent, not at all as if he were caught in a web of deceit and duplicity. Correct?"

"Correct," I replied. "He sounded totally normal, and trust me, I was listening for that telltale pause or crack in his voice."

"Nice work, Sherlock, but you didn't hear anything suspicious because Brian didn't think he had to cover anything up—because he didn't think there was a problem with what he did."

I digested this revelation. "I guess that is an alternative way to look at it."

"So you might not like the fact that he kept his mother in social quarantine, but you can't turn his different point of view into a lie."

"Okaaaaaay," I said, feeling childish about my chiding.

"And second of all, and I don't think this will come as a shock to you, you're a mama's boy."

Flynn was right. I wasn't an apron clutcher who expected my mother to be my surrogate wife, cooking my meals and sprinkling the perfect amount of Downy in my laundry, but I was one of those sons whose mother would always be a large part of his life. Flynn made me realize what every frustrated Republican already knows: no matter how hard you try, you can't force your lifestyle on someone else.

So Brian didn't have a great relationship with his mother or think it was important to introduce her to his boyfriend. Was that reason to audition for the role of high-maintenance drama queen? I didn't want to be that type of person and I didn't believe Brian was interested in dating such a man either. So I, like Donna decades before me, made a realistic choice—I chose to ignore Brian's actions and move forward. But I also accepted my reality and made another choice. I recognized that I am of the suburbs born and just because I ignore doesn't mean I forget.

Luckily I had other things to occupy my mind, like preparing for Gus's fortieth birthday roller boogie party. What a coup that Sebastian was such a slut. Otherwise, there was no way that we would have been able to have Splash to ourselves for a few hours on a Friday night. Jean-Luc, the ripped French muscle-boi PR rep for Splash and Sebastian's Thursday night fuck buddy, loved the '70s disco idea so much that he pitched it to the owners, who loved it even more and decided to have a whole retro weekend. This meant we didn't have to spend a dime on decorations and DJ Pasquale would already have opened his vinyl vault and pulled out all those funkalicious vintage sounds. The gay gods were wrapping us in gold lamé hugs so we could ring in Gus's fortieth year by shakin' our groove things in style.

And although I had what I considered a fair amount of style as a gay man, I had absolutely no style as a gay man in drag. Standing in front of Brian dressed up as Samantha Sang, the Bee Gees' very own Eliza Doolittle, I had to confront my worst fears.

"Tell me the truth, Brian, does this dress makes me look fat?"

"I haven't even been able to look below your neck," Brian replied. "You really are frightening as a blond."

Ripping off my Tova Borgnine superblond, super-'70s wig I cried, "I told you I don't look good in drag."

"Then we won't do drag, let's go as something else. It's not like the disco police will arrest you for showing up as your own gender."

"The police! That's it!"

"Um, Steve, the Police aren't really considered disco."

"No, not Sting's police, the gay police. Let's go as the Village People!"

Not to beep, beep, toot, toot my own horn, but sometimes my ideas are brilliant. And this one most certainly was. What better way for Gus's friends to celebrate his birthday than as a unified group, a collection of random gay stereotypes? I called the boys and they were all on board. The thorny part, however, came when we had to actually decide which village person's persona we were going to don. We hashed it out over coffee.

"Everyone knows that I have had sexual fantasies about John Wayne since grammar school," Flynn declared. "I should be the cowboy."

"But I have Western blood in my name," Lindsay said. "I should represent the wild, wild West."

"Speaking of things Western, I want to make a political statement and come as the police officer," Gus said.

"And how would that be political?" I asked.

"Because I'm a foreigner. It would be a statement about America's misguided foreign policy."

"I have a feeling that subtle political irony is going to get lost when your friends are trying to push their bush into the nearest tush."

"Well, I'm sure we can all agree on one thing," Sebastian said. "I should be the Indian chief."

"I don't think so!" Lindsay shouted. "I have an Indian headdress from *Ice Reservations*, the skating show I did in New Mexico."

"And I have a loincloth," Sebastian added.

Flynn rolled his eyes. "Of course you do."

"Anyway, you want to be the wild cowboy," Sebastian reminded him. "So it's decided, I am the Indian."

"But Sebastian," Lindsay said exasperatedly, "if *you* have half the costume and *I* have half the costume why should you automatically get to wear the full costume?"

"Because I look better naked."

And that was true. For even though Lindsay had a smooth, muscular body which I had now seen way too up close and personal, Sebastian's was a bit smoother and a bit more muscular. Having seen the penises of both friends in the flesh—and not while accidentally stumbling upon pictures of them online while cruising for sex—I had to admit I wanted Sebastian to be the one wearing nothing more than a loincloth that would flop up and down as he turned his beat around on the dance floor. But Lindsay's ego was as huge as Sebastian's uncut manmeat so this couldn't be admitted out loud. Fortunately another brilliant idea came to me.

"Sebastian is also Latin, which on the skin color wheel is closer to Native American Indian than Anglo-Saxon, so he'll look more authentic."

Lindsay digested this information. "Fine. The Puerto Rican can be the Indian."

"Thank you," Sebastian said with a smile. "Now I have to go home and practice putting war paint on my body. Maybe I'll paint my phone number on my ass!"

"Copycat!" Lindsay cried. "Now listen up, people, if I'm not the Indian chief I should be the cowboy."

"I want to be the cowboy!" Flynn cried.

"I'm going to be the cowboy," I informed them, then waited for Flynn and Lindsay's high-pitched shrieks to finish. "My mother bought me a complete cowboy outfit for last year's Salvatore DeNuccio Tenants' Group's first annual hoedown. I even have a lariat."

"When did the old hoes have a hoedown?"

"The event had to be canceled thanks to that friggin' Sylvia Dumbrowski."

"Steven, you're starting to talk like your mother."

"Sorry. Sylvia snuck into the community room the night before the hoedown and broke her hip while riding the electric bull. She was trying to get in some extra practice so she could win the bull-riding contest. First prize was a free dinner at the Outback. Before five p.m., of course. But I kept the outfit so I'm the cowboy."

"Then I'm the leatherman," Lindsay declared.

Some of the other Starbucks regulars were startled by our howls of laughter and stared. What they saw was three men hysterically laughing and pointing at one blond man-boy with delicate facial features who thought he could pass for a big bad leather daddy. Gus snorted back some latte drizzle that was seeping out of his nose and said, "Blimey, Linds! Not even under gay disco standards could you pass as a leatherman."

"Excuse me! I love the leather lifestyle!"

"Sure you do," Flynn said, wiping his eyes. "Leather cock rings under hot pink undies, leather thongs with the word SEXY spelled out in rhinestones."

"That was a gift!"

"It's my birthday and I'm going to be the leatherman."

"I thought you wanted to be political!"

"I'd rather wear leather chaps and expose my beefy arse."

"Is that the same as ass?" Flynn asked. "Because if so I just got hard."

"I figure I'm forty, I'm in the best shape of my life, why not show a little arse? Sebastian reveals more when he goes to church."

"You think Sebastian goes to church?"

"The priests probably pay him to go to confession. It gives them a week's worth of fantasies to wank off to."

"I do not want to hear about priests wanking off," I said.

"Sounding like your mother again."

I quickly changed the subject. "Now Linds, didn't one of your long programs have a military theme?"

"Oh yes! I skated to the soundtrack from *Private Benjamin* and wore army fatigues."

"Ice-skating is so bloody gay!" said Gus.

"I lived a very sheltered life when I was training. I thought the movie was a glimpse into the early life of Benjamin Franklin."

"He wasn't a soldier! Even I know that and I'm not American."

Lindsay was stymied. "I'm limited, *okay*?! All I know is what takes place on the ice!"

"Calm down Linds, at least you have a costume," Flynn said. "Who the hell is left for me?"

"You'll be the cop," Gus said with a wink. "I have a cop's hat and shirt at home that you can wear. I dated a policeman a few years back."

"When you were still dating adults?" Flynn cracked.

"Don't be jealous 'cause I'm riding the boyhole."

"Then it's settled, we all have our roles."

"Wait a second," Lindsay shouted. "Isn't there a construction worker too?"

"For crissakes, just how many Village People are there?" Flynn asked.

"If it's all right with you guys, I'll ask Brian to put on a hard hat."

"Only if that's all he wears," Gus said. "You landed yourself a cutie, Stevie."

I blushed a little. "I know."

"Is he as nice to you as he is sexy?" Gus asked.

Flynn was the only one who noticed that I paused for a split second. "Yes, very nice."

A few days later when Brian and I walked into Splash dressed up as two parts of the musical group that made Culture Club look butch, I felt like I had entered a time machine and been transported back to the good old gay days. The whole place truly resembled a boogay wonderland. Hanging from the ceiling was the de rigueur silver disco ball that slowly revolved, creating little specks of light that trickled down onto the revelers. Rainbow streamers fell from the center of the ceiling and were draped to create inverted arches that were tied back in the corners of the room by balloons shaped like huge, sparkly red platform shoes that could have been worn by the Wicked Witch of the East if she had had a little more funk in her soul.

Everywhere you looked there was a visual homage to a disco icon. In the center of the dance floor–cum–roller rink was a life-sized cutout of a white-suited John Travolta in his *Saturday Night Fever* dance pose and strategically placed throughout the hall were mannequins dressed up as disco royalty. There was Grace Jones in thick purple eye shadow and a leather one-piece bathing suit with a neckline that plunged below her belly button, Andy Gibb in tight purple bell bottoms and a billowy white shirt that was unbuttoned below his belly button, and even those two tons of fun, the Weather Girls, wearing purple raincoats and holding umbrellas that sprouted two naked male mannequins that had fallen from the sky.

Even DJ Pasquale was dressed up like Sly Stone in polyester, gold chains, and a 'fro so big it could be used in the next decade to house a flock of seagulls. The bartenders, all of whom passed Sebastian's soon-to-be-patented *I Really Do Suck Cock* test, were clad in one-size-too-small tighty-whitey underwear emblazoned with such logos as KNOCK ON MY WOOD and HOW DEEP IS YOUR LOVE HOLE? And then there was the Altar of Summer.

It was only fitting that the undisputed queen of disco, LaDonna Adrian Gaines Sommer Sudano aka Donna Summer, should have her own special place where the grateful could worship. (It also doubled as the birthday gift table because whenever possible gay should be fabulous *and* practical.) Lindsay had constructed the altar and he had done an outstanding job. In the center of the table was a papier-mâché bust of Donna from her *Live & More* album underneath a rainbow adorned with hundreds of fairy lights and the words ONCE UPON A TIME written on it in silver Mylar. There were several Sugar dolls—Barbie's mulatto girlfriend—dressed up like hookers standing under a street lamp, a naked doll swimming in a bowl of hot stuff, which was actually Anjanette's jalapeño salsa, and another doll sitting on a cotton-ball cloud hanging from the other side of the rainbow wearing a HELLO MY NAME IS HEAVEN name tag with a thought bubble over her head that said, I KNOW. To top it off, a light switch was rigged so the rainbow lights would dim every thirty seconds. Although I knew this perfect piece of summer-love was created by Lindsay's talented hands, I felt it could have been done by magic.

"Lindsay! This is a work of art!" I cried. Lindsay's outfit, however, was working a different kind of art. I had forgotten that his army fatigue skating costume would have made a four-star general's head spin. Obviously Lindsay had put on a few pounds since his competitive skating days so the olive-green satin costume was skin tight, which was acceptable in the current surroundings, but his red, white, and blue epaulets were created with the Bedazzler and down both sides of his legs ran the bespeckled phrase I ♥ UNCLE SAM. An incredibly fey costume, however, didn't stop him from arriving with a good-looking man-in-drag on his arm.

"Steven, I think you know Donald."

"*This* is Fuck Cou . . ."

"No, it's Donald!" Lindsay loudly corrected me.

"Oh yes," I stumbled. "I didn't recognize you."

Donald had made a very clever costume choice, coming as Olivia Newton-John as skanky Sandy from *Grease*. Black tube top, spandex pants, slutty heels, permed wig, and Pink Ladies satin jacket, his outfit was almost as gay as Lindsay's. And I had to admit his Olivia could whoop my Samantha's ass in the Miss Drag Queen contest. Which incidentally was set to begin at three a.m.

"Are you the guy who counts cock thrusts?" Brian asked.

"You've heard of me?" Donald asked proudly.

"I thought it was an urban myth. Wait until I tell Rodrigo."

"Make sure to tell him I'm up to seven-fifty."

"Really?" Brian and I said simultaneously.

"Owe me a Coke," I said to Brian.

"I do need a drink," Brian announced. "Can I get you guys anything?"

"I'll come with you," Lindsay said. "I want to see if the bartenders are as gay as Sebastian claims."

"Linds, get me a Bud, please," said Donald.

"Steve, Absolut and tonic?" Brian asked knowingly.

"Absolutely."

"And later on you can tell me how you recognized Mr. Counter," Brian teased.

Brian's fake moustache tickled when he kissed me. Donald smirked at me playfully and I smiled back.

"I really am up to seven-fifty now," Donald whispered. "I'd love to prove it to you some time."

"That sounds great, but I've been dating that construction worker for a few months."

"Good for you. But when you break up with him give me a call." Olivia strutted off, then turned back. "See ya later, stud."

Me break up with Brian? Was I subconsciously sending out signals? Had his lie affected me much more than I cared to admit? Or was I just the cliché New York gay who spends half his time searching for a boyfriend so he can experience the joys and pains of a monogamous relationship and the other half of his time searching for ways to get rid of the boyfriend so he can be free to start his search all over again with someone new? My head was spinning like the disco ball overhead. Where was Brian with my drink?

Two Absolut and tonics later and I felt a little better. I felt much, much better when Gus arrived with his latest boy toy, looking like the lead in an S/M leather video and true to his word with his beefy British butt exposed for all to see. I kept my Gus-crush in check and my hands to myself as Gus introduced the latest in his string of boy toys.

"Mates, this is Al. Alex Peter Keaton."

"Are you kidding me?!" I screamed.

"That's my real name," the incredibly underage-looking Alex P.

Keaton replied. "My parents named me after some famous Republican kid."

"They named you after a character played by a Canadian actor in a mediocre American sitcom who happened to be a teenaged Republican?"

"Yeah, something like that," Al replied. "But how should I know? The show was canceled before I learned how to talk."

Touché. "Brian! Get me another drink!"

"Coming right up, old-timer."

An hour later and everyone had arrived. Flynn made a perfect gay boy in blue and was doing an admirable job keeping up with Lindsay as they roller-skated around the disco floor. My heart leapt when I saw Lucas (who actually accepted my invitation and arrived in winged-back hair and plaid cuffed jeans as one of the Bay City Rollers) skate behind Flynn and grab his billy club. Very quickly the two were skating in the happy lane.

As for Sebastian, well, he was skating in the center of the floor surrounded by some Bee Gees, a Diana Ross, and an ugly Sledge sister. As he did a scratch spin that would have made Lindsay jealous he showed us all that he wore no shame and no underwear under his loincloth. Who could blame him for advertising, though? He had to make up for lost time now that his asshole was no longer poisonous.

But when I rolled past the bar I was the one who got stung, as I saw Grace Jones fondling my boyfriend's tool belt. Screeching to a stop inches from Brian's skates I saw that Grace was downing my drink. Just who the hell was this harlot who obviously wanted to make Brian her very own Dolph Lundgren?

"Steven, this is Rodrigo."

In my mind I stumbled back through time and saw the face of the guy who pulled Brian back onto the dance floor the first night we bumped into each other at Marys. It was the same face except now his hair was all slicked back and he wore heavy makeup. But the eyes were the same. They were the eyes of a friend determined to become a lover. Maybe the Absolut had given me extrasensory perception, but I knew in that instant that Rodrigo was in love with Brian. And there was no way in this hellish disco inferno that I was going to lose my man to a woman who couldn't even keep her career.

"Rodrigo!" I said extra cheerfully. "How nice to finally meet you."

"You too. And I'm sorry, I think I stole your drink."

"No problem. It's not like you stole my man!"

I laughed so hard the other two were forced to join in. Despite his laughter Rodrigo's eyes didn't change; they still glared at me as if he were Debbie Reynolds and I was Liz Taylor and Eddie Fisher was a fresh wound that time and Carrie Fisher's *Star Wars* paycheck hadn't yet healed. I knew I was in trouble when my mind raced back to pop culture of the '50s, but I couldn't help myself. The nagging doubts in my own head were hard enough to squelch, and this devil dressed up like Ms. Jones could not be ignored.

"I think it's time for us to put on our show, Brian."

"You sure you want to do it in public?"

"What are you going to do, Brian?" Rodrigo asked. "Get another blow job on the bar?"

Brian went red. "That was one time during spring break in college!"

"Sorry, Rod, but all Brian's sex acts are now invitation only. And I'm the only one invited." Score one for Liz. "C'mon Brian, it's showtime!"

In honor of Gus's birthday we had wanted to do something really fun and really gay. After much debate we decided that we would simply bring our impersonation of the Village People to the next level and perform one of their most popular tunes, one that has been sung at bar mitzvahs and bathhouses across the country since the '70s. DJ Pasquale started the karaoke version of "Macho Man" and Flynn, Lindsay, Sebastian, Brian, and I got up on the stage to perform for Gus and the rest of the roller boogieing crowd.

As the beat began to pump louder and the lights ricocheted off the dance floor, I finally got to feel what it was like to be a real disco diva. I felt empowered as I looked out at the sweaty half-naked crowd and saw them cheering for me and my friends. I looked over at Flynn, then at the rest of the boys, and we were no longer our boring selves, we were macho Mary men and we had an anthem to sing.

By the end of the song every person in the bar was singing along. Standing up on that stage, a few things penetrated my drunken mind. We had made our friend Gus happy on his pivotal birthday, we'd given our friends a memory that would make them smile for years to come, and as silly as it sounds we declared in song that just because we were men who liked to do girlie things like get manicures, apply self-tanners, and give blow jobs, we were still men, macho, Mary, or otherwise, and no matter what anyone ever tried to do or say, that fact would never change.

Another fact that would never change is that men give mixed signals. One minute Gus was groping Sebastian's loins under cloth and the next he was getting his unclothed ass gripped by Alex P. Over the requisite end-of-the-party tune, "Last Dance," I swore I heard Gus proclaim that later on that night he would give himself a birthday present and bottom for the very first time. Elsewhere, Lucas finally proclaimed his homosexuality differently, with a mouthwatering kiss on Flynn's lips. Before Flynn could even think about pulling away, Lucas had wrapped him in a tight hug and lip-smacked him. Lucas stunned himself, but Flynn was more stunned when Lucas pulled back and said feebly that he had to leave. Before I could get to Flynn to counteract Lucas's callous action, Flynn too had fled the party. That left me and Brian. And Rodrigo.

"So where to now?" Rodrigo asked.

"I don't know," Brian said. "What do you feel like doing?"

"Not sure, but it's not every night I get dressed up like a woman."

Brian smirked. "Oh, really?"

"Well, except for that one time. Remember?" Rodrigo said, touching Brian's now-bare chest. "You said I looked like a slutty version of Jenny McCarthy."

"My exact words," Brian said, grabbing Rodrigo's bare shoulder, "were that you look like a sluttier Jenna Jameson."

"That's right! You remember everything about us, don't you?" And he touched his chest again. "I'm so glad we've stayed friends after all these years."

I was actually standing next to my boyfriend watching him flirt with another guy. And I was allowing it to happen. *Waiter! Where the fuck are my balls?*

"I hate to interrupt this absolutely charming trip down memory lane, but it's late and I'm horny. What are you going to do about it, Brian?"

I pulled the sex card. I wasn't proud of it, but in desperate times pride has no place. Rodrigo might be a good flirt, but Brian and I both knew I was a good fuck. It was time we let Rodrigo in on the secret.

"Well, Rod, I have to listen to my own rod and it's pointing east."

It took me a moment to realize that I was standing on Brian's right, which meant that from his point of view I was eastward. Liz: Two. Debbie: Zero.

"See ya 'round, Rod."

We left Grace standing forlornly amid a cloud of machine-made fog. From out of the smoke appeared an old man who looked like a holdover from the original days of disco wearing red satin shorts, yellow satin jacket, headband, and sunglasses. He skated by Rodrigo and stopped to give him two complimentary toots on his disco whistle. Repulsed, Rodrigo cringed and skated off into the fake cloud to search for a Brian substitute. I clutched the hand of the real thing knowing that while Rodrigo would spend the next hour trying to catch a little night fever, tomorrow morning I would wake up with a splitting love hangover.

Two weeks later and my hangover was still the sweetest. Brian and I were moving along at a nice pace, sleeping over at each other's apartments a couple nights during the week, having affectionate and superhot sex, and making sure we made time in our schedules for date nights—nights spent doing something silly just to get to know each other better. One night we played

Trivial Pursuit and surprisingly I did much better in Science &
Technology than I did in Arts & Entertainment. And Brian's
knowledge of all things historical was astounding. I was very
much looking forward to bubble bath night for reasons that
should be self-explanatory. All bubbles aside, these nights were
important because they were our private time. For a new relationship this was the perfect defense against outside forces such
as Rodrigo, who had emerged from the fog and was still trying
to maintain best-friend status. Of course I never expected him to
disappear completely, but I was hoping that he would get the
hint that Brian was pursuing other interests. But best friends can
be like bad songs that get stuck in your head. Turned out the
real test to our relationship was soon to come, as it was time for
me and Brian to spend our first real holiday together—Thanksgiving.

"So how would you like to spend a good old-fashioned Italian Thanksgiving with me and my family?" I asked.

"That would be really nice," Brian said. "Except . . ."

"Except what? You don't like turkey?"

"No, silly. I would love to spend Thanksgiving with you, but
Rodrigo and I always spend it together. His family's in Argentina
and my mother is not thankful and/or giving so years ago we
wound up spending the day together. I'd hate to give him the
boot on such short notice."

I heard the words form in my head, and couldn't stop them
from pouring out of my mouth. "Rodrigo can come too."

"Really?"

"Absolutely. My mother loves a crowded table."

"You're sure it won't be an inconvenience? Because we're
kind of used to having Chinese on turkey day."

"No boyfriend of mine is having mu shu pork on Thanksgiving. Tell Rodrigo to prepare himself for his first Thanksgiving
in Jersey."

"Thank you," Brian said. "I wasn't sure if you really liked
him."

Damn, my man was perceptive. "Not like Rodrigo?!" I said,

using my higher-pitched shocked voice. "Why, that's as crazy as you not liking Flynn! You do like Flynn, don't you?"

"Yeah, he's cool. All your friends are nice. Sebastian's a little out there. . . ."

"I told you, totally second tier. And tell Rodrigo not to worry about being a third wheel or anything because Flynn is going to be joining us for dinner too. He's like my mother's other gay son."

"Oh, don't worry about Rodrigo. He knows that my best friend never has to feel like a third wheel."

Damn, my man was thoughtful. I know it was information that should make me happy, but at that moment all I could think about was how I was going to convince Flynn to join us for Thanksgiving dinner.

"Thanks, Steve, but I'm really not up for a Ferrante holiday meal this year," Flynn said.

I sipped my SU to calm my nerves. "I will buy you anything you want."

"I make more money than you do."

"I will clean your house. Naked. Admit it, Flynn, you've always wanted me to do that."

"Honey, I've seen you naked when you were in your prime and I giggled."

"You did not giggle! You smiled at me very tenderly."

"As I suppressed a giggle."

"Why, Flynn? Why would you laugh at my naked body?!"

Once again a conversation I was engaged in at a Starbucks café forced a family of tourists to flee.

"Oh, you laughed too. Listen, thanks for the invitation, but I would just rather spend a few days on my own."

"The thing with Lucas got you down?"

"The thing with Lucas reminded me that there is no thing with Lucas."

"Sorry about that. I haven't had a chance to talk to him because his character's doing undercover work in Bolivia, so he hasn't been at the studio for the past few days. But I did think that kiss he gave you might actually turn into something."

"Because you're now playing the role of the optimist." Awkward pause, then, "I have to get back to the office."

I grabbed Flynn's arm and asked him not to go. It was a little melodramatic, but it worked. Without going into excruciating detail I explained that he had to put his feelings aside, table his disappointment and depression, and help me out of a jam that I had gotten myself into single-handedly.

"You want me to rescue you, while I'm at the lowest ebb I've been at in years, because you told your boyfriend that he could bring along his platonic boyfriend to Thanksgiving dinner and that I would be sitting across from them at the table before you consulted me?"

"Lawyers really do have advanced comprehension skills."

"This is not what I would have expected from you, Steven."

"I'm sorry! I know I'm being selfish, but if it makes you feel any better I will force myself to be majorly depressed on Christmas."

Flynn studied me and sipped his gingerbread latte. Despite the tense atmosphere the aroma of ginger goodness permeated the air and caressed my nostrils. Personally, I was dying to try one of the special holiday drinks, but I need order in my chaotic life so I only allow myself to taste specialty coffee drinks from Thanksgiving to New Year's. Discipline would be needed for a few more days.

"Will your mother make her mashed turnips and squash thingumajig?"

"She's mashing them as we speak."

"Will you provide round-trip transportation?"

"My mother is already in Sparta and I'm borrowing her car."

"Will your brother wear those tight Levi's that hug his ass?"

"I'll dress him myself."

"You got yourself a deal."

Thrilled, I tried to hug Flynn, but he stopped me. "No, I'm still annoyed with you. I'll be over it by tomorrow, but I don't want you to touch me right now."

"I understand. And I owe you, Flynn, just name your price."

He studied me again more seriously, then said, "You can't put a price on friendship, Stevie."

Just like disco music, Thanksgiving is misunderstood. In the latter instance, however, it's a misunderstanding as a result of the nationwide cover-up of the crimes of our forefathers. Bitter pilgrims learned how to till the land and make it productive, then stole said land from its original owners. But to prove they were generous they invited them to a thank-you dinner, though I'm sure anyone wearing feathers was relegated to the children's table. Despite its scandalous origins, Thanksgiving is still one of my favorite holidays because it marks the beginning of the holiday season and is a time of good food, good will toward men, and days off from work. The only potential for disaster is spending an extraordinary amount of time with your family.

My brother Paulie was three years younger than me and heterosexual. Therefore my relationship with Paulie was and would always be that we loved each other, we would be there for each other in moments of crisis, but we didn't understand each other and really had no desire to be close friends. The typical hetero-homo brother relationship. However, despite our differences we respected each other and I was especially proud of the life he'd created for himself. He had a gorgeous house in a ritzy part of Jersey, a lovely Italian wife with a hair-styling degree from the Bergenfield Academy of Hair who in an emergency could erase all traces of gray from my otherwise chocolate brown locks, and a thriving dental practice with an incredibly high family discount. Most important, he was good to our mother. He wasn't involved in her daily life as much as I was, but she knew that when she needed him, he'd be there. The one trait that we did have in common was that he often lacked subtlety. In fact he'd told me just the other day, "I might have to make a quick exit after the lasagna to bring the wife upstairs to, you know, do her."

My brother and I were the only male Ferrantes left, which meant he was the only one in the family capable of carrying on the Ferrante name. I knew Montgomery and Leilani-Anjanette might make an appearance in my life at some point, but in all reality the burden of keeping the Ferrantes from extinction lay on my brother's shoulders. And it must have been a particularly heavy burden because Paulie and his wife, Renée, had been trying to have a baby for the past two years and although the doctors said both of them were healthy and fertile, a new Ferrante had yet to arrive. So now they were using fertility charts and on Thursday Renée would be ripe for the picking. So they might have to excuse themselves in between courses to attempt to fertilize her eggs. I told Paulie that as long as they didn't mix up the turkey basters they had my blessing and I would entertain the family downstairs while they entertained each other upstairs. Interestingly, during their quest to become pregnant my mother had been uncharacteristically quiet and had not been badgering them incessantly to make her a grandmother. I think she enjoyed her freedom and knew that the minute a newborn was ripped from Renée's vagina she'd be on babysitting duty. Maternal instinct sometimes ventures off to the dark side.

Her instinct toward cars was also off-target. A two-toned black and cream Honda Element is not the type of car that you would expect a senior citizen to drive. But that's the type of car Audrey's son-in-law sold, so that's the type of car Audrey's friend bought. With Brian next to me and Rodrigo and Flynn in the backseat of Honda's sportiest SUV, I felt like we were driving to an excursion in the mountains and not a holiday dinner in the suburbs. By the sounds of silence that clung to the soft leather interior, however, it seemed as if we were driving to a funeral.

"Um, so, how's um, the ride back there?" I asked.

"Good," Flynn said.

"Yeah. Good," Rodrigo added.

We had another thirty minutes to go before we could shove food in our faces, thereby making it unnecessary to talk. I had to think of a conversation starter.

"Do you think it's windy enough so that another balloon in the Macy's parade will commit manslaughter?"

"I hate parades," Rodrigo offered.

"Oh, I see. I didn't realize that," I said.

"Almost as much as I hate soap operas."

Brian's head snapped so hard to glare at Rodrigo in the backseat that I thought it was going to break off. "Steven, do you think your mother will like the flowers? I got the idea to turn the pumpkin into a vase from an old Martha Stewart magazine."

"Yeah, sure, she'll love them."

"So Rod," Flynn started, "have you ever seen *If Tomorrow Never Comes?*"

"You mean that insipid piece of —"

I made a split-second decision to play the adult and not allow the conversation to disintegrate into a debate over the pros and cons of my livelihood—because as much as I love the genre of daytime drama, I knew from experience that it was foolish to try and convert nonbelievers.

"Rodrigo, don't answer that question on the grounds that it could incriminate you," I said. "I'm a producer of that show and while I know soaps aren't everyone's cup of tea, I love what I do."

As a gesture of thanks, Brian put his hand on my knee and smiled sheepishly.

"Anyhoo, what exactly do you do? I don't think Brian's ever mentioned."

"I'm a translator at the United Nations."

"Really?" I said.

"That's fascinating," Flynn added with genuine interest.

"Some days I can't believe it myself."

"What languages do you speak?"

"English, of course, Spanish, French, and Russian. Oh, and Mandarin. I keep forgetting that one."

Twenty minutes in the suburbs and I was already thinking like a conniving, manipulative, desperate housewife. Was I impressed that the guy in my backseat spoke five languages and worked at one of the most prestigious institutions in the world? No. Did I even think to ask him if he ever translated really important documents that he couldn't talk about because they would risk our nation's security? No. The only thought that kept repeating in my brain was, *Now I understand why Brian knows so much about history!*

"... so even though Putin is a homophobe, he's really hot."

"Tell them the story about his bodyguards and the gymnast," Brian suggested.

Before Rodrigo could regale us with a report on randy Russian rescuers, I turned into my brother's circular driveway.

"And here we are," I announced, speeding to the front entrance.

"Wow," Brian said. "They don't make houses like this in Alabama."

"We're in Jersey, Brian," Rodrigo said. "Home of the McMansion."

I wanted to correct Mr. McLingual and tell him in five different languages that he was wrong. McMansions are those ostentatious houses that are built on every available inch of a person's land and adorned with stone columns, poorly sculpted lions, and oversized fountains. My brother's split-level A-frame house, while big in the square foot department, was surrounded by five acres of beautifully landscaped grounds and the only animal on the property was Trixie Trueheart, Renée's beloved long-haired dachshund. I wanted to say all this, but I didn't because I was still trying to act like an adult. Before anyone could make another remark, adult or juvenile, my mother and Audrey ran up to the car like crazed Italian paparazzi.

"Happy Thanksgiving, boys!" they both cried.

Everyone got out of the car cautiously, like Jennifer Aniston and her personal staff on their way into the Stop 'n' Shop. Anjanette wasted no time taking center stage, "You must be Brian."

"Yes," Brian said, allowing Anjanette to hug, kiss, and inspect him. "What a pleasure to meet you."

"Likewise. I have heard so much about you. Steven just goes on and on, I try to tell him to hold a little bit back, but it's like he has diarrhea of the mouth. Once he gets revved up he just can't stop. I have no idea where he gets it from. Oh, are those flowers for me? That is so sweet. Mums are my favorite. Maybe

because I'm a mum! And in a little pumpkin vase, they're adorable."

"Ma!" I screeched.

"Yes, Steven?"

"Can we please go inside?"

"Of course! What do you think? We're going to have dinner
on the front lawn? C'mon now, everybody inside." She took
Brian's arm and escorted him into the house. "I haven't forgotten about you, Flynn, I'll hug you when we get inside."

"I'm counting on it," Flynn said, ever the trouper.

"And Steven?" Anjanette called out.

"Yes?"

"Who's the little Spanish boy?"

Inside it wasn't much better, but for completely different reasons. Now that I was finally at a holiday gathering with a
boyfriend other than Jack I felt awkward and nervous. I knew
my family was making a judgment about Brian and I wanted to
know if they were giving him a thumbs-up. My brother's lack of
subtlety sometimes is a godsend.

"I give your boyfriend the thumbs-up, Steven," he said after
chatting with Brian. "He's got clean fingernails, he knows the
definition of a hedge fund, and he's got good teeth."

"Perfect. When we try to sell him at the next slave trade, he'll
bring in a good price."

"Shut up, you know how important teeth are to me."

"Almost as important as his wife," Renée said, holding Trixie
Trueheart in her left hand and a tray of food in the other. "I've
got stuffed mushrooms in one hand and the most precious dog
in the world in the other. Who wants what?"

"I want Trixie!" I yelled, grabbing my niece and immediately
making those sounds only appropriate when in the company of
an infant or a dog.

"She's all yours," Paulie said under his breath.

"Paulie! If Trixie goes with Steven so do I!"

"Who are you kidding? You couldn't fit your shoe collection
in his apartment."

"That's true," Renée admitted. "Sorry, Steve, Trixie has to stay here."

"As long as I get visitation rights."

"Hey, Steve," Paulie whispered.

"Why are you whispering?"

"I just wanted to tell you that I'm glad you found somebody. It's a nice thing."

Taken aback by my brother's sincerity, I wasn't sure what to say or do. "Thanks. Do I have to hug you now?"

"No, Renée gets jealous when someone better looking than her touches me."

"You're insane. Now turn around so Flynn can see your ass in those Levi's."

Paulie did a straight-guy imitation of a male model walk in front of Flynn. "Mama like?"

"Mama love!" Flynn said. "But mama hungry. Waitress! I'll have a 'shroom."

"Have two, I didn't make them."

"In that case I'll have three."

"Psst," Renée whispered. "How're you feeling?"

"Really well," Flynn whispered back.

"Good, I'm glad. And psst: you look fabulous."

"Me! You must have Anna Wintour tied up in the basement doling out styling tips."

And as always Renée did look fabulous. She was wearing an ivory man-tailored shirt that made her ebony hair appear darker, a brown tweed miniskirt with the most miniscule stripes of orange and a gold chain belt, mocha textured stockings, and brown alligator-skin shoe boots. Renée paid attention to fashion, which was one of the reasons we got along so well.

"How 'bout you, Brian?" she asked. "Mushroom?"

"I'd love one. Steven wouldn't let us eat in the car."

"Are they made with garlic?" Rodrigo asked.

"My mother-in-law made them, what do you think?"

Rodrigo grabbed Brian's hand before he could pop the mushroom into his mouth. "Brian, maybe you shouldn't. You said garlic was bothering you lately. You don't want to spoil your dinner."

"You're right. Here, you have it." Then Brian did something he probably thought was quite innocent and not at all jaw-droppingly provocative, he popped his mushroom into Rodrigo's open, eager mouth. Jaws dropped.

Renée, like most Italian girls who grew up in gritty, urban Hoboken, New Jersey, then moved to one of the state's more up-scale neighborhoods, could lose the demure dentist's wife shtick and become the gum-chewing, teased-haired, tough girl of her youth in 2.5 seconds flat. Renée bent her knee, jutted out her hip, and cocked her head. When she spoke she looked at Brian, but pointed at Rodrigo. "Is he boyfriend number two?" Once again I felt the need to break the awkward silence.

"So Paulie, is now a good time to fertilize Renée's eggs?"

We are not the type of family to pray before a meal, but I said a quickie asking God to send Rodrigo off to Spain or Russia or wherever they speak Mandarin on a six-month highly confidential work-related translation project. So confidential that he wouldn't be able to have contact with the outside world. Renée wasn't praying, she was eyeing Brian and Rodrigo as if she were Lil' Kim and they were her former rivals from the big house. Even Trixie knew that her Mama was sending off ugly vibes and re-fused to leave my lap even when Renée waved the Thanksgiving wishbone from across the table.

After a while I was able to push images of Brian finger-feeding Rodrigo out of my mind and the day became more en-joyable. Paulie was a bit more social than usual (possibly be-cause he knew he was going to get laid before the dishes were dried) and my mother seemed taken by Brian's easy charm. She kept giving me not-so-secret winks whenever she caught my eye. Most of the time, though, she and Audrey flitted from the dining room to the kitchen and back again bringing in trays of food, then removing empty dinner plates, taking hostess duties away from Renée, which was perfect because she was clearly more in-terested in examining my boyfriend and his boy friend than in serving dinner. During a break in the meal Renée snuggled up beside me on the couch while I tried to feign interest in the football game that was unfolding on Paulie's fifty-inch plasma TV screen.

"Steven?" Renée whispered just like her husband previously.

"Yes, Renée."

"I do not trust him."

"Paulie is not having an affair."

"Please! Paulie's lucky he got me. I'm talking about Miss Alabama."

"Brian?"

"Keep in mind this has nothing to do with my hatred of the South. I just think you should invest in a private investigator. Though I have never employed one for personal use, I can pass on to you the names of several reliable private eyes from my very own Rolodex."

"Since when do you hate the South?"

"*You* represent your state in the National Hair Colorists Competition in Pelahatchie, Mississippi and wind up spending two days in jail because some homegrown bitch claims you transported illegal hair-care chemicals across state lines and see if you don't come out cussing anyone with a drawl. Bottom line, Steven, your boyfriend's a little too friendly with the Rican."

I didn't get a chance to correct Renée and tell her that Rodrigo was actually from Argentina because at that very moment Brian wedged his way into the whisperfest.

"What are y'all talkin' about?"

"You," Renée said. "And your adorable Southern accent. Have I told you that I spent some time in the South?"

"Ma! Do you need any help?" I asked.

"Why do you even ask?" Paulie asked. "You know she's going to say no."

"No, you boys relax. You too, Renée. Audrey and I can handle it."

"That's right," Audrey said. "Today on this most thankful of days you people are my family. Thank you!" Then she burst into tears and ran into the kitchen.

"What the hell's wrong with her?" Paulie asked as a spokes-person for us all.

My mother explained that Audrey's daughter, Lori Ann, had taken her family to spend the holiday with her husband's rela-tives in Colorado this year and ever since "the nine-one-one" Audrey refuses to fly, so she was left alone this year.

"But as long as I'm alive, Audrey, you will never be alone!" Anjanette yelled into the kitchen. "Now stop the friggin' crying and baste that turkey!"

I watched the tears well up in my mother's eyes. Her relation-ship with the crazy woman basting the turkey, whose tears were probably falling into the gravy, was most certainly stronger than the bond that had kept my parents' marriage together for over thirty years.

So why was Brian's friendship with Rodrigo any different? Because I felt threatened in the knowledge that my brief time with Brian couldn't compare to the years he and Rodrigo had spent together cultivating a closeness that wasn't based on some-thing as ephemeral as mutual physical attraction? Or was it all the years I'd spent reading scripts filled with dialogue wherein a friend suddenly proposes undying love for another friend and they realize their friendship was a mask for their true love?

Later that night, in bed, unable to keep my inner dialogue within any longer, I asked Brian if he was aware that Rodrigo had the hots for him. Kudos to him for not denying it.

"I think on some level there's an attraction. Just like with you and Flynn."

"Flynn and I are not attracted to each other!"

"Yes, you are. And that's why you're friends. Are you going to act on that attraction and have sex with him?"

"No. Absolutely not."

"Then why do you think Rodrigo and I will?"

Damn, my man was clever. I guess it was possible that Flynn and I weren't the only best friends who knew our friendship was more important than a quick fuck. But then why couldn't I get out of my mind the image of Rodrigo alone in his own bed jerking off while thinking of Brian dressed as a hot roller-skating construction worker?

"Rodrigo's flirty," Brian said. "He's got a stressful job and that's how he blows off some steam. But you don't have to worry, he isn't blowing me. You're the only one who gets to do that."

"Okay, I get it."

"Good. Now I have to visit the latrine. Your mother sure does like the garlic, doesn't she?"

"Hey, did you have a good time today?"

"Yeah, I did. You must've figured out by now that I'm not really the family type, but yours is entertaining."

"That's an understatement."

"Especially when we could hear your brother banging Renée while your mother was serving dessert."

Left alone in bed, I was conflicted. If I expected Brian to deal with my neurotic family and friends, the only fair thing to do was temper my objections toward Rodrigo and make an effort to get to know him as something more than my boyfriend's inappropriately flirty friend. I thought for a moment, stubbornly held on to my own neurotic nature, and made yet another choice—I decided to look at Rodrigo as the guy who wanted to steal my boyfriend. Because enough was enough—I WAS NOT STUPID.

So I turned up the volume on the TV to drown out the sound of Brian having a touch of diarrhea thanks to my mother's garlic-infused cooking and with apologizes to God knelt at the Altar of Summer. I thanked Donna for teaching me as a young boy that there were bad girls in the world and that a fairy tale high may lead you faster and faster to nowhere, just like it had in my first major relationship, with Jack. And I prayed for the strength to get my love life back under control, because this time with Brian I knew it was for real and I didn't wanna get hurt by another guy. By the time Brian crawled back into bed I felt better knowing that I had Donna on my side in my fight to keep my boyfriend.

Chapter Ten

In 1964 Christmas turned gay. It was the year Rankin/Bass's now-classic stop-motion TV special, *Rudolph the Red-Nosed Reindeer,* premiered. To the layman, the program was just a holiday special based on a popular Christmas song. But to gay men, this animagical musical featuring thinly-veiled gay anthems like "We're a Couple of Misfits" and "Silver and Gold" was the first in-depth full-color televised examination of what it truly meant to be a misfit in the closeted 1960s. This song-and-dance version of the Rudolph story would go down in gay history.

The first time I watched this Christmas masterpiece, it was with wide eyes and a heavy heart. As a six-year-old I couldn't comprehend that Rudolph's red nose and Hermey's desire for unconventional employment were symbols of the alternative lifestyle I would lead as an adult, but I still felt sad. Even at that age I knew what it felt like to be called names and I understood the wish to run away to a place where I belonged. In that respect Rudolph, Hermey, and I were kindred spirits. And fat old Santa was our archenemy.

I had been taught that Santa was a gentle, kind-hearted man who loved all children. But that is a lie. In that TV special it was made clear that Santa was selective in doling out his love and was nastier than the Abominable Snowmonster before his first dental visit. SC represented every adult I ever met—with the exception of my mother—who I intrinsically knew would shun me if I didn't keep my own red nose a secret from the world. The big fat gift-giver was actually the mob ringleader who ran Rudolph out of Christmas Town just because he was different. He was as evil as my Aunt Katey who snidely referred to me as "The little Mary boy who plays with dolls."

So evil, in fact, that in the original version of the special he ignored his promise to include the misfits in his annual Christmas Eve delivery run. It was only after a write-in campaign championed by angry viewers expressing their disgust at Santa's obvious sexual-orientation bias that a scene was included wherein Santa scatters the inhabitants of the Island of Misfit Toys (an obvious homage to Greenwich Village) throughout the world. Despite this attempt at redemption, Santa's despicable actions toward Rudolph and his friends left an indelible impression on my young gay brain. There's a reason Santa is an anagram of Satan.

But while Satan, or Santa, only pops up once a year, best friends are just the opposite. Thus far Brian and I had attended three holiday gatherings and Rodrigo had piggybacked an invite to all of them. Not only that, but he clung to us like a koala bear cub with separation anxiety. I tried introducing him to some eligible bachelors. I tried setting him up with some not-so-eligible bachelors. I even tried to convince him that a very handsome, strong-jawed woman would make an interesting yulehole.

"Are you trying to get rid of me, Steven?" Rodrigo asked.

"Of course not!" I lied. "I just want you to be as happy as I am with Brian," I lied again.

"That is so sweet," he gushed. "Bri, you are one lucky man."

"I know," Brian said as he pushed me under the mistletoe to seal his comment with a kiss. "But you're pretty lucky too, Rod. Or should I say Mister I-Have-the-Entire-Month-of-December-Off."

"Rodrigo has off for the entire month of December?" I gasped.

"Yeah. Nothing much happens at the U.N. in December so this year they gave a lot of us time off. With pay."

"Of course," Brian said. "The government wouldn't have it any other way."

"That's right," Rodrigo agreed. "So not only do I have a lot of free time, but I have lots of spending money too. What should we do first, Brian?"

I felt as fretful as Rudolph did when Comet—the athletic, burly, manly-man coach of the reindeer team—announced in front of all the other reindeer that he could never, ever join in any reindeer games again. I took a deep breath and tried to remember a happier time, like when it was just Rudolph and that strapping young blond buck, Fireball, before that stupid Clarice showed up and told Rudy he was cute.

"Are you going back home to visit your family?" I asked hopefully.

"I wish. Technically I'm still working so I have to stay in the city. Which just means Brian and I will do some day trips."

"Yeah, the magazine shuts down the last two weeks of the year so I'll be free. What about you, Steven? Does the studio shut down for the holidays?"

"Just on Christmas," I replied, then added feebly, "And, you know, the day after."

"Oh, that's too bad," Rodrigo said. "You're going to miss all the holiday fun."

"Well, there are always the holi-nights," I said.

"Perfect! We can share Brian. You can have him at night, but during the day he's all mine."

Rodrigo clinked our glasses and a little bit of eggnog foam splattered into my eye—not enough to blind me to what was truly happening right in front of me. I flicked away the foam and forced myself to laugh along with Rodrigo and his boyfriend, I mean *my* boyfriend, but underneath that smile a desperate plan was forming. You could keep your gold, your frankincense, and your myrrh; this holiday season I would be giving the gift of revenge.

"Stevester, I would love to help destroy your boyfriend's relationship with his best friend, but I leave tomorrow for two weeks," Lindsay announced. "I'm joining the *Stars on Ice* tour."

"Really?"

Lindsay slammed his fist on the table so hard my Venti cup tipped over. I grabbed it a second before it was horizontal and once again my eye was hit with foam. "Does that surprise you? Did you think I was all washed up? Did you think the public wouldn't have any interest watching an Olympic loser skate?!"

"Shut up, Linds," Flynn said. "And tell us how you got the gig."

"It's all thanks to my friend Dick Button."

"Your *friend*?" I squealed.

"Once I let go of my hatred for him, I realized he's quite a nice man. And he arranged it so I can sub whenever they need a replacement for the tour. I leave tomorrow, but before I go maybe I can help you rid yourself of the Ladyfriend of Spain."

At that moment Sebastian showed up out of nowhere and plopped his floppy mocha brown ass down at our table. Not surprisingly, he thought it was him we were speaking about.

"Steven, why would you want to get rid of me? Are you finally tired of the competition?"

"We're talking about a different señorita," Flynn said helpfully.

"What are you doing here, Sebastian?" I asked. "Following us?"

"Don't flatter yourself, puppy. Papi just came in to get some coffee to give himself a coffee enema later on tonight, but then I realized it's Thursday."

A moment of silence followed this remark. "And by that do you mean that Thursday is herbal tea enema night?" Lindsay asked.

Rolling his eyes, Sebastian explained, "I forgot that my Thursday night fuck buddy has to switch to Wednesdays and my Wednesday night blow job will now be on Tuesdays. *Dios mio*, I need a BlackBerry to keep up with my own sex schedule."

"You need a blackberry with penicillin shots," Lindsay declared.

"I get those on Fridays."

"So what are you going to do with a free night?" I asked.

"Maybe I'll fuck Gus now that he's a power bottom."

"Getting fucked once doesn't make you a power bottom," Lindsay corrected.

"Turns out Alex P. Keaton is packing a ten-incher."

"And Gus took every inch?" I asked.

"*Sí, señor.* Ooh look, I'm hard now!"

"So am I," Flynn, Lindsay and I said simultaneously.

Sebastian jumped up, "I'll let you know what it feels like to be inside the great Briton!"

"Even though I'll be skating under the spotlights straining to hear my music over the deafening applause of my fans and won't be around to watch you get your revenge on the boyfriend stealer, I will help you plot against him."

"Me too. Ever since Lucas shoved his tongue down my throat and then ran for the nearest exit, I've been miserable. And misery needs company, so count me in."

"That's the holiday spirit, guys," I said. "Now let's brainstorm."

"Don't start working those brain cells without us. The Jersey bitches have arrived!"

And for the second time that night someone popped up out of nowhere and plopped their ass at our table. This time it was two someones, my sister-in-law Renée and her faithful companion, Trixie Trueheart. Earlier that day I had called Renée to fill her in on the latest Rodrigo incident, or as we called them, *Los Incidentes de Rodrigo.* She had just been on her way into the city to attend a hair coloring seminar at the Color Annex of the Vidal Sassoon Beauty Salon and said she would meet me for coffee before she and Trixie headed home.

"Have you started to strategize?" Renée asked.

"Not yet," I said grabbing Trixie, who barked and rolled on her back in my lap so I could rub her belly.

"Good, because I learned something today that is the answer to your prayers."

There was another moment of silence.

"With the help of Vidal Sassoon's protégés, I learned that you can color hair . . . with colorless dye."

And yet another silent moment.

"Trixie might be distracting me, but I don't follow."

"Concentrate, Steven!" Renée barked. "Rodrigo has been

Brian's friend for years, you've been dating him for barely three months. So Brian is not just going to dump his friend because he's got a boyfriend no matter how extra special you are. What you need to do is make Rodrigo dump Brian. Or at least not want to hang out with him."

"And how do the superbly coiffed spawn of Sassoon fit in?" Lindsay asked.

"With the help of Vidal's vinions . . ."

"I think you mean *minions*," Flynn corrected.

"Vinions sounds more dramatic," Renée countercorrected. "The *vinions* have developed a color-free hair coloring gel, which means you can dye Rodrigo's hair—any color you want—without him ever getting suspicious."

"You don't think Rodrigo will be suspicious if I'm wearing rubber gloves and rubbing gel into his hair just because the gel is color-free?" I asked.

Renée tossed a plastic tube onto the table. "He won't be suspicious if you put the gel into his shampoo."

The fourth moment of silence descended upon the table.

"Will you marry me?" Lindsay asked.

"I cannot marry a man who wears more sequins than me."

"So all Steven has to do is get this gel into Rodrigo's shampoo and before he can rinse and repeat his hair will turn a vibrant orange?"

"I actually chose green dye, Flynn, to keep it Christmasy."

"Can't you get orange? That way it can perfectly mimic the final episode of *The Brady Bunch* when Cousin Oliver and Bobby sell Greg mail-order shampoo and his hair turns orange the day before his high school graduation."

"Oh, that would be so symbolic," I said. "But risky. Brian knows the Bradys were my salvation growing up."

"It's green or it's nothing," Renée announced.

"Fine. How long will it last?" I asked.

"It's still being tested," Renée answered. "But long enough to put a dent in Rodrigo's holiday activities."

"Brian won't want to set foot out of his apartment anyway

and Rodrigo, as the superficial gay we know he is, won't want to spend time alone with Brian if his hair is completely green."

"But how are you going to get this stuff into his shampoo?" Flynn asked.

"Well . . . Brian and I are going to Rodrigo's for dinner tomorrow night. I'll just slip into the bathroom and put some in his Head & Shoulders. How much should I use?"

"Half the tube, just to be on the safe side."

Finally, my conscience intervened. "This is a terrible thing I'm doing, isn't it?"

"Yes, it is," Flynn said. "But the Argentinian deserves it. Your relationship with Brian will never fully develop if you don't take drastic action. Plus he'll never be able to trace it back to you, so I say go for it!"

Even though my instincts as well as my years of working as a soap opera producer told me that Flynn was wrong and that no one ever gets away with such harebrained schemes, I couldn't think of another breakup plan.

"Okay, I'll do it. But I need you all to take an unbreakable Christmas oath on this tube of colorless green hair dye that you will never expose my secret."

Four hands and one paw touched the plastic tube in the center of the table. All but one of them repeated the same solemn vow: "I swear on all that is holy, holly, and homo, that I will never expose Steven Bartholomew Ferrante's secret that he was the one who caused Rodrigo's hair to turn Christmas green."

Later that night I felt as befuddled as the little Misfit Girl Doll. Why was she on the Island of Misfit Toys? What was her imperfection? Could it be psychological like mine? Was I that crazed by Rodrigo's presence that I was actually going to change the essence of his hair in an attempt to loosen his grip on my boyfriend?

I still didn't have any answers by the next night. I also didn't have any control over my motor skills and I stood frozen next to Brian in front of Rodrigo's apartment. He clutched a bottle of red wine while I clutched the tube of colorless hair dye that was stuffed into the pocket of my olive green corduroy cargo pants—green in case the tube accidentally opened. Brian flashed me a smile and I was consumed with guilt, convinced that I wouldn't be able to go through with it. But when my nemesis opened the door all happy and Hispanic I got lucky because he took a moment to give Brian a hug, which gave me a moment to will my body into action.

From somewhere deep inside my head I heard a tiny voice whisper "Put one foot in front of the other." And because I always listen to the voices inside my head I did. And as a result soon I was walking 'cross the floor and into Rodrigo's apartment as if I was just a guest and not some vengeful winter warlock.

Somehow I got through dinner without self-destructing and exposing my diabolical scheme. Finally I couldn't take the suspense any longer and right before dessert was served I announced that I needed to use the little boys' room. Once again I put one foot in front of the other until I was inside ground zero. I made sure the door was locked and surprised myself by how quickly I slid back into Electra Woman undercover superhero spy mode. I surveyed the area, commented to myself that gray, yellow, and beige do not make an attractive color grouping, pulled back the shower curtain making sure not to let the metal shower curtain hooks scrape against the metal shower curtain rod, and grabbed the bottle of shampoo from the shower caddy without making a sound. It's difficult to say if I was more repulsed by my actions or by the fact that Rodrigo shampooed with Original Formula Suave.

As I poured half the contents of the hair dye into the bottle of cheap, generic brand Suave, I caught a glimpse of myself in the bathroom mirror. For a moment I felt like Lorna's character Ramona, who had once tried to drug her sister, Regina, by mixing the powder from her sleeping pill caplets into her facial cleanser. But the next moment I regained control and hoped my attempt would be more successful, for Ramona only succeeded in giving Regina an allergic rash.

The rest of the night was spent with me half-listening to Brian and Rodrigo's activity schedule for the rest of December, half-chastising myself for not having a job that has a better time-off policy, and half-erect because I have to admit playing Electra Woman gets me excited. When I fucked Brian later on that night I was half-smiling not only because I thoroughly enjoy topping my guy, but because I had a dirty little secret.

The next few days were more suspenseful than any episode of *ITNC* ever filmed. The weekend passed and Rodrigo still had not been cast as My Favorite Martian. By Tuesday there was still no word and I grew convinced that Argentinians had a different approach to hygiene and simply never washed their hair. Tuesday night Brian left for a business trip, which meant I would probably not hear about the transformation until he returned that Saturday. Fortunately, between Christmas shopping and helping my mother with the last-minute details of her Christmas extravaganza I was too busy to dwell on my misdeed. And before I knew it Saturday night had arrived.

"Where the frig is Baby Jesus?" my mother shrieked.

"Here he is!" Audrey replied, cradling the statue of Baby Jesus as if it were a real infant. "I gave him a little bath, he was very dirty. Made me feel like Mary Magdalene."

"Audrey! He's supposed to be dirty! He's sleeping in a manger next to farm animals."

"I am sorry, Anjanette, but you know that I cannot bear a dirty child."

Anjanette yanked the statue of Baby Jesus from Audrey's arms and raised it overhead. When she spoke it was as if she were auditioning for the role of the Blessed Mother in a film to be directed by Mel Gibson. "This baby is a symbol, Audrey! A symbol of how cruel and hateful people can be to one another. Don't you know the true spirit of Christmas?"

"I apologize, Anj, I just wanted to wash my Lord."

"Well, knock it off! Now go find Betty Occhipinti. She smokes. Smear some of her cigarette ash all over Jesus so it looks like he spent the night in a barn! Steven!"

Involuntarily I flinched. I was used to my mother's powerful personality, but she was starting to get Santa-nasty. I needed to channel my inner Rudolph and save the holiday.

"Mother! You need to take your own advice and knock it off. Your attitude is becoming frightful."

It was harsh, but it did the trick. "I have become frightful, haven't I? Oh, Steven, I'm sorry." Then she turned to her people and cried, "I'm sorry, everyone!"

And her people cried back, "That's all right, Anj!" "We still love you!" "You're the joy to our world, Anj!"

"Thank you. I couldn't do this without your support. And that tree has too much garland!! Steven, I've just been on edge. So many decisions, so many details, and all the while I have the evil eye of that friggin' Paula D'Agostino on my back just waiting for me to fail. At least this event has gotten me closer to God."

"By being dictatorial and dreadful to your subordinates?"

"By understanding how difficult His job is. I now know the pain of leading people."

I felt my eye twitch. I had to learn to let my mother's comments skim off my skin and not permeate my central nervous system. If not, she would succeed in leading me to an early grave. "God must be so proud that he created you in His image."

"I'm done!" Audrey shouted, entering the community room. "I've restored Jesus to his former glory."

What she did was turn the statue of Baby Jesus into Al Jolson's offspring. His entire body was covered in cigarette ash. Regardless, my mother's demeanor softened.

"He's beautiful," my mother sighed. She then put her arm around Audrey and whispered, "Only a few of us know that Jesus was really a little mulatto boy."

An hour later, the room was as unrecognizable as my mother's revisionist views on religion. She might be maniacal, but she got results. The community room where the tenants played bingo, poker, and harmless mind games as they regaled each other with hyperbolic stories of their glory days was transformed into a winter wonderland. A seven-foot Douglas fir was propped in the corner of the large room, its branches adorned with an array of red and silver decorations of every shape and size imaginable, and topped with the porcelain red-robed, white-haired angel that sat on top of every Christmas tree we ever had growing up. She, like my mother, was a little frayed and tattered at the edges, but still the queen of the holiday season.

There were also red and white poinsettia plants on every table, mistletoe hung from the ceiling (one was conveniently thumb-tacked to the top of the doorjamb at the entrance of the community room), and one entire wall was covered with hand-crocheted stockings—one for each resident of the Salvatore De-Nuccio Towers. On opposite sides of the stage where Lucas would make his New Jersey debut in less than an hour were near-life-size figurines of the Christmas season's two opposing figures. Stage left was the Nativity, complete with the blackface baby Jesus, and stage right housed fat Santa in a semi-airborne sleigh being pulled by two of his slavedeer. I would be sitting stage left because in my book mulatto beat overweight every time.

And openly gay beat closeted hands down. Finally, Lucas had figured that out for himself. When he arrived—sans eye patch and arm cast—he didn't seek me out first, nor did he wait to introduce himself to my mother; his eyes scanned the room until they landed on Flynn.

"I need to talk to you," I heard Lucas tell Flynn.

"So talk," Flynn replied.

"In private."

"So you're still afraid to be caught in public with me?"

"That's what I want to talk to you about," Lucas said. "Please."

An emotionally conflicted Flynn studied Lucas's face to determine if Lucas was acting or acting real. He decided it was the latter and led Lucas to the bathroom. The residents were so excited to see a bona fide soap opera star offscreen that they didn't even comment on the fact that two men just entered a bathroom with seating for one. I pushed an elderly woman wearing reindeer antlers out of the way so I could press my ear up against the bathroom door. I heard nothing except the bathroom fan whirling and the bells on the woman's antlers jingling.

A few minutes later the door opened and Lucas came out looking as if it were the most wonderful day of the year; Flynn looked more like a traumatized Margaret O'Brien after Judy Garland sang the completely depressing "Have Yourself a Merry Little Christmas." Whatever they had talked about ended with a difference of opinion.

"He told me he has not stopped thinking about me since the first time he saw me in Starbucks."

"I knew it! They should rename that place the Love Café!"

"And despite the fact that his agent wants him to keep his homosexuality hush-hush, he asked me out to dinner tomorrow night," Flynn said. "And then he gave me probably the most romantic kiss I have ever received in or out of a men's bathroom."

"Then why do you look like you just had a mouthful of figgy pudding?" I asked.

"Because, Steven, once I tell him that I'm HIV-positive all romantic kisses and dinners will be a thing of the past."

"Flynn, you don't know that."

"I know that he's a celebrity."

"Demi-celebrity."

"Who is anxious to move up in the ranks. One surefire way not to do that is to date a man with a non-glamorous disease."

"And there are diseases with hints of glamour?" I questioned.

"Diabetes, any cancer in remission," Flynn said.

"You're nondetectable, that's just like remission."

Flynn gave me a patronizing look. "It's not the same thing and you know it."

I didn't know what to think. I felt like my mind was split in two and one half of me was Heat Miser and one half was Snow Miser. The snowy part of me was happy that Lucas was actually gay and had finally asked my best friend out on a date. But the hot, enflamed part of me was sad because I wasn't certain that a happy ending would ever be part of Flynn's future. Sometimes I was more scared about HIV than Flynn, and he was the one living with it. So I decided to act snowy.

"This isn't a time to be scared," I said, more for me than for Flynn. "This is a time to be joyful."

"I am," Flynn declared. "Right now I'm as joyful as a lord a-leaping in a field of other naked lords. But once I admit my status to Lucas I'll be as depressed as a lonely, pear-hating partridge."

I took my friend's hand and peered into his eyes. "At least you're not pear-shaped."

Flynn laughed, but then Sebastian and Gus entered and Flynn tried to turn his laughter into a cough because Sebastian's face was as long as his dick.

"Hey, Sebastian, why so sad?" Flynn asked. "Isn't your *navidad feliz?*"

"He's just a little . . . irritated," Gus giggled.

"Gus, you promised!" Sebastian shouted.

Sebastian was so superficial that it was very easy to read between the lines. "I guess the bottom couldn't rise to the top of the occasion," I surmised.

Gus smirked. "Something like that."

Ah! Clearly Sebastian had tried to fuck Gus and couldn't get it up. It was the perfect comeuppance for Señor Sluttyslut. Unfortunately, we didn't have time to bust Sebastian's chops for not being able to bust a nut all over Gus's butt, because my mother was announcing that the concert was about to begin. We all sat down next to Paulie, Renée, and Trixie, and I saved a seat for Brian, who was going to come here directly from the airport.

"Hello, everyone, and welcome to the fourth annual Salvatore DeNuccio Tenants Group's Christmas Celebration," my mother shouted into the microphone. "I would like to thank each and every one of you from the bottom of my heart for celebrating the spirit of the season and making this year's party the best ever. And by *season* I am referring not only to Christmas, but to the lesser holidays too like Hanukkah and Kwanzaa."

It was finally clear why there was a photo of Martin Luther King, Jr. next to a menorah.

"This year is extraspecial," my mother continued, "because as I promised you so many months ago, tonight is not only a celebration of family and tradition, but also a celebration of music. Thanks to my son, Steven, we will be entertained by a major actor from the television community whose soap opera gets much better ratings than Katie Couric's nightly news program."

Even without a microphone, Paula D'Agostino could be heard cursing under her breath.

"Making his musical debut tonight is none other than Lucas Fitzgerald, that handsome young man who is the star of the TV show *If Tomorrow Never Comes*, which my son—another handsome young man—produces." My mother beamed as the De-Nuccio denizens applauded wildly. "Steven, why don't you stand up and take a bow."

Begrudgingly I stood, but I drew the line at bowing. I smiled and waved at the crowd shyly, which made the applause grow even louder. At that moment I saw that Brian had finally arrived, still wearing the baseball cap he always wears when he flies. As the applause died down, he sat in the seat next to me and then all the joy that I was feeling suddenly died too. I saw green. And not in the symbolic, envious way. I literally saw strands of green hair peeking out from underneath Brian's baseball cap.

"I'll explain later," Brian laughed nervously. "It's really kinda funny."

My heart fell to my feet faster than Yukon Cornelius fell over the side of an arctic cliff. But unlike Yukon I didn't have a bouncing Bumble to break my fall. So while my heart lay squashed and hemorrhaging on the ground, all I could do was maintain a quizzical gaze and pray to Baby Jesus and Martin Luther King, Jr. that my expression came off as sincere and not sinful. I leaned back in my chair to give Flynn, Renée, and Trixie a clear view of Brian's greenery and they were less successful in hiding their expressions. My mother, for once, interfered at just the right time.

"Ladies and gentlemen, let's give it up for Lucas Fitzgerald!"

Flynn, Renée, and Trixie's sounds of horror were drowned out by the applause. We exchanged glances that said, "How the hell did Brian's hair turn green?" "What the hell are we going to do now that Brian's hair has turned green?" and "Are we on a one-way trip to hell because we turned Brian's hair green?" The string of nonverbalized questions would have to wait to be answered, since Lucas was already asking the musical question,

"Do you hear what I hear?" All I heard was a voice deep inside my head telling me "I told you so."

The next hour was more painful than the time I volunteered at the Lower Hudson County Special Needs Institute to help out with their holiday party and got stuck singing "The Twelve Days of Christmas" with a kid who had a severe stutter. He couldn't get past five golden rings without me slapping him across the side of the head. Although the kid was grateful, I was never invited back to the school and I had a feeling that Brian would never invite me back into his life once he found out I was the one who was responsible for his green locks. But then it hit me like a ton of green bricks—why was Brian washing his hair with Rodrigo's shampoo?

My intestines wrapped themselves around each other even tighter as I imagined Brian naked in Rodrigo's shower as Rodrigo massaged dime-store Suave into his scalp. The dread I felt that my secret would be exposed was quickly being replaced by anger. I couldn't believe that my original fear—that Brian was cheating on me with Rodrigo—was coming true. I also couldn't believe that Lucas was a damn fine songstress, but that was also true.

At the same moment that I was consumed with fright, hatred, and/or remorse, I was able to hear Lucas singing a string of holiday classics in a beautiful tenor voice that would have made Bing Crosby proud and brought tears to the eyes of many of the senior citizen spectators. When Lucas sang "There's Always Tomorrow" directly to Flynn I saw a rainbow of hope that this yuletide would truly be gay. Flynn saw something else.

"Doesn't he totally put the dick in melodic?" Flynn whispered.

Lucas ended his performance with a sing-along version of "We Wish You a Merry Christmas" that got the seniors singing at the top of their congested lungs. When his performance was over and the cheering finally subsided, I needed to end my torment and find out the truth.

"Brian, what happened?" I asked.

"I'm not really sure. I didn't notice anything weird until I was on the plane and people were staring at me. At first I thought people in Ohio just aren't used to seeing a real live gay."

Something wasn't right. "I thought you said you were going to South Carolina?"

A split second pause. "Columbus, *Ohio*, not Columbus, *South Carolina*." Another pause. "Is there any food? I'm starving."

Brian made a beeline for the breadline as Flynn pointed out the geographical glitch in Brian's story.

"Sweetie, it's *Columbia*, South Carolina. Not Columbus."

My lungs felt as congested as those of the elderly celebrants surrounding me. I wanted to breathe freely but couldn't, and I knew that the reason was bad karma. I looked over at my boyfriend making small talk with a woman who was wearing a Christmas sweater the same color as his hair and wondered how much longer I'd get to call him my boyfriend. I just hoped the karmic reaction to my actions didn't screw up Flynn's chance of a happier tomorrow.

A mere five minutes later I was thrilled to discover that the karmic buck had stopped with me.

"Did you tell him?" I asked Flynn.

"Tell who what?" Brian asked with a mouthful of lasagna.

"Yes, I told Lucas that I'm HIV-positive."

"And what did he say!?" I demanded.

"That he's fine with it and in fact he's dated positive guys before."

"Good for him," Brian said. "And you."

"And then I went into this long rambling paragraph about how I was so nervous because I didn't think someone with an up-and-coming acting career would want to date someone of my status and he just smiled at me and said, 'I'm not a moron, I just play one on TV,'" Flynn said, beaming. "And then he gave me the second most romantic kiss I've ever had in my life."

"Which was the most romantic one?" Brian asked.

"The one he gave me earlier this evening in the bathroom."

"Of course. Love among the ruined tiles."

"Flynn, I am so happy for you," I said. "I just knew it would work out."

"Of course it was going to work out," Brian added. "If Steven's willing to go out with me in my condition there's no reason why Lucas wouldn't want to go out with you in yours."

Stymied, Flynn asked, "What do you mean?"

To illustrate, Brian took off his cap. "Honey, in the gay world, imperfect health is acceptable, imperfect beauty is not."

"Ay papi, did you dye your pubies red, too, so you could be a little gay Christmas elf?" Sebastian asked as he and Gus came back to the group after sampling the buffet.

"It must be a reaction to this new gel I used," Brian said, not so convincingly.

"Have you switched shampoos?" Gus asked. "Maybe you bought one of those bloody kid shampoos by mistake, the kind that temporarily dyes hair green to make shampooing fun."

Brian thought about this for a moment and then called out, "Hey, Renée!"

"Yes," Renée answered, stroking Trixie's hair faster in an effort to calm herself.

"You work in the hair industry. Any idea how this could have happened?"

"Well, there are so many factors that can cause a hair malfunction," Renée began. "But in this case I'd say there are only two ways this could have possibly happened. Either you tried to dye your hair and it went terribly awry, or you're the Grinch."

"You got me!" Brian joked. "I'm Mister Anti-Christmas. So as a hair-care professional, is there anything you can do to restore my hair to its former glory?"

"Of course. Come over by us after the party and I'll work my magic. If you're good I might even put in some highlights."

"Thanks, Renée, you're my Christmas angel."

Which made me the Christmas devil. Or just Santa. I thanked Renée for agreeing to dye Brian's hair back to its beautiful shade of blond.

"I'm really doing it for me," Renée said. "It'll be like penance."

Something in my expression must have told her that I could use a dose of penance myself.

"Are you going to confess?"

"I don't know. If I do, that's going to make Brian confess how Rodrigo's shampoo got on his head and I'm not sure if I want to know."

"The holiday sure is getting off to a great start, isn't it?"

But as Tommy Tune once warbled in a bygone Broadway musical, it's not where you start, it's where you finish. And unfortunately, the Salvatore DeNuccio Tenants Group's Christmas Celebration was not over. For one member of our group the real drama had yet to begin.

When the hoopla surrounding Lucas's concert died down, all eyes turned to Santa, who made a grand entrance pulling behind him a sleigh full of gifts. Despite my previous encounter with him, Lenny Abramawitz had ignored my threats and donned a red suit to impersonate jolly old Saint Nick. I was disgusted. I didn't care for Santa, but I knew what he represented to the world and I hated that Lenny was hoodwinking my mother and her pals into thinking he stood for the same ideals that their Santa did. However, I didn't feel I had the right to judge.

"Leonard!" Sebastian shouted.

All heads turned to see who dared call Santa by his real name.

"You gave me the gift that keeps on giving!"

"Lenny, that is so sweet," my mother shouted. "But I thought you said the foot massager was for Loni?"

While Lenny's face turned two shades redder than his costume, I turned to Sebastian to find out why he wanted to reveal that his former trick was lavishing him with gifts.

"Can I please tell 'em, mate?" Gus asked gleefully.

"Tell 'em what?" I asked.

"Oh, go ahead if it'll make you feel better," Sebastian said.

"The old man gave Sebastian herpes!"

Immediately icky thoughts of a naked, entwined Sebastian and Lenny penetrated our brains and we all made the same face. Sebastian explained that even though he was promiscuous, he was diligent when it came to his sexual health. We all made the same facial expression we had two seconds before. Right before he'd had sex with Lenny, he'd tested negative for every STD in the

Physicians' Desk Reference. On his next visit he tested positive for herpes.

"I'm sure you had sex with more people than just Lenny during that time," Flynn suggested.

"Only my regular weekly fuck buddies and we share all our medical results with each other," Sebastian said. "I'm a smart slut."

"Steven always said you were," Brian commented.

"Shut up, greenhead!" Sebastian roared. "When I went over to Gus's to fuck him, I took my dick out and I had an open sore— and it's all that old geezer's fault." He turned to the man in red. "You want to know my wish this Christmas, Santa? Take back your gift!"

"Honey, you should keep it," my mother responded. "Your feet might not hurt now, but trust me, in a few years you'll be begging for Lenny's gift."

Just as Sebastian went to undo the top button of his jeans, Lucas (ever the performer) jumped into action and diverted the attention away from the Spaniard with the STD.

"I think it's time for another sing-along!"

Lucas then led the crowd in a very loud rendition of "Santa Claus Is Coming to Town." For a few of us, the song now had an entirely different meaning. We were able to calm Sebastian down long enough to get him to promise that he would not strip down, and to convince him that any sort of confrontation would not only embarrass Lenny, but my mother and her friends as well. I was quite impressed when Sebastian said that he would never do anything to hurt a friend's mother and that he would wait to confront Lenny at the proper time. The slut had scruples.

"Didn't you see Lenny's dick when you had sex with him?" I asked.

"I half-close my eyes when I'm turning a trick," Sebastian confessed. "But it wouldn't have mattered. Have you ever seen a seventy-year-old dick? With or without herpes, a dick that old is all skanky and scabby anyway. Oh, *Dios mío!* Gus, can you take me home now? This situation is stressing me out and I feel another outbreak coming on."

* * *

Two nights later as Brian and I sat on my couch watching my absolute favorite Christmas special, *The Year Without a Santa Claus,* I was overcome with guilt.

"I have a confession," we both said.

"Let me go first," I said.

Once again Brian and I repeated each other word for word. I had to speak quicker before I lost my courage.

"I'm the one who turned your hair green."

"What?"

"I flipped out, Brian. I put hair dye in Rodrigo's shampoo so his hair would turn green and he wouldn't want to go outside in public and be with you every single day while I was at work and somehow his shampoo got on your head. And I know it was childish and stupid and I'm sorry and I really, really wish I hadn't done it and that I wasn't so jealous, but I did and I am."

"I didn't go to Columbus, Ohio or Columbus, South Carolina."

"I know."

"How do you know?"

"It's Columbia, South Carolina. Your geography isn't as good as your history."

It was Brian's turn in the confessional. "I've had plans to go away with Rodrigo to Mount Snow for some time now. It was completely platonic as is my relationship with him, but I know you're jealous of him and I knew you'd freak out if I told you we were going away on a long weekend so I lied and said I was going on a business trip. It was juvenile and stupid and *I'm* sorry and I wish I hadn't done it either."

So we both lied. It either made us even or through.

"So where does this leave us?" I asked.

"I had a talk with Rodrigo this weekend and told him that he needs to back off. Not just because it upsets you, but because it upsets me. I like you, Steven. A lot. I've been single for a long time and I'm rusty, but I want to see where this relationship can go. The problem is I can't guarantee Rodrigo is going to change overnight, so it's really up to you. Can you trust me?"

I looked into Brian's blue eyes and saw the sincerity of his words. I pulled him close and kissed him tenderly.

"Yes," I answered. "And you can trust that I won't flip out again."

"Good, because I really like the highlights Renée put in my hair."

"I'm sorry I doctored Rodrigo's shampoo."

Brian laughed. "I know. And I'm sorry I washed my hair before he did."

We made love on my couch—and then again on my bed. Rodrigo was true to his word and kept his distance, giving Brian and me the chance to have our first Christmas together and rediscover the true joys of an adult relationship. It felt good to "let go and let gay" and just embrace the man who was trying very hard to embrace me. For the first time in years I didn't feel like such a misfit, I felt like a normal gay man in a normal gay relationship. A relationship I hoped would be as beautiful and unique as Rudolph's shiny red nose.

Chapter Eleven

New Year's Eve is the perfect children's holiday. It's one of the few times kids can stay up until midnight, have a sip of champagne, and blow on a noisemaker. Good times. For adults, however, it can be a good time gone bad. Staying up past midnight is no longer a novelty, Veuve Clicquot champagne doesn't have the same kick as a kicky cosmotini, and blowing on a noisemaker is just another Saturday night. By the time the twelfth chime chimed, I was longing for the New Year's Eves of my childhood.

About two hours before midnight Brian and I showed up at Marys bar. We'd decided to ring in the new year with our friends at our favorite bar instead of spending a quiet evening in my bed with Brian's balls striking my asshole when the clock struck twelve. Actually, Brian decided and I reluctantly agreed. He promised to goose me at midnight, but it just wasn't the same thing as a good old-fashioned turn-of-the-year fuck. So when I entered Marys, it was with a forced smile.

But my smile became genuine when I saw a beaming Flynn and Lucas waltz into the bar followed by Lindsay and Donald. Two of my best friends were also going to start the new year off on the arms of new beaus. Our futures looked promising. And then the door opened and the promises of the future scrambled for the nearest exit: framed in Marys' doorway was Gus flanked by the two people I despised most.

On Gus's left was Rodrigo, who was supposed to be spending

the night with Jörgen, a six-foot-four, blond-haired, blue-eyed Swedish interpreter who spoke ten languages, one for each inch of his cock, or so his business card claimed. And on Gus's right was the woman I feared more than my mother, Gus's sister Wendolyn.

The last Gus had told us, Wendolyn was on vacation at a spa somewhere in the south of France. We all knew that *vacation* meant *doctor-mandated rest* and *spa* meant *obscure mental health-care facility that only took cash* and as always we didn't tell Gus that we knew Wendolyn was having electric shock treatments by a most likely unlicensed European psychiatrist and not having seaweed infusion treatments by a probably uncut European masseur. It didn't matter as long as it meant that we didn't have to deal with the letter-G-hating fem-Brit. A few hours before the year's end and our luck had finally run out.

"Odd-dammit!" I shouted to Flynn.

"Holy fuckin' shit," he replied, flabberhasted.

And Lindsay added, "Fellas, this is not ood!"

As Gus grabbed their coats and headed to the coatroom, Rodrigo grabbed Wendolyn's hand and headed toward us. My spine went cold. I felt like I was seven years old again and my mother was playing the *Sophie's Choice* game with me, except this time instead of being forced to give up either my beloved Big Jim doll or my *Battlestar Galactica* playset complete with Cylon fighter ships in an attempt to clean out my toychest, I had to choose between befriending what was behind Evil Door Number One or Evil Door Number Two. Once again, Brian made the choice for me.

"Roddie!" he cried. "Why aren't you fuckin' the Swede?"

"Wrong positioning," Rodrigo said, not noticing Wendolyn twitch twice. "To him, being versatile meant fucking me doggie style or fucking me on my back." Wendolyn twitched a few more times, grabbed the drink out of my hands, and chugged it down.

"Sounds like my kind of Swede," Lindsay added.

"I'll give you his card."

"So you didn't want to end the year as a bottom?" Flynn asked.

"I'm all for that, but I'm homoflawed—no matter how hard I try, I can't take ten thick inches of cock!"

"I can!" Gus shouted as he rejoined the group. "And I have!"

"Oh 'us!" Wendolyn said. "You've become so bloody American!"

I closed my eyes for a moment and said a quick prayer to Saint Stephen, my patron saint who, according to Catholic history, was the world's first martyr. I asked him for an anti-nasty blessing so I could enjoy the evening. I thought I heard Saint Stephen laugh at my request, but I couldn't be certain because Brian distracted me by tugging on my arm.

"I told you to take a nap."

"I'm not sleepy, I was saying a prayer."

Brian's smile faded and his voice become cold. "You know, I didn't plan for Rodrigo to be here."

Obviously Brian did not ask Saint Stephen for an anti-nasty blessing. Stung, I stuttered an apology for what Brian thought I was praying for and told him that I was just upset because Wendolyn was here, as whenever she's around disaster strikes. He tilted his head slightly to the left like my father did when I told him my grammar school *required* me to have an Easy Bake Oven to conduct scientific experiments. In retrospect, I believe it was my request to also have a pink Barbie Chef apron that triggered his disbelief.

"Could we make a New Year's resolution?" Brian asked.

"I'd love that."

"Let's take all our petty jealousies and insecurities, put them in a box, tie them up in a pretty little bow, and toss them into the Hudson so they can disappear from this relationship completely."

The faint whiff of bourbon mixed with a Southern drawl floated up my nostrils and I realized Brian was, at best, predrunk. I didn't want to end the year in an argument so I nodded in agreement and gave him a kiss.

"Now, sugar, you wait here for me. I'm gonna rustle us up some more of this here magic potion."

This wasn't a New Year's Eve celebration, it was the first

scene out of a lost Tennessee Williams play. Brian was starring as the Southern floozy, Wendolyn was featured as the insane grandame, and I was left to play the newspaper boy who has one scene, kisses the star, and gets booted off the stage. It was enough to make my mouth water with fury. Well, if Brian wanted a New Year's resolution that's exactly what he would get.

"Roddie, buddy!" I said, cozying up to my new best friend. "So sorry the Swede was inflexible."

"That's okay, I'm sure I'll find someone who's way under ten inches," he replied. "Are you free later on?"

Saint Stephen, where the fuck are you?! How the fuck did Rodrigo know I was way under ten inches? And why the fuck was Wendolyn suddenly arm in arm with some busty blonde?

"Steven!" Wendolyn shouted, her normal tone of voice. "This is my lady friend Lenda. Lenda Ilchrist-Oolie."

Actually her name was Glenda Gilchrist-Goolie and besides being Wendolyn's lady friend (whatever that meant), she was also a favorite subject of the British tabloids. According to the *Daily Mirror,* Lenda was the love child of the lead singer of Douche, the revolutionary Brit punk band of the '80s, who died of a heroin overdose when Lenda was two, and a British Petroleum heiress who committed suicide when Lenda was twelve. The orphan's story made Wendolyn's tortured past seem idyllic. Wendolyn explained that the two women met while she was doing PR for Lenda's soon-to-be-released tell-all tome, *Vinegar and Oil.*

"Wendy made me realize I can't run from the slippery ooze of my past," Lenda said in a bored Princess Di-ish British accent. "I have to, you know, let it enter me like cool rain on a summer's eve."

Acting as if Lenda had turned into a giant letter *G,* Wendolyn's glassy eyes filled with tears and she cried, "I need the loo!" Lenda informed us that "her Wendy" was a bit balmy these days as she had just learned she'd been fired from her stint as host of the BBC's new show *Glorious Green Gardens of Greater England.* The firing, of course, was inevitable, but it hurt just the same.

"I thought she ran off because she was wiping from back to

front again," Lindsay said. "A pussy can be dangerous, you know."

"You don't know dangerous until you've met Steven's mother," Brian said, rejoining the group. "She could teach a pussy like Wendolyn a thing or two!"

I turned to look directly at Brian to try and determine what would prompt him to make such a comment. All I saw was an unembarrassed smile as he handed me my drink.

"Hey, Stevie, maybe Wendolyn's actually your long-lost sister!" Brian shouted, then actually high-fived Rodrigo.

I'm the first one to admit that my mother is crazy, but she's my mother and I, as the offspring of crazy, have that right. Even my friends who know her understand her eccentricities and love her anyway and would never make a derogatory comment about her in or out of my presence. I looked at Lindsay and Flynn, and their hanging jaws told me that they too heard something besides the words Brian spoke. They heard something unkind.

Suddenly I heard myself mumbling, "I don't know . . . you know . . . if I would . . . um . . . put my mother and Wendolyn in the same category."

"Well, of course not," Brian said, much to my relief. "Wendolyn has a long way to go to be your mother's equal." My relief was temporary.

Brian and Rodrigo's howls of laughter were drowned out by the squeals of laughter coming from the bar. Sudden mood swings are another of Wendolyn's list of symptoms and it turned out that DJ Esqualito's real name was Medwyn Wintersham and he hailed from Sheffield, England, the same town where Lenda's father grew up, and he was a major local celebrity. So in honor of his daughter's presence at Marys, Esqualito/Medwyn decided to play Douche's biggest hit, "Yeast Infection," from their second album, *Scratch the Itch*. Very much like Twyla Tharp, Wendolyn turned her most recent personal pain into dance and pushed Lenda on top of the bar, where they both danced like it was 1984.

I tried as well to act as if it were a much more uncomplicated time and joined the dancers of Marys' makeshift mosh pit. As bodies jostled against me, thoughts jostled inside my head, angry as the lyrics that were being shouted into the air. I mentally beamed positive energy rays at the negative vibes, concentrating on the fact that I was not boyfriendless this New Year's Eve instead of the fact that my boyfriend was acting less like the boyfriend I had come to really, really like. I wasn't the only one with a boyfriend problem.

"How dare you say the O-word in my presence!" a drunken Lindsay shouted, as Douche sang about "unshowered Taiwanese."

"How dare you make me *do* the O-word last night . . . prematurely!" an equally drunk Donald shouted back, as Douche rhymed their previous lyric with "stinky cottage cheese."

"So that's what this is about! You're pissed that I made you shoot several hundred thrusts before your goal number."

"You knew I wanted to reach one thousand before the end of the year! You deliberately clenched your asshole so I couldn't make it past eight hundred."

"That's still no reason to remind me that this is an Olympic year! That's spiteful, Donald, just spiteful! And I cannot help it if my asshole is tight. I am an athlete," Lindsay spat.

"You're not an athlete!" Donald spat back. "You're a *figure skater.*"

The venom coming out of Donald was so palpable it was as if he were a life-sized plastic Massengill applicator.

"You want to see an athlete, Mr. Fuck-by-the-Numbers!? I'll show you an athlete!"

Lindsay stormed over to the DJ's booth, yanked *Scratch the Itch* from the turntable, and instructed Esqualito/Medwyn to put on a new album. Shocked but submissive, Esqualito/Medwyn acquiesced and soon the patrons of Marys were hearing the opening notes from the music of Lindsay's Olympic long program—*Yanni Live at the Acropolis.*

As the new age electronic sounds filled the air, Lindsay stood in the center of the dance floor and proceeded to do his entire pewter-award-winning skating routine, determined to prove that he who can do a triple lutz shall be called an athlete. Mouths agape, we watched Lindsay spin, leap, and jump with surprising agility and grace for a man several points over the legal drinking limit. When he launched into the straight-line footwork section of his routine, looking like Zorba's gay son, we automatically started to clap to the beat of the techno Greek music and when he took his final pose we responded with enthusiastic applause.

"If only he had skated that well in Lillehammer he might have come away with a real medal," I said.

"Wellshhugar," Brian slurred. "Ya can o'whays get whatcha wan'."

As if he were standing on center ice, Lindsay bowed to his fans one section of the audience at a time. When he got to the section that included Donald, he paused and the two men contemplated each other. After a moment, they simultaneously tilted their heads in acknowledgment that their relationship had ended right there in the midst of the cheering crowd. Lindsay turned to the next section and grandly bowed before them, not even watching Donald leave the bar. I wasn't going to romanticize their relationship as I knew it was nothing more than a fuck-buddy-with-the-occasional-dinner sort of thing, but I still felt sad that it ended so casually and with very little effort or emotion. The way I had ended many relationships.

"Looks lahk thahs one couple down," Brian said, then turned to look at me. "I wonder who's gonna be the next tah go kuhr-plunk?"

My father's face flashed before my eyes. Not because he was gay or Southern, but because there was a period of his life when he was drunk or on the verge of becoming drunk very often. I don't consider him a full-fledged alcoholic and he never missed a day of work because he was hungover (a fact of which he was quite proud), but during my early teenage years he would start his morning with a little anisette in his coffee and end his day with a little rum in his Coke. My mother made excuses for his behavior and tried to shield us from his outbursts and tirades, but I still remember the things he said to me while he was drunk. "Steven the Sissy" was his favorite barb. Even though he apologized for his remarks years later, the words—and the hatred behind them—still hung in the air and rang in my ears. I never thought anyone would make my ears ring like that again.

But now, standing next to the man I had thought I could fall in love with, my ears started ringing. A sly Alabaman drawl could hide many things, but not hatred. And that was what I heard coming out of Brian's mouth. That was what I'd been hearing in smaller doses all night long and intermittently throughout our relationship, but now the sound was strong and unmistakable. I believed that the true self often emerges when you're at your most vulnerable—sick, frightened, or, like Brian, drunk.

"Everything okay over here?" Flynn asked.

"Nothing another drink won't cure," I said.

"Now yer talkin' baby," Brian added and walked as straight as he could to the bar to get us another round of drinks. I watched him throw his arms around Wendolyn and Lenda and I prayed he wouldn't order a gimlet.

I desperately wanted to pull Flynn off into a corner and ask for a reality check, but he and Lucas looked so happy and homoesque with their arms around each other I didn't want to ruin the mood. Anyway, Lindsay beat me to it.

"Gold! Gold! That's what I should've won in Norway! A fucking Olympic gold medal!"

This sudden outburst didn't faze any of us as we've heard it all before, but Wendolyn was different. And when Lindsay shouted "Gold!" right in her face she screamed, "Bad letter! Bad letter!! Please mother of odd take the bad letter away!" As the patrons stared, perplexed but thoroughly entertained, Lenda picked her lady friend up off the floor and raced her out of the bar. If Gus had been American he might have raced after his sister or gotten upset with Lindsay for pushing her once again over the edge, but being British he just raised an eyebrow.

"I see Wendolyn's had a bit too much of the sauce," he said. "Mates, you remember Alex."

"Of the ten-inch club," Flynn said.

"Actually it's ten and a quarter," Alex responded.

"Ouch!"

"Speaking of taking ten-plus inches, has anyone seen Sebastian?" I asked.

"His sores cleared up so he decided to gather his fuck buddies and have an end of the year sex party," Gus replied with complete nonchalance.

"I hear they're serving Valtrex and Viagra as the hors d'oeuvres," Lucas quipped.

"Not to change the subject, but Alex is studying political science at NYU grad school," Gus explained. "And I thought we'd take a cue from him and end the year by discussing something important and relevant to the state of our world instead of always chattering on about sex and pop culture."

"So you want us to enter the new year bored?" Flynn asked.

"Sod off, Flynn. I want us to discuss things that matter. For instance, Alex and I were just discussing on the dance floor which group has the better rationale to win their war—the Sunnis or the Shiites?"

"Are you serious?" I asked. "There is no answer to that question. That's like asking who had the better career, Judy or Audrey Landers."

"Steven! That's exactly the type of bloody nonsense I'm talking about."

"You're absolutely right, Gus, it is nonsense," Lucas agreed. "Everyone knows Audrey Landers was the star of that family."

"How can you be so certain?" I asked.

"Audrey was a regular on *Dallas* for several seasons and was the Tits and Ass girl in *A Chorus Line: The Movie*."

"But they did some fancy editing and cut her out of the big dance number."

"That's because she had the tits and the ass, but not the dance moves."

"I guess you're right, but Judy was in *BJ and the Bear*."

"When a bear gets better billing, it's safe to say your career isn't successful."

"Okay, Audrey wins. Let's all raise our glasses in honor of Audrey."

Gus pulled Alex closer to him. "I guess we can talk politics later while you're fucking my arse again."

"Oooh, another ten-inch night?" Flynn asked.

"Ten and a quarter," Alex corrected.

Suddenly DJ Esqualito/Medwyn's voice boomed over the loud-speakers, announcing that it was five minutes until midnight. Lindsay scrambled over to us holding the hand of some twink who he announced had spent a year as a skating gargoyle with *Disney's Hunchback on Ice,* and seconds later Rodrigo scrambled over to us to announce that Brian was hunched over a toilet puking.

How perfect! Brian had spent the evening spewing bile at me and now bile was spewing from him. For a moment I thought I should let Brian puke on his own, but then I realized he was still my boyfriend and as such it was my duty to comfort him in his time of need. When he was sober I would of course blame him for ruining our first New Year's Eve together.

On my way to the bathroom DJ Esqualito/Medwyn stopped me and handed me a rose and a card. Some guy had asked him to give it to me just before midnight, then left.

"Did he give his name?" I asked.

"No, he said it was a secret."

Frank, the Starbucks Regular, flickered in front of my eyes.

"Was he by any chance . . . drinking coffee?"

"No."

"What did he look like?"

"He had a baseball cap on so I could hardly see his face. Just be happy that you have a secret admirer, eh, mate? It's kinda sweet, no?"

Yes, it was kinda sweet. But since I was on the way to the bathroom to help my puking boyfriend, it was also kinda disturbing. What was more disturbing was seeing Brian on his knees in front of the toilet throwing up about a gallon of bourbon and a splash of lime juice. He leaned back to rest and saw me standing there holding a rose which of course he thought was for him.

"Mah baybee got me a rose. Thahtsshnice."

Brian plucked the rose from my hands, sniffed it, and proceeded to throw up all over it. I opened the card and read the unfamiliar handwriting: *I've been thinking about you.* Could it be really be from Frank? Who else could be thinking about me? Thoughts of secret admirers were drowned out by the sound of the crowd counting down to midnight. While they cheered for the arrival of the new year I watched my rose swirl down the toilet bowl to the sewer below. Sitting in the stall, Brian wiped his mouth with some toilet paper and wished me a happy new year, and I managed a weak smile back. Happy Fucking New Year.

I spent the next few days exhausted from all the backpedaling. I didn't want to admit that I was having serious problems in my relationship with Brian. I didn't want to admit that the more I got to know him the more I didn't like him, because I didn't want this relationship to wind up like the rest. I was determined not to become the commitment-phobic gay guy I'd heard so much about, so I did the only thing I knew to make things better. I ignored all of Brian's bad aspects, convinced myself there were rational explanations for everything he'd said and done, and plunged myself into my work.

It was perfect timing too, since this Monday was going to be a tougher one than usual: it marked the return of Loretta Larson. We were all curious to see how a few months in a rehab center might have changed our tempestuous diva. Would she be a kinder, gentler version of herself? Would she be sober? Would she at least be a better actress? When she sashayed onto the set— and I do mean sashay—we realized immediately that Loretta had indeed changed. Her hair was now a dark espresso and her nose no longer had those thin red veins crawling all over it. The most remarkable change, however, was that Loretta was smiling and the cameras weren't even running. Laraby and I exchanged glances, and the thought occurred to me that the day might not be that bad after all. It was a premature thought.

Loretta stood in the middle of her palatial living room set and acted as if she were Gloria Swanson's stand-in. "It's so good to be back home. Why, everything's as if I never said good-bye."

"She never did say good-bye," Laraby whispered. "She just spat at all of us."

"I want to thank you all for standing by me during this most difficult time. And as I climb the twelve steps that so many others have climbed before me, I have decided to embrace my illness the way my fans have embraced me all these years."

"Oh God, I need a drink," Lourdes whispered from my other side.

"I am not going to cower in the shadows like a frightened lamb. I am stepping into the light like a proud lioness to share my story. Today I have invited the editors of *Soap Opera Digest* magazine to follow me around as I begin this new journey in my life. The journey to sobriety."

"Steven, do you know what this means?!" Laraby shrieked.

"Loretta's got herself another cover on the *Digest*?"

"Everyone's going to know that daytime's biggest star is nothing more than a drunken boozer! We cannot let that happen."

"So we just ignore the truth of what Loretta's gone through?"

"Yes! We keep up the story that she was visiting a sick uncle, has nursed him back to health, and is now able to return to work."

I thought about my own personal situation. "I don't know, Laraby. Maybe it's time to tell the truth."

"This is daytime television, Steven! Our audience doesn't want the truth. They want to see the heiress transform the bad boy into the perfect husband, they want the heroine who tragically died on the operating table to miraculously come back from the dead, they want every good citizen to have an evil twin, they do not want to know that the woman they have adored for almost thirty years is nothing more than a bitter, foulmouthed alcoholic who's tasted her own vomit more than a mother bird with ten chicks."

"Well, when you put it that way . . ." I started.

"That's the only way it can be put. Now I want you to stop this madness. Talk some sense into Loretta and get those magazine people out of here!"

"Shouldn't you do it? Loretta likes you better."

"I can't," Laraby whimpered. "I have to go to my office and cry."

Maybe Laraby was right? Maybe the truth had no place in

our job. It wasn't like I was allowing honesty to fester in my personal life, why should I let it live in my professional world? I watched Loretta being photographed on the set; she had never looked happier. As producer, it was my job to destroy that happiness.

"Excuse me, Letitia, may I have a word with you?"

Letitia Dumonde was the long-standing editor-in-chief of *Soap Opera Digest*, but she looked more like the desperate, wannabe actress she really was. She had secretly screen-tested for nine different soap operas over the past fifteen years only to be told every time that she was a far better journalist than she was an actress. And she sucked at being a journalist. The only reason she was editor-in-chief was because she was awarded the title in the divorce from her first husband, the publisher.

"You're gay, aren't you?"

And here I thought I could pass. "I beg your pardon."

"My first two husbands were gay, so I've learned to be more aware when it comes to the opposite sex."

"Kudos to you, but I don't see what that has to do with—"

"My current husband, I believe, is bisexual. He knits, but he also enjoys professional wrestling."

"Does he knit those cute little wrestling trunks? You know, the one-pieces with the straps that always shift so you can see some nipple."

"No, those he gets online."

"News flash, honey—you're three for three."

"Damn! You gays are ruining my life!"

"Well, I hate to do further damage, but I have to ask you to leave the set."

"But I'm conducting an interview with a star."

"Without permission from the network . . . so you and your homosexual photographer need to vamoose."

"Lloyd! You're a homo?"

"You cannot ask me questions about my sexual orientation."

"I'm surrounded by you people! Loretta!"

Loretta politely excused herself from Leon, the director, who

was going over the day's shooting schedule with her, and waltzed—
and I do mean waltzed—over to me and Letitia.

"I am being forced to leave the premises by this gay man."

"Why, Steven? I thought you were different from the others. I
thought you recognized honesty."

"I do recognize honesty, but I also recognize job security. And
when my boss gives me a direct order I follow it through."

"Laraby!" Loretta shrieked in a perfect mimic of her old
drunken, shrewish self. "Laraby Simmonson, get your chicken-
shit ass out here right now!"

Laraby stumbled out of his office wiping tears from his eyes.
"Y-yes?"

"Why are you trying to suppress me, Laraby?"

"Why are you trying to destroy me!? You know the show
can't take any bad publicity."

"You mean *you* can't take any bad publicity. You're so frightened of your own shadow that you refuse to allow anyone else
to push back the lace curtains and let the sun shine in."

"I just don't want the world to know about your . . . problem."

"Don't whisper, Laraby! Everybody knows my name is
Loretta Larson and I am an alcoholic."

Some of the crew spontaneously applauded.

"Hear that, Laraby? That's applause because they aren't
afraid of a character flaw. They understand people need a helping hand. Give me your hand, Laraby."

I didn't know where Loretta was going with this, but I knew
she was going to make Laraby climb a few steps of his own.

"Now repeat after me," Loretta said as she clutched Laraby's
hand. "My name is Laraby Simmonson."

"My . . . name . . . is . . . Laraby . . . Simmonson . . ."   Laraby
repeated.

"And I am a flaming homosexual."

"And I am a flaming homo . . . what? I am not!"

"Laraby, don't fight it, take that first step."

"Lots of straight men enjoy cooking and collecting antiques!"

"Just speak the truth, Laraby, it will set you free."

"No! Let go of me!"

Laraby wasn't the only one who wanted to let go. Poor homophobic Letitia also found herself in an extremely uncomfortable situation.

"Have all the straight men died?"

"Nope, they just went to gay heaven," I declared.

"Loretta! I'm outta here."

The rest of the month chugged along without too much drama. Loretta did wind up on the cover of *SOD,* in an issue that included an exclusive in-depth article about how she had battled the devil's brew since she was a teenager growing up in Montana. She embellished a little of her past history and hid some of the uglier moments, but she basically told her truth. It was a brave thing to do and although the set was far from a love-in, it became a place that was a bit calmer and less volatile. Lourdes wasn't thrilled by this change, but the network brass was ecstatic when *ITNC* shot up two full points in the ratings and maintained that increase going into the all-important February sweeps period.

My personal life was less of a ratings bonanza.

I still didn't know who had left the rose and card for me on New Year's Eve so I wasn't sure who was still thinking about me. The only rational explanation was that it was someone's idea of a practical joke so I turned over a mini–new leaf and refused to concentrate on it. Since I also refused to concentrate on Brian's shortcomings, he and I were getting along perfectly well. It helped that he had to go away on another business trip (this time a legitimate one) and that I was working overtime a lot and that we stayed away from bars and alcohol. It did still irk me that Brian never apologized for his behavior on New Year's Eve. I didn't want to bring it up because I, like many gay men I know, can be a coward. I didn't want to get into an argument because I knew that Brian didn't think there was anything to apologize for, and if he didn't apologize then I didn't want to be the one to say that I was wrong in the first place because deep down I knew I wasn't wrong. But I chose to sweep it under the relationship rug and let it fester, knowing full well that at some point I would either have to confront him about his behavior or he would simply get drunk, badmouth my mother, blame me for being hostile toward Rodrigo, and throw up during a special occasion. Deep down I knew I would be waiting for the latter to occur. But until that time arrived it would be personal business as usual.

Since our four-and-a-half-month anniversary coincided with Valentine's Day I thought it would be fun to have a romantic dinner. Brian thought so too and even volunteered to cook—and not order—dinner. He was going to cook my favorite meal—chicken cutlets, with mashed potatoes and corn. Maybe this was Brian's subconscious way of apologizing. If nothing else at least he remembered what my favorite meal was. When it comes to romance, beggars sometimes can't be choosers, so I was going to accept this dinner as an apology and be done with it.

On my way to Brian's for our celebratory dinner I felt like I was walking in sunshine even though the February sky was gray and overcast. When I turned into Rainbows & Triangles to buy Brian a mushy anniversary card, the artificial sunshine grew so bright I thought it was going to permanently blind me. For right there in front of Chelsea's premiere gay stationery store, I had bumped into my all-time favorite adult film star, Aiden Shaw.

Let this be said and understood for the generations to come: Aiden is way, way, way, way hotter looking in person. His green eyes sparkled to emit enough light that the flecks of gray in his hair looked like the silver tinsel on an angel's wings. His puckered ruby red lips were so puckery that I instinctively wanted to trace them with my tongue. And his bulging muscles bulged right out of his leather jacket and low-waist super-tight jeans. When I looked down at what appeared to be size-13 black motorcycle boots I almost shot my load right then and there in the doorway. As was to be expected, my mouth had become so dry I couldn't even speak, so Aiden spoke for me.

"Hello, sexy," he cooed.

I smiled.

"I hope I didn't hurt you. Perhaps I could take you back to my place to check for bruises."

"Huh?"

"Sorry, mate, too strong? You remind me of the first lad I ever fucked and I'd fancy a romp with you in my flat."

What poetry. Hell had just frozen over, the sky had just fallen, and Dr. Laura had just announced she was an antifamily bull dyke with an incurable lust for girl pussy. Aiden Shaw was pro-positioning me. Correction, Aiden Shaw wanted to take me home and fuck the shit out of me. I had dreamed about this moment ever since I saw his first porn video, *Night Force,* and now my dream was about to come true. So no one was more surprised than me when I said, "I can't."

"Aw, come on. We could do whatever you want. As long as I get to fuck your bum."

What a charmer! I felt like Julia Roberts in some formulaic romantic comedy where she has to decide between two incredibly hot guys and only has a second to make the decision. Why couldn't life really be like the movies? Then I could vamp while a musical montage played highlighting the special moments Brian and I had shared as well as the special moments I shared with myself watching Aiden's porn movies, and by the end I'd know what I should do.

"So what's it gonna be, sexy? You wanna get naked with me so I can relive some hot memories and give you some new ones?"

God is absolutely, positively cruel. And obviously a little bit gay because a straight man would never understand what a dilemma I was facing. Go with Aiden, get laid, then have dinner with Brian and feel guiltier than I had ever felt before. Or go to Brian's and celebrate while thinking about Aiden's ultra-fucking-hot naked body intertwined with mine.

"You have no idea how much I would love to go home with you, but I can't. My boyfriend is cooking me an anniversary dinner and I'm expected in five minutes."

Aiden looked at me as if he could see through to my soul.

"I wish I were lucky enough to have a boyfriend like you."

And with that profound statement he leaned over and kissed me full on the lips, his tongue confidently licking mine, his manly hand holding the back of my neck. He smelled and tasted as divine as he looked. He pulled away and tucked a card in the front pocket of my pants.

"If you break up with your boyfriend, call me."

I watched Aiden walk away and could not believe that that hot motherfucker was almost hotter from the rear view. I caught my breath, wiped away the sweat that was bubbling on my brow, bought Brian a very provocative card, and picked up flowers. All the way to Brian's apartment I kept turning back in case Aiden was the tenacious type and might be following me.

Dinner was wonderful, conversation was easy, and Brian was on his best behavior. Ultimately, I was glad I had chosen dinner with him over a hot steamy fuck with Aiden. At least I thought I was happy. Later than night when we were having sex and Brian's face was buried in my neck, I closed my eyes. To my surprise I didn't see Brian's face or even Aiden's, I saw Frank's. What the hell was my problem? I hadn't thought about Frank in months, but ever since I got a rose and a juvenile secret admirer card I'd automatically leapt to thinking it was this guy about whom I knew nothing. I didn't even know his last name; why was I picturing his face and not my boyfriend's? Was our relationship that screwed up and beyond repair? And why oh why can't men fake an orgasm?

Five minutes after Brian shot his load, and after much concentration, I finally came. Brian started kissing me and cuddling and I responded. How could I not respond to being treated so wonderfully and gently? But I hated myself too, because part of me wanted to push him away.

By the time I got to work the next day I had come to a decision. I could play the coward no longer. I had to talk to Brian about our relationship, to try and mend it before it got too out of shape. I wanted to know what he was thinking; was he remorseful for the things he'd said and done? Why had he said and done them in the first place? I also wanted to know if I'd been doing things that were upsetting him. Now that I had made a decision I felt good; I felt responsible, like an adult. Exactly one minute later I would feel like a scared, frightened child.

I didn't recognize the caller's number when my cell phone rang. "Hello?"

"Steven, this is Audrey. Meet me at Meadowlands Hospital as fast as you can. Your mother's had a stroke."

Chapter Twelve

My earliest memory is from when I was six years old and my parents took me to Alexander's, a now-defunct department store that was located somewhere off the New Jersey Turnpike. I remember thinking it was a magic store where all your dreams could come true. When I walked through the revolving door, my little jaw dropped as I was immediately thrust into sensory overload. The store was palatial and no matter where you looked you saw shiny chrome and bright colors all accompanied by a conflicting soundtrack of languid Muzak and the efficient, staccato rhythms of busy cash registers. I looked up at my mother, who was holding my hand, with wide-eyed innocence and joy. She understood the feeling and smiled back at me.

We walked down an aisle that was decorated on both sides with perfectly manicured mannequins wearing the most sophisticated outfits. I wanted to touch the mannequins' clothing, the fur trim, the smooth Qiana, but I thought if I made contact they would disappear. We kept walking until we reached the most amazing sight I had ever seen in my entire six-year-old life: the toy department. I wanted to rush into this magical land and grab and touch and play and fulfill every wild six-year-old dream I had, but my mother squeezed my hand to slow me down. She wanted me to stop for a moment and take in the beauty that stood before me. She wanted to give me a little moment of magic.

The only other thing I remember from that day is the ride home from the store, my brother sitting next to me rolling a huge red Tonka truck all over the car seat and me clutching the box that contained my bright yellow, two-story, Fisher-Price dollhouse. My father was yelling something that I couldn't understand, but I clearly heard my mother's reply, "There is absolutely nothing wrong with Steven. He just likes houses."

When the bus pulled up in front of Meadowlands Hospital, I had a split-second urge to stay in my seat and ride back to New York. I had not been frightened in a very long time. It's an odd feeling, being frightened, sudden and with a steel grip. And it's devious. Every couple of minutes it will release its hold and allow your mind to think of other things—the new billboard that wasn't there the last time you took the bus, the muffled sounds coming from the iPod in front of you, your first memory—but then the feeling comes back even stronger than before, along with guilt for allowing yourself to be anything but frightened.

Just before I entered the hospital I tried to call Brian a third time. The first message I left on his voice mail at work was relatively calm, the second one I left on his cell phone was serious in tone, but this one was a frantic and detailed message telling him that my mother had had a stroke and had been rushed to the hospital. On the elevator ride up to the ICU, I was able to reach Flynn.

"My mother's had a stroke, she's at Meadowlands."

"I'll be right there."

And then the doors to the elevator opened. There was no more time for phone calls or any other diversions; it was time to confront reality. I heard Audrey before I saw her.

"Steven! Over here."

She looked just as frightened as I felt.

"Where is she?"

"In the ICU. The doctors are with her now."

"Can I see her?"

"You have to ask. They won't let me in because I'm not a blood relative. As if I need blood . . . I love that woman more than I loved my sister."

"How is she, Audrey?"

Audrey looked at me with that face that you really never

want to see. It's the one that tries to, but can't, hide the pity and sorrow, the one that is always accompanied by tragic news.

"Not good. We were watching an old *Merv Griffin* on cable and his guest was Totie Fields, you remember her, don't you, Steven? Not a pretty woman, but funny. Merv asks her how she's doing since her amputation and she says she's taking it one leg at a time and actually takes off her artificial leg. I laughed so hard and I thought your mother was laughing too until she fell."

"Thank God you were there, Audrey."

"I will always be there for your mother," she said, then gave me that look again. "And for you."

Just when I thought Audrey was going to burst into tears, she shouted, "Doctor! Here's the son."

The doctor, a serious-looking Asian man, introduced himself to me, but since my mind was still filled with images of a one-legged female talk show guest, he sounded as if he spoke in the same language adopted by the adults in those Charlie Brown TV specials. The only words I could make out were *stroke, unconscious,* and *monitor.*

"At least she's stable," Audrey said.

"He said stable?"

"Yes."

Before I could quiz Audrey further about what Doctor with the Asian Last Name had said, my brother and Renée sprinted out of the elevator.

"Don't worry, she's stable," Audrey proudly exclaimed.

Renée threw her arms around me. "How is she, Steven, really?"

I could feel my voice starting to shake. "Stable like Audrey said. Other than that we don't know anything."

Renée hugged Audrey and Audrey hugged Renée back and then Audrey hugged Paulie who sort of hugged Audrey back and then it came time for Paulie and me to hug. I expected Paulie to half-hug me, which is typical, but was surprised to feel my brother's arms embrace me tightly. He held me to him close and long, the heat of his cheek warming mine, his sharp breaths tickling the nape of my neck. I was startled, but I didn't let go. I needed that hug just as much as Paulie did.

Then we waited. We drank surprisingly good hospital coffee, which Audrey took as a good sign. "If they care this much about coffee, imagine how much they care about their patients." We asked several nurses how my mother was doing, but each one merely replied with the same automated response, "I'll check with the doctor." Problem was Doctor with the Asian Last Name must have skipped out via the ICU's back door because we never saw him reemerge. So we did what every family does who's unfortunate enough to have to mark time in a hospital waiting room; we made small talk.

"You okay?" I asked Paulie.

My brother looked at me with the same anxious expression he'd worn when he was seven years old and asked me if there was a Santa Claus. Although I didn't care for the duplicitous Mr. Claus, I knew that Paulie, like most children, loved the fat liar so I asked him if he believed deep down in his heart that Santa Claus was real and he whispered, "Yes." I told him that as long as he believed in Santa, the fat man would always visit him on Christmas Eve and bring him toys. Now looking into his fearful eyes, I wished I could reassure my brother that as long as we believed deep down in our hearts that our mother would recover, she would.

"Not really," Paulie responded. "You?"

"Not at all."

I put my hand on top of my brother's and rested it there. Paulie didn't make a move to hold my hand—that would have been completely out of character—but he didn't pull away. He let my hand cover his and I believed he welcomed the connection as much as I did. My mother, whether she was conscious or not, would be happy.

Almost two hours later we still hadn't seen the doctor. Just as I was on the verge of understanding the rage behind Shirley MacLaine's character in *Terms of Endearment*, Flynn got off the elevator. He wasn't my mother's doctor, but he was a friend and I really needed one at that moment. Everyone muttered hellos and I updated Flynn on the little bit we knew about my mother's condition, then I took him aside and informed him of the other pressing matter that was causing me additional stress.

"And you're sure you were specific and told Brian that she had a stroke? You didn't just say 'call me'?"

"I explained everything. And I've sent him two text messages updating him."

Flynn took a deep breath. "Let's stay focused on your mother and worry about him later."

I wanted to spend the next hour bitching about Brian, but once again reality interceded and Doctor with the Asian Last Name finally entered the waiting room. Like no-name actors in a low-budget George A. Romero zombie film, we mechanically rose to hear the news from our leader.

"I'm sorry it's taken me so long to get to you, we had several emergencies back-to-back; it hasn't been a great day for the ICU."

The news from our leader was not starting out good.

"Anjanette's suffered a mild stroke. It doesn't appear that there has been any permanent damage. We'll monitor her overnight and she'll have to be on some medication to increase blood flow, but I think she's going to make a full recovery."

For a second there was silence as we all said our thank-yous to God, but after that solemn second the zombie spell was broken and the ICU waiting room was filled with cheers. Audrey roughly embraced Doctor with the Asian Last Name, Paulie grabbed Renée and hugged her tightly and I stood there and watched. Before today I had thought I had someone to hug at such a moment, but I was wrong. That person couldn't even respond to me no matter how hard I tried to reach him. I'm not sure what I felt first, the tears spilling down my cheeks or Flynn's arms pulling me to him. I was grateful for both.

By the time we got to see my mother, she was propped up in bed eating boiled chicken with boiled potatoes and a medley of boiled vegetables, and watching *Oprah* on a little TV the nurses wheeled over for her. Other than the two machines next to her bed and the IV tube sticking out of her arm, she looked like she was lounging in her own bedroom.

"Come quick, Oprah's gained her weight back!" she cried.

Upon closer inspection her pallor did look gray and her eyes a bit glassy—my mother's, not Oprah's—but she really did look like the mother I remembered and not a mother who had just had a stroke. We surrounded her like type-A bees around a hive, asking her repeatedly how she felt, had she been feeling poorly recently, and the usual hospital chitchat. She responded by asking where her granddog was, telling us all how much she loved us, and making a point to thank Flynn for coming.

Not long after, the nurses told us that we had to leave, but could come back tomorrow at nine. When it was just me and my mother, she took my hand and smiled at me like she did when we were strolling through the aisles at Alexander's. "I'm sorry I scared you."

"I'm just glad you're okay."

"Mama'll be fine. I'm not so sure about you, though. What's wrong?"

Even a few short hours after suffering a stroke, she could tell something was amiss in Stevenland. "I'm fine. Just worried about you."

"You're worried about something else too. Or is it a certain someone?"

I turned away, pretending to be very interested in the larger of the two machines next to her bed in order to avoid answering. Not original, but effective. "Listen to me, Steven. A mother's job is to make her children happy, so my advice is if something's worrying you . . . throw him away."

I didn't want to cry in front of my mother, but sometimes you have to do things to remind yourself that you are connected to someone else on this planet. She didn't say anything else, she didn't have to, she just put her arm around my shoulder so I could feel her connection. I felt as protected and loved as I did while sitting in the backseat of our car on the drive home from Alexander's.

That night I was forced to grow up and act like an adult. Brian finally called me back and while our conversation was not long, it was definitive.

"Hey, Steven," Brian chirped. "I have had the craziest day. Three deadlines and I had to squeeze in two production meetings. We're doing an extra double issue this year and a special stand-alone for the latest tech products so everything is hyper."

"Did you get my messages?"

"Oh yeah, I did. I just didn't have a free moment to call back." Pause. "How's your mom?"

"Well . . . she had a stroke."

"I know that. How is she?" I was hoping to hear concern in Brian's voice, but I just heard clicking. "Are you typing?"

"Sorry, this article was due yesterday. All about reverse discrimination from the gay community toward the straights, you know, heterophobia."

"She's going to be okay."

"What?"

"My mother, remember? The stroke was mild. She'll need to be on some maintenance drugs, but otherwise she'll be fine."

"Great news."

"I'm going to take off a few days and be with her so—"

"That's perfect. I am so swamped with work that I'll be living in my office. I probably won't be able to see you for a few days."

This was not the response I expected or deserved so I thought I would take one more shot. "What about the weekend? My mother'll be back home by then."

"Sorry, I can't. We have an emergency layout meeting all day on Saturday."

I was about to inquire about his Sunday schedule when he mentioned that he just got an e-mail from the primary source of his article who refused to sign a release form so he would have to throw out three-fourths of what he'd written thus far. Just throw it away. It was then that I remembered my mother's advice.

"You know something, Brian, that's not going to be a problem," I said. "Because I don't think we should see each other at all any longer."

Was that relief I heard? "Steven, don't get excited, we put the issue to bed in a week and my schedule will totally clear up after that."

"Good. Then you'll have lots more time to ignore your next boyfriend's desperate messages when he calls you to say his mother had a stroke and might be dying in the hospital!"

This time I heard a heavy sigh along with the clicking. "So that's what this is about. I told you I don't do the mother thing very well."

"You also don't do the boyfriend thing very well! I may not be perfect, Brian! I know I make lots of mistakes when it comes to relationships and I made some with you, but if someone I care for reaches out to me I'm damned well gonna respond!" At this point I had absolutely no control over my anger so I just let it all out. "You didn't even call me back to find out if she was dead! How could you be such a prick?"

The clicking continued. "I didn't think it was my place. It's not like I really know your mother."

"Cut the shit, Brian—you know *me*! What the hell have you been doing the past several months if it hasn't been getting to know *me*?"

"I've been having a great time with you, Steven. But I think . . . I don't know . . . sometimes I want more, and then sometimes I . . . sometimes I just don't."

"You know what, Brian? This isn't even about the problems in our relationship, this is about the problems with you as a person!"

"Blame it on me if it makes you feel better."

"I'll blame it on you because it's your fault! You're the one who's wrong!"

"The real problem, the way I see it anyway, is that we're on different wavelengths. We want different things."

"You're absolutely right, Brian, we do want different things," I said. "I want a boyfriend who will call me back when I tell him my mother's had a stroke! If you could have only done that I would have thought there might be some hope for us. But you didn't and there isn't, so that's it."

"Just like that?"

"Yeah," I said. "Just like that."

By the time I put down the phone I was single once again.

The next morning I knew Brian was officially a sidebar to the main article that was my life because I had no desire to call him to rehash the situation, beg his forgiveness, or tell him that my words were the result of stress. My feelings for him were just as strong as they had been yesterday and the week before, but his actions had forced me to realize he wasn't the guy for me. I could have made excuses for his behavior, but I guess when you're a gay man of a certain age you start drawing lines in the sand and if people cross them you need to put them on a raft and send them out to sea. I wished Brian bon voyage and exciting travels, but travels that would take place without me riding shot-gun.

In perfect sync with our skewed relationship, Brian had a different way of sending me out to sea. He sent me a text message saying, *Thanks for a few great months.* Actually, the message read, *Thx4fewgr8mos.* His good-bye, like our relationship, was abbreviated. In completely selfish terms, my mother's stroke-lite was a good thing as it gave me a diversion from dwelling on my failed queeromance. And when my mother was once again healthy, my job would always be there to occupy my time.

"Ssssteven," Laraby hissed over the phone. "*Ssssoap Opera Digessssst* did a ssssuper-duper job on Loretta'ssss up clossssse and persssssonal feature in thissss week'ssss issssue."

"Um, that's great news."

"She'sssss ssssuch a geniussss! Her twelve ssssstepssss changed my life!"

Obviously, Laraby had taken Loretta's advice and flung open his closet door, ripping it from its hinges—but it sounded like he was either confusing femininity with homosexuality or overnight he'd developed a speech impediment. "That's great, Laraby, but you can be gay and not talk with a lisp."

"I'm not talking with a lisssssp."

"Yes, you are. You sound like you have a slow leak."

"I'm sssssorry if you dissssapprove Sssssteven," Laraby leaked. "But thissss issss the new me. Newsssssflash: I am a homosssssexual."

"Laraby, I have to hang up. I'm at the hospital. And newsflash: the revelation of your sexual preference is not news."

"Don't be nassssty, Mary!" Laraby scolded. "And give your mom a kisssy kissss for me!"

I tried to think positively. Even though Laraby sounded like an embarrassing stereotype at least he was being open and honest about his true nature. And now that he was Loretta's disciple, maybe the soundstage would be a quieter place. Who was I kidding? He was much easier to take when he was closeted, self-hating, and afraid of Loretta's drunken shadow. It had been fun to watch him scamper around the set whenever Loretta self-destructed.

When I arrived at the ICU waiting room, Paulie and Renée were already there. Sweat appeared on my brow and palms as I immediately thought the worst. Renée passed me a napkin and quickly explained that the nurses were making the morning rounds delivering multicolored pills in Dixie cups to the patients. We waited for ten minutes, Paulie silent, Renée chatty, until we were allowed in to see my mother.

The first thing I noticed before my mother noticed us was that she looked a little scared. Not big scared like something bad was imminent, more like concerned that something bad could have happened and that something bad will probably happen very shortly. We all get that feeling every once in a while when we are forced to contemplate our own mortality. When Flynn told me that he was HIV-positive I, of course, initially thought of how this would change his life, but very soon after I thought of my own lifespan and had a look on my face similar to the one my mother was now wearing. I upped the wattage in my smile to beaming and greeted my mother with the cheeriest of cheery hellos.

"What's wrong, Steven, you look terrible. Did the doctor tell you I'm going to die?" my mother asked.

"No! I haven't even spoken to your doctor. And I don't look terrible, this is my cheery face."

"Cheery? You look terrified."

"Ma, my smile might be masking concern, but definitely not terror."

"Paulie, is he hiding anything from me?"

"No, Ma. We're just really happy you're okay."

I could see Renée touch Paulie's arm, very gently, but strongly enough to remind my brother that he wasn't alone. His expression was generally one of utter malaise so it was sometimes hard to tell what he was feeling, but now it was clear by the crack in his voice and the attentiveness of his wife that Paulie was much closer to terrified than cheery. Once again I was reminded that my brother had deep feelings, his wife truly loved him, and I was the single gay brother aka the Loser who desperately wanted someone to touch his arm gently during a moment of crisis. *Try not to be so egotistical,* I reminded myself, *there is a woman in the hospital bed in front of you who just had a stroke.*

"I'm a very lucky woman," my mother announced. "I'm not going to lie to you, this has shaken me up a bit. But I will get through this with the help of my two wonderful sons and my beautiful daughter-in-law."

"And your gorgeous friend too!" Audrey added, bursting into the ICU.

"You're a handsome woman, Audrey, but I would not go so far as to call you gorgeous."

"Someone's feeling better today."

"How *are* you feeling, Ma?" I asked.

That look of seriousness took control of her eyes once again. "I'm much better, honey. I know it's a big deal, but I'm trying not to make a big deal out of it. But it is scary."

"Yes, it is," Paulie said.

In response, Renée's gentle touch became a firm grip on her husband's hand. My mother reached out a hand to me and I took it. She reached out her other hand to Audrey and then told us all to hold hands. We stood around my mother's bed holding hands and looking like a scene from a very special episode of *The Waltons,* but none of us felt awkward or silly. We were a family and this was just one of the stupid little things families do every once in a while. The other thing they do every once in a while is speak the truth.

After the fourth time my mother asked me what was wrong I told her that I had broken up with Brian. She asked me how I felt about it and I told her that I thought it was the right decision. I was more upset that another relationship had failed than I was sad that this particular relationship had gone kaput.

"You're a good man, Steven, you'll find someone worthy. In the meantime you still have your mother."

I laughed so loud that I was chastised by one of the nurses.

Despite the antiseptic surroundings, the day was quite pleasant. We were reassured that the stroke didn't cause any permanent physical damage and my mother would only have to take one pill a day. We couldn't help but feel thankful when Audrey informed us that she would make it her duty to ensure that Anjanette took that daily pill because Anjanette—and this is where Audrey lowered her voice to a raspy whisper—sometimes forgets. While Audrey tried to convince my mother that she should keep some of her pills in her apartment as backup in case she ever ran out, I updated Renée on the Brian situation. True to her brusque New Jersey heritage, she was sympathetic but realistic.

"I'm sorry it's over," she said. "But not for nothing, I never liked him."

"He's not a bad guy."

"But he's not for you. You're worth a lot more, Steven. You need to know that."

I did know that, in theory anyway.

That night the boys and I gathered for a Starbucks summit so I could convey one mo' time what went down between Brian and me and see if I could turn that theory into practice. Halfway through my retelling I could tell they were growing bored. I could accept the fact that my love life was boring to my boyfriends, but to my friends as well? I took it as a sign—maybe I should shut up about the past and move toward the future?

"You need to get laid," Lindsay declared. "And by laid I mean fucked blind."

"I could ring Alex up and see if he's free tonight," Gus offered.

"I have a broken heart, I don't need a broken anus," I said, sounding like a character out of an X-rated gay Lifetime movie.

"Your heart isn't broken, Steven," Flynn said. "If it were you'd be home right now sulking and trying to decide if you should call Brian and beg him to take you back. You had a boyfriend for a few months and it didn't work out. You're feeling guilty because you lied to yourself that it was something more."

"Your compassion is overwhelming, Flynn," I said. "Have you considered a career in hospice care?"

"Listen to me, Steven," Lindsay bellowed. "You don't need compassion, you need a big fat dick up your ass to make you feel a little more and think a little less!"

Some of the Starbucks customers nodded in agreement and one horny-looking kid wearing an NYU sweatshirt applauded. This was not the pro-Steven summit I was anticipating. This was what Gorbachev must have felt like when he accepted Reagan's invitation. "But Ronnie, I thought ve ver juss going to have vodka and reminisce."

"You want a relationship so badly, or you think you do, that you're getting a little desperate," Flynn said.

"Face it, Steven, you knew for a long time that Brian wasn't the guy for you, but ever since Jack—"

"Flynn! You're not supposed to say the *J* word!" Lindsay said as he and Gus gasped.

"Stop it, Linds, this isn't funny. Ever since Jack dumped you you've been trying to replace him. Maybe you should just call him up and reconnect."

I felt sucker-punched, like Betty Ford's pharmacist the day she stopped refilling her prescriptions. But like Betty, if I embraced the truth it would make me stronger.

"I'm not going to apologize for wanting a boyfriend. I love being in a relationship."

"With the right guy."

"Yes. And you know Jack announced to the world that he isn't the right guy for me."

"All I know is you were extremely happy with him and you haven't been that happy since you guys broke up."

"I don't want to backtrack."

"Then move forward! And stop getting in a relationship with guys simply because you want to be in a relationship. That's very suburban. Those pseudo-relationships are really nothing more than extended hookups."

"Not that there's anything wrong with extended hookups, fellas," Gus said.

"Do you get it, Steven?" Flynn asked.

I did get it. I had gotten it before and this wasn't anything new. I knew that Brian didn't love me and I didn't love him, but I needed to create a love affair to feel connected to someone, to feel that I was worthy. Why, God, why do we put so much importance on nonfamilial, nonplatonic connections? I was faced with the reality of my life—my friends and family were supportive and dependable—why wasn't that enough to make me feel whole? Why did I have such a burning need to have a boyfriend? Was I nothing without one?

"Promise me that Brian will be the last one," Flynn said. "No more fake, inflatable boyfriends."

"Not that there's anything wrong with fake, inflatable boyfriends," Gus said.

"I promise. I will seek out a man who is genuine and not settle for one who is breathing."

"Or you could do what I do, mate, and go from one random boy to the next," Gus began. "It's completely superficial and shallow and not for the long term, but I've had more hot young arse in the past few months than I've had in my four decades on this beautiful gay earth."

"In other words," Lindsay translated, "YOU NEED TO GET LAID!"

"You have to lighten up, Steve," Flynn advised. "Maybe focus on your job and Anjanette and leave the romance thing alone for a while."

"Or I could find out if the latest college graduate I'm poking has a friend," Gus suggested.

"What's this one's name?" I asked.

"Fred."

"As in Flintstone?"

"No, silly!" Gus replied. "Sanford."

Gus explained that he was doing Fred Sanford for more than just the "stunning ebony junk" in his trunk. The kid was actually a paralegal at the Greenland embassy and he was hoping to find a legal shortcut so Wendolyn and Lenda could arrange a quickie adoption.

"Your sister wants to adopt a baby from *Guh*-reenland?" Lindsay asked.

"She feels compelled to rescue a child from a lifetime of cold weather and cross-country skiing."

"Why don't they do what all real lesbians do and adopt a baby girl from the Far East?" Flynn asked. "Because I swear to God the lesbos are trying to create a super race of dominant, flat-chested women. They take these girls out of China and Malaysia, teach them how to verbally emasculate men, use a power drill, and brew the perfect cup of tea. I tell you right here and now, their spawn will one day rule a man-free world."

"I'm not really sure if Wendolyn's a lesbian. I suspect she's a bit envious of my carefree gay lifestyle. In any event, she's got a thing against straight black hair."

"Your sister's got a thing against a lot of things, Gus," Lindsay said. "And just like Steven, it's time you ponied up to the truth bar. Wendolyn's—"

I had to cut off Lindsay before the evening turned into Gus's summit and not my own. "Thank you, boys! I really appreciate your advice and concern."

"Brilliant! So are you going to work on your emotional well-being or shall I ask Alex to fuck you six ways to Sunday? Either way, may I hold your hand during the process?"

"Gus, it might be my sudden emotional maturity, but I don't think holding your hand while getting fucked is going to help my self-esteem."

"It's always about you, Steven, isn't it?" Gus said, eyes twinkling.

"Very soon it will be."

But before I could focus on me, I had to focus on my mother, who'd been released from the hospital. The Salvatore DeNuccio Towers was disquietingly quiet for a Saturday morning when we arrived. No one was milling about in the lobby area, the community room was vacant, and the hallway was empty. When we turned the corner, however, we saw Audrey waiting in front of my mother's apartment.

"Audrey, what the hell are you doing camped out in front of my door?" my mother asked. "Did you lock yourself out again?"

Once more Audrey used her rasp-whispery voice. "I am here to tell you that everybody is in your apartment—we're throwing you a surprise Welcome Home party!" Trixie started barking her approval until Renée grabbed her snout and told her to ssh. "But they wanted me to warn you in case the surprise gave you a heart attack on top of your stroke."

My mother's eyes welled up with tears and she turned to us. "This right here is the true meaning of friendship."

I couldn't agree more.

When we opened the door we saw that Audrey was not exaggerating when she said *everybody* was attending the Welcome Home party. Every single tenant was crammed inside my mother's apartment underneath a huge WE LOVE YOU, ANJANETTE banner. There were Rosemary and Lenny, of course; and Alberta and Antonia, the seventy-five-year-old Italian twins whom my mother had known since grade school and who were dressed in identical leopard print velour track suits; Ruthie the crazy paraplegic who won the talent competition at last year's Miss Senior Secaucus beauty pageant by popping wheelies in her wheelchair while lip-syncing to Kanye West's rap ode to Evel Knievel—"Touch the Sky"—and even my mother's nemesis Paula D'Agostino, who looked like anger wrapped in a gabardine pantsuit.

As I watched my mother hold court among her peoples, I thanked God for her quick recovery. I could tell she was a bit shaky and I would have to keep a more watchful eye over her, but she would soon be on the road to being her old self again. I also thanked God for the blessing of friendship. Not just for my mother, but for me as well. We both might be single, but we had great friends. And just as my mother was listening to her friends coo and caw it was time I listened to my friends' advice and not pooh-pooh their suggestions. It was time for me to go home and douche.

If I were a financially savvy gay I would buy stock in Fleet enemas, for every gay man has, at all times, a few bottles stashed away in his bathroom. I will spare you the details, but just know that when I started to dial Aiden Shaw's phone number my colon had never been cleaner. My heart skipped a beat when numero uno porn star answered.

"Hallo," said Aiden in a voice that suggested accented gravel.

"Aiden, it's me, Steven, from Rainbows & Triangles."

"Sexy Steven who stole my heart?"

My face flushed. "One and the same."

"How are you, mate?"

"Single."

"That's brilliant!"

Then I decided to do what Flynn suggested and feel more and think less. "So I'm calling on that rain check. You want to come over and fuck me?"

"Baby, I'd love to."

Bingo!

"But I'm back in the UK."

Loser!

"May I take a rain check on the rain check?"

My heart and dick deflated. "No problem."

"Tell you what. Why don't you go out, find some hot man, take him back to your place and while he's fucking your arse, put in one of my DVDs and imagine that it's really me doing the fucking. It'll be like practicing for the real thing."

The blood poured back into both my heart and my dick. "Um, that sounds like a plan."

"I'll be back in New York in a few months. I'll call you then."

A few months!? I couldn't believe that a few days before, I had had the chance to have mind-blowing sex with my sexual fantasy and I had chosen to have dinner with Brian instead. Since I was horned up and hosed out, I decided I should fulfill Aiden's sexual fantasy and go out to hit the bars. Just as I was about to leave, however, I realized that I could bump into Brian and/or Rodrigo and as firm as I was in my belief that breaking up was the right thing to do, I wasn't ready to confront either one of them just yet. But I simply couldn't ignore the fact that I was very, very horny and an evening of self-pleasure would not cure my itch, so I decided to check out Manhunt to see if there was anyone online who resembled Aiden in the ways that were most important. After a few e-mails I turned off the computer and waited for Hank to arrive. If his dick was as big as the one in his pictures, my spleen would soon be having company.

The next day my mother noticed that I was walking funny. Were the doctors wrong and did the stroke screw up the censors in her brain? She was already quite blunt and often spoke without thinking, but could my mother turn into the real live version of Dorothy's mother, Sophia, on *The Golden Girls?*

"You have more bounce in your step. You're happier, I can tell."

"I am counting my blessings."

"And you have many."

"Yes, I do. Instead of focusing on what I lack, I am making a very conscious effort to be thankful for what's mine."

My mother gushed, "Like mother, like son."

On the way to work the next morning I was still walking funny, but funny happy and hopeful, not funny like my ass was so stretched out and hyperextended that it hurt to take a step. The magic of Alexander's Toy Department had returned. I was

in charge of my life; I had chosen to break up with Brian and return to singlehood, I had chosen not to be one miserable half of
a couple just because society likes people (gay and straight) to
be paired up. I was a proud, gay American who did not have to
settle.

The magic feeling grew stronger when I entered my office. I
took a deep breath and imagined that my mother was holding
my hand, forcing me to stop and appreciate the moment. On my
desk was another rose and card from my secret admirer. The
card read, *I think it's time we meet.*

Chapter Thirteen

If I hadn't already been standing less than fifty feet from the set of the number four daytime drama in the country, I would have felt that I had just been thrust into the surreal, sudsalicious world of the great American soap opera. A world of extreme highs and lows with all the boring stuff in the middle cut out. In the past week I had dealt with the unexpected health emergency of a loved one, I unexpectedly broke up with my boyfriend, and now I was staring at yet another unexpected missive from a mysterious stranger. The one thing I could expect: the secret storm was approaching.

I deliberately tried to ignore the fact that I had a secret admirer because as addictive as I knew it could be to an audience, I did not want my life to be a potboiler with endless storylines that only got exciting and resolved during certain sweeps weeks in November, February, and May. I wanted my life to be viewed as a neat little episode, beautifully written, but with a plot that could be wrapped up in under an hour. But whatever network was running the serial of my life had a different idea. My plotline had just thickened.

Who would send me red roses and cryptic messages?

I examined the note card more closely to see if it prompted a memory. None emerged. The handwriting remained unfamiliar and at first glance appeared to be delicate calligraphy, but upon closer assessment was revealed to be merely swirly cursive. My secret admirer might be romantic, but he was lazy. Or was he a she? Could I be sending off hetero vibes without knowing it? I did love my pleated Dockers and there had been times when I didn't wash my hands after peeing, but that was only when I peed in a very steady stream and didn't get any on my fingers. Could that be enough to fool a straight woman? They are gullible creatures.

No! My storyline was already revolutionary enough, seeing that it uniquely focused on the romantic exploits of an attractive gay man, so it didn't need to add a straight twist to the mix to make it breakthrough material. My secret admirer was definitely a man, but which man? It was time for me to be bold and once again adopt the persona of that Saturday morning superheroine, Electra Woman, who incidentally was played by soap opera icon Deidre Hall of *Days of Our Lives* fame. But this time I needed backup; I had to find my very own Dyna Girl.

"Lourdes!" I shouted into my phone. "I need you!"

Within seconds the fiery Latina was in my office.

"*¿Que pasa, jefe?*"

"Are you up to playing junior detective?"

"Do I get to carry a piece, homoslice?"

"No. But I'll buy you a slice of pepperoni pizza from Ray's for lunch."

"*Amiga,* you just bought yourself a South American sidekick."

It was true. Her people would do anything for a little something spicy.

First, I made Lourdes put her hand on my Jack Spade bag and swore her to secrecy. Second, I filled her in on the details of my secret admirer. Third, I demanded she stop giggling. Fourth, I informed her that a secret admirer was not gayspeak for stalker. Fifth, I told her that from now on we would be known as Electra Woman and Dyna Girl. And sixth, I accepted her counterproposal that henceforth we be known as Electro Papi and Latyna Girl. Sometimes immigrants could teach.

"Electro Papi?" Lourdes said.

"Yes, Latyna Girl."

"We have to get ourselves a catchphrase. We can't be a dynamic duo without one."

Would the teaching never end? The Dominican crime-fighter was right, we did need a catchphrase, but how to decide on one?

"I got it! *Beam me up, gayboy!*"

"Excuse me, but do I look geeky enough to be allowed entree to a Trekkie convention?"

"*Who loves ya, papi?* While you suck on a lollipop."

"That's a bit too homoerotic even for me."

Her black eyes almost jumped out of their sockets like they had when she found out that Juanito, the hero of her favorite Mexican telenovela, *Los Crucifixiones de Juanito,* was not a poor orphan boy who had overcome poverty and polio to become Mexico City's highest ranking lame bishop and sometime advisor to the Pope, but was actually Juanita, a wealthy post-op transsexual, who came over to Mexico from Palos Altos, Texas to escape her family of religious fanatics, hellbent on exposing the Catholic Church as the lame organization he/she deemed it to be. "How about *Watchootalkinbout, Homo?*"

"Perfect! You're ethnic and I'm not exactly tall!"

Now that we had settled on a catchphrase we could begin our investigation. Lourdes as Latyna Girl flirted with Luther, the security guard whose teeth ranged in color from ash gray to gold, and found out that there had been no visitors to the set the night before or that morning. Next she flirted with Lorenzo in the mailroom, whose hair followed the same color spectrum as Luther's teeth, but this time she had more success. She learned that a dozen roses had been delivered to the set early that morning.

"Who received them?"

"Brace yourself, Electro Papi. The roses went to Laraby."

"*¡Dios mio, no!*"

Laraby couldn't be my secret admirer, he was my boss. Plus, he had a lisp. I must find the head writer and demand a rewrite.

"I know how we can find out if Laraby is your *admirador secreto,*" Lourdes claimed.

"*¿Cómo, Latyna Girl, como?*"

"Follow me, Papi."

I followed Lourdes as she tiptoed down the hallway, her back pressed up against the wall, her index finger pressed to her lips. She dashed behind a flat that served as one of the walls to Regina's penthouse set, then down a makeshift alleyway so narrow that we had to turn sideways in order to get through to the other end. Before exiting, we did a superheroinesque slo-mo look to the left, then one to the right to make sure we weren't being watched. The few people who were dressing the set were so engrossed in their jobs we were able to dash unseen down the hallway until we came to Laraby's office.

His door was open, but from our angle we couldn't tell if he was inside. We each put an ear up against the wall, but could only hear silence. Lourdes dug into the back pocket of her one-size-too-small Lucky jeans and pulled out a slightly bruised Hershey's Kiss. I know Latinos like their sugar, but I thought it odd she would satisfy a craving while on a stakeout. Then I remembered that Laraby had a wicked sweet tooth and had been known to interrupt taping if he could smell chocolate.

As if it were a tiny silver-wrapped grenade, Lourdes bit the paper string that wraps around every Hershey's Kiss and pulled it out with her teeth. She then tossed the candy so it landed perfectly in the doorway of Laraby's office. No response. There was no explosive roar from within the office indicating that he heard, saw, or smelled the chocolate decoy. Location Laraby was empty.

"Quickly, Electro Papi, quickly."

We slinked into Laraby's office and hardly needed X-ray vision to see the beautiful bouquet of red roses in a crystal vase displayed smack dab in the center of his oversized faux marble desk. Of course my first thought was, Why couldn't *I* get a desk like that? But my second, more relevant, thought was, Why were there only eleven roses in the vase?

"Latyna Girl, count the roses."

"*¡Ay, Papi!* One's missing."

The beautiful bouquet was flawed. One of its robust red roses was missing, taken from its group and placed on my desk in an attempt to spread its message of love. The unlovely truth had to be that it was placed there by Laraby. If it were ten years ago, this storyline would have dragged on for weeks. Latyna Girl and I would have followed the scent of increasingly more complex clues; we would have crossed paths with eccentric day players, one of them most definitely played by a dwarf, perhaps even an albino dwarf; and we would have gone somewhere exotic on location. But times have changed and soap opera budgets have tightened, so this storyline was wrapped up quickly and we found our evidence before the opening credits rolled. The mystery of my secret admirer was resolved and while the audience might be titillated by this plot twist, I was horrified.

"Are rosessss sssso beautiful becaussssse they're the ssssymbol of love? Or are they the ssssymbol of love becausssse they're sssso beautiful?"

Laraby stared at us from the hallway and while he waited for our response to his lispy riddle, he popped the Hershey's Kiss in his mouth. My secret admirer was a pasty effete who would eat stray chocolate found on the ground.

"*¿Qué pasa, Papi?*" Lourdes whispered to me. "You look pale."

I took a ten spot out of my wallet and stuffed it into Lourdes's hand. "You go have that pizza, Latyna Girl. You earned it."

Before my faithful sidekick left she turned to Laraby and said, "You take good care of my papi." It was close-up worthy.

Laraby looked confused . . . or was he faking it? "I'll never undersssstand the minoritiesssss."

Once Lourdes was gone Laraby closed the door and walked toward me. I instinctively moved in the opposite direction. He kept walking and so did I, so we appeared to be playing a very slow version of musical chairs around his desk.

"I'm glad you ssssaw the flowersssss, Ssssteven."

"Before you say another word Laraby, I must insist you stop the lisping."

His stare intensified. "As you wish. I don't need a speech impediment for the world to see that I'm gay."

"No, Laraby, your gayness speaks volumes without special effects."

Laraby beamed coquettishly, but then something interesting

happened. His coquetry grew into confidence. This was a new, stronger Laraby. "These simple, yet exquisite roses mark a new era in my life."

No matter how catty I had to get, I had to break him. "I'm glad that you've decided to start a new diet."

It didn't work. "Better than that! As that prophetic nutritionist and one-time *General Hospital* contract player Richard Simmons once suggested, I've decided to Live-it."

Self-assurance was an admirable trait, but right now I wanted the old insecure, stuttering Laraby to magically appear. Obviously the writers had decided to take his character in a new direction. Damn the regime change!

"Ever since Loretta forced me to step out from the darkness of my closet my life has bloomed like one of these delicate, yet muscular, roses. I'm happier, I'm not stuttering any longer."

"I-I-I hadn't noticed."

Laraby didn't stop moving nor could he stop talking. "And the show has gone up two more points in the ratings thanks to *Soap Opera Digest*'s in-depth cover story on Loretta in which I was mentioned as 'one of Miss Larson's cadre of homosexual supporters and close friends.' They called me *homosexual*, Steven . . . in print! I'm having that page framed and placed on that wall behind you. What this all means is that I am out, proud, and ready to revel in the man-to-man love that is my right as a homo *Homo sapiens*. These flowers are a thank-you to Loretta for changing my world. I'll hand-deliver them to her after we finish taping."

I couldn't take the suspense any longer. "Why are there only eleven roses?"

Laraby finally stopped moving. He stared at me and although I tried to look away I knew it would make a better shot if I stared back at him and so I did. It was a well-produced scene and I could hear in the back of my mind, softly at first, one note of music build until it became an ominous sound.

"As a symbol of my love I sent the most beautiful rose to a man. A man I have been interested in for a very long time. I'm not sure if that man is interested in me, but I had to make a gesture. I told that man I think it's time we meet. What do you think that man will say, Steven?"

"Watchootalkinbout, Homo?" I love when a catchphrase actually fits neatly into the dialogue.

"Do you think he will respond with a romantic gesture of his own?" Laraby asked, then gasped as his puppy dog eyes grew teary and he clutched a recently manicured hand to his throat. "Do you think he will send me a box of chocolate?"

Like sands through the hourglass, Laraby inched, one step at a time, toward me, and every inch of my body wanted to move away, but that would have put me out of frame. Remarkably, I didn't flinch when he touched my arm. "Do you think my sweet will send me a sweet?"

The perspiration that began in my armpits was now speeding down my arms and the sides of my chest. I shivered. "What's wrong, Steven? Your hands are like ice," Laraby said. "Do you need me to warm you up?"

"Uh, uh . . . my mother's had a stroke!"

"Another one?!"

"No, but I think I'm getting sympathetic pains. I have to go."

I couldn't take it any longer. I wrenched myself from Laraby's hold and made a quick ungraceful exit. It was an awkward end to the scene, but the dazed expression on Laraby's face would make for a good cutaway. The boys in the control room would be pleased. I, however, needed a jolt of Starbucks and some company, so I called the only person I knew who would be free in the middle of a workday.

"Lindsay, what the hell am I going to do?"

"You're going to Iceland."

I tilted my head and raised my eyebrows much in the same way that Alexis did when Fallon came back to the Carrington mansion with bigger boobs and a British accent. "Don't you think relocating to the Arctic Circle is a bit drastic?"

"Just for the weekend."

I took a long, comforting sip of my SU and once again adopted what could become my trademark catchphrase. "Watchootalk-inbout, Homo?"

Lindsay explained that he had just been asked to skate in a by-invitation-only professional figure skating competition that weekend in Reykjavik, Iceland and that I should join him as one of his people. "They sent me two first-class tickets and since Fuck Counter is part of my very colorful past, I want you to come with me." I was intrigued, but I couldn't accept. "I have a sick mother to attend to."

"The same mother who you said was laughing it up with the crones at her welcome back party like virgins getting ready for their first panty raid? Listen, your brother and Renée will be there and the doctors said she was going to be fine. Nothing bad will happen if you go out of town for a few days."

"Iceland isn't out of town."

"It's a few hours on a plane. It takes longer to get through the tunnel to Jersey during rush hour. We leave Friday afternoon and you'll be back in your office Monday morning with a fresh new outlook and the chutzpah to tell the flaming queen cast as your boss that you want a raise, not a rose, and if he doesn't give you one you'll take the floral evidence to his boss and get his faggoty ass fired! Now go home and pack yourself a thermal thong, Steven, we're going to Iceland."

My mother insisted that I go and I knew she would be in good hands—and paws. Renée and Trixie were sleeping over on Friday and the girls were going to make lasagna for Paulie on Saturday to celebrate his five-hundredth root canal. On Sunday if my mother was feeling up to it she and Renée were going to use Paulie's money to shop for Renée's five-hundredth handbag. My mother would definitely be in good, capable hands so I jetted off to Iceland to hopefully lose myself in the hands of a good, capable Icelandic male.

Reykjavik is an odd city. Look one way and you see what resembles a typical American urban landscape, but look the other way and you see hot steam boiling up from the ground. It's disconcerting. Who wants his world to look like an entrance to the fiery pits of hell? Unless, of course, that entrance is guarded by bare-chested hunky men with chiseled features, jet black hair and ice blue eyes. And that's just what we found at our very first hot spring in the center of town. You have to love a country whose people start their day with a near naked dip into a communal pool. And thanks to Lindsay's online research we found the homo-hottest hot spring in all of Reykjavik.

"It's like a Turkish bath without the hairy backs," Lindsay squealed as hot bubbles erupted around him.

"Did you fart?" I asked.

"No, it's the spring's way of saying hello to strangers."

"A better way to say hello to strangers is like this," said a stranger in the spring. "Hi, my name is Eric."

"Hi, Eric," I said, shaking his wet hot hand. "Are you a local? Eric doesn't sound very Icelandic."

"It's actually spelled with two *i*'s and a *k*."

"Ahhh, Eriik. This is my friend . . ." When I turned to introduce Eriik to Lindsay I saw that he had drifted away into the arms of a tall, muscular man.

"I see Jason has also turned a stranger into a friend," Eriik said.

"You know Jason?"

"He's my brother. And Jason's with two *a*'s and an *e* instead of an *o*."

"Eriik and Jaasen," I said. "Two gay brothers from Iceland. Hmmm."

Eriik smirked, "Must be something in our water."

That corny line that I'm sure he used on all the gay male strangers who stumbled into his spring worked and soon I found myself staring at Eriik from the comfort of his bed. Iceland might be on the verge of bankruptcy, but very soon we were on the verge of orgasm.

An hour later I found myself at Ice Land, Iceland's only ice rink, giving Lindsay a last-minute pep talk via cell phone, when my blood went icy.

"Dick!"

"Seriously, Steven, haven't you had enough sex for one day?"

"Not that, it's Dick Button!"

"Oh, say hi for me! Tell him he's my salvation."

"He's also Laraby's obsession."

"Are you on crack?"

"No, on target. Dick's sitting at the commentators' table with Peggy Fleming, who looks absolutely stunning, I might add, and he's fixing the most beautiful red rose in his lapel."

"Steven, the hot springs have been known to cause hallucinations. It's probably his bow tie."

"I'll prove it to you."

Certain that Dick would remember me from our last memorable encounter, I put Lindsay on speaker and walked up to the commentators' table for the denouement of my mystery date storyline. Just as I was walking up to the skating legends I was hit with another huge realization—I was on location! Maybe despite the decline in ratings that started the day O.J. decided to take a spin in his Bronco, soap opera's glory of yesteryear could be relived.

"Hi, Mr. Button."

"Steven, how nice to see you again. May I introduce my colleague—"

I blushed. "Miss Fleming needs no introduction. Hello."

"Hi, Steven, welcome to Iceland."

"Oh, I've already been warmly welcomed to this gorgeous country, thank you very much. Mr. Button, may I speak with you for a moment?"

Like the first-class lady she is, Peggy knew Dick and I needed some privacy and left us. She could definitely teach Katarina Witt, two-time Olympic gold medalist and *Playboy* covergirl, about decorum.

"What would you like to speak about?" Dick asked.

"I wanted to know about your rose."

"My Irish maid?"

"No, the one in your lapel."

Dick couldn't hide a huge grin. "Ah, this rose. Young man, can you keep an old man's secret? I have a secret admirer."

"Didja hear that, world?" I shouted loud enough for Lindsay

to hear, then shut off my phone, satisfied that I had proven my point.

"It's nice to know that I can still turn a head. However, I am dedicated to the sport that has been so very, very good to me and I have no time for affairs of the heart. I have accepted this rose, but I cannot accept my admirer's request that we meet."

I was as happy and relieved as Susan Lucci the night she finally won a Daytime Emmy after her eighteen-year losing streak. Laraby was a secret admirer, but he wasn't mine and that's all that mattered. Of course there was still the matter of who my secret admirer was, but prime suspect number one was falsely accused. It didn't say much for the track record of Electro Papi and Latyna Girl, but perhaps it was time to retire my superhero cape and go back to being a full-time gay who was open to new and increasingly exciting possibilities. But my personal adventures would have to wait for the moment, as the competition was about to begin.

One after another the skating legends took the ice. I held my breath each time a skater attempted a triple salchow, flip, or loop or some combination thereof, not because I was afraid they would fall, but because I hoped they would. It's not that I had anything against Viktor Petrenko and his ice posse, but I wanted Lindsay to have all the help he needed to win.

Most of the skaters, while not as flexible and powerful as they had been in their early competitive days, skated clean programs. Some of them even reached new artistic heights—although if Flynn were in the audience he would have ripped the mic out of Dick Button's hand to tell Rudy Galindo and the packed Icelandic stadium that Stephen Sondheim's "Send in the Clowns" was not, in fact, about circus clowns and therefore the wearing of a silk pink-and-purple harlequin costume was inappropriate. It was finally Lindsay's turn to skate and as always I had to force myself to watch him with both eyes open. At least this time he didn't enter the ice with a raging hard-on or a rage against the world, he actually looked calm and composed. Maybe he realized how important this competition was. It was fine that he had been asked to perform in exhibitions and touring shows, but at the heart of every great skater is a fierce competitor. And a fierce competitor always wants one more chance to win.

Skating to the iconic music of *The Mission,* Lindsay looked incredibly trim and buff in a simple black long-sleeved shirt and pants ensemble. The shirt was adorned with a simple cross and nothing more. Even Alexei Yagudin, the former Russian Olympic champion, wore a bugle-beaded top that Peggy Fleming found to be quite *busy*.

One minute to go in his program and Lindsay looked like he might finally take home gold instead of pewter. Dick had run out of superlatives after Lindsay completed a huge triple axel, so he simply gushed about his clean edges and effortless grace. And then Lindsay fell. It was what skating insiders call a hard fall. Not one of those simple falls on the bum where the skater almost bounces back up from the ice and continues on with his program as if nothing happened, but a crash belly-first onto the ice that takes the skater careening uncontrollably twenty yards on the ice, through the protective barrier, and directly into the front row of startled fans. It's an ugly fall and it means the difference between first and fourth place. Which is exactly where Lindsay finished.

Standing once again next to, but not on top of, the podium, Lindsay clutched his pewter medal and flashed back to the horror of Norway. With the Russian national anthem playing in musical homage to Yagudin's win, Lindsay's psyche couldn't take a replay of his worst failure and he let out a guttural scream. He blindly flung his pewter medal into the audience, where it hit Nancy Kerrigan right in the shin. Nancy and Lindsay simultaneously screamed, "Not again!" but their painful cries were drowned out as Dick instructed the sound man to turn up the volume on the music.

The silence on the ride home from the airport was interrupted by the ringing of my cell phone. It was Lucas. I didn't really want to don my producer's hat for a few more hours, but talking to Lucas would be better than not talking to Lindsay.

"Flynn's in the hospital."

My first thought was irrational. It's general knowledge in the soap opera world that one hospital storyline shouldn't piggyback another. It's overkill and the audience finds it depressing. Then I went into action mode, rerouting the driver and informing Lindsay of the news, calling Gus to meet us at the hospital.

Entering the hospital room, I could only see Flynn from the waist down, lying motionless on the bed, but I could very clearly see Lucas hunched over him sobbing.

When I saw Flynn's arm reach up to stroke Lucas's back, I cried out. Flynn wasn't dying! The next moments were a jumble. I was crying; Lindsay was crying; Lucas was crying, then laughing, then crying again; and even Gus was wiping a tear from his eye and blaming us American softies for crumbling his British resolve. I hugged Flynn so hard I didn't think I'd ever let go.

I cried more in those few moments in my friend's hospital room than I had cried the whole time since I first learned my mother had a stroke. I guess you expect your parents to die; hopefully you don't spend too much time dwelling on it, but the idea is part of the parent-child contract. Friends, however, aren't supposed to die; they're supposed to make you forget about unpleasant things like death. I would forgive Flynn for this breach, but make him sign an updated version of the friend contract wherein all mentions of death were forbidden.

"Are we done with the hysterics?" Flynn asked, propped up in bed.

"What happened?" I asked.

"I started some new medicine and it gave me the dizzies."

"He passed out," Lucas corrected.

We pressed Flynn for more details and he explained that his doctor had said that the new combination of medicines Flynn had started to take sometimes triggered an adverse reaction. His was a bit more severe than usual, but it was not a cause for alarm, just an indicator that the new medicine would have to be substituted with another that had less harsh side effects. Much to Flynn's disapproval, his doctor had insisted that he stay in the hospital overnight so his response to this new medicine could be monitored.

"What's that noise?" Flynn asked.

"My stomach," Lindsay said. "I didn't eat on the plane."

"Too upset to eat because you won another pewter?" Flynn asked.

Lindsay's body language spoke volumes. "You, my friend, are so lucky I am minutes away from thinking you might die."

"We're all lucky," Lucas added.

I couldn't tell if everyone caught Flynn's reaction, but I did, and I knew that Lucas said something wrong. I couldn't imagine what it was, but I was certain that Lucas's intent and Flynn's interpretation were as disparate as J.R. and Bobby's views on who should run Ewing Oil.

"Lucas," I said, "why don't you and the boys go get us some food? We can have hospital room potluck. I'll stay with the patient."

I couldn't tell if Lucas knew that I wanted him out of the room, but like the good actor he had evolved into, he did as he was directed. When it was just Flynn and me, I found out that he and Lucas had more in common with the wayward Ewing brothers than I originally thought.

"I'm breaking up with Lucas."

"Haven't you learned not to make big decisions when you're dizzy?"

"Please put on your serious hat." I did. "Look at me, this is my future."

"Look at Lucas, *he* is your future."

"He is a very sweet man and I have fallen in love with him quicker and more deeply than I have ever fallen in love before and that is why I have to break up with him."

"Repeat after me: 'I am a stupid gay.' "

"How long do you think it's going to be before Lucas realizes an HIV-positive boyfriend who makes frequent trips to the hospital is not the type of baggage an actor needs when he's on the brink of success? I'm a liability."

"You are not a liability, you're a wonderful man! How long's it going to take for you to realize that Lucas loves you despite your illness, despite the fact that every once in a while you might have to spend a night or two in the hospital, despite the fact that you're stupid enough to even contemplate pushing him away? So you're HIV-positive! So what? It's not the best hand to be dealt, but it's not a reason to push away a chance at happiness."

"I'm afraid."

"You told me very recently to stop being afraid of being alone. Now I'm telling you that you need to stop being afraid of *not* being alone."

I knew Flynn had heard me, but like Miss Ellie after she scolded J.R. for yet another unscrupulous act, I just wasn't sure my words had any impact. Flynn wouldn't make eye contact and he wouldn't answer me when I wanted him to promise he wouldn't push Lucas aside out of fear. When the boys returned with a Chinese smorgasbord, I still didn't know on what side of the Lucas-fence Flynn was standing.

"Well, here's to another relationship gone bust," Lindsay announced.

Was Flynn and Lucas's breakup already a spoiler alert on some soap opera blog? Could bad news travel that fast on the Web? Would Pamela enter the bathroom to find her dead husband alive and showering and realize the past year was an incredibly long and specific dream? Alas, the truth was nothing quite so entertaining or unbelievable as Lindsay clarified: "Gus gave Fred the boot."

"The Greenland gay?" I asked.

"I guess I shouldn't have asked him to bend the rules for my sister's adoption as I was bent over taking his dick up my arse."

"Isn't bottoming wonderful?" Lindsay asked dreamily.

"Your sister should stick to the Far East," Flynn said, looking nothing like the despondent man he had seemed just moments earlier. "They're giving babies to anyone with a mullet."

"I'll suggest it to her," Gus said. "Once I break the news, though, I may have to hop a flight to London. Mates, I have to admit I'm noticing Wendolyn's starting to lose her grip on reality a bit."

"Starting to!" Lindsay shouted.

"Just little things, you know, besides her little thing about the letter *g*."

"Oh yes," I said, "that little thing."

"Speak of the devil," Gus declared, answering his cell phone. "It's Wendolyn. I'll take this out in the lobby."

After Gus had left, Lindsay's face held an expression that meant he was either caught with his hand in the cookie jar or with his hand on some big boy's cookies.

"I think Wendolyn's going to unravel a wee bit further."

"What's the worst that can happen?" I asked. "She and Lenda won't be able to vacation in 'reenland?"

"No, a different kind of unraveling," Lindsay said. "I did something."

I almost choked on my egg roll. "What the hell did you do?"

Lindsay swallowed a healthy mouthful of moo goo gai pan, then confessed that he had bought a large selection of vintage G-Man comics on eBay and shipped them to Wendolyn hoping they might shock her back to normal. As one who understood what it's like to be held back by a terror from your past, he was trying to help her come to terms with her own irrational fear.

"I think you done good, Linds," Flynn said. "Sometimes you need a little dose of reality to make you come to your senses."

I didn't like the tone of Flynn's comment, but I couldn't press him further since Gus came back into the room.

"How is she?" Lindsay asked.

"Not good. But she just got a note from the mailman that a post came the other day that was too large to deliver. She has to pick it up tomorrow. Maybe that'll cheer her up."

It wasn't the edge of night, but suddenly darkness crept into the room. Flynn was the only one who seemed to react favorably to the news and that worried me. I didn't know what was going on in his sort-of-young and definitely restless mind, but I sensed it wasn't full of many-splendored things. Lucas, however, once again proved me wrong and reminded us that we have one life to live so we should do our best not to fuck it up.

"I'd like to say something."

"Let's go, mates, the boys want some privacy."

"No, I'd like to say this in front of Flynn and his friends."

If we were being watched by housewives in the Midwest, the next word that would be heard would be from our sponsor.

"I'm an actor and I have a certain image to uphold, at least that's what my agent tells me."

Our sponsor had never been so shocking. And our writers had never been so bold. I couldn't believe Lucas was going to break up with Flynn in front of his friends. Maybe he was being accommodating since he knew Flynn would want the support of his friends? Or maybe beneath that aw-shucks exterior was the evil heart of a daytime supervillain?

"So I fired him and got a new agent. I told him what I'm going to tell you, Flynn. I am a gay man in love with another gay man who just happens to be HIV-positive. If the world finds out and it means the end of my career, so be it. I will not live in fear."

Aw shucks. There were no traces of evil blood in his heart.

"Does that make you afraid?"

Flynn didn't flinch. "Yes."

"Good. Then together we can find some peace."

Watching Flynn take hold of Lucas's hand inspired me. I could do the same thing. Starting tomorrow I would search for my own peace. It might involve my secret admirer, it might involve my family, it might even involve taking a trip to Dallas, Knots Landing, or Melrose Place, but wherever my search took me, I knew I would go. Because from now on, no one else was going to write the story of my life but me.

Chapter Fourteen

The most nerve-wracking moment in the life of a soap opera producer had finally arrived: it was time for the Daytime Emmy Awards. Everything that my colleagues and I had worked for during the year, every episode that we had created, was about to be judged. And not judged by an impartial panel of our peers, but by a group of bitter, desperate-to-keep-their-jobs, would-prefer-to-work-in-primetime sons o' bitches. Yes, daytime television is a nasty business.

Although many of those who worked in my industry considered it a stepping-stone to a more lucrative job, there were a handful of us who truly loved the medium of daytime TV and didn't have aspirations of producing one of the ubiquitous and now repetitive *Law & Order* franchises. We preferred to create drama in the harsh light of the sun. Unfortunately, the harsh reality was that the soap opera industry was on the critical list and while winning an Emmy wouldn't reel in more viewers, holding one while standing on the unemployment line would make you look that much more impressive. It was an accessory that I didn't yet possess, but now that *If Tomorrow Never Comes* had been nominated for Best Daytime Drama, this might be the year I, as one of its producers, brought home the winged statuette.

As expected, my emotions surrounding the event turned out to be unpredictable. I spent a day feeling post-Brian depressed because I didn't have a serious boyfriend to bring to the ceremony, but then decided to ask Lindsay to be my "date" since he would definitely do something to make me forget about my nonpartnered life. I was also able to snag two extra tickets for my mother and Renée. My mother only watched *ITNC* out of loyalty to me so she was only excited to come because there was the possibility that her son could win an award and thank his mother on national television, something Paula D'Agostino's daughter had never had the opportunity to do. Renée, in contrast, was a rabid, lifelong soap viewer and was beyond thrilled to be going to what she referred to as "*the* most important television event of the year."

"Steven," she said breathlessly, "if you see me and that hot British guy who plays Lionel on your show sneak off to the ladies' room together, you must promise never to tell Trixie."

"What about Paulie?" I asked.

"My husband understands I have certain fantasies that even he cannot fulfill."

So much for the sanctity of hetero marriage.

Regardless of what Lindsay did while among the soap opera elite or which member of the soap opera elite Renée did, the surprise of the evening would definitely involve Lucas. Not only had he been nominated for Best Actor (because ever since the eye incident his acting had vastly improved), but he was also bringing Flynn as his date. And Flynn would not be introduced as his brother, college roommate, or president of his fan club, he would be introduced as his boyfriend. When Laraby found that out, his newly opened mind shut tighter than an Italian virgin's legs while on one last fling before her wedding day and old stuttering Laraby returned.

"S-s-steven!!" Laraby screamed. "You m-m-must put an end to this!"

"I'm a producer, not a crisis manager."

"What the hell do you think p-p-producing is? You put fires out! And this flaming inferno needs to be doused with c-c-cold water before it spreads out of control and we all get burned!"

"What happened to saying good-bye to your closet, Laraby? I thought you had put your homophobia to bed and covered it up with a baby blue cashmere duvet."

"Oh, that sounds lovely, Steven! Do you think I can find one at Gracious Home?" Laraby said, then covered himself. "Oh, will you stop diverting my attention from the issue. Lucas cannot attend the Emmys with his b-b-boyfriend!"

"Well, that's what he plans to do and there's nothing you or I can do to stop him."

"You're half right. There's nothing I'm going to do, but as your boss I demand that you make him take a woman. I am!"

"What woman are you taking?"

"Loretta."

"She's not a woman, she's your beard."

"Enough, Steven! You make Lucas straight for the night and that's an order!"

Had I recently said that I wanted the old Laraby back? What the hell was I thinking? And what the hell was I thinking by actually dialing Flynn's number to ask him to *not* attend the Emmys with Lucas?

"Steven, you'll never guess where Lucas and I are right now!" Flynn said, before I could even say hello.

Could Lucas and Flynn be on some deserted island without television reception? Could I be that lucky? No.

"At Georgette Klinger for a day of beauty before the Emmys! I'm going to walk down the red carpet with my boyfriend with blemish-free skin."

"I thought you stayed away from all things red since the color clashes with your auburn hair."

"Simple solution—after my mud bath, Lucas scheduled me to have my hair highlighted with chocolate brown streaks. Hasn't he thought of everything?"

Well, not everything. "Could you put him on the phone, please? I'd like to wish him good luck in case I don't see him before the ceremony."

"Would if I could. Currently he's wrapped in cellophane from head to toe to sweat off an inch from his waist. Did you know the camera adds ten to fifteen pounds? I have to remember not to lower my chin tonight."

I wanted to tell Flynn that no one would look at his chin if he arrived holding the hand of one of the Best Actor nominees, but that would lead him to think that I thought he shouldn't be Lucas's date, which isn't what I thought. Or was it? Was I being a hypocrite? Was I as homophobic as Laraby? The answer was a very definite maybe.

Anyone in my company for two minutes knows I'm out and proud, but Lucas, whether it was deliberate or not, was still passing. I wasn't afraid for myself or for the show—Lord knows we could have used the publicity—but I was afraid for Lucas. If he were realistic he would be wrapping his head around the idea of returning to his previous career as bartender instead of wrapping fat-reducing cellophane around his body.

Suddenly I was angry. This was the twenty-first century and if American soap fans couldn't handle watching a man who likes men in real life play a man who likes women on TV, then they should just turn the channel and pray a rerun of *McMillan & Wife* wasn't airing.

"You tell Lucas I'm proud of him and even if he doesn't win, he's the best actor daytime's ever had."

"I've already told him that, but I'll let him know you agree."

I felt better about myself, having handled the crisis the only way I knew how, by admitting to myself that there really wasn't any crisis to handle. I would have to take a different approach with Loretta, who like Laraby had regressed.

In what was supposed to be a poignant reconciliation scene between Regina and Ramona, Loretta relied on old habits and went off script. Instead of acting humble, she stumbled around the set, under the influence, and called Lorna slutty, scandalous, and South Carolinian.

"How dare you!?" Lorna screamed. "I am from *North* Carolina!"

Loretta must have jumped off the wagon because she was clearly drunk. We gasped when she pulled an Absolut bottle out from underneath her skirt—I'd thought she was retaining water, not vodka. Just as she was about to chug what was left, Lourdes leaped onto the set and ripped the bottle out of Loretta's hands. How happy I was that my sidekick couldn't bear to watch a victim suffer. How sad I was when it turned out my sidekick was the victimizer.

"I'm sorry, Miss Loretta," Lourdes cried. "I turned your orange juice into a screwdriver."

Loretta's mind slowly digested this information. "You screwed with my breakfast? That's why my vodka craving came back! You lowlife immigrant, I'll fucking have you deported . . . in a body bag!"

Loretta lunged at Lourdes, who did a dive roll to the left, which resulted in Loretta crash-landing onto the floor and grasping Lorna's ankles firmly with her hands. Then Lorna lunged at Lourdes, who did a floor roll to the right, which resulted in Lorna crash-landing onto the floor grasping the ankles of Larry the cameraman firmly with her hands. As a result, Larry lunged forward and lost control of the camera, which luckily landed on Loretta's bumderwear-clad butt and bounced onto the carpet without breaking. Boozed-up and padded, Loretta never felt the impact.

There was no other direction Lourdes could roll in and she was finally subdued by security. I didn't approve of my Latyna Girl's actions, but I was proud of how valiantly she tried to escape.

A half-hour later I found myself holding a drunk and incredibly angry Loretta in the shower hoping the cold water would sober her up so she would be presentable to be a presenter later on that evening. I didn't care that I was soaking wet, Loretta would represent *ITNC* in prime time and it was my duty to do everything possible to make sure she was flawless. Even Lorna understood how important the Emmys were and volunteered to make a pot of coffee. Of course, in the middle of all this drama my mother decided to call me.

"Burgundy or black, Steven?"

"Did you try to make meatloaf again, Ma?"

"Dresses! Should I wear the burgundy dress I wore for your brother's wedding or the black one I wore to your father's funeral? I had a good time at both, so they each hold pleasant memories."

"You had a good time at Daddy's funeral?"

"I mourned for that man for two years while he was sick, I deserved a night out!"

"I was going to announce tonight that I was three months sober," Loretta slurred in between gulps of shower water. "I'll be lucky if I'm three hours sober."

"Wear the black, Ma. More than one career might die tonight."

"I can always count on you, honey," my mother said, which was exactly the same thing Loretta said to me right before she fell asleep in the shower stall.

Several hours later Loretta was dry, sober, and compassionate. Once she heard that Lourdes only spiked her juice because she missed Loco Loretta, whom she dearly loved, Loretta decided not to have Lourdes arrested or fired, but did request that she be fitted with an ankle bracelet that would give her an electric shock if she came within twenty feet of her. Loretta loved her fans, she just wanted them to fawn over her from a distance.

Before we all left to go home and change for the festivities, Laraby cornered me. He used his Tony-Soprano's-long-lost-gay-brother voice so I knew he was trying to be serious.

"Did you take care of things, Steven?"

"Yes, Loretta's alcohol free."

"I mean the other thing we talked about when we were talking about things."

"Oh, that thing."

"Yes, that thing. Did you take care of it?"

"Yes, it's been taken care of."

"I can always count on you, Steven."

Radio City Music Hall is one of those landmarks in New York that a New Yorker will walk by thousands of times and not even notice. Yeah, it's big, iconic, and has a huge neon sign, but unless it's showcasing the talents of, say, Liza, an '80s reunion band, or the Daytime Emmy Awards, who really cares? Okay, perhaps I'm speaking only about myself and the subset of gay men who are over 30 and love *Cabaret*, Kajagoogoo, and daytime television. We may be a small subset, but we're vocal.

But not as vocal as die-hard soap fans. When Lindsay and I arrived at the red carpet, the iron-lunged teenaged girls were already out in full force. Each time a hunky young soap actor touched down on the red runner, they let loose with piercing screeches that would have made a banshee proud and ignited passion in every dog from New York to the outer banks of Long Island.

Needless to say, when Lindsay and I walked down the redness there was silence. Until, of course, my mother spotted me. She raced down the runway with her black tea-length dress hiked up to her knees screaming, "Steven! Mama want an Emmy!" followed by Renée and Trixie chasing after her dressed in matching hot pink one-shoulder Grecian silk gowns. The look was pure over-dressed fan club presidents stalking a soap star. Naturally security intervened and I had to explain who I was and that the stalkers were relatively harmless relatives, though Luigi, the larger of the two security men who blocked our entry into the Music Hall, didn't hear a word I said because all his attention was focused on Renée's rack. Luckily my sister-in-law's got a nice set of jugs and Luigi accepted her story that Trixie was a service dog and allowed us to enter. I started a prayer to the Blessed Mother asking her to make the rest of the evening less bumpy, but before I could get to the Amen I overheard my mother asking Lindsay if he was happy now that he had found his real daddy, and I knew that even Jesus's mother was powerless when it came to protecting me from mine.

We did luck out and get primo seats ten rows from the stage and far away from the screaming teenaged girls. To my right sat Lucas and Flynn. "I don't care how much it costs, Flynn," I said, admiring his bronzed and glowing skin, "but for my next birthday you are getting me a spa day at Georgette Klinger."

To my left sat Laraby and Loretta. "I don't care how much it costs, Steven, but you must split those two up!" Laraby hissed at me, his face red and glowing. "So far we've gotten lucky."

It turned out that the moment Lucas and Flynn had begun their red carpet journey as a couple, they were separated. The daytime paparazzi descended upon Lucas (the absolute hottest Best Actor nominee in the past three years) with such gusto that Flynn (who was not accustomed to being photographically assaulted) was momentarily blinded by the flashing lights of the cameras and in his desperate attempt to reconnect with Lucas, found himself clasping the hand of the sturdy, horse-faced female star of *As the World Turns*. Both Flynn and Horse-face were startled by their unexpected clutch.

By the time Flynn's sight returned, Lucas was at the other end of the carpet being pushed inside by an overzealous Emmy intern. They didn't reunite until they were inside the Hall and far away from the prying eyes of the general public. I took it as a sign that perhaps the whole male-actor-with-a-boyfriend thing was really no big deal.

Then Laraby added, "And you must find out what kind of facials they got. Lucas's pores have all closed up."

I acted as if I couldn't hear the hypocritical homosexual next to me, while I couldn't help overhearing the hyperactive and hyperhormoned heterosexuals—my mother and Renée—behind me. Anjanette was talking the ear off of Susan Lucci's publicist as Renée flirted with an actor from *One Life to Live*. They both sounded as if they were enjoying themselves so heartily, I didn't have the heart to tell them the truth about their companions. Susan's publicist wore ear plugs during these functions because she was bombarded with requests from fans to be sent pieces of Susan's wardrobe or fallen strands of hair, so the woman wasn't hearing one word of my mother's monologue. And the actor Renée was hot for was being written off his show next week in the worst possible way, via a *non-exit*—industry slang for when a character simply goes down to the basement to check on the furnace or up to the attic to find an old box of photographs and is never referred to again. Such an exit is usually reserved for a character the audience does not care about, played by an actor the producers do not care about. It's cruel and unusual punishment, almost as cruel and unusual as Lindsay's commentary.

"That one over there holding the microphone, the one with the sunglasses, and those two," Lindsay said. "I've seen them all naked. And despite what outward appearances might lead you to think, it wasn't pretty."

As we sat waiting for the ceremony to begin, Lindsay pointed out that the boom operator, an usher, and two actors from the same West Coast soap had all attended the sex party he'd been at several months back. And they had a flabby butt, matching hairy ass-moles, and groin pimples, respectively.

"Wasn't there mood lighting to keep things all dark and sultry so no one could be identified in the real world?" I asked.

"I have spent my life skating in dark arenas with lights blazing in my eyes," Lindsay said. "I have excellent vision."

"Well, don't try to organize a reunion if my mother's around; she's still obsessed with your daddy."

"Isn't she sweet? If she only knew the spanking he gave me last night! I'm surprised I can sit down."

Speaking of men with open sores, out of the corner of my eye I saw Sebastian two rows in front of us holding the hand of an elderly woman, none other than Lucinda Clarke, an Academy Award nominee for best supporting actress in 1962 and grandame of *Emergency Hospital* for the past thirty-five years. How in the world had Sebastian wound up as her escort? Was superfag suddenly bi?

My thought-questions were interrupted when a fan screamed out "Lucinda, we love you!" The ancient actress stood as upright as possible and waved to her admirers, causing the freaks to let loose with a shrill siren song that could have reawakened former soap starlet Meg Ryan's career. They loved the frail and grandmotherly look; if they only knew that Lucinda was actually a chain-smoking shrew who's had plastic surgery on every inch of her body and tried to cop a feel from every actor she's ever shared a scene with. At that very moment her non-waving hand was freely exploring Sebastian's ass. And he was letting her. Was Sebastian that desperate for spending money? And why was he two rows in front of me?

"How much is she paying you?" I asked Sebastian when he scurried over to gloat that he was closer to the stage than me.

"It's a freebie," he said. "She bought me this tux and she's introducing me to Lincoln Smalls, the guy who plays her long-lost great-grandson who, she tells me, is anything but small."

"So she really does feel up the new recruits?" Lucas asked.

"*Sí, sí, chica,* she makes all the new boys strip down in her dressing room. They think it's some sort of initiation."

"Did you have to be initiated?" Lindsay asked.

"No, I just had to massage her bunions."

"Gross!" Flynn cried.

"Honey, when you've given hand jobs to eighty-year-old dicks, a bunion is like a gift from the sex gods."

"Sebastian!" my mother cried, and I prayed she hadn't heard the dick-to-bunion comparison. "Aren't you using Lenny's Christmas gift for those bunions?"

"Only once, Mrs. Ferrante, when the pain was too much to bear."

"But he will surely have another outbreak soon," Lindsay added. "Probably next month."

"That's wonderful news! I'll let Lenny know that his gift hasn't gone to waste."

Renée interrupted the unnerving bunion-disguised-as-herpes conversation to announce that Lorna Douglas had arrived on the arm of Lionel Smythe, looking like the hottest May/December romance since Demi and Ashton. They were followed by Lourdes, who was being escorted by Lorenzo from the mailroom. Lindsay whispered to me that Lorenzo was the host of the sex party he'd mentioned and that underneath his suit he was wearing the most elaborate cock ring 'n' Prince Albert combo he'd ever seen. But I finally got to trump one of his sex revelations by informing him that Lourdes's rhinestone-studded anklet was actually a court-ordered monitor.

Lindsay's eyes glazed over. "Do you think she'd let Lorenzo borrow it for the next party?"

*   *   *

After the first twenty awards were given out, *ITNC* was still empty-handed. We lost in every category from Makeup to Sound Editing to Best Original Song, which was a real surprise, because I think the lyric to our entry, "Silent Love," which rhymes *infernal needing* with *internal bleeding,* is inspired. But we had another chance to grasp the gold when Loretta, sober and smashing in Oscar de la Renta, took the stage to announce the nominees for Best Actor.

The only person in our area who looked calm was Lucas. He really didn't care if he won or not; he was truly amazed that he was even nominated and was extremely proud that he was becoming a better actor. The rest of us were experiencing the type of anxiety typically reserved for murder trial defendants when the jury foreperson passes the little piece of white paper to the judge.

Right before Loretta opened the envelope I heard Flynn whisper to Lucas, "I love you." It was the calm before the storm. The next words I heard were from Loretta, who shouted, "My costar, Lucas Fitzgerald!" He had actually won. The guy who one year ago was only expected to say his lines while unbuttoning his shirt had just taken home the Emmy for Best Actor.

Renée and Trixie were the first ones to stand up and cheer and soon our little group was jumping up and down and shouting riotously and I didn't even care that I had become one of those annoying, loudmouthed fans whose voice boxes I had wanted to rip out with my bare hands mere moments before. We were all huddled so close together jumping up and down and hugging one another that no one saw Lucas give Flynn a sweet kiss before he bounded up to the stage to accept his award from Loretta. When the crowd simmered down, Lucas began his speech.

"Thank you, Loretta, and I'd like to thank the Academy. I've always wanted to say that."

The audience hahaha'd.

"Ever since I was a young boy I've only had a few goals. One was to become a really good actor. I don't know if I've achieved that goal yet, but I hope this means I'm on the right track."

The audience hooted.

"I want to thank Loretta, Lorna, the rest of our wonderful cast and crew, my agent, my friends . . . I would not be up here on this stage without you."

The audience hurrahed.

"There's another thing that I've wanted ever since I was a young boy . . . to fall in love."

The audience hushed. I stared straight ahead, but I felt Laraby's eyes boring into me like two angry lasers and I felt Flynn's hand squeeze mine.

"And that's finally happened. I am proud to say that I have fallen in love with the most wonderful man in the world. Flynn, I love you too."

It was as if an immense vacuum had sucked every last molecule of oxygen out of the building. Every jaw dropped, every eye bulged, and I finally knew what it must have felt like to be sitting in the audience at the Academy Awards when Jack Palance announced, "The Best Supporting Actress Oscar goes to Marisa Tomei."

Flynn's hand squeezed mine tighter, Laraby's eyes seared my head, the startled audience members looked at each other in disbelief, but through it all, Lucas smiled. He was so in love and so happy at winning an award he never thought would be his, he really had no idea of the effect of his words.

Slowly, several members of the audience started to clap. Then the clapping grew and soon the entire audience was applauding and the suburban housewives in the cheap seats at the back of the house found their voices and started screaming and shouting their approval. Over the clamor one lone voice bellowed, "We love you, Lucas!" and it somehow morphed into the chant, "It's okay that you're gay!" Within seconds the entire population of Radio City Music Hall, straight, gay, and undecided, was chanting, "It's okay that you're gay!" The only voice that remained silent belonged to Laraby.

I would deal with him later; right now I had to join in a chant to celebrate my best friend's boyfriend. Despite the distance between them Flynn and Lucas were staring into each other's eyes.

Flynn was crying; Lucas was fighting back tears but looked extraordinarily relieved. He didn't have to say another word, he just held his Emmy high over his head and the crowd erupted once more.

It took a while for the audience to settle down and for the ceremony to continue. And it was a testament to how thrilled I was for both Flynn and Lucas that I didn't even care when *ITNC* lost the Best Drama award to *The Rich and the Powerful*. I felt that my show had received a much bigger prize, a place in gay history. After the ceremony we spotted Lucas being interviewed by some *Entertainment Tonight* hottie.

"That guy fucked me at the sex party!" Lindsay declared. "Twice."

"Am I the only gay who wasn't at that sex party?" I asked.

"It *was* a sold-out event."

We all joined Flynn as he stood on the sidelines while Lucas was being interviewed. We huddled together and got as close as we could to hear Lucas's responses, while not being intrusive. Well, not too intrusive. I suddenly forgot that I was a TV producer who was surrounded by daytime actors every day and instead felt like a lame member of some demi-celebrity's entourage. I had to admit that it was fun to stand on the side and watch somebody else be glorified. I felt like my mother watching me.

"How does it feel to be the first openly gay daytime soap star?" said the *ET* hottie.

"Almost as good as it feels to be the first openly gay daytime Emmy winner."

Every member of Lucas's entourage laughed and applauded except for Laraby.

"Do you think that your coming out will affect your career?"

"It might, but you know, that's not something I can control. All I can control is how I live my life and I choose to live it openly and honestly."

Once again, everyone except Laraby voiced his approval. I noticed the volume had gotten much louder and I turned around to see that our entourage had grown tenfold. Lucas's self-outing was turning out to be bigger than the Emmys themselves.

"Well, I have to say," the hottie continued, "you're an inspiration."

"I don't know about that, I'm just an actor."

"You were an actor! You're fired!"

I heard the voice, I knew the voice belonged to Laraby, but I couldn't believe the voice was actually articulating such incredibly stupid, not to mention lawsuit-invoking, words. The *ET* hottie proved quite agile (as Lindsay probably already knew) and in seconds he and his technical crew had shifted position away from Lucas and in front of Laraby to capture the latest twist in what was quickly becoming the biggest story in daytime TV history.

"Are you firing Mr. Fitzgerald because he's gay?"

"I'm an executive producer; I don't fire anyone," Laraby stammered. "*He's* firing Lucas!"

As one unit the *ET* hottie and his camera crew swiveled to the left and zoomed in on me. Now I had become Marisa Tomei and I hoped, like her, I would find the will to speak intelligently while being stared at by hundreds of dumbfounded faces. If only my cousin Vinny were around. Luckily I found my inner Marisa before there was any bloodshed.

"No one is getting fired, especially not Lucas."

"Steven, your job is on the line," Laraby said, seething.

"Then go ahead and fire me, Laraby. Do it on national television so I can sue you *and* the entire network for discrimination."

"Awwwww, shiiiiit!!!!"

That wasn't the cry of a shocked network executive, that was the cry of a shocked Lourdes. She overheard the ruckus and joined our group at precisely the same time Loretta did. While Lorenzo dragged Lourdes to a safety zone, I felt myself leave mine. I felt passion and conviction and it had nothing to do with the fact that the *ET* hottie was inches from my face, it had to do with doing the right thing. When I spoke I spoke from the heart and, of course, remembering Flynn's earlier comment, with my chin raised about a quarter of an inch.

"What Lucas Fitzgerald did tonight took guts. But it shouldn't have. He simply said that he was in love, end of story. But unfortunately our society has turned love into something controversial and wrong and I for one will never take part in helping perpetuate that myth. So I urge every gay man and woman who is hiding in a closet and living in fear to follow in Lucas's footsteps and be honest. It's time we stopped asking for approval and started telling the truth. I'm a gay man. So what? Being gay doesn't mean that you can't be an excellent TV producer or an Emmy Award–winning actor. And it definitely shouldn't mean that you're going to get fired."

At this point I actually paused and looked at Laraby, who shrank about three inches in response to my leer.

"In fact, the only things that are being dismissed here tonight are deception and hate. I suggest we replace them with truth and love. Because starting right here and right now it's time that we all just let go and let gay!"

The cheering and applause were thunderous. I had struck a chord with the entire daytime industry, straight and gay, and my little catchphrase—freely borrowed from Lindsay—would be repeated on every news channel from Anchorage, Alaska to Zolpho Springs, Florida.

"Your father always said it, Steven," my mother cried. "You're a good man."

"I strayed, Steven! This gay strayed!!" Laraby bellowed, then fell to his knees before me. "Please forgive me!"

"Ruff, ruff!" Trixie declared, and of course my attention was immediately diverted from the demented to the dachshund.

"Steven, please!" Laraby begged. "I need forgiveness."

"Oh, for crissakes!" I cried. "You're forgiven."

"Thank you! Thank you!" Laraby mumbled, clutching my legs and causing Trixie to bark maniacally.

I shoved Laraby off of me before Trixie could do any damage and shoved my way through the crowd until I reached the real man of honor.

"You didn't have to do that," Lucas said. "But I'm grateful that you did."

"Thank you," said Flynn. "You're the best friend a person could ever hope to have." Flynn gave me a hug and I gave him a kiss on the cheek.

We couldn't get near Lucas and Flynn for the rest of the evening; every news team in the city swooped in to get up close and personal with daytime's answer to Doogie Howser. Finally, around two a.m., some network brass ordered Laraby to escort Lucas and Flynn out of the media's web and they left surrounded by a gaggle of six-foot-tall security guards—one of whom Lindsay identified as a very enthusiastic and popular member of the infamous sex party.

I had suspected the evening would be memorable, but I had no idea that I would utter the sound bite that would be at the center of that memory. It's funny how most of the things you feel good about doing are things you never imagined you would do. I was still filled with joy as I waved good-bye to my mother, Renée, and Trixie and watched their limo whisk them off toward Jersey.

Bounding off the elevator back at my building I was all happy and smiling, but when I turned the corner of the hallway I saw something that changed all that. I saw another beautiful red rose in front of my door. This time the rose was held by my ex-boyfriend Jack.

Chapter Fifteen

I remember standing on a chair in my kitchen and staring at the clock over the sink when I was nine years old. I was willing the big hand to tick-tock faster to the twelve and the little hand to ease on down to the eight because then it would be the magic hour, the time for that once-a-year television event—the annual airing of *The Wizard of Oz*.

I wasn't just a friend of Dorothy, I was her BFF. I loved (and still love) everything about her and her movie. I think it's brilliant, flawless, fabulous, and every other gay adjective you can think of. I remember my mother telling me that the clock wasn't going to move any faster by me staring at it, but I didn't care, I had to do whatever I could to make Dorothy and her fellow Ozians arrive as soon as possible.

Like many a gay boy, I was fascinated by the fascinating world of that MGM classic. Not just by the flying green witch and ruby red slippers, but by the movie's dramatic themes. I connected with Dorothy on a very emotional level and understood her restlessness. Maybe even as a little boy I knew that some day when I grew up I would have to leave home in order to return. For as much as I loved my family, when I teetered on adulthood I knew I had to get out of my house and go away to college to assert my independence and accept the person I truly was. If I hadn't, I would not be able to embrace them and my childhood as I do today.

My favorite part of the movie is when Dorothy is whisked

away by the tornado and plops in Oz. Her life, like mine before coming out, was dull and shrouded in shades of gray. After I opened my closet, my world took on a Technicolor brilliance. As I stood before Jack, I once again felt like Dorothy, yanked out of everything familiar and plunged into a world that might be pretty to look at, but was also terrifyingly confusing.

"What the hell are you doing here?" I asked, sounding more like Dorothy from *The Golden Girls* than the one from Kansas.

"Stevie B.," Jack said, offering me his rose, "I'm your secret admirer."

Jack DiRenza had been many things to me—first real love, first live-in boyfriend, first destroyer of my heart. I never expected him to be my first secret admirer as well. The last time I had seen Jack was almost five years ago, when he told me that he was bored with the whole commitment thing and I was preventing him from living the life he was meant to live or some such existential bullshit jargon that simply meant "I can't stand the sight of you any longer so please get the hell out of my life." And here he was now, the guy who'd been sending me cryptic messages and flowers for five months now, standing before me holding a rose. I hadn't been so shocked since I found out Jed Clampett was the original Tin Man.

"Is Ashton Kutcher hiding somewhere?" I asked. "Am I being punked?"

"No, silly, you're being courted."

"Courted! That's what you call five months of stalking me!"

"I wasn't stalking you," Jack protested. "I was trying to get up the nerve to do this, to reveal myself to you in person."

"We were boyfriends, remember? You've revealed yourself to me before. You've even relieved yourself in front of me on more than one occasion."

"And because of all that I had to make sure this was the right thing to do."

My head was spinning faster than Dorothy's tornado. I was still a bit tipsy from the Emmy extravaganza, and it was only a few hours before dawn, so whatever language was coming out of Jack's mouth sounded to me like Munchkinese.

"I don't understand what the hell you're talking about. Is this some sort of game, Jack?"

"No, I've never been more serious in my whole life."

"More serious than the night you threw me out of your life?"

"That was a mistake."

"Oh, is that what you're calling it these days? I heard through the grapevine that you used to call it an epiphany, a turning point, a message from God."

"I never called it a message from God."

"So you think you can get from epiphany to mistake with a few clever messages and some roses?"

"No, I made that journey after years of wondering why I wasn't happy, why I was only happy when you were by my side. I screwed up, Steve, letting you go . . . correction, breaking up with you was the biggest mistake of my life and I'm glad I finally have the guts to admit that to you in person."

I wasn't in Kansas anymore. I was completely lost. I had waited to hear those words or words oh-so-similar for years, and every time I imagined Jack speaking them to me, I'd imagine myself rushing into his arms and giving him a big welcome-back-into-my-life kiss. We'd fall to the ground in each other's arms and in love and resume our life where we left off without missing a beat. But now that I was hearing those words actually spoken by Jack, I wasn't moved to move. Surprisingly, I had no desire to move within touching distance of him. It was as if I were standing at the beginning of my very own yellow brick road and I could not make my ruby slippers move one step down the road.

"Why should I believe you?" I asked.

"Because it's the truth. I don't expect you to jump for joy or forget about the past, but I've thought about this long and hard and I didn't want to be hasty, that's why I took so long to come back. I wanted to make sure my feelings weren't fleeting, that I really missed you and wasn't just missing having a boyfriend."

He was good. Or maybe he was crafty? Like the traveling salesman who sneaks into Dorothy's bag and sees a picture of

Auntie Em and tells her that someone back home loves her very much. Was I being tricked by a street corner huckster?

"So you entered into an act of duplicity to find out the truth?"

Jack flashed me another smile. "Ironic, huh? I thought that if I played secret admirer from a distance that might be enough, and I'd get over these feelings and realize that I was just being nostalgic, nothing more. But that wasn't the case, Stevie B. I fell in love with you all over again."

I took a step back and had to catch my breath. If Jack's gorgeous hazel eyes weren't completely serious I would have laughed in his face, but his sincerity was palpable. He believed what he said, but should I?

"I don't know what you expect me to do. How the hell am I supposed to react to this?"

"Just think before you make any decision. Remember what we shared, the good and the bad, and ask yourself if it's worth a second look."

By this time, Jack had moved closer to me and since my back was against the wall I had nowhere else to go. He was inches from my face and I could smell that he smelled the same way he used to smell: fresh and clean, with just a little hint of musk. I used to call it the good boy/bad boy scent. God, how I loved waking up with that smell clinging to my skin. I had missed it so much and here it was, lingering in the air right in front of me.

Neither of us could think of anything to say so we just stared at each other. Me, as lost as Dorothy in a strange, stupid, colorful world, and he, as serene and calming as a really handsome Glinda. He brushed the rose across my lips playfully and we both tried not to smile, but couldn't help it. Then my façade crumbled and my face must have softened, because the next thing I knew his forehead was leaning against mine and I could feel his warmth pressing into my body. I closed my eyes for a second to process what was happening—the guy I had loved more than any other in the world, and later, hated more than any other in the world, was back in my life, leaning against me, seconds away from kissing me passionately. Sanity did not intervene and soon I felt his lips softly kiss my cheeks, then my eyes, then my lips. I would like to say that I was repulsed that this phantom from my past would try to worm his way into my present with fervor and flora, but I wasn't. I was delighted and overjoyed and my passion was uncontainable.

Part of me wanted to give myself to him right there in the hallway of my building, but like Auntie Em, I too was a good Christian woman and I knew how to be a lady when need be, so I just threw my arms around him and kissed him back. Five minutes later I was still returning his kisses until I finally had to physically push him away. He stumbled a bit.

"I'm sorry," I said. "I didn't mean to push so hard."

"That's okay," Jack replied. "Somebody had to come to their senses, before, you know, one of us started to come."

And then it hit—the awkwardness after sexual repartee. What else do you say after you make out passionately with your ex-boyfriend whom you've tried for years to forget? Is it appropriate to say, "When can I move back in 'cause really, there's no place like home?" No, you find the courage to hold on to the last shred of dignity you have and ignore the welcoming pangs in your heart and the raging hard-on in your pants—both begging you to open your apartment door, undress your ex-boyfriend, and let him fuck you senseless—and you do the only proper thing, you step back into your happy bubble. Once inside that bubble you can think clearly and remember all the pain, the heartache, and the fury you felt over being dumped. But then through the lining of your bubble you see his smile. I don't think Jack had stopped smiling once since I turned the corner of my hallway. That stupid grin could still melt my heart.

"I don't know what you want from me, Jack," I said softly.

He touched my cheek, reddened by his five o'clock shadow. "I don't want anything except the chance to make things right between us."

"You made things really wrong, if you remember."

"I do. I remember every stupid thing I did and said and I don't blame you if you tell me to get lost. And if that's what you say, I won't bother you again," he said. "But if you think there might be the slightest chance . . . then I know I can make you happier than you ever thought you could be."

Charming *and* egotistical. Very much the Jack I remember.

"I have to think about this," I said, finally.

"Of course, take your time. I've waited this long, a bit longer isn't going to kill me."

I felt his rough beard once more and for some reason I had to fight back the tears. Was I vulnerable or grateful? I wasn't sure, but I knew I had to make a speedy exit before I did something insanely dumb like beg him to spend the night. As always, Jack could see right through me.

"I want to spend the night with you too, baby, but there are times in a man's life when he needs to be a gentleman."

Right before he turned the corner to get on the elevator, he looked back at me and said, "Sweet dreams, Stevie B." Sweet dreams!! How the hell was I going to fall asleep after that?

Once again I found myself staring at the clock, willing the big hand to haul ass toward the twelve and the little hand to make haste and reach the eight so I could call Flynn to ruin his morning after by telling him about my night before. Maybe it was the absolute desperation in my voice, but Flynn only hesitated a moment when I asked him to meet me at Starbucks without Lucas. He's obviously grown used to the SAMSEM, aka Saturday A.M. Starbucks Emergency Meeting.

Flynn stared at me in disbelief. "I cannot believe you already trumped Lucas's TV outing. If *Inside Edition* finds out about this they're going to bounce his segment."

"What the hell am I supposed to do?"

"About what?" Lindsay said, sitting down at our table with his usual grande vanilla skim latte in hand.

"I sent Linds a text when you called me," Flynn explained. "This sounded uber-important."

"And I purchased my coffee at the rival Starbucks across the street so I wouldn't waste any time," Lindsay said. "Does that finally make me the thoughtful one?"

"Steven's secret admirer is Jack," Flynn said.

Lindsay spit out a mouthful of vanilla skim latte. "You have got to be fucking kidding me." So much for thoughtfulness.

"Part of me wishes I was," I said.

Flynn made a face that resembled that of a member of the Lollipop League after accidentally sucking on one of his own sour members. "Only part of you?"

Lindsay wiped up his mouth and his mess and asked for a time-out. "My Starbucks combo of chemicals and caffeine has not yet penetrated my bloodstream so I'm still a bit groggy from spending the night with the boom operator from *The Rich and the Powerful,* whose dick incidentally could be dubbed 'The Thick and the Mouthwatering,' so forgive me if I need to step back and take this all in. Jack DiRenza, that no-good fuck who dumped you like a bad shit, has been stalking you for months to engage in a second-time-around relationship and only *part* of you wishes it t'weren't so?" Lindsay took a pause to stare at me. "Is Bobby Brown a barista? Are you drinking crack?"

"Mama concur."

"I know what it sounds like," I said trying to explain the un-explainable to myself as well as them. "And I didn't get any sleep trying to make sense of it, but . . . well . . . you know how I felt about Jack."

"And we also know how Jack made you feel," Flynn reminded me. "Uncoupled, unwanted, undone."

Lindsay continued, "Underappreciated, unnecessary, ugly. So very, very ugly. Remember how I had to practically drag you to get your unibrow waxed? Jack turned you into Ugly Steven and I will not let him do it again."

"Mama agree."

"Mama agree about what?" Gus asked, as he stood next to us holding the hand of an extraordinarily handsome six-foot-two, 225-pound (give or take) African-American hunk. My mind might be a tornado of emotions, but my homo-perception skills were as sharp as the pleat in a freshly ironed gingham skirt.

"I forwarded Flynn's text to Gus," Lindsay said. "The ex-boyfriend is the new secret admirer."

"Blimey! Jack's back."

"Armed with roses and stale bon mots," Lindsay declared. "Ooh, listen to me, I sound British."

"Jefferson," Gus said to his hunky mate, "could you get me an espresso?"

"Sure thing, babe," Jefferson sealed his comment with a kiss on Gus's lips and glided over to the Starbucks counter.

"Apologies, Steven, but Mama must know. Gus, does Jefferson own a chain of dry cleaners?"

"No, he's an actor. And a bloody good one. I saw him in a show downtown, an all-black version of *Come Back, Little Sheba*."

"What are they calling it?" Lindsay asked. "*Sheba, Where You At?*"

"Guys, could we refocus?"

"Sorry, mate. So how'd it feel to kick his sorry arse to the curb?"

"He only kicked with one foot."

"Is Flynn right?"

What's more attractive—hemming or hawing? "My, um, feelings for Jack are, well, you know, complicated."

"They bloody well shouldn't be. Not after how he treated you, Steven. One day it's *I love you*, the next it's *You're suffocating me so get the fuck out of my apartment*."

"You're all absolutely one-hundred-percent right, I know that, but last night when I looked into his eyes and saw how sorry he was, how contrite . . ."

"Contrite? Mama no like this, Steven, mama no like!"

"Despite everything he did to me it was nice to feel his arms around me again."

The three of them gasped at the same time.

Lindsay found breath first. "Tell me he did not fuck you. Or that you fucked him. Or any combination thereof."

"There was no fucking. Just some kissing."

"But you wanted him to fuck you, didn't you? You wanted him to fuck you blind!"

Jefferson gave Gus his espresso and pulled over a chair to join us. "Now that's my kind of dialogue."

"This isn't dialogue, actron," Lindsay berated him. "This is real life. Steven, continue."

"I admit it, if Jack wanted to spend the night I would have let him."

Flynn grabbed my hand, then squeezed it until he almost broke more than a few bones. "Are you insane, Steven?"

"No, just lonely."

They all looked at me with the same expression the Tin Man gives Dorothy when he realizes he must have a heart because he feels it breaking. But that expression was soon replaced with the look the Wicked Witch of the West gives her flying monkey flunky when she sees the snow-covered poppies.

"Not this lonely shit again!" Lindsay cried. "We're all lonely, Steven! We're gay men, it comes with the territory. Jack's playing games with you; if he really wanted romance and not a mind fuck he would've been up front with you and not hide behind some secret messages."

I explained to them how Jack had explained his decision to go the secret admirer route and see if he could get me out of his system. This too was greeted with skepticism, even from Jefferson.

"My last boyfriend tried to get back together with me during a scene from *Romeo and Juliet* at the Royal Shakespeare Academy in London. I was playing Tybalt and he was playing Mercutio and during one fight scene, he—"

"That's a lovely piece of theater lore, but it would be most effective if we could concentrate on the specifics of *Steven's* story. Steven, it's like ice-skating. When the ice hits your ass one too many times it's time for beer and Dick."

"Random sex isn't always the answer," Jefferson said.

"A relaxing drink and a chat with Dick *Button*! Someone much, much wiser," Lindsay explained. "Gus, will you please control your acquaintance du jour?"

Instead, Flynn took control of the conversation. "Steven, I know you want an LTR ASAP and that you're still disappointed

that it didn't work out with Brian, but desire and disappointment are no reasons to give Jack another try. He doesn't deserve
you."

"Flynn's right, mate. Jack served his purpose in your life. He
helped you realize that despite what straight America might
want us to believe, two men can set up house and live together
monogamously if they so choose."

"And they, like straight America," Lindsay continued, "can
also fuck up and destroy one another and go their separate ways
never to meet again. This is what you need to do."

The part of me that should have embraced their words had
shut down and instead I decided to ignore them.

"Guys, I hear everything you're saying and I hope you don't
hate me when I say that I'm not going to listen to one word of it.
I don't know what happened to me last night, but I haven't felt
that alive since . . . well, since I was with Jack before, and I owe
it to myself to see if the moment was fleeting or forever. So
please raise your Starbucks cups with me and put the kibosh on
those cynical looks. Remember we're friends of Dorothy, which
means we're friends of optimism."

I raised my SU and for a moment it hung alone in the air.
Then one by one my friends found the courage, the heart, and
the knowledge and raised their cups too, for they realized they
couldn't betray their friend as he was about to set out into the
unknown territory of the second-time-around romance.

The first hour of my first date with nuJack was going rather
well. He took me to a new Italian restaurant in Chelsea, *Meat &
Balls,* and we started the process of getting to know each other
all over again. Jack told me that he had been promoted and was
now the retail planner for Abercrombie & Fitch, which meant
he's the guy who decides how low jeans will ride on a boy's hips
and how much public pubic cleavage is acceptable.

Then I told him about my promotion to producer of *ITNC.*
He offered his congratulations and told me how fortunate we
both were to be succeeding in our chosen professions while not

having to hide our sexuality. We were lucky that shopping and soap operas are two gay mainstays. I was doubly impressed with his enthusiasm because I clearly remember Jack telling me that he wouldn't watch a soap unless he were in a nursing home, hooked up to an IV, and in the last stages of dementia. Obviously he was making an effort.

When job talk was exhausted, the conversation inevitably turned personal. I gave him a brief synopsis of my love life since the day we'd broken up, deleting the low points, embellishing the highs, and ending with my most recent stint as Brian's other half.

"Did you love Brian?" Jack asked bluntly.

"No, I didn't love Brian," I said with a mouthful of meatball, "not the way I loved you anyway. . . . I'm sorry, I didn't mean to say that."

"Don't ever be sorry for being honest. I told you, Steven, that's what I love most about you."

Self-consciousness crept in, at least for me anyway, and I felt every gay in the restaurant had stopped chewing and was waiting for Steven's next statement. Should I allow the angry voice deep inside me the freedom to rise and shout, "If you love honesty so much, why did you deceive me when we were living together?" Or "Why didn't you have the balls to call me up instead of sending me stupid notes?" But I decided the boys had seen enough drama for one meal and quashed those comments.

"What about you, Jack? What's your personal life been like?"

For the first time all night, Jack struggled. Was he searching for the right way to express the truth of his life or the right lie to cover it up? I wasn't sure—until he started speaking.

"It's been a mess. It's been one random hookup after another. I've had a long series of really hot twenty-minute relationships with every kind of guy you can dream up. Hunky, hefty, bigdicked, little-dicked, overeducated, underfed—you name it, I've fucked it. I even tried to extend some of those twenty-minutes into a couple hours. But none of them ever worked out."

"Why?"

"Because none of them could make me forget about you."

It was Jack's turn to be way too honest. Much to his credit, he didn't run away from it.

"When we were together I thought it was too good to be true; I convinced myself that it was playacting and would never last. I had to get out before you left me, as I was sure you would." Jack smiled sadly, but it wasn't for my benefit. "Once I was on my own I figured out pretty quickly that the only thing in my life that had any worth was my time with you. I'm sorry it took me so long to let you in on my secret."

I tried not to think about what I should say next, but concentrate on how I was feeling right at this moment. "I wish you had never left us."

"Me too."

Jack paid for dinner and I asked him to stay the night. The sex, as expected, was mind-blowing. Imagine a filmic montage of the reunion between Dorothy and the brainy farmhand if they'd been having an illicit affair behind Auntie Em's back. Jack and I started out rough and passionate, with clothes being torn off and tossed aside; then there was the pause when we were completely naked and realized that after five years apart we were really doing this. The frenzied pace slowed down and we kissed and giggled and mumbled about how incredibly fantastic our bodies looked and I commented that Jack still had the little scar on the inside of his thigh and Jack kissed the two birthmarks on my hip; first one, then the other, like he always used to before sucking my dick. He spent a great deal of time down there before coming back up to plant wet kisses on my mouth. Then I retreated south to return the favor and found myself smiling while sucking on a mouthful of Jack's thick slab of a dick. When I was licking his big, hairless balls I heard my inner and more rational voice ask, *Is this really such a good idea?* but before I could answer Jack pulled me up, rolled on a condom, and fucked me silly, if not blind. When it was over the only thing that separated us was a thick layer of mutual cum.

"This is what I've missed most of all," Jack sighed.

And with that he wiped away the cum, threw the towel on the floor, and kissed me on the lips before saying, "G'night, Stevie B." He shifted our positions so we could spoon and drifted off to sleep. Me? I lay there unable to get his last comment out of my mind. What he missed most from our relationship was a hot fuck before bed?

After a restless night torn between loving the familiar feeling of Jack's hard biceps holding me close and the equally familiar feeling of wanting to rip the bicep flesh off of his bones, I had decided to tell Jack that if the most important thing to him was fucking me, then round two of this relationship was over before it could begin.

"That's not what I meant."

"It's what you said."

"And when did I say it?"

"Right after you fucked me."

"And while I was holding you. That's what I missed, Steven. The emotional connection after the physical, which I know sounds like therapist BS, but it's what I meant. Do you know how happy you made me last night, Stevie, when you let me fall asleep holding you? That's what I want in my life, you and me sleeping next to each other again. And not me running out of some nameless guy's apartment in the middle of the night so I can wake up in my own bed alone."

"Flynn, we have a problem," I cried into the phone an hour later.

"Did Jack dump you again?"

"Are you taking bitch lessons from Lohan now that you're half of a celebrity duo?"

"Mama, sorry. I'm just a bit ticked off because Lucas had to cancel our weekend plans. His agent booked him on a flight to L.A. to do *The Tonight Show*."

"Aren't you going with him?"

"Yeah, but this weekend we were supposed to go to that cute bed-and-breakfast in Vermont I told you about."

"So you'll have breakfast in bed at the Beverly Hills Hilton instead of the Vermont Arms, where should I send my sympathy card?"

"Assholishness duly noted. Now what's the problem?"

"Jack wants to make me dinner. At his place."

"He's domestic, that's nice."

"He's still living in our old apartment."

The pause was thick and long. "If you're able to reconnect with the guy who kicked you to the curb, you should have no problem revisiting the apartment in front of said curb."

"Is that the whiff of an asshole I smell?"

"What do you want me to say, Steven? You're going to have to face up to it sometime, might as well get dinner out of it."

"I thought you might be a little more supportive, especially after the hand-holding I gave you when you were freaking out about Lucas."

"I don't support you and Jack! I told you that. If you're having misgivings about having dinner with him at the apartment you guys once shared, that should tell you something."

The only thing I knew was that the truth must sometimes be blocked. "You know what I'm hearing from you, Flynn? A superiority complex. You've turned into Mister I'm-so-important-and-smart-'cause I-have-a-boyfriend."

"Who's giving off asshole emissions now?"

"Whatever! Go hop your flight with Lucas and have a great time with Conan. I don't need your help or your friendship!"

In some ways the apartment was the same and in other ways it was unrecognizable. Jack still used the same chocolate brown ultrasuede pillow as an accent to the sand-colored couch, but the abstract painting over it must have been a more recent purchase. I also recognized the multicolored throw on the club chair as the one his grandmother made, but the crystal vase that held a dozen red roses was a heretofore unseen heirloom or some knockoff he'd picked up at Bed, Bath & Behind.

"The place looks great," was all I could muster.

He knew I was hedging. "You're okay being here?"

"I'm not sure. Maybe you should ply me with some wine."

Before Jack could uncork the bottle, the most unexpected thing—to anyone living in a New York apartment, anyway—occurred. There was a knock on the door.

"Have you become friendly with the neighbors?" I asked.

"Not that friendly." Jack peeked through the peephole. "It's Lindsay and Sebastian."

"What?"

A second later Lindsay and Sebastian had invaded the apartment.

"What are you two doing here?"

"Flynn told Lindsay you were having dinner with Jackie Jack and we just had to see for ourselves if retro romance had made a comeback," Sebastian announced. "I hope you have enough meat for four, Jack."

"I'm sure Steven's told you all that I have more than enough meat to go around."

Sebastian squealed. "You know Steven doesn't suck and tell. I, on the other hand, like to share my good fortune with the world."

"Guys, I appreciate whatever it is that you're trying to do here," I started, "but—"

"No buts," Lindsay said. "We are joining you two for dinner. If Jack is back in your life, Steven, then he's back in ours too."

Jack shot me a playful grimace. "It's fine with me. I'll open up another box of pasta."

"Are you making puttanesca?" Sebastian asked. "That's whore pasta, you know. Whores used to make puttanesca and put it on their windowsills to attract men with its intoxicating whorish smell."

"Sorry, this is just plain old red sauce," Jack said.

"Which cries out for red wine!" Lindsay shouted. "Steven, come with me so we can get some red wine."

"I have wine. I was just about to pop the cork."

"You have to pop *my* cork, Jack," Lindsay said. "I'm the guest and guests bring the wine. We'll be right back. Steven, come on."

Confused and a bit suspicious, I found myself being pulled

out of Jack's apartment by Lindsay and just as I turned around I saw Sebastian close the door. Then I heard him lock it.

"What the hell is going on?"

"Hold this."

Lindsay pulled out a bottle of red wine from behind the potted plant in the hallway and thrust it into my hands. He was either stealing Jack's neighbor's secret stash of spirits or this was all part of a grand plan.

"It's all part of a grand plan, Steven," Lindsay whispered.

"What plan?"

"To show you Jack's true colors. Right now Sebastian is in there seducing him. He has exactly ten minutes to get Jack to reveal his duplicitous, disgusting self—which is nine minutes longer than Sebastian usually needs—so you can get over this stupid fascination with reliving the past."

I was stunned. And surprisingly grateful. "You would do this for me?"

"Steven, do not repeat this to anyone or else I will kill you. You are my best friend and I love you and if this is what it takes to make you realize you're making a mistake, so be it. Truth be told, I've done worse."

For some reason I didn't protest, but allowed Lindsay to push me so my ear was against the door and I could hear Sebastian attempting to seduce my ex- and current boyfriend. What concerned me most was not whether Sebastian would succeed, but that I wasn't at all certain he would fail.

"You look mighty muthafucking hot, Jack," Sebastian purred.

"Well, um, thank you. And you look, you know, pretty good yourself."

"You think so? I do try to take care of myself. I work out a lot, can you tell?"

"That shirt isn't leaving too much to the imagination."

Lindsay whispered, "Oh my God, it sounds like he's taking the bait."

"What's in your imagination, Jackie Jack? This?"

"Sebastian . . . I think you should put your shirt back on."

"Come on, tell me you don't like what you see."

"That has nothing to do with it. You know what you look like."

"Do you want to see the rest?"

"Uh . . . look, Steven is going to be back here in a minute."

"Baby, my hole is so tight I'll make you come before your balls hit my nether parts."

"Ahhh . . . Sebastian . . ."

"That sounds like he's gonna take more than the bait!" Lindsay whispered excitedly.

"Thank you, Fag Whisperer," I replied. "I might be stupid, but I'm not deaf."

"Listen, Sebastian," Jack said. "You need to get dressed right now."

"Must I remind you that it's Friday?"

"What's so special about Friday?"

"If it's Friday it's high-colonic day. I am clean as a whistle. And I need some loosening up 'cause I film my first porno tomorrow. The fucking IRS still wants their back taxes."

"Sebastian, I know what you're trying to do and yes, you are a hot man, but I do not want to fuck you. The only hot guy I want to fuck is Steven, so please get dressed before he gets back here and you make an awkward situation even more awkward."

"You turn down the Sebastian? I do not understand."

"That's because I don't think you understand anything about love."

That's all I needed to hear. I pushed open the door and stumbled in.

"Sebastian, I think it's time for you to leave."

Jack turned around and saw not only me standing there holding a bottle of wine, but Lindsay crouched in his doorway.

Lindsay tried to divert attention away from his compromising position and called out in a booming, authoritative voice, "Ignore the man crouched in your doorway." And, as always, Sebastian ignored the oddness of the situation and focused only on himself.

"He passed the Sebastian test, Steven. I do not know how he did it, but he has passed where so many, many men before him have failed. Come on, Lindsay, let's go, our work here is done. And I need to find someone to work over my waste-free heinie-hole so high-colonic Friday isn't wasted."

Sebastian didn't even bother to put his shirt back on before he and Lindsay left and I faced Jack, who was wearing a much different expression than a man who is in love would typically wear.

"I hope you enjoyed testing me. I think you should go now."

"Wait a second, I had nothing to do with this."

"They're your friends."

"Lindsay's my friend, yes, but Sebastian's just a slutty accessory you like to wear every once in a while. Look, I didn't even tell them about tonight, Flynn did."

"But you think this is kind of funny, don't you?"

I shrugged my shoulders. I knew Jack well enough to know that it would piss him off, but that's how I felt. "It is funny. And sort of sweet, in a strange way. My friends care about me, Jack, and they don't want to see me get hurt. Like it or not, you hurt me."

"I know that, Steven! But I don't feel like being constantly reminded of it."

"It won't be constantly, but every once in a while something's going to happen or someone's going to say something that will remind us both that you told me to get the hell out of your life so you could be alone in this nice apartment with all the nice little things while I slept on Flynn's couch trying to figure out what the hell I was going to do with my life. I don't like being reminded of it either, but sometimes when I look at you I see the same face I saw seconds before our final conversation."

"Could you stop being a soap opera producer for just a second?"

"Don't make fun of me, Jack, this is serious!"

"I know this is serious! I don't take taking you back lightly!"

And suddenly, as if I were stepping from a house that had crash-landed in a strange place, the landscape of our new relationship changed. The happy delight of making love to an old lover had been replaced with the recognition that the old lover came with the same old unhappy baggage.

"*You're* taking *me* back?" I asked, stunned. "Is that how you see this?"

Jack let out a groan and almost started to stamp his feet. "Don't do this again, don't harp on my every word!"

"If anyone is taking anyone back, I'm taking you back!"

I wasn't sure if he understood my words, but he understood that his answer was extremely important. He took a deep breath and I could tell he was searching for the most perfect response.

"Yes, I understand that, Steven. Now can we just sit down and have a nice dinner?"

Very, very far from perfect.

"No! No, we can't. This isn't going to be easy, Jack. Learning to live without you wasn't easy and learning to live with you again isn't something I can do overnight."

"I'm sorry. I don't mean to rush things, but I've missed you. I've missed having you in my life. So come on, let's start small, one little dinner, that's all I ask."

There really is no place like home. But often we fill our memories with dreams of happy laughter and rainbow colors to overshadow the wickedness and the cruelty. It works very well until you wake up and stare directly into the black-and-white reality.

"I think I'm going to have dinner without you tonight, Jack," I said. "Just like I've done for the past five years."

Chapter Sixteen

Cinematic hubris was committed in 1985. That was the year some moronic film studio president gave the green light for *Return to Oz*, the sequel to what I've already stated is one of my favorite films. If only that studio head had had a brain, he would have realized that tampering with a classic is not the way to box office gold or critical acclaim.

The movie actually asked the question, "What if Dorothy was insane?" and opens with the popular singing farm girl from Kansas as a patient in a mental hospital. But maybe the dumbass film honcho was trying to teach us all a lesson—do not meddle with the past. If that really is the lesson to be learned from the sequel, maybe I should follow Dorothy's footsteps to the nearest Duane Reade and fill my prescription for thorazine.

My relationship with Jack was not a classic love story, but like *The Wizard of Oz* it was a product of a specific time and place and perhaps any attempt to revisit that time and place could only end up in failure, like the critically trounced box-office flop *Return to Oz*. These were the thoughts floating in my head like a hot air balloon in a windstorm as I read yet another of Jack's text messages asking me to meet up with him.

When I was away from my friends their voices were only louder and more effective. I heard every one of their words of caution, and understood that those words were intelligent and just. I had a great life without Jack; I had survived, prospered even, and it had been quite some time since I had even thought about him and had those pangs of "If only?" and "What if?" But could my life be even better if I were with Jack and not without him?

"Hi, it's me, Steven."

"I know it's you, silly," Jack said. "Thank you for calling me."

"You know, it really is a fine line between secret admirer and stalker."

"I'm sorry, but the way you left . . . I couldn't let it end just like that."

"Who said anything about ending?"

I actually heard Jack smile.

"That's the best news I've had all day. Could I come over? I know it's late, but I would like to see you before I go to bed."

Without hesitation I lied. "I have to get up really early in the morning. I have to go to Jersey to take my mother to a doctor's appointment before work." At that point I started pacing my apartment to give God a moving target in case he wanted to strike me dead for using my mother's illness as an excuse not to meet Jack.

"I could go with you, I wouldn't mind."

I started moving faster.

"The truth is, I haven't told her about the new us yet, so it might be a bit awkward. She just needs to have some tests done anyway, no big deal, but I want to be there just in case."

"You didn't tell her about me?"

I stopped moving because I could finally resume truthful talk.

"No. I figured I'd tell her if we decided this was going to be permanent."

"You mean if *you* decide this is going to be permanent."

I decided to speak more truth and let God aim elsewhere. "Yes, that's right. When I decide."

Whoever said the truth shall set you free was a liar. All it does is make you think more and sometimes thinking is not the answer; sometimes porn is. As I sat on my couch with my sweatpants rolled down to my ankles, one hand stroking my lubed-up dick, the other fast-forwarding to all the close-ups of Aiden Shaw's superior piece of lubed-up manhood, all I could think of was Jack. And not the Jack who fucked me or French-kissed me, but the Jack who wanted me to decide. The only decision I wanted to make was if I should come at the same time Aiden did or let the Britstud shoot first. I decided to let Aiden explode first, then I followed up with a lukewarm ejaculation that would have gotten me banned from any respectable porn set. Decisions suck.

And sometimes so does work. Before my SU could even do its job and soothe, delight, and invigorate me and my tonsils, Laraby pulled me into his office and informed me of his latest ill-conceived decision.

"Lucas is going to be gay," Laraby declared.

"Lucas is already gay."

"Lucas is going to be gay on TV."

"He is already gay on TV, you were at the Emmys. He's gay on TV, he's gay off TV. He's an all-the-time gay!"

"Lucas is going to be gay on TV," Laraby repeated, "as Roger."

Listening to this man (who, as infuriating as he could be, was still my boss and fellow homosexual), I felt betrayed, like Toto must have felt when Uncle Henry awarded Miss Gulch canine custody. "Lucas is gay, but Roger is straight."

"Not after next Wednesday's episode! That's when his secret affair with Rick is finally revealed."

"Since when is there a secret affair? Roger pledged his undying love to Ramona just last week."

"He was lying. We're going to shoot a flashback scene that shows Roger declaring his love to Ramona, but then looking past her to where we see Rick peering out from behind the curtain. That's who Roger was talking to. It's brilliant!"

"It's fucked up! And furthermore it's wrong!"

Even though I was completely repulsed by this blatant attempt to exploit Lucas's recent personal triumph, I wasn't sure if the rage I was feeling was a byproduct of my own personal crisis. Mentally I had done a lot of screaming and venting, vocally I was silent. I welcomed the opportunity to be able to channel some of that silent screaming and direct it toward Laraby and his ridiculous scheme.

"You will not use Lucas's coming out to spike the ratings. I would think as a gay man you'd have a little more integrity."

"Don't be silly, Steven, like every other good television producer, I leave my integrity at the door. This is an opportunity to seize the drama of real life and turn it into something good—a controversial plotline. Can't you see the beauty in that?"

All I could see was a desperate fag trying to hold on to his job. "This isn't even your idea. The suits upstairs told you this is what they wanted and you didn't have the balls to tell them to fuck off."

It was Laraby's turn to pale. "I . . . I . . . I . . ." And to return to the stuttering. And my turn to return to my dramatic homosexual roots. I walked into the middle of Loretta's lavish living room set and looked around to make sure I had an audience. Lucas, Loretta, Lorna, and Lionel were just coming out of makeup, ready to shoot the first scene of the day; Lourdes was lingering a safe distance behind them, and Leon was consulting with a cameraman. In the distance I could see two of the powers-that-be loitering near the control booth, looking a little bit anxious. They had good reason. When I knew attention would be paid, I began. "Lucas Fitzgerald is gay!" Someone muttered, "That is so last week's episode."

"Roger Renault is not."

"Not unless Ramona is silicone and duct tape," Lorna shouted.

I could hear some laughter, but I kept my eyes on the two PTBs in the back of the studio. They weren't laughing at all.

"If the network has its way that might just happen."

"Watchootalkinbout, Homo?" Lorna asked.

My catchphrase was catching on. "Laraby has informed me that the network wants to turn Roger gay simply because Lucas is gay, in a revolting attempt to force art to imitate life. I don't know about you, but this makes me sick and I will not stand for it."

Lucas's voice broke through the din of chatter. "Neither will I!"

"Good. Because *If Tomorrow Never Comes* is not a side show. We are not here to turn an actor's personal life into a ripped-from-the-headlines plot twist. Otherwise Regina would be a drunk and Ramona would be a coldhearted shrew. So listen up, network brass! Roger will not bed Ramona's nephew Rick next Wednesday as planned. He will keep on fucking Ramona, because that's what Roger does and that's what the audience wants to see."

"You tell 'em, Electro Papi!" Lourdes shouted from well over twenty feet away.

"Thank you, Latyna Girl. Our audience might be made up of a bunch of housewives, but they're not stupid and they will never believe that Roger would give up a hot piece of ass like Ramona for a skinny twink like Rick."

"Thank you, Steven," Lorna said. "I *have* been doing some extra squats at the gym. And I would also like to remind the network brass that my contract states that while Ramona may turn another character bi-curious, she will never turn two men one-hundred-percent, jumped-over-the-fence gay. FYI—that goes for off-camera as well."

"They wouldn't let me put that in *my* contract!" Loretta cried. "Laraby!"

"This is how you reward me for winning the Emmy?" Lucas cried. "Laraby!"

"I am *not* gay-for-play!" Lionel cried. "Laraby!"

The bloodcurdling shriek that was next heard wasn't, as we all immediately thought, from Laraby. Lourdes, in her excitement, rushed toward me, but the minute she got within twenty feet of Loretta her ankle bracelet kicked in and several volts of electricity joined the adrenaline pumping through her veins. As the crew carried her a safe distance away she could be heard mumbling, "Papi really is electric."

When I looked up I saw that the two PTB had disappeared. An hour later when the network bosses called Laraby and me into a closed-door meeting, I thought it would be the end of my career as a soap opera producer, but I walked proudly into that meeting and closed the door behind me, determined not to bend. I would not allow my colleagues to belittle something so brave as Lucas's public coming-out by turning it into a publicity stunt.

Surprisingly, the network honchos agreed with me. Before I

could launch into a Julia Sugarbaker-esque homily about respect, one of the PTB apologized for making it seem as if they were suggesting Roger become homosexual as a result of the actor's recent public announcement. They in no way wanted to create a work situation where anyone felt as if they or their lifestyle was being unjustly exploited or they were in any way being harassed. Obviously, someone had made a quick phone call to a labor attorney. Roger would remain heterosexual, but one who is philandering and possibly homicidal, you know, just to keep the character interesting. Upgraded from homosexual to homicidal? For a moment I felt Ms. Sugarbaker's passion stir and demand articulation, but then I remembered what my father used to tell my mother: "Sometimes, Anjanette, you just have to shut up." And so I did.

Leaving the meeting, I had one of those fleeting moments of pure joy—like what Dorothy experienced when she woke up in her own bed and was surrounded by her loved ones. The feeling is like wind: it rushes in, completely overtakes you, but flees before it can be caught. The meeting had made me feel good, as if I had made a difference. All by myself. It also made me realize I did not need Jack in my life. I could feel happiness on my own. Before I told the cast and crew the good news, I took another moment to remember this feeling before it got lost amid the regular demands of the workday. The next time I saw Jack I would be a little bit closer to making a decision.

"The *H* in HGTV no longer stands for *Homo,*" Jack declared.

We were lying on my couch sharing a bowl of popcorn and watching some real estate show on the House & Garden channel, and we were quite disappointed that the little cable station we had loved so much had changed so much.

"It's all about hetero home-buying instead of homo house-decorating," he continued. "Who cares which house a couple in Arizona buys?"

"Not me. I miss the days when you could make treasure from someone else's trash."

Somehow Jack took that comment as foreplay.

"I've got a treasure you can trash."

And with that subtle segue we tossed aside the popcorn, turned the channel until we found a *SpongeBob* repeat, and started to make out. The kissing turned to undressing, which in turn turned to sucking, a little rimming, and a finale of flip fucking. But the sex was a bit different this time. It was a bit quieter than it had been and I got the distinct impression that although we were connected physically, we were separated emotionally.

I didn't know if Jack was bored or grateful that I was allowing this relationship to move forward, but I knew that I was not able to let go of myself. While Jack was blowing me and tongue-lashing my testicles, I closed my eyes and thought it was interesting that I had been so powerful at work a few hours earlier, but now was too weak to tell Jack that something felt a bit off. Maybe I had already made the decision, but wasn't completely ready to say it out loud.

The next day, however, I had no choice but to be more vocal.

"Steven, is there something wrong?" my mother asked.

"I'm dating Jack again."

I braced myself for a barrage of maternal warnings, but instead Anjanette was oddly quiet. Every once in a while she did this and I hated it. As much as I complained that my mother was loudmouthed and intrusive and blunt, that's what I expected. And that's what I wanted, because any other response would be unfamiliar and therefore unsettling.

"It doesn't sound like that's making you happy."

"It's making me nervous."

"Nervous isn't happy, honey. And that's all I want for you."

"For me to be nervous? Don't worry, you've taken care of that."

"All I want is for you to be happy. If Jack can do that, I'll make him lasagna the way he likes, without the hard-boiled eggs."

"You remember that?"

"I remember everything that has to do with you."

We talked silently for a few moments. I could hear my mother saying that life is too short to waste it with people who make you unhappy. And I'm sure she could hear me saying that life is too short to waste it alone. Where was that feeling of joy when you needed it?

"Thanks, Mom. I haven't decided what I'm going to do yet, but I appreciate the support."

She had one more tidbit of post-stroke wisdom: "Don't complicate things, Steven. Keep it simple and do what makes you happy."

Once upon a time happy meant gay. Now it means something you have to visit a shrink to discover. My mother was right though, happy is uncomplicated, it's simple. Everything was so much easier when it was simpler. Even salad—iceberg lettuce and a tomato. Simple, delicious, basically healthy. Now you can add every type of vegetable, nut, dressing, and spice to your salad and what do you have? Lettuce in hiding. I took another deep breath and felt like I was closer to turning my life into a happy salad.

The next stop on my path to a happy life was a visit to the Gay Life Expo with Lindsay and Gus. This annual event at the Jacob Javits Center was a trade show for all things gay and a perfect way to be reminded that gay can equal happy. Everywhere you looked there were rainbows, leather, dazzling displays of unnecessary grooming products, impeccably dressed and coiffed men, and no-carb snacks. There were also nonstop live performances from a slate of no-name disco artists of mixed ethnicity. Come to think of it, the Gay Life Expo wasn't as simple as I had hoped it would be. Luckily, Lindsay was the queen of simplifying.

"Where's the black boy?" Lindsay asked.

"Jefferson has a matinee," Gus replied. "And if I weren't so concerned about Wendolyn, I'd publicly spank you for being so rude."

Lindsay sneaked a glance in my direction.

"As much as public displays of humiliation have been known to turn me on," Lindsay said, "I have to ask: what's up with Wendolyn?"

Gus couldn't hide behind his typical staunch British veneer; this time emotion actually showed on his face. "I got another e-mail from her asking me to meet her at *ylf xp*."

"What the hell is *ylf xp?*" I asked.

"Gay Life Expo without the *g or* the vowels!" Gus explained. "She's off her biscuit, I tell you. I know I've ignored it all these years, but my sis has got problems."

"The *g* thing," I offered.

"Yeah, and now . . ." Gus said, hardly able to finish his sentence, "she can't even say her vowels!"

"*Y* is sometimes a vowel," Lindsay reminded him.

"I just know it has something to do with that mysterious package she got in the mail."

Lindsay gasped, then tried to cover. "I hate the post office!"

"What was in the package?" I asked, already knowing the answer.

"She never said, but Lenda translated one of her e-mails and said Wendolyn felt the contents of that package had forced her to question her entire existence."

Lindsay shot me the same kind of look that Katie Holmes reportedly shot to her mother right after saying "I do" in front of a church full of Scientologists.

"Mates, I think it's time I faced facts," Gus said. "Wendolyn is not well!"

"Wendolyn is dead, big brother! But *Gwendolyn* is back and she's here to stay!"

That announcement wasn't just shouted to the hysterical British hunk, it was proclaimed over the loudspeaker, so that all the Expo attendants could hear.

"I got my groove back, Gus!" Gwendolyn gushed from a nearby stage.

"Thank God, it's a miracle!" Gus gushed back.

"It wasn't God, it was the bloke who sent me every G-Man comic ever printed," Gwendolyn explained. "It almost broke me, but then it made me shout 'Gee, I want to live!' "

Lindsay clutched my hand and tears sprang from his eyes. "Steven, I'm a miracle worker!"

Glenda joined Gwendolyn onstage and they introduced themselves as the new hostesses of "Gay Girls A-Go-Go"—Logo's latest foray into lesbian reality TV. Each week they'd be inviting a bunch of lesbians to their London pad, turning on the cameras, and capturing all the lesbian goodness. Not something I would personally watch, but I felt sure there was an audience for it.

A few booths away, I glimpsed someone I had paid good money to see. It was Aiden Shaw. He looked even better than he had the last times I'd seen him—in person and in video while masturbating that morning.

"Make your move, Steven," Lindsay demanded.

"No," I said, dry-mouthed. "He looks too busy."

"I found Gwendolyn's G-spot, I can find yours too."

And without a second thought, which is usually how Lindsay works, he pushed me through the crowd that was gathered at Aiden's booth until I was face-to-face once again with my porn idol.

"Hi, Aiden," I squeaked.

"Steven! So you got my messages?"

What? I had felt my cell phone vibrating in my jeans all day, but I hadn't picked up because I'd thought Jack was trying to get in touch with me.

"Yes," I improvised. "That's why I'm here."

"Great, I get off at seven. Come back and we can get off together?"

Cheeky! But totally hot at the same time.

"It's a date, mate."

Cheekier! And hopefully Aiden thought my ass looked totally hot as I pushed my bad self through the crowd to rejoin Lindsay.

"Who's gonna get porn-fucked tonight?" I asked. "Oh, that would be me!"

We both laughed and I realized that some phrases would never find their way into the hetero lexicon. Or some images. A few aisles away Lindsay and I spotted Gus looking helpless next to Flynn, who was crying in front of a huge dildo. Now while it's true that Flynn can't really take more than seven inches without discomfort, the giant eight-foot, rainbow-colored dildo was obviously a promotional display and not meant for practical use.

"Don't cry, Flynn," Lindsay said. "We're not all meant to be power bottoms."

"Gus, what's going on?" I asked.

Gus made a *this-is-really-bad* face and Flynn made a half-hearted attempt to wipe away his tears before shoving a piece of paper into my hands. It was a printout from a Web site with a picture of Flynn and Lucas from the Emmys. They both looked so handsome, how could this be a bad thing? Then I saw the headline: *Daytime Superstar And His HIV+ Boyfriend.*

Flynn started crying again. "I've been outed, Steven, all over again."

I hugged my friend. "It's going to be okay."

My friend pushed me back. "No, it's not."

"Lucas knew this might happen," Gus offered.

"But I never did! How stupid was I to think something like this would remain a secret? Look at him up there, getting interviewed as if nothing's happened."

We turned around to see Lucas on a stage being interviewed by every member of the gay and gay-friendly media.

"He's probably telling them right now that his boyfriend's HIV status doesn't concern him. That he'd love me even if I were negative."

"And you know he means it, don't you?" I asked. "It's not just PR talk."

"I know he means it and I love him for it, but Steven, you know how hard I try to rise above this every day. It's been a struggle and that's with only a few people knowing. I don't know how the hell I'm going to handle the entire world knowing I have AIDS."

"You don't have AIDS, asshole," Lindsay corrected. "You're HIV-positive, that's a big difference."

"Tell that to the clients who fired me this morning."

"You lost clients over this?" I asked rhetorically, then added even more rhetorically, "They can't do that, it's illegal."

"It's immoral," Gus said, "but not illegal."

"It's the American way! Admire those living with the disease, just don't get close to them. I'm sure this is just the beginning; once the word gets out I'll lose some more clients and then my job and what'll I have then, nothing."

"You'll have your friends and a boyfriend who loves you," Lindsay said.

"Who the hell are you?" Flynn asked. "You know as well as I do that without your career you're nothing. I am an attorney: if I can't practice law, I can't do anything."

The dildo stand was starting to draw a crowd, so we guided Flynn away from the plastic loveshafts. We didn't realize that we were guiding him right into the lion's den.

"There's the boyfriend!"

Before we could make an exit we were surrounded by thrusting microphones and eager, well-groomed reporters. Under different circumstances and less obtrusive lighting, I might have thought I was in a back room somewhere.

"When did you tell Lucas you were positive?"

"Do you always practice safe sex?"

"Will your status endanger Lucas's role on the show?"

I saw Flynn open his mouth, but heard nothing come out. He squeezed my hand tighter and I could see his face turn white and beads of sweat form on his brow. He was scared and I felt helpless. Lindsay, Gus, and I could physically whisk him away, we could try to claim our inner-Sean Penn and punch out one or two reporters, but what good would that do? The damage was done. Flynn was outed for being positive and he was devastated.

"Get the hell away from that young man!"

The voice that commanded the media to back away from Flynn was none other than my mother's. Before I could even ask what in the world my mother was doing at the Gay Life Expo, she told everyone that Lenny Abramawitz, who was standing on her left, wanted to check out the End of the Rainbow Retirement Home for Gay Seniors, but hadn't wanted to come alone so she and Audrey, who was standing on her right, had joined him.

The reporters were so shocked by the vision of three people

over the age of sixty-five at a Gay Life Expo not dressed in head-to-toe leather that they did as my mother asked. Then she asked me what was going on and for the second time in recent memory I found myself under harsh lights and near a microphone. I squeezed Flynn's hand tighter before I spoke.

"They found out that Flynn's HIV-positive."

Neither my mother, nor Audrey, nor Lenny changed their expressions. They simply responded in unison, "So?"

I tried to explain the gravity of the situation. "They, um, seem to think this is newsworthy."

By this time Lucas had made his way off the stage and was standing next to Flynn. When he looked at Flynn's terrified face, I could tell Lucas loved him because he looked just as terrified. Despite the terribly awkward situation, I felt happy to know that my friend had found something so wonderful.

"And I keep trying to tell them it doesn't change a thing," Lucas said. "I'm in love with Flynn and I'm proud to be his boyfriend."

"But Lucas, do you think this is going to hinder your career?" shouted a reporter. "Is anyone going to want to hire you if they think you could be positive?"

"That's ridiculous!" my mother shouted. "My husband was diabetic and I didn't get it from him. And trust me, we had lots of sex."

"Ma!"

"Honey, everybody knows your father was diabetic, it's not a secret."

"And even though I too am a diabetic," Audrey said, "I did not get it from Anjanette's husband. I never had sex with Tony."

If I hadn't still been trying to make sense of my mother's diabetes-as-STD comparison, I would have had to acknowledge that I was no longer going to die without hearing a word about my father's sex life. Sometimes you just have to let go of things. And that's just what Lenny did.

"I have herpes."

The hardened journalists gasped and one newbie almost fainted.

"It is not something I like to share with people, it's something

I wish I didn't have, but it's something that I have to deal with on a daily basis. Some days I deal with it better than others, but it's my something to deal with, not the world's. Wouldn't you agree with me, Flynn?"

"Yes, I would, Lenny."

"Since when does every personal secret have to be aired on national TV? The only people who need to know if Flynn is positive or negative are himself, his doctor, and Lucas. And Lucas doesn't care, so why does anybody else?"

There was a silent pause, then one by one the reporters lowered their microphones, closed their notebooks, and walked away, some of them shrugging their shoulders at Flynn as if to say, "Hey dude, I'm only doing my job."

"Lenny," I said, shaking the old man's hand. "You're very brave."

"Nah," he said, not letting go of mine. "I'm just old and at some point you have to stop caring what the world thinks of you."

"I would like to apologize," I started.

"For what?" Lenny asked. "For thinking I'm a dirty old man? I *am,* but just because I'm a dirty old man doesn't mean I can't treat myself and my friends with respect."

Flynn, Lucas, Lindsay, Gus, my mother, and Audrey were engaged in a group hug that they pulled me and Lenny into. Nothing had really changed—Flynn was still positive and he and Lucas would still have to deal with the fallout from this breach of privacy, Lenny was still a lech with herpes and would still have to take medication to control his outbreaks, Audrey was still diabetic and kind of stupid (my mother later explained to me that when Lenny said he had herpes Audrey thought he was talking about a Hermes scarf)—but I felt that rush of joy again. I was surrounded by goodness, in spite of it all.

On my way home I tried to push all thoughts of the disquieting events of the day from my mind and concentrate on how absolutely perfect and perfectly surreal my night was going to be. Finally, after years of fantasizing and masturbating, I was going to cross the line and have sex with Aiden Shaw. I had three hours to douche, shower, and get just a little bit drunk so I wouldn't chicken out. Unfortunately, the disquieting events of the day weren't over.

On my walk to Aiden's hotel I knew who was calling, but I answered my phone anyway. "Hi, Jack."

"So you invited your mother to the Gay Life Expo, but not me."

Jack explained that our impromptu media showdown was all over the media, and I explained how Lindsay had dragged me there and how my mother and company happened to show up at the wrong place at the right time.

"I love your mother, she's got some big balls. But who's the old dude with herpes?"

At that moment I got a text from Aiden that read: *It's waiting for you.* I clicked on the attached photo: it was a close-up of his suckalicious, maybe-more-than-ten-inch, uncut dick. My mouth watered and I was lost in a familiar fantasy. Somewhere I could hear a guy calling out to me. "Steven! Steven, are you there?"

I was still looking down at Aiden's dick, ignoring Jack's questions, when I bumped into a guy on the street. I was right smack-dab in the middle of fantasy and reality. Right in front of me was Frank, the Starbucks Sunday Regular.

Chapter Seventeen

Would someone please page John Edward, because I believe I have crossed over? Truly, the moment I saw Frank I felt as if I had died. Images of my entire life for roughly the past year flashed before me. I saw myself sitting across from Lindsay at Starbucks, Lindsay throwing Frank's *New York Times* to the floor, Frank's gorgeous green eyes for the first time, Frank sitting by himself staring at me, Frank approaching my table with his confident sexy swagger, the Patti LuPone article, Frank's denim-clad ass leaving Starbucks. Frank, Frank, Frank, Frank, Frank.

Then (still thinking I ought to be looking for the light) I saw myself obsessing over why Frank never called me back; myself near tears with Flynn trying to figure out why I was obsessing; Flynn near tears trying to get me to realize that I had to stop obsessing and take control of my emotions; Frank's beaming face as I had obsessively imagined it so many times when I was at work, at a bar, or having sex with Brian. Then I crossed back and was no longer dead, dying, or obsessive. I was alive and I saw Frank right in front of me.

"I never thought I'd see you again," Frank said.

"Had you returned any of my phone calls you would have," I replied.

If gay men, especially those living in Metropolitania, want to transcend the image of the polygamous, emotion-free sex hound, they need to return a phone call every now and again.

"I'm sorry, I've been in a coma."

"*A coma?*" I said.

"Right after I left you at Starbucks I turned the corner and was hit by a taxi. I was in a coma for about eight months."

When Sid Fairgate didn't survive his season-two car crash cliff-hanger on *Knots Landing,* I was shocked. When *Bare Essence* crashed in the ratings and didn't even make it back for a second season, I was stunned. But this was even more bizarre.

"You've been in a coma?" I asked. "That's your excuse for not calling me?"

Frank nodded and pointed to his cheek. "See this scar? This is where I had twelve stitches." Then he rolled up his left sleeve. "And this one? This is where a loose piece of the taxi's fender cut three veins." And then he pulled up his T-shirt and pushed his jeans down a bit to reveal a thin, long scar that I could only imagine was from being punctured by the taxi's hood ornament.

"Okay, I believe you!" I shouted before Frank had to strip naked on the street just to prove his point. "I believe you were in a coma. I am so sorry. And all along I thought you just weren't interested."

"That's the furthest thing from the truth," Frank said, blushing. "The first thing I did when I woke up was ask if the guy from Starbucks had called."

"I did call you," I protested, "several times! On your cell phone, your home phone—"

"My cell phone was crushed in the accident. The taxi ran over it right after it rolled over my ankle. And my mother retrieved all my phone messages, but my mother isn't what you'd call a technological genius. She's not really a genius at anything, except, of course, being a mother."

My knees buckled a little bit like when the kind Asian doctor told Karen that Sid died on the operating table. Frank and I really had shared more than a passing Starbucks moment, we also had a maternal connection. But then when Brian first talked about his mother I thought we shared a connection too.

"My mom's wonderful. I couldn't have survived the accident without her. From what the nurses tell me she practically took up residence at St. Vincent's."

But Brian never talked about his mother like that.

"I can't believe you've been at St. Vincent's . . . in a coma . . . all this time. I thought you might be in St. Bart's or St. John's cavorting on the beach with some other guy you picked up at Starbucks talking about Patti LuPone's career. I have to say I'm much happier to know that you've been in a coma."

"Thank you," Frank said, holding my gaze even though I could see his eyes watering up.

"I guess it's been pretty tough going."

"The past few months have been difficult; rehabilitation isn't fun no matter how muscular your therapist is."

"Please tell me you at least had a guy therapist and not some burly woman."

"I demanded a man. I said I hadn't felt a man's touch in way too long and, of course, that girls have cooties. To which the lesbian nurse replied, 'Only if they've recently returned from South America.' Keyshawna was cool, though, and hooked me up with Rutger, a twenty-five-year-old Swiss-German bodybuilder, whose hands are weapons of torture, but whose nipples could cut stone. So the pain was worth it."

"I'm glad you're all right."

"Me too."

"And I'm glad you're right here."

"Me too."

"*Beep!*"

I was so startled that I dropped the cell phone when Jack called back. Frank and I bopped heads when we both bent down to pick it up. Frank reached the phone first.

"That looks like Rutger."

It was my turn to blush. Aiden's cock photo was still on my screen in all its uncut glory. I tried to make light of it. "Oh, you know how gay boys love their Photoshop." What wasn't funny was that Jack was calling me and I had absolutely no desire to pick up. Wasn't I just saying something about the link between gay men and bad phone etiquette?

My fingers fumbled around the keypad for the OFF button while my mouth mumbled something about the phone call not being important and the cock in the photo being a practical joke. Then I decided to stop being diffident and emulate one of my idols—resident *Knots Landing* vixen Abby Fairgate Cunningham Ewing Sumner—and be a man.

"Let's go to our Starbucks."

I was very relieved to discover that Frank's Starbucks drink of choice was a grande double-shot latte. I would have been very disappointed if his signature drink had been something girlish like a Caramel Macchiato or, God forbid, something boring like house blend.

"I'd ask you what's new in your life, but I already know that standing vertical tops the list," I said.

"I'm never going to complain about not getting enough sleep ever again."

"Who needs sleep when you've been in a coma?" I joked. "Sorry! Are coma jokes okay?"

Frank laughed. "Coma jokes are fine. After your nurse tells you that your mother has been applying ointment to your ass to prevent bedsores, nothing is sacred."

"I know the feeling. My mother would jump at the opportunity to spread anti-bedsore ointment on my ass. Are you by any chance Italian?"

"Half. My mother's from Merano, but my dad's German. Was German, he passed away a few years ago."

"Mine too. Dead, not German. I'm one hundred percent Sicilian. But we have no links to the Mafia, even though my cousin Vito has connections"—and when I said connections I actually put the word in finger quotes—"so I might be able to put a hit on the taxi driver who hit you."

"No need, he died in the crash."

I had a mental image of one of those *New Yorker* cartoons (which is very odd because it's a well-known fact that no one reads *The New Yorker* beyond the front cover) where a slightly-fleshed-out stick figure opens its mouth and inserts its foot. I was that stick figure and my mouth was stuffed with an Adidas Samba.

"I'm really sorry," I said in my most serious of serious voices. "I had no idea."

Frank started laughing. Perhaps inappropriate laughter was a coping mechanism. "More coma humor! The driver was fine, not a scratch on him. Though he might need some ointment on his ass by now; he's been in Rikers Island for two months, convicted of reckless vehicular endangerment or something like that."

"Well, good! If taxi drivers can't be put away for not using deodorant in August, at least they can be put away for reckless driving."

"Hear, hear!"

We clinked our Starbucks cups and shared some more basic information. Frank's full name was Frank Anthony Gunnerson, which meant he grew up with the unfortunate initials of F.A.G., a fact that did not go unnoticed by his classmates while he was growing up in North Dakota. "Until this day I have a fear of schoolyards," he confided.

"How'd you wind up in New York?" I asked. "Was it the typical 'gay-boy-needs-to-surround-himself-with-other-gay-boys'-syndrome?"

"Not at first. I got a scholarship to New York University and fell in love with everything the city had to offer. The whole experience was a revelation. I don't even like to think about the person I would've become had I gone to my number-two choice."

"Which was?"

"North Dakota School of Dentistry. I was going to be a dentist like my brother."

"Get out! My brother's a dentist!"

So many similarities. A mother with questionable sanity, a brother with a dental drill, what else could we have in common?

"Does any relative have a dachshund?"

"My sister's got a chihuahua." Close enough.

Just when I didn't think the conversation could get simpler or more spontaneous, we started talking about Patti LuPone and how we both wished we knew how to write a musical (instead of just criticizing them like every other gay man) so Patti could create

another original musical theater wet dream like her portrayals
of Eva Peron and Mama Rose. We thought she'd make a great
queen of some sort, perhaps Queen Elizabeth without the alpha
forehead or Katharine of Aragon, King Henry VIII's first wife,
since Patti could once again tap into her Spanish side, or even
Queen Latifah since we decided Patti could do anything onstage
if Patti really wanted to. We were laughing so hard I didn't even
notice right away that Frank's hand was resting on mine. I think
we both noticed it at the same time, but neither of us flinched.
Until Jack walked through the door.

Reflex took over and I pulled my hand away just as Jack
sauntered up to our table.

"When you said 'Let's go to our Starbucks' I knew exactly
which one you meant," Jack said.

I was just like Frank's mother—unable to master technology!
I must have hit the wrong button and instead of sending Jack to
voice mail, I answered the call and he heard me ask Frank to go
to our Starbucks. How much else had Jack overheard? The way
Jack kissed me, naturally and not as strategy to show Frank that
I was taken, I was led to believe he hadn't heard more. At least
that's what I was going to go with until proven otherwise.

"Hi, I'm Jack. Steven's boyfriend."

Or proven a two-timer.

Disappointment had a brief cameo on Frank's face, but was
then replaced by dignity. "I'm Frank. An old friend of Steven's."

I watched Frank and Jack shake hands and I couldn't believe
that our reunion was being ruined. I wanted to scream, but as
usual I kept silent. I didn't want to cause a scene or make anyone uncomfortable, which was an idiotic thought since Frank
and I were already uncomfortable, so basically I was just saving
Jack from discomfort. Maybe since being gay usually puts me in
the minority I had forgotten that majority rules, and if the two
of us were awkward the third party should have awkwardness
thrust upon him as well. Then again, maybe I was just a pussyboy.

Frank stood up and extended his hand to me. I took it and
welcomed the warm flesh, which did not prepare me for the cold
good-bye. "It was great to see you again, Steven. Take care."

Jack was jabbering about something, while I struggled with the urge to run after Frank. I was paralyzed, but with what—fear? Was I so conditioned to think that every relationship will end up badly that I was frightened to run after the man of my dreams, the gay sleeping beauty who'd awakened from his coma to walk back into my life? Had I become that much of a robot that I was willing to let the possibility of true love just walk out the door? Was I going to end all my sentences with question marks, but refuse to answer any life questions?

"I have to go to the bathroom." And off I ran.

The porcelain tiles seemed to be closing in tighter around me and the coffee beans in the Starbucks diorama appeared to be swirling around my head. I took a few deep breaths and caught my reflection in the mirror, but quickly turned away. I couldn't even look at myself. I knew I was acting like a child, but I wasn't exactly sure why. So I did something childish and called my best friend for help. Flynn's voice message said he would be out of the office all day without access to voice mail, so I called Lindsay, an even more childish thing to do.

"Are you riding Aiden's dick right now?" Lindsay hyperventilated.

Aiden! I had totally forgotten about my guest appearance on *Fucking with a Porn Star*. I filled Lindsay in on what had happened, but he couldn't see above his waist.

"Step away from the Starbucks, Steven, and go get fucked!" Lindsay ordered.

"I just let Frank walk away!"

Lindsay totally ignored me. "Just go get fucked! By a dick, not an asshole like Jack."

"Lindsay, please, I need advice."

"That is my advice! Forget about asshole and coma boy and all the uncertainty surrounding them and go to Aiden's hotel suite where you know what you're going to get. The fuck of your life!! No uncertainty, expectations fulfilled, ass full of dick, it's all good, my friend."

I tried to get Lindsay to focus on the problem at hand. "Why am I so confused?"

"Because you're like every other citizen in the United States of Gaymerica, you're creating drama where there is none because you spent a lifetime feeling like an outsider and now you want to make up for lost time and constantly be in the spotlight. Not everyone can be Meredith Baxter-Birney and have above-the-title billing! Some of us have to realize that no matter how important we think we are, Barbara Walters is never going to call us up and invite us to be one of her Ten Most Intriguing People of the Year. And I should know, I've been waiting for that lisping bitch to call me since the fiasco at Lillehammer and my phone has yet to ring! Am I making myself clear, Steven?"

Not really. "Well, sort of."

"I know you crave a life filled with soap opera twists and twirls."

He was right. "That's not entirely true."

"It is too! And by thinking it you create it."

"You think I somehow conjured this all up?"

"How many guys do you know who turn the corner and bump into a man from their past not once but twice? How many guys do you know whose ex-boyfriend and secret admirer are the same person? And how many guys do you know who have a porn star waiting to be their big bad uncut top?"

"That still doesn't make me the star of my own soap."

"Let me ask you this. When you bumped into Frank, did you immediately compare it to scenes from nighttime soaps of the eighties?"

Lindsay truly was an honor student at the Dionne Warwick Psychic Academy. "I can't help myself, Lindsay. As much as I want a simple life, I can't make it happen. It's like you and your Olympiphobia, you can't say Lillehammer without having a spasm." Hold on. Lindsay did just say *Lillehammer* and I didn't hear foam gurgling. "You just said *Lillehammer,* didn't you?"

"Yes, I did."

"And how come I don't hear you writhing on the floor in gut-wrenching emotional pain?"

"Because I have decided to move on with my life. Actually my very expensive therapist and my favorite G-woman Gwendolyn helped me realize I wouldn't be able to move on with my life until I moved away from the emotional frigidity of Norway."

"How did Gwendolyn help you?"

"When she got my batch of G-Man comics she could have filled out an application for a lifetime membership at London's premiere rest home for the very, very anxious, but instead she chose to stare those comics down, accept that they had crippled her, and allow the past to remain in the past. And that's exactly what I'm doing. I am an Olympic pewter medalist and damn proud of it!"

What the hell was wrong with the world? If you couldn't count on Lindsay to freak out every time the Olympic fanfare was heard, what could you count on? I was more uncertain than ever. I thanked Lindsay for his frankness, washed my face, looked at my reflection with repugnance (which is the formal use of the word *disgust*), and went back to join Jack.

"I thought you fell in."

"You know how coffee affects me sometimes."

"We shared a bathroom, how can I forget?"

Before the scatological references got too distasteful, my cell phone rang. Illogically I hoped it was Frank, but then I realized Frank didn't have my number. It was Flynn inviting me to dinner with him and Lucas. I told him I was with Jack, and Flynn said that it would be fine to bring him along. At some point during dinner I would have to figure out a subtle way to get Flynn alone to update him about Frank.

Not surprisingly, the décor of Lucas's apartment was metrosexual meets Midwest. A Bo Concepts black leather recliner and ottoman were next to a tan and black plaid Ethan Allen couch, which was next to a mahogany and glass cocktail table. On the walls, abstract art mingled with oil paintings of farmlands and the crisp antique white walls allowed the wildflowers in the various vases throughout the room to capture your eye with their glorious colors. It all worked together to create a unique, but relaxing, atmosphere of urban cowgay.

Flynn handed me and Jack glasses of merlot in delicate, oversized wine glasses. He made a bit of ceremony out of it, presenting the wine—and his goodwill. Jack knew that Flynn wasn't a fan of our relationship, but Jack also knew that any long-lasting relationship with me would have to include civility toward Flynn. And so he met Flynn's formality with cordiality. "Thanks, Flynn," Jack said.

"You're welcome," Flynn replied, just as cordially.

"I'm sorry to hear about the whole outing thing. That really sucks."

"I wanted to sue," Lucas said, "but Flynn wouldn't let me."

"I might be a lawyer, but I'm not a suer," Flynn said. "Besides, things are already getting better."

One of the good things to come out of our ultrafast-paced society is that not only do the good times rush by, so do the bad. Yes, Flynn lost some clients due to his moment in the tabloids, but only a few. The next day at work his partners informed him that they stood behind him unequivocally and if they were to lose any clients over an HIV status, they were clients they didn't want to represent in the first place. *How non-lawyerly of them,* I thought. Flynn's career bled a bit, but didn't hemorrhage. And the whole reprehensible incident made him feel liberated.

"I don't have anything else to hide," Flynn declared. "I don't have to worry any longer if someone is going to find out that I'm positive. I'm on the Internet, my biggest secret is downloadable."

"You're like Paris Hilton," Jack joked.

"Except *my* carpet matches my drapes."

"Not so much since the Emmy highlights," Lucas remarked.

Like a long-married wife, Flynn ignored Lucas. "But seriously, folks, I'm going to be doing double duty on my shrink's couch to deal with the public humiliation."

Lucas raised his voice sternly. "You have nothing to be ashamed of."

"Except my unmatching drapery. But as my boyfriend has pointed out to me, there is always a silver lining."

"It's an actor thing," Lucas explained. "Any publicity is good publicity."

"Same goes for pubicity," Flynn said.

During a scrumptious homemade meal of veal piccata, crispy fried brussels sprouts, and some sort of citrusy rice thing (and by homemade I mean made in the Home of Italy, a mangiarific restaurant two blocks away from Lucas's pad), Flynn said he wanted to get my mother a thank-you gift for standing up for him when he couldn't stand up for himself. I told him that wasn't necessary since she considers Flynn a third son and was merely doing her motherly duty, but he wouldn't hear of it.

"Does she still wear thongs?" Flynn asked. "Victoria's Secret has some great ones in cotton and lace."

"Why must you always put X-rated images of my mother in my head?!"

"Because that's what friends are for. I want to send Lenny something too. Maybe a hustler."

Then Lucas fag-teamed with Flynn to torment me. "Steven's mother would say 'mama like' to a hustler!"

"Perfect! I'll send them one bisexual hustler and give them the gift of the three-way!"

When I got up to tweak Flynn's nipple seriously hard, I noticed a photo on Lucas's mantle right next to his Emmy. The photo was of me and Flynn on a New York spring break fling during college. We were at Uncle Charlie's, the first gay bar I ever visited in the City, and the photo was taken by an apple-cheeked former ranch hand from Wyoming, who became my first gay lay in the Big Apple. We looked so happy and relaxed. We got doubles made and I have the same photo in my bedroom.

"I see someone is personalizing Lucas's apartment."

"It's actually my apartment too now," Flynn announced. "I'm moving in."

Schoolgirl-like screams pierced everyone's ears. My best friend had finally found someone he loved enough to live with. I couldn't be happier and I couldn't help but feel more responsible.

"All this is because of me, you know."

"How could we forget?" Lucas asked. "You remind us all the time."

"Shut up, you! I could drive your car off a cliff or let you get caught in a house fire so you're burned from head to toe and completely unrecognizable."

"You're talking in soap opera terms, right?" Jack asked.

I demurred coquettishly. "Perhaps."

As I made everyone get up to toast Flynn and Lucas's decision to commit, I decided it was time to end my indecisiveness or else Jack and I didn't stand a chance.

Later, when Jack was in the bathroom and Lucas was in the kitchen putting away the leftovers, Flynn and I had a few moments to ourselves. "I'm so happy, Steven."

"I can tell."

"Despite all the angst and heart palpitations I've had since meeting Lucas, it has been the most wonderful time of my life. I've actually fallen in love with someone who loves me and doesn't consider my health a reason to make a hasty exit."

"You deserve all this happiness and much more, Flynn."

"So do you. And I hope you get it with Jack."

Frank was not only in the forefront of my mind, he was also on the tip of my tongue, and I was just about to tell Flynn the details when Jack flushed the toilet and came back into the room. Maybe that was a sign. Any chance I had with Frank had already gone down the drain.

I was glad to see that Flynn had chosen to send my mother a huge fruit basket and chocolate sampler as a thank-you instead of a hustler, when I went to visit her the next day. This visit, however, did have an ulterior motive. My mother was babysitting Trixie since Paulie and Renée were at a dental convention in Aruba, so I would also have a chance to bond with my niece.

"How come we never had a dog growing up, Ma?"

"Because your father hated dogs."

"He did?"

"A German shepherd bit him on the face when he was six."

I couldn't believe this was the first time I was hearing about this. "That's how Daddy got that scar? He said it was from the war."

"Your father was never in the war."

"He was *never* in the war?! How many lies did the man tell?"

"Well, he was in the war, but not *in the war*. He was a cook. The only action he saw was when the soldiers would fight over the last biscuit."

"Really?"

"Your father made a very good biscuit."

How we got from biscuits to marriage I don't really know, but I guess I'd come for more than Trixie-bonding and a cup of tea.

"You loved him a lot, didn't you?"

"From the first time I laid eyes on him. Across the counter at Woolworth's."

"What did he order from you again?"

"A chocolate egg cream and a crumpet. He didn't have enough money for the crumpet too, but I gave it to him anyway."

"So all you knew was that he was cash poor, yet you still loved him."

"What else did I need to know? You either love someone or you don't."

"But how did you know that he was the one you wanted to marry? That you could have a life with him?"

"That I didn't know. Honey, nobody ever knows if a marriage is going to work out until they've lived together for a few years. We were lucky, we fell in love in an instant, but it took some time to find out that we liked each other too."

"So you believe in love at first sight?"

"I'm living proof."

My mother gave me a cup of my favorite orange tea and gave Trixie a carrot to nibble on. She sipped her own tea quietly.

"I think I've been so willing to give Jack another try because it would mean an instant relationship. I already know that I enjoy living with him, that we're compatible, so the future wouldn't really be guesswork. As long as I can trust that he won't leave me again, it could be a perfect life."

"But can you trust him?"

My answer was immediate. "No. He betrayed me big-time

and I suffered big-time. Maybe it's the Italian in me, but I just can't forgive or forget what he did."

"It has nothing to do with being Italian; it has everything to do with self-respect. Your father and I yelled at each other, we fought and bickered, but we always respected each other. If you don't have that, you've got nothing."

And then I found myself talking to my mother more openly and honestly than usual. "After Brian and I broke up I gave in to the feeling that I would never have another good relationship again. That every guy would be a loser or cheat on me or just not measure up to the idea I had in my head of what the perfect man should be like, so if I met someone and they weren't absolutely perfect in that very first meeting I'd cut them loose. I wouldn't even give them a chance. I'd say to myself, 'Well, if they aren't perfect now, imagine how bad they're going to be in six months . . . or ten years from now.' I convinced myself that the best thing to do was just say good-bye before I even got to say hello. So when Jack showed up I think part of me felt like I'd done this already and even though it turned out bad at least I knew how it would turn out. But I don't feel that way with Frank."

"And who is this Frank?"

I filled my mother in on Frank pre- and post-coma and quite quickly her expression changed.

"You light up when you talk about him."

"But I don't even know him."

"So what. Get to know him."

"You make everything sound so simple."

"Because Steven, honey, life really is simple. Why is Trixie such a happy baby? Because she's simple. All she wants is a carrot and some love. People are no different. It's just when we start questioning every little thing that we want or don't have, that's when we screw it up and make it all complicated."

My mother knew her son. She tapped into exactly what I had been feeling and was able to make me understand that what I was feeling was right and good and not something I should run from, but something I should act upon. She did—and I'm using her own words—what she was put on this earth to do: make her children happy.

"It's over, Jack," I said simply.

"Not this again," Jack sighed. "Steven, we're never going to move forward if you keep making us take these little steps backward."

"There isn't going to be any moving forward. I'm sorry, but I don't want to be your boyfriend again. It's that simple."

"No! It isn't that simple. It's never that simple with you!"

"Well, now it is. And please don't yell. I know this isn't what you want . . . breaking up with you wasn't what I wanted either, but things happen . . . actually things don't happen, people make decisions and I'm making one right now."

I could see that Jack wanted to fight me, yell and argue his points; but, though I couldn't be certain, I was hopeful he could see a change in me. Something had shifted inside me and maybe it was already making its way to the surface.

"You really don't want to try anymore?"

"I really don't. What we had was wonderful, but it's over. I want to thank you for trying to make this work again, though."

"But why? Isn't this what you want?"

"No, it isn't. And now I can put an end to wondering if it *was* what I wanted. And you can put an end to wondering if it would have ever worked out again. We can both move on."

Jack couldn't help but laugh out loud. "You still like to put a positive spin on everything, don't you?"

"I find that it helps."

We stared at each other for a few seconds, both of us okay with the silence, which was refreshing, until one of us had something to say.

"I am really upset over this and I'm going to miss you."

"Give it some time. Trust me, you really will be okay."

I ran all the way home. I was a man on a mission and I was praying that my luck would hold out. Luckily, I'm Mister Mary Organized and I have all my old cell phone bills. I pulled out the one from October and found Frank's number, dialed it and prayed that his carrier had allowed him to keep his same number. When the taped greeting began I recognized his voice.

"Frank, it's me, Steven! I'm sorry for yelling, but I'm a little excited. I would really, really like to see you so I can explain about Jack and me. Well, there actually isn't a Jack and me. . . . I want to talk about me and you. It may not sound it, but it's all very simple; if you'd just give me a chance I think I can make both of us very happy. I'm going to our Starbucks right now and I'll wait for you until it closes. Please come meet me."

I walked over to Starbucks slowly and tried not to think too much about what might or might not happen. I tried very hard not to play the soap opera couple game, which is when you compare you and your boyfriend to a famous soap couple based on similarities in the relationships. Would Frank and I be like Krystle and Blake? Solid and strong in the beginning, then boring and separated in the end. Or more like Val and Gary? Passionate and tumultuous and ultimately together in the end, but with huge gaps in between. Nope! I pushed all those crazy, unrealistic thoughts from my head. I wanted a fresh start, to base a decision on what I was feeling and not on some unseen head writer's creative imaginings. I wanted a chance with Frank.

Frank must have been feeling the same way because when I opened the door to Starbucks, he was already sitting at our table.

Chapter Eighteen

Everybody repeat after me—"Happy One-Month Anniversary, Steven and Frank!" Doesn't that have a nice ring to it? When I was dating Brian and even when I was living with Jack, anniversary reminders would pop up on my PDA, causing thoughts to pop up in my head like "I must now do something incredibly special to commemorate this occasion," or "What is the modern-day gift for a three-month homosexual anniversary—pleather?" Looking back, I was forced to admit I had reacted that way because the landmark date was more special to me than it was to the other person I was sharing the landmark with at the time. Happily, things were different with Frank.

Why? Because I'd had a relation-shift—a change in how I viewed my personal relationships. Honestly, I couldn't take all the credit for this emotional growth since it wasn't a conscious change, but one that grew organically, out of necessity. Like when I realized I could no longer masquerade as a heterosexual; women I liked, pussy not so much. Somehow I grew out of that self-destructive, high school mentality of searching for a boyfriend, finding one, and then worrying so much about our future together that I ignored the present. I let go of thinking "Steven + Frank = 4ever, 2gether" and by doing so gave Steven and Frank a fighting chance to actually have a future together. Once again I had to give credit to Lindsay: let go and let gay.

The more interested I became in Frank, the less anxious I became about Steven 'n' Frank, which also allowed me to let go of the idea of perfection. Gay men love perfection—perfect abs, perfect ass, perfect future, perfect relationship—but there is no such thing. Perfect relationship is a lie, and not a good one like *toilet water*. Relationships are as difficult and annoying as they are fulfilling and comfortable, and thankfully I had become fully aware that for a relationship to thrive you had to deal with it in the present and not dream about its future. And Frank had been the best present I'd ever received.

So here we were. At the beginning of who knows what might be. But so far I liked what I knew. For instance, Frank and I shared the same passion for television and pop culture. He answered every one of my *Brady Bunch* trivia questions correctly, including "What is Alice's last name?" and "Who gave Bobby his first kiss?" (The answers are Nelson and Millicent, played by Melissa Sue Anderson who, for the uneducated, would go on to much larger acclaim as blind Mary on *Little House on the Prairie*.) He knew how many seasons Donny & Marie's effervescent variety show ran, the names of Barbara Mandrell's sisters, and the breed of Captain & Tennille's beloved dog Broderick. (Three, Louise and Irlene, bulldog.) He only got stumped when I asked him to name the now-defunct soap opera that the actor and actress who played Blair Warner's parents on *The Facts of Life* (Nicolas Coster and Marj Dusay) starred on in the '80s. (The answer: the groundbreaking, hysterically funny, and much-missed *Santa Barbara*, as Lionel Lockridge and Pamela Capwell Conrad respectively.) He thanked me for that trivia tidbit with a sexy tongue kiss so there was no way I could hold his mistake against him.

What else did I know? While Frank gave up on a career in dentistry, he did wind up as the marketing manager for a public relations firm that handled pharmaceutical accounts and was currently working on a campaign for a revolutionary toothbrush that flosses and brushes at the same time. Frank's current task was to come up with a new name for the product since the working title—*Flush*—just doesn't sound like something you'd want to put in your mouth. He was also bored with working out at the gym and preferred to ride his bike and practice yoga to keep his body supple, toned, and oh-so-touchable. Plus he had a past.

"I've had a lot of fun in my life," Frank informed me. "Lots."

"Are you talking *Guinness Book of World Records* fun?" I asked. "Or just typical gay male, been around the block several times, wearing a whole bunch of different outfits and using a whole bunch of different names, kind of fun?"

"Let's just say that you'll probably hear me say hello to a lot of guys when we walk around Chelsea," he replied. "And the West Village. And if we're ever in West Hollywood. Or Boise."

"You had sex in Idaho? I didn't think anyone had sex in Idaho."

"Honey, some might say I put the 'ho' in Idaho."

So I knew Frank had a past filled with promiscuity. Did that bother me? Only if I wanted to be a hypocritical gay, as I had my own string of one-nighters, afternoon hookups, and quite a few dates that started off with me announcing, "I only have twenty minutes because I have to get home to watch *Friends*." But he also informed me that he always practices safe sex, treats his partners with respect, and believes in monogamy when in boyfriend mode.

"Are we in boyfriend mode?" I asked, after our second date.

"We were in boyfriend mode five minutes before I went into my coma."

Good answer! Bottom line, I liked him, I really liked him, and without a doubt Sally Field would like him, but most important, my friends like him too. In fact, on our first real date Frank and I had dinner at East of Eighth and the boys, acting like less butch Nancy Drews, decided to crash the party.

Over appetizers of fried calamari and baked clams Frank and I shared food and childhood stories. I explained that for some reason I peed my pants in school until the fourth grade, causing my mother to more than once have to come to St. Ann's Elementary with paper towels and a dry pair of pants. I thought it might have been because of separation anxiety; Frank thought it was because I was into water sports early on. Then Frank told me how his mother caught him playing doctor with his cousin

Albert in their toolshed when he was seven. She completely ignored the fact that they were coughing and cupping each other's testicles and proudly informed the neighborhood that her son would grow up to be a respected surgeon. He thought it was because his mother was traumatized; I said it sounded as if his mother was Jewish.

As Frank was telling me how he lost his gay-ginity backstage during a high school production of *Bye Bye Birdie,* I noticed a pair of binoculars peering through the large potted plant a few tables away. The only person I knew who owned a pair of binoculars and who had the audacity to bring them out of his bedroom was Lindsay. I wasn't sure if Lindsay saw me, but I knew I didn't want Frank to see Lindsay behind a pair of binoculars and a potted plant so I kept quiet. Soon after, Frank whispered that all this talk about peeing had gotten the better of him and excused himself. Quiet time was over.

Pulling apart the plant leaves, I peered through and caught not one, but three, peeping Toms in action. Lindsay might have been on lookout, but Flynn and Gus were providing backup.

"See anything you like?"

"My eyes!" Lindsay shrieked, so startled that he dropped his binoculars and fell stomach-to-the-floor trying to break their fall.

"I see someone's recreating an Olympic moment," I said.

"Steven!" Flynn exclaimed, with arms stretched high over his head like an attention-hungry showgirl. "Fancy meeting you here."

"Blimey!" Gus added. "What are the odds?"

"Oh shut up, all of you," I hissed. "You're terrible actors. And I'm a bit surprised at you, Flynn. Has Lucas taught you nothing?"

"Damn! My gestures are still too big, aren't they?"

"Before we continue," Lindsay interrupted, "may I remind everyone that in Lillehammer I never once fell on my stomach. Twice on my ass, once on my side, and despite the French judge's skepticism, the fall to my knees was part of the choreography."

"What the hell are you three doing here?" I demanded.

Flynn, Lindsay, and Gus looked at each other like three nervous schoolboys wondering if the strange man in the schoolyard was telling the truth and really did have several bags of candy in his station wagon. Wary, hopeful, and just a little bit aroused. It was an odd and admittedly discomforting expression each wore. But there was nothing odd or discomforting about the reason behind their stakeout.

"We had to see if Frank was friendworthy," Flynn said.

"We didn't want you to get your heart broken again," Gus added.

"I wanted to see if Frank had any ugly scars from the accident," Lindsay finished. "Beauty sleep is one thing, but a coma can have terrible consequences."

My friends: an odd bunch, but good-hearted and well-meaning. They were spying on an intimate moment between me and Frank on our first date just because they cared about my emotional well-being. Who could be upset by that? Not me. But who could fuck around with that? Absolutely me.

"Well, I'm really glad you guys are here," I told them.

"Why? Is it not going well?" Flynn asked. "Do you need to be rescued?"

"Maybe I expected too much. Maybe my expectations were so high that nothing Frank could do would excite me or make me want to date him beyond tonight."

"But he's your Starbucks Sunday Regular!" Lindsay reminded me. "And he doesn't have one scar on that gorgeous face of his."

"I know, but he's just not doing it for me," I said. Then I showed Flynn and the boys how an actor really takes control of a scene. "I think I made a mistake. I think I'm going to call Brian."

"What?" Flynn shrieked, once again adopting his showgirl pose. "That Southern floozy!? That is ridiculous. Why are you constantly backtracking? The next thing you'll say is that you want to give Jack another chance."

"Well . . ."

"Don't even say the *J*-word!" Lindsay shouted, shaking his binoculars like an overstressed English nanny. "Can't you see how hot Frank is for you? Do you know what I saw through these binoculars when I was invading your privacy? I saw pure chemical attraction. And honest-to-goodness love growing between two men. The last time I saw that I was in the steam room at the gym before the mist took it all away. Don't be like the mist, Steven!"

My charade was working. "I don't know if I can, Lindsay. I honestly don't see anything growing between me and Frank."

"Except your nose, Pinocchio!" Gus bellowed, putting an end to my charade. "Can't you see he's wanking our chains?"

"Are you playing me, white boy?" Lindsay asked.

"Steven!" Flynn cried.

"Oh, put your hands down, Nomi. Of course I'm faking it and it serves you guys right for spying on me."

Flynn finally gave the actress routine the hook and he seemed truly sincere when he asked me if Frank was proving to be as unforgettable as I had remembered.

"For once, Flynn, the real thing is actually surpassing any fantasies my overactive imagination may have dreamed up."

"Glad to hear it, Steven."

"Score one for team homo," Gus said.

"Well, it's about time!" Lindsay added. "Maybe all that endless droning of 'I want a boyfriend! I want a boyfriend!' can finally be put to a merciful end. Right here and right now, Steven, the dreaming stops and the living begins! And if you regress and start whining again I'm going to take these binoculars and use them as a dildo so you can see what an asshole you've become."

"Don't pay any attention to him," Gus advised. "He had a hard night."

"No sex?" I asked.

"Bad sex," Flynn said.

"Sorry to hear that. Did he have ass pimples? I know how much you hate boys with ass pimples."

Flynn and Gus chuckled as Lindsay's neck started to turn red.

"What's so funny?"

Flynn tried to give me a clue. "Imagine Lindsay as the star of *Nine*."

If *Password* was ever redone on Logo and featured gay celebrities and their partners, Flynn would not be involved. "That's not funny," I said. "Didn't you always say Broadway's blackest day was when *Nine* beat *Dreamgirls* for the Tony award for Best Musical?"

"Of course it is!" Flynn proclaimed. "That all-black musical was a perfect ten compared to the sixes-and-sevens of the black-and-white costumed Tommy Tune superficial glossfest. But think of the casting."

I did. All I could get from Flynn's clue is that Lindsay had had sex with Raul Julia since he was the only male character in the show except for the little boy. But Raul Julia is dead; so if Lindsay didn't have sex with his corpse he must have had sex with another *Nine* cast member. But the only other cast members were female. Lightbulb!

"Oh my God! You had sex with a *woman*?"

"Please! I am one hundred percent, grade-A homosexual!" Lindsay shouted. "I had sex with a trannie!"

I was curious homo. "I have never known anyone who's had sex with a transgendered person before. How could you tell?"

"I couldn't. He looked like a guy, he sounded like a guy, he even smelled like a guy."

"Then how do you know he was a trannie?"

"Because when Lindsay was fucking him—" Flynn began.

"And just so there's no room for doubt, I was fucking him *good*!"

"You're fucking women now *and* you're a top?" I asked.

Lindsay's face got even redder. "I am trying to incorporate change into all areas of my life!"

"So as Lindsay's fucking him *good*," Gus continued, "the guy starts getting really vocal."

"Which turns me on even more so I fuck him harder."

Flynn highkicked it back into his showgirl routine. "And the guy starts yelling, "Fuck me! Oh yeah, fuck me, sir! Fuck me so fucking hard!"

Then Gus joined Flynn for the finish: "Fuck me like the woman I used to be!"

"What the hell did you do?"

"The only thing I could do," Lindsay said. "I acted more like a woman to make him feel comfortable. I faked an orgasm, cuddled with him for five minutes, then asked if he had any moisturizer since my T-spot's been dry lately."

"I'm sure that made him feel downright nostalgic."

"So stop your bitching, Steven," Lindsay scolded. "Your reality could be a helluva lot worse."

"Lindsay," I said with total sincerity, "my reality has never been better. And I owe it all to Frank."

"And Frank demands payment on a daily basis," he said, striding up.

I introduced Frank to everyone—much to my relief and Lindsay's disbelief Frank didn't remember him from our Starbucks encounter—and before I knew it Frank and I had joined the boys at their table to continue our date.

"I've had group sex before," Frank said, "but never a group date."

"Despite his inability to remember me, I approve of him," Lindsay said.

Flynn agreed. "Me too."

"Me three," Gus added.

"Well, I'm glad I get the friends' seal of approval," Frank said.

"Me too," I said. "Because you might as well know that if you're dating me, you're kind of dating them too."

That had been a month ago and now instead of planning a celebratory dinner, Frank and I weren't going to do anything special; in fact, we weren't even going to be able to see each other, as Frank was on a plane flying back from Boston, where he'd attended a dental trade show. He had promised to bring back samples for my brother, who kept telling me every chance he got not to fuck this one up as he could use the connections for his dental practice. Brotherly love was a beautiful thing.

But even though we had no intention of turning our one-month marker into a party, Flynn had other ideas.

"I don't care if you don't want a party, I do."

"But Flynn, I don't want to make a big deal out of it. I'm trying to approach this relationship with a bit more maturity."

"Mama no like Mature Steven, Steven! Saturday night I'm throwing a party for you and Frank. You can tell Frank it's actually a party for me and Lucas since we're officially co-homotating and I've signed Lucas up for domestic partner insurance at work. Your BF doesn't have to know a thing."

Fortunately, I knew Flynn too well. "Fine, but promise me you won't make a *Happy One-Month Anniversary* banner."

Flynn pouted. "I had to go to Chinatown to find the perfect glitter glue!"

"And there will be no cake shaped like the Starbucks logo."

Flynn protested, "I would never be that tacky."

"Or shaped like a cab hitting a pedestrian."

Flynn proclaimed, "How did you know?"

"Because I know *you*! Promise you'll take it back."

"I'll have them turn the cab into a limo and say it's Lucas driving incognito and me stopping traffic."

"What about the strawberry icing representing Frank's blood on the pavement?"

"Damn you, Steven! I'll have them turn Frank's blood into a red carpet."

"Thank you."

"You're like the big-budget blockbuster British import musical of the '80s that ruined Broadway. Are you happy now that you've ruined my party?"

"Nope. I'm actually *very* happy."

The mood at work, however, was not as festive. We were losing one of our own. Lorna Douglas had decided not to renew her contract since the pilot she'd shot six months before had been picked up as a midseason replacement. After she filmed her final scene today she would hop on a flight to L.A. to start her new acting gig in *Shrink Wrapped,* an ABC dramedy set in a rehab center that could only be described as *The Love Boat* meets the Betty Ford Clinic. The premise was that each week B- and C-list actors would guest star on the show as celebrities, politicians, and athletes who check in to dry out, regroup, or attempt to rejuvenate a sagging career with a fake personal scandal. Lorna played Mitzi McCall, the center's events planner (a twenty-first century Julie McCoy for the coke and booze set) who would help the patients discover the joys of backgammon and cribbage while on the road to clean livin'. Since her character was a recovering sex addict, she'd no doubt also help them discover the therapeutic powers of the anonymous fuck.

"Steven!" Lorna hissed right before she started filming her celluloid swan song. "I'm counting on you to thank the gay community for helping me unlock the secrets of my new character."

"I'm sure my fellow gays will be so happy to hear that we're your role model for sexual compulsive behavior."

I was obviously a better actor than Flynn, since Lorna didn't detect a note of my sarcasm. "Thank God you people are practical—if you can't love the one you want, fuck the one you're with."

During the farewell party Lorna raised her glass of champagne and toasted her coworkers and crew. "I hope I make you all proud."

"You've *already* made us proud, Lorna," Loretta said. "Simply by leaving."

Lorna's left eye twitched as she noted the jab. "How ironic that I'm leaving for a fictional drying-out clinic and when you leave it's for a real one."

It was time for Loretta's left eye to twitch. "It's at times like these that I wish I was still a raging alcoholic so I could throw up."

"Laraby!" Lorna shrieked.

"Y-y-y-y-yes, Miss Douglas."

"Why don't you pull out the reel of Loretta's scenes that failed to get her an Emmy nomination—for the twelfth time! I'm sure watching them will make her hurl."

"Laraby!" Loretta countershrieked.

"Y-y-y-y-yes, Miss Larson?"

"Why don't you pull out Lorna's twelve-inch-thick medical

file? She's going to want to burn the proof once Hollywood hurls her out on her ass when they realize she acts with her tits!"

"Hollywood already knows I tit-act, you washed-up hag! And they know that I have more talent in my right tit than you have in your entire shriveled-up old woman's body!"

"Women twenty years younger than me would sell their souls to have a body like mine!"

"*Sixty*-year-old women already have sagging knockers and cellulite! What the hell do they want yours for?"

"Miss Loretta does not have cellulite!" Lourdes cried as she raced toward Lorna. "She had all of it sucked out! Ahhhhhh!"

That was the last thing Lourdes said before she crashed into the Kraft service tray and then crashed to the floor, doing the horizontal electric boogaloo. And then Langley, the kindly stage-hand, did what no one else had thought of doing before, and what Lourdes hadn't thought to do herself; he gave her a tape measure.

"Now maybe she can stay far enough away from Loretta and stop shocking herself," Lucas said to me.

"Too bad," I replied. "I think she's come to like it."

"Do you think Flynn would be willing to wear one of those ankle bracelets and bring electro-sex into our relationship?"

"Flynn's very vanilla. He doesn't like props in the bedroom."

"You'd be surprised, Flynn's changing."

"TMI about my BFF. And incidentally, I'm sorry I couldn't change their minds and stop them from making your character a philandering and possibly homicidal heterosexual."

Lucas shrugged. "What was the alternative? A happy and content homosexual?"

"There is no such thing!" Laraby chimed in.

"*Au contraire, mon cher,*" Lucas said Frenchly. "May I introduce you to the happy and content Steven Ferrante."

I guess I *was* happy and content in a really-real, not-trying-too-hard-to-feel-it sort of way. I was even happy and content to be the silent guest of honor at Flynn's quote-unquote moving-in party. He was true to his word, and nowhere in their apartment could be found a Happy Anniversary party favor, so Frank and

I were able to mingle as just another couple and not the couple du jour.

As Frank spread some Brie on a Ritz for me, Gus, who I still thought was the best-looking over-forty gay I knew, but who I no longer thought of X-ratedly, joined us with his date du jour. Something was amiss, however, as this miss was well over the legal age limit.

"Can I guess his name, Gus?" I asked.

"It's a bit unique."

I love a challenge. "Gilligan?"

"No."

"Gomer?"

"Sorry, mate."

Names of sitcom characters raced through my mind, but I was a bit stymied. "Gidget?"

Gus's older-than-usual boy toy brought my guessing game to an end. "It's Gatsby."

Would wonders never cease? I never thought I'd see the day when Gus upgraded from sitcom trash to classic literature. Maybe this aging gracefully thing was catching on.

"Gatsby works at the hedge fund my company just bought."

"So this is sort of your own personal merger," Frank said.

"Spot-on, mate!" Gus replied. "I made a wise investment in my future." Gus clinked Gatsby's wineglass with his own, making his new boyfriend's intense black onyx eyes soften.

"Why Gus," I gushed, "our little playboy is all grown up."

Meanwhile, some playboys just kept playing with the boys.

"Full-fledged porn star coming through," Lindsay announced, waving a DVD high overhead.

Could the former ice-skater have given up lamb's wool sweaters for lambskin prophylactics? Could my unpredictable friend have gone the predictable gay midlife-crisis route and begun a second career as a porn star? Would I be seeing Lindsay's dick again? All hopes of seeing Lindsay parlay his ice-skater's flexibility into a blue-movie actor's repertoire were dashed when Lindsay stepped aside to reveal Sebastian who, so that there was absolutely no confusion, wore a spandex T-shirt with the message *Me. I'm A Porn Star Now.*

"Isn't this going to destroy your chances of becoming a full-time professor at NYU instead of being just an adjunct?" I asked.

"*Chica,* I had no choice."

I shook my head. "Sebastian, we all have choices."

"No papi, not when you fuck with the Cabbage Patch People."

Being Sicilian, I had heard many of the Mafia's code names, but Cabbage Patch People was not one of them. I made a mental note to ask my mother, who would be arriving momentarily, if she knew of a connection between the mob and the supertoy of the '80s. Turned out, however, the legendary dolls were connected to another group of ball-breaking, unscrupulous law-breakers—the IRS.

"You know how back in the day doctors gave the little Cabbage Patch babies real birth certificates?" Sebastian explained.

A pop culture tidbit had slid past me? "No, I did not know that."

"*Es verdad.*"

"He means it's true," Lindsay translated. "And Sebastian has been collecting government-issued disability checks on account of the fact that Nathaniel Thomas Applethistle was disabled in 1985 in a terrible doll factory accident that severed both his legs, and could no longer work."

Frank gasped. "The Cabbage Patch Scam is not urban legend, it's *verdad.*"

Another thing I really liked about Frank was that he caught on quick and played along.

"As real as the sixty thousand dollars I owe in back taxes to the fucking IRS," Sebastian cried.

Lindsay held up Sebastian's DVD. "Which means Sebastian will be filming IRS, or Incredibly Real Sex as we say in the porn biz, for quite a long time."

I caught a glimpse of the DVD cover and it was my turn to gasp. "That's my Aiden!"

Of course it was only fitting that Sebastian the slut would have sex with my porn idol before I did. I looked at Frank and thankfully reflected on the way the real world could actually be better than fantasy if you gave it half a chance. I did experience one twinge of "what if" as I glimpsed the cover photo of Sebastian and Aiden, naked and oily, each with one hand on the bony shoulder of a twinkish Eurasian boy who looked as if he barely passed the mandatory age requirement the porn industry rigorously upheld. The title, *Mind the Jap,* hovered in big letters above their heads.

"Aiden and I play international spies based in London who have to protect an orphaned Japanese boy who is the only witness to his parents' murder by an underground splinter group bankrolled by an unnamed foreign government."

And I thought the plots on *ITNC* were convoluted.

"Every time we save his life we fuck him."

"And that, people, is the true meaning of gratitude," Lindsay declared.

I mentally pushed the metaphorical parallel and realized I was like that Japanese orphan with the well-lubed hole. I was grateful that Frank was in my life. I was also grateful that my family and my friends could merge and I didn't have to compartmentalize my life like so many gays were forced to do. The special moments of my life crossed borders even if the participants of my special moments sometimes attempted to cross the line.

"Steven!" my mother shouted. "I'm going to be a grandmother!"

"Is Trixie having puppies?" I asked hopefully.

"No, stupid, I'm pregnant," said Renée, beaming. She confessed that there hadn't been any trip to Aruba; she and Paulie had gone to a clinic to fast-forward past their fertility problems. Renée had been having trouble conceiving, so they went to South America for a few days of sun and in vitro and voilà, Renée was pregnant with twins.

"Are you sure it's only twins?" my mother asked. "You're not having quintuplets like those women in the Midwest, are you?"

"No, Ma," Paulie answered. "It's just two, a boy and a girl."

"Anj!" Audrey cried. "You're going to have a grandson and a granddaughter all at the same time. You're a very lucky woman."

Even in the throes of her own unexpected joy my mother always placed me first.

"Those two kids are the lucky ones. They're going to have the best uncle in the whole world!"

I congratulated my brother, hugged Renée and whispered to Trixie that she would still be my favorite no matter how many babies Renée and her fertility drugs popped out. Trixie licked my nose; Paulie, conversely, licked his lips in gratitude when Gwendolyn and Glenda asked Renée if she wanted to guest star in the New York installment of "Gay Girls A-Go-Go."

"It's okay if you want to be a lesbian for a few days," Paulie mentioned casually. "As long as you film it."

A friend as an adult reality star I could handle; a pregnant relative, not so much.

"Sorry bro, your wife only speaks hetero."

The party, however, spoke hetero, homo, and every shade of gay in between. My mother had tears in her eyes when she gave Flynn and Lucas her housewarming gift. Flynn didn't dare tell her that they didn't need another Mister Coffee and said he couldn't wait to get up and brew a pot of Colombian roast. Lenny had tears in his eyes when he wished me and Frank luck on our anniversary. I had misjudged the guy, which often happens when you judge people. Yes, he was sort of lecherous and STD-ish, but he was also thoughtful and worldly wise.

When Frank was off refilling our drinks, Lenny put his hand on my shoulder and said, "If you want to grow old together, treat him with respect and demand the same from him."

I guessed that Lenny wished someone had given him that same advice when he was a younger man. I no longer viewed him as an old gay with a depressing future, but as a man who had lived a long life and was still trying to live it despite some hard knocks. Next week I would set Lenny up with the gay actor on *The Rich and the Powerful* who was a former chorus boy and

Jerome Robbins's one-time boyfriend. Sure, elders wanted respect, but they also wanted companionship.

Standing around the chocolate fountain with them, it seemed to me like all my friends had found both. Sebastian and Aiden. Gus and Gatsby. Flynn and Lucas. Me and Frank. That left Lindsay.

"I know what you're thinking, Steven," Lindsay chided. "And I am not wasting the best years of my life or the best bubble butt in all of Chelsea."

"I know your ass isn't being wasted."

"It's also not being shared by the public at large. My hole only serves one these days."

How could people say homos weren't romantic?

"You have a boyfriend?!"

"Keep it down. We're on the down low."

"You're in a relationship and you're not flaunting it? That's not like you."

"For the first time in my life, Steven, I'm thinking about someone other than me."

The cold made my nipples erect, for hell had surely frozen over.

"Come again?"

"My boyfriend is a former child actor and he's trying to make a comeback. He'll know in a week or two if his movie deal goes through and if so we're going to go public. Until then he doesn't want his personal life to overshadow his work. He wants to get this job based on his worth as an actor, not because he's tabloid-worthy."

I was impressed. "It looks like we're all growing up."

I looked around the room at my friends and family, and life was as it should be, filled with hope, laughter, and smiles. Then, I took a good hard look at Frank and got a rush of happy adrenaline when I caught him looking at me first.

That was over two months ago. My life seemed to only get better. Frank liked me a lot. How did I know? He told me before I had to wonder.

"I thought of you at work today," Frank said, as we lay in bed facing each other.

"You're going to get caught jacking off in the bathroom one of these days."

"Shut up. My boss said his favorite movie is *Caddyshack*."

"I love that movie."

"I know. I told him it makes you cry."

"Bill Murray's character is a very lonely man. Underneath the laughter is sadness, you know."

"He said he'd never really thought of it that way. I said that's what I like so much about you—you make me look at things differently."

"And that's what I like about you so much."

"What?"

"You let me have my different point of view."

"Promise me you'll always be yourself. Always be a little neurotic and quirky and interested in seeing the world as you see it and not how everybody else thinks it should be seen. Promise me you'll always just be yourself."

"I've realized I can't be anything *but* who I really am. I've tried and it just doesn't work."

"Good. Because I've fallen in love with the real Steven."

"And I've fallen in love with the real Frank."

There was nothing more to say so we kissed each other good night and fell asleep, two happy and contented homos who would wake up and work together to have another happy and contented day. Sometimes we would succeed, sometimes we would fail, but together we would wake up the next day and try again.

I don't know if it's that simple or if it's really super complicated and we're both being naïve and deluding ourselves that this is it—the rest-of-our-lives, long-term relationship we've both searched for. All I know is that my name is Steven Bartholomew Ferrante and my boyfriend's name is Frank Anthony Gunnerson and we've been dating for three months, two weeks, and four days. We hope it's the beginning of our very own happily ever after. Wish us luck.